INSIDER THREAT

Book 1 in the Deep Cover Series

MARLISS MELTON

James-York Press
Williamsburg, Virginia

Edited by Jeanne Olynickj
Cover Design by Teresa Cabañas
Print Layout by BB eBooks

Dedication

For Steve, without whom this tale could never have been told. I am humbled and touched that you would share your knowledge with me so selflessly and with such dedication. What a blessing you have been to me! And thank you, dear Aunt Ellie, for finding me such an incredible resource!

List of Acronyms

BUDs—Basic Underwater Demolition and SEAL Training

RGB—Reconnaissance General Bureau, North Korea's equivalent of the CIA

DPRK—Democratic People's Republic of Korea

The Bu—The FBI

FISA—Foreign Intelligence Surveillance Act

PD—Police Department

SDR—Surveillance Detection Route

SOGs—Special Operations Group members

CART—Computer Analyst Response Team

ELSUR—Electronic Surveillance

UCO—Undercover Operation

SOCOM—Special Operations Command

PROLOGUE

North Korea, One Year Ago

ALL THE LEADER'S cabinet members stood at attention in Kim Il-sung Square, forced to watch the execution.

Moon Min-yun huddled with his remaining peers as they braced against the frigid wind whipping across the Taedong River. Snowflakes twirled between them and the victim, the Minister of Agriculture, handcuffed to a pole jutting up in the center of the square. Quaking and blindfolded, Ahn-ju sobbed in vain for Kim Jong-un to spare him.

None of the cabinet members had the slightest idea what Ahn-ju's offense had been. Was it public corruption? A glib comment uttered thoughtlessly and soon regretted? Or had the Glorious Leader realized someone in his midst was passing secrets to the Americans?

Moon Min-yun locked his knees to keep them from giving out suddenly. He exerted every ounce of control to keep his expression impassive while concealing his inward terror. How long could he keep informing the CIA before Kim Jong-un suspected *him*?

A volley of gunfire shattered the frosty air. Ahn-ju's body jerked and twitched, and Moon Min-yun knew it was only a matter of time before he was next to die. The most he could hope for was that the CIA swept him away from his country before that happened.

CHAPTER 1

San Diego, CA, Present Time

ONLY AN ASIAN fusion restaurant could surpass the variety of fare in Charles Suzuki's parents' house at Christmas time. Chuck had heaped bulgogi, sweet potato noodles, sashimi, tempura, and dumplings on his plate, but eating it with his heart and mind in turmoil was proving impossible.

He sat in the same chair he had sat in his entire childhood, with his younger brother Seiko across from him, his grandmother at the head of the table, his parents on either side of her. Fond memories of the past two and a half decades floated through him, compounding his grief. He forced himself to eat, ignoring his sudden queasiness.

Christmas music played softly in the background, and a refreshing San Diego breeze wafted through the open windows to cool the adjacent kitchen. Surrounded by all that was dear and familiar, Chuck searched himself. *Am I really going to say good-bye?*

One by one, he memorized the faces around the table. To an outside observer, his family appeared ordinary, if ethnically diverse. Reality could not be farther from the truth. His grandmother, Sobo, stooped and harmless looking, was the great aunt of North Korea's current dictator. She had been spying on behalf of her native country for nearly seven decades.

Chuck's gaze focused on the framed photos of his ancestors staring back from the wall next to him. Chuck's great-grandfather, born in America, had been thrust into a Japanese containment camp during WWII. He had shared his resentment with his first-born son Hiroshi, who later became an Air Force pilot and fought in the Korean conflict. When Hiroshi's plane went down in enemy territory, instead of being made a POW, he was invited into the home of North Korea's leader and indoctrinated.

At the war's end, Kim Il-sung sent Hiroshi back to America with his sister for a bride.

Sobo had been a beautiful woman back then, given the portrait of her and Hiroshi together. They had been assigned a sacred mission—to uphold the Ten Principles for the Establishment of the One-Ideology System. They did so by feeding Pyongyang with information and later with food, as Hiroshi established Suzuki Shipping Enterprises.

Their son, Chuck's father, was educated likewise, then expected to follow in their footsteps, as were Chuck and his younger brother. For Chuck, the secret, sacred mission had to end. He was risking his career for a country he had never seen.

Laughter shattered Chuck's contemplation as his father continued his tale. Chuck mustered a smile, then caught his mother studying him. Diane Suzuki, the only white face at the table, had noticed something was amiss with her eldest.

She cut his father off. "Chuck, is that all you're going to eat? I'm going to have a ton of leftovers if you can't do better than that."

"I'm still stuffed from last night." The murmured excuse failed to drive the worry from her eyes.

Chuck's brother, a twenty-three-year-old post graduate student, urged their father to continue. Pushing a dumpling around his plate, Chuck waited for just the right moment to deliver his parting speech. Sorrow clogged his throat, preventing him from taking another bite. Tears pressured his eyes. He loved his family—even Sobo, whom they all secretly feared.

His family had cheered him through SEAL training in Coronado. They had toasted his success when he'd graduated from BUDs, then wept at the airport when he'd been assigned to SEAL Team 12, all the way on the other side of the States. He'd called home every Sunday since to talk to them.

The physical distance hadn't excused him, however, from the commitment imposed on him. A North Korean case officer working for the Reconnaissance General Bureau, their equivalent of the CIA, had befriended him, then acted as his handler, a liaison between the RGB and Chuck. On his first dead drop, he received a tiny camera for taking pictures of hi-tech gear, maps, and navigational systems. Chuck had learned from Sobo how to conceal those photos within his own personal photographs in a process called steganography.

His life became a balancing act between risking his life for his country and feeding the RGB misinformation that looked real enough to keep them complacent. Between the fear of getting caught and the fear that the RGB would realize he was duping them, he could barely sleep at night. One morning, several months ago, he had decided he was done being a North Korean spy.

His family would be stunned, furious, disbelieving, and hurt that he had chosen service to his country over loyalty to his family.

Time crawled. Their dinner seemed to last forever. Chuck glanced surreptitiously at his watch. He had packed his bags before the meal in anticipation of having to leave at once. It was stuffed with the gifts he'd received for Christmas, including a book on photography from his mother and a new diving watch from his brother, Seiko. Now he would have to check his bag as it would no longer fit in the overhead compartment.

"Well," his father declared, "my hip is killing me

from all this sitting. What do you say we help the women wash up then retire to the living room for board games?"

It's now or never, Chuck thought. "I have something I need to say first."

Four sets of eyes fastened on him. Only his mother appeared worried, as if she'd already guessed what was on his mind. He hesitated, wondering how he would cope without calling them on Sundays.

"Well, what is it?" Seiko prompted.

Chuck cleared his tight throat. "I have to say goodbye." He pushed back his chair and stood over them. He'd gotten his height of six feet from his mother's side of the family.

"Are you being deployed again?" Diane Suzuki jumped to the most logical conclusion.

Chuck shook his head. His chest constricted. "When I became a SEAL, I swore an oath of loyalty to my Country and to my Team. I've since realized I can't serve two masters." He met his father's pain-filled eyes. "I'm so sorry. But the ideologies of this household are not compatible with my beliefs. I have to cut ties."

He had thought he could get through his speech without crying, but his voice cracked, forcing him to be succinct. "I love you all, and I'll never stop thinking of you, but I won't call, and I won't visit. You won't be able to reach me. My phone number, my address—

all of that has changed."

His mother pushed to her feet. "Chuck, please, stop right now. This isn't necessary." She rounded the table with a stricken expression and threw her arms around him.

Chuck returned her embrace, burying his nose in her hair, smelling her shampoo one last time.

Diane directed an appealing look at Sobo. "Please, Chun-ja. Tell Chuck he has no more obligation to the family. Tell him so he doesn't have to leave us."

"Mom," Chuck chided, "it makes no difference whether I'm obligated or not. I still can't associate with you." He braced himself to look back at Sobo.

Kim Chun-ja sat ramrod straight in her chair, mouth pinched. Her dark eyes, although sunken with age, blazed with betrayal. "You know the ten principles of the One-Ideology System. You must give your all to the Glorious Leader."

Chuck squeezed his mother one last time then stepped resolutely away. "I am a front-line servant of the United States of America," he said to his grandmother. "I give my all to my country."

The crestfallen expressions on his father's and Seiko's faces kept Chuck from shaking their hands. He spun away from the table and hurried down the hallway of the one-floor contemporary toward his old bedroom. He'd left his stuffed duffel bag on his bed. Snatching it up, he crossed to the sliding glass door that led to a walled garden.

The weather was clear and cool, the darkening sky the only indication it was early winter. A full moon lit the bonsai plants and koi pond where his father spent so much time practicing the gardening methods taught to him by *his* father.

Figuring his family would try to detain him if he left by way of the front door, Chuck had planned an exit strategy. He slung his full bag over the four-foot wall running the perimeter of the small back yard, then hopped over it with the grace of a Ninja. His heart felt heavy, but his conscience felt light.

I did it. Weighed by guilt for years now, his soul rose up on wings of righteousness.

He landed on the curb, hefted his duffle over one shoulder, and started walking. No one could call him and plead for him to change his mind. He'd taken every measure possible to ensure his break was a thorough one. Nothing from this time on would connect him to Sobo's spy ring.

Yes, he had lost his family and he would mourn that loss for years to come. But in Echo Platoon, he had a new family, comprised of unswerving patriots.

He walked stoically away, murmuring a portion of the oath he'd spoken upon graduation from BUDs when he'd been issued his Trident. "By wearing the Trident, I accept the responsibility of my chosen profession and way of life. It is a privilege that I must earn every day. My loyalty to Country and Team is beyond reproach."

Now he could say those words without cringing.

Virginia Beach, VA, Two Months Later

SPECIAL AGENT KELLY Yang wasn't easily intimidated, but the bar full of broad-shouldered Navy SEALs and beautiful, bodacious babes had her slipping into the bathroom in the lobby of the restaurant to check her appearance.

Inexperience put butterflies in Kelly's stomach. She'd been a Special Agent for just five years, making her among the youngest Special Agents ever to work undercover. Her advantage over those with more experience was her fluency in Korean. It didn't hurt that she was also cute and female, and the target was a male of Asian descent, just a year older than she was.

He was also a Navy SEAL who knew a hundred-and-ten ways to kill someone, but Kelly didn't want to dwell on that just then.

I can do this. Through almond-colored eyes, she critiqued her outfit. A blood-red sweater dress outlined her modest curves. Heeled ankle boots added three inches to her petite stature. She wore her hair down. It fell, black and glossy to her hips, concealing the tiny earpiece that allowed two-way communication between herself and the two key members of her special surveillance squad, currently parked in the lot outside. She looked nothing like an undercover agent.

"Are you good, Munchkin?" The question sounding in Kelly's ear came from Hannah Lindstrom, the case agent.

Kelly rolled her eyes. If there were a moment in history that she wished she could redact, it was admitting to her peers at the FBI academy that her only acting experience came from playing a munchkin in *The Wizard of Oz* back in high school. She'd been called Munchkin ever since.

"Of course. Just checking my lipstick." She withdrew said item from her tiny purse and painted her lips deep red to match her dress. The simple act helped to subdue the fear swirling in the pit of her stomach.

"Time to roll," she murmured, leaving the restroom for the noisy restaurant.

The Hawaiian theme of Calypso Bar and Grille appealed to the eye. Its high cabana-style roof, however, made the acoustics terrible. Kelly winced at the cacophony of boisterous voices.

"Can you hear me?" she asked under her breath.

Calypso, being the nearest ocean-front bar/restaurant to two Navy bases, appealed to servicemen for its mosaic of red, white, and blue bottles lying end to end to take the shape of the American flag, not to mention its scenic views of the

Atlantic Ocean. Ignoring the men who tried to catch her eye, Kelly scanned the noisy area for her target's dark head.

"Barely," came Hannah's affirmation in her ear. "Look for Lexi at the bar. She's holding a seat for you."

Lexi was a twenty-year-old who babysat Hannah's three sons. She never knew the details of a case, but got paid to act as an FBI asset, since her looks opened doors without raising suspicions. Kelly spotted the young blonde sitting on a stool between the target and his roommate. Both were still in uniform, having come to the bar directly from work.

"I see her. Going in."

Fighting her awareness of the target, Kelly zeroed in on the roommate. Charles Suzuki loomed in her field of sight, larger and more virile than his photos had suggested. While his back was to her, she could see him watching her approach through the mirror on the backbar.

Exotic attributes betrayed his mixed heritage— deep-set hazel eyes, strong cheekbones, firm jaw, nice lips. He didn't look like a traitor, but according to an informant within Kim Jong-un's own government, a Navy SEAL was feeding Pyongyang military secrets. The CIA had requested that the FBI find and deal with the insider threat. Kelly had combed through thousands of military personnel files looking for a

SEAL with even the flimsiest of ties to the Korean Peninsula. Charles Suzuki was her one and only candidate.

Interestingly enough, his roommate, Austin Collins, was half Russian, though looked as all-American as any man could with golden-brown curls, gray eyes, and symmetrical features. What set Austin apart was his formidable IQ. He sat with one arm on the bar talking to Lexi, who looked more overwhelmed than flattered by Austin's attention.

As Kelly walked right up to them, Austin paused mid-sentence. Through the backbar mirror, Kelly's eyes connected with Charles Suzuki's stare, and her stomach gave a backflip.

"Excuse me." She wrenched her attention back to the couple. "Sorry to interrupt, but some guy over there told me you speak Korean," she said to Austin, "and I just want to know if that's true."

"Oh." He turned to Lexi who started slipping off her stool. "Wait, where are you going?"

"I have to run." With that breathless excuse, Lexi was gone.

Kelly didn't wait for an invitation. "I'm Katy." She offered Austin her hand as she helped herself to the vacated stool. Both the driver's license and credit card she carried identified her as Katy Tang.

"Austin." His handshake held just the slightest reservation.

"So, is it true? You speak Korean?"

"Who told you that?" He drew his hand back.

"Some dark-haired guy over there." She gestured toward the far side of the bar where Suzuki's platoon leader was having a drink with another SEAL.

Austin swiveled and searched the bar. "Oh, you mean Sam." He swung back around to regard her with more interest. "You speak Korean, too?"

"Badly." She grimaced. "I'm second generation, so of course I understand it, but I don't get the chance to practice much." *Am I talking too fast?* She could sense her target listening in on every word.

Austin ran a discreet gaze over her sweater dress. "Can I get you a drink?"

Apparently, she met his requirements as a potential date. "Well, thanks. I'll take a glass of Chardonnay."

As Austin relayed her order to the bartender, Kelly kept her back to Charles and tried to guess what Austin was drinking—it looked like a gin and tonic.

He faced her again, his expression friendly. "Do you want to speak Korean now?"

"Why not?" she answered in the language of her parents.

"I hope I don't disappoint you," he said, following her lead. "I don't speak it that well."

"Yes, you do. I don't even hear an accent."

"It's a difficult language, nothing like the other languages I know."

Kelly gestured at Charles, using her thumb. "What about him? Does he speak Korean?"

Austin leaned back and addressed his roommate over her shoulder. "She wants to know if you speak Korean," he relayed in English.

Bracing herself, Kelly swiveled on her stool to smile at her target. His hostile gaze hit her like a punch in the gut.

"No," he stated, with as much warmth as an icicle. "I'm one-quarter Japanese. I speak English."

"Oh, too bad." She affected a pout of disappointment and wondered why he would lie to her. His military records, which she had perused in detail, stated him proficient in Korean, Japanese, and English.

Austin introduced them. "Chuck, this is Katy."

So, he preferred Chuck, did he? All she got was a cool nod, no handshake. He turned his shoulder on her and stared down at the tumbler in his hand. Dismayed to have been rebuffed right away, Kelly turned back to Austin with a raised eyebrow.

He leaned closer, assailing her with the scent of sea spray and gun oil. "Just ignore him. His manners are rusty."

Interesting, Kelly thought, that Austin hadn't exposed Chuck's outright lie.

"Truth is, he thinks you're pretty," Austin added.

Clearly not, Kelly thought. Getting to know

Charles Suzuki, let alone befriend him, was going to be a challenge.

She decided to win over Austin first, following his cue to continue in English. "So, where did you pick up your Korean? Were you stationed overseas?"

"Oh, no. Language school." Austin lifted and lowered his powerful shoulders. "The Navy sends me for three months at a time, and I come back semi-fluent."

"Well, thank you for your service," she told him. "How many languages do you speak?"

A man's raised voice tore his attention from her briefly. "Er, a few," he said.

"Like what?" She acted engrossed, though she could have listed them herself.

He blinked at her. "You are so cute. Let's talk about you. That's got to be more interesting."

"Hardly. I'm a student. I don't even have a career yet. So, what languages?"

He blew out a breath. "Well . . . my mother is Russian, so I grew up speaking Russian and English, then Spanish, which I took in high school."

The raised voice came again, cutting him off. This time, they both looked at the burly, bald man yelling at his girlfriend.

Frowning in the man's direction, Austin added, "Since then, I've learned Korean, French, and Arabic."

He was talking to her, but Kelly could tell he was listening to what the man had to say.

"I suck at Arabic." Austin cited a particular linguistic feature that gave him trouble. All the while, he kept an eye on the bristling bully.

Someone told the jerk to tone it down. Big Meany shot back with some not-so-nice-words that caused Austin to put a hand on the bar.

"I'm sorry," he said. "Please don't go anywhere." Pushing off his stool, he started to walk away.

"Austin, don't!" Next to her, Chuck Suzuki called his friend back.

Austin ignored him.

Kelly watched with a held breath as he crossed the room and grabbed Big Meany by his T-shirt, hauling him around. Kelly read Austin's lips. *Come with me.*

The bar fell quiet as Austin, who was several inches taller and in much better shape, wrestled the tattooed, beer-bellied bully toward the exit to the deck. Someone darted forward, opening the door for them. A gust of frigid, salt-laced air blew into the bar as the pair went outside.

Once there, Austin released the man, who whirled to face him, swinging wildly. Austin sidestepped the swing. A swift counterpunch sent Big Meany sprawling onto a picnic bench. He remained there, unmoving. Kelly resisted the urge to cheer with the rest of the onlookers.

"Great." Chuck started to head in Austin's direction when another man—Kelly recognized him as

Sam, the platoon leader—pushed through the crowd, headed for the deck.

With a whispered "Shit," Chuck backed down.

Kelly girded herself to talk to him again. "Is Austin going to get in trouble?"

"Newton's third law," was his response.

She thought she'd misheard him until she remembered what Hannah had relayed from her husband, who was, by pure coincidence, the operations officer on the target's SEAL Team. According to *him*, Charles Suzuki tended to speak in metaphors, a habit that had given him the code name Haiku.

Newton's third law. Kelly thought back to her undergraduate physics class. She wasn't entirely sure, but . . . "You mean for every action there is an equal and opposite reaction?"

His sidelong glance betrayed surprise. "Exactly."

Just like that, the ice between them seemed to thaw. His lips twitched toward a smile, and a feeling of camaraderie stole over her.

They both looked back at the patio, where Austin stood with his eyes downcast. Sam, the platoon leader, slightly taller, was chewing him out. That man pointed toward the parking lot, clearly telling Austin to walk that way. He turned his head, catching Kelly's eye through the glass, grimaced his apology, and raised a hand good-bye. Then he followed Sam off the deck.

"Aww," she lamented. "He's being sent away."

"History repeats itself." Chuck swiveled to face the bar.

Finding herself alone with her target, Kelly's heart started thudding. She needed to be careful. Spies tended to be narcissists, contemptuous of authority. They didn't like to be interrupted or challenged—all of which she had a tendency to do. Picking up her wine, she articulated the obvious question. "How many times has Austin done this kind of thing?"

Chuck tried to catch the bartender's eye. Wait, was he leaving already?

"Plenty." He didn't even look at her.

Kelly slid Austin's glass closer and sniffed it. Yep, gin and tonic. "Is he drunk?"

"That's his first drink. Tony!" Chuck raised his voice for the bartender to hear him.

Tony moved even farther away.

Kelly sought to get on Chuck's good side. "If you really need to go," she said, "I'll pay your tab, and Austin's too. That way you can check on your friend."

He raked her with an inscrutable once-over and put his wallet away. "Okay. Thanks."

"Katy," she reminded him. "And no big deal." She flashed him a winning smile, then promptly turned her shoulder on him. No need to show excessive interest.

Without another word, Chuck walked away, his footsteps inaudible. Kelly waited for him to disappear from view, then braced both elbows on the bar and let the tension flow out of her. "Well, that was brief," she said under her breath.

"You did well," Hannah replied. "When you move into the apartment across from his, it'll just seem like a coincidence."

"Right." Remembering her promise to pay their tabs, Kelly flagged down Tony as he walked in her direction. She left Calypso Bar and Grille knowing the target had nursed a single tumbler of top-shelf bourbon on the rocks while his roommate preferred Tanqueray gin. Clearly that kind of intel wasn't going to implicate Charles Suzuki of spying, but she could still use it to her advantage.

What she really wanted to know was why a Navy SEAL would risk all that he'd accomplished to help out a hostile nation like the Democratic People's Republic of Korea. She'd learned at FBI Academy there were four reasons why people became spies. Number one was money. If Chuck was being paid for sharing military secrets, he had to be keeping his money in an offshore account. Number two was ego. Chuck's leaders, in their yearly evaluations, had described him as quiet and self-effacing. That left number three, ideology, or number four, coercion, as the SEAL's motive for betraying everything he was supposed to stand for.

It was hard to picture the broad-shouldered, stoic Suzuki being coerced by anybody. Whatever his reasons, her instincts had insisted from the moment she first pulled his file that Charles Suzuki was a spy. And in good time, she intended to prove it.

✕

AUSTIN ACQUAINTED HIMSELF with the features on the dashboard of Sam Sasseville's Lexus. "What's this do?" He went to push a button by the stick shift.

Sam slapped his hand away. "Don't touch that. Jesus, Austin, can't you keep your hands to yourself?" The lieutenant's jungle-green eyes glinted with aggravation. "Look, you have got to stop getting into bar fights."

"That wasn't a fight," Austin replied, still trying to fathom what the button did. "That was a lesson in etiquette. You don't yell at a woman, let alone in a public setting."

"It's not your job to teach people lessons, man. This is the third time I've had to drag you away from a brawl."

"It's not a brawl if you only beat up one guy."

"Shut the hell up and listen to me. In public settings, you represent the Team, not just your personal beliefs of who deserves or doesn't deserve to be hit. Trust me, if you keep this up, you're going to find yourself facing captain's mast or, worse, court martial."

Austin pictured himself in military court and

gulped.

"I'm sending you to mandatory counseling," Sam announced.

"Counseling?" Austin gaped at his leader.

"Don't even try to talk me out of it." Sam scowled as he accelerated toward Austin and Chuck's apartment only seven blocks up Atlantic Avenue. "Counseling is exactly what you need. Do you want to get promoted? Do you want to remain a frogman?"

"Yes, of course."

"Then you'll go to counseling, and you'll fix your problem now. Don't worry. I'll find you a therapist you'll like, someone who'll get results. You're going to see him twice a week on your own time, and you're going to take your sessions seriously."

Austin scowled. "For how long?"

"Until you're cured."

Austin looked out the window, swallowing a sigh. He didn't have a problem, so what was he to be cured of? He'd done nothing wrong. The fat bald guy would think twice before yelling at his girl in public again. In fact, Austin's only regret was leaving that cute-as-hell Katy at the bar without paying for her drink like he'd said he would. Chuck would cover the tab, he assured himself. And Katy, though she'd tried to hide it, was actually more interested in Chuck, so perhaps it was a good thing they'd been stuck with each other.

Was it too much to hope Chuck had gotten her

phone number? Of course, it was. His roommate rarely talked to strangers, let alone the female kind. Lately he'd seemed more introverted than ever.

Chuck's the one who needs counseling, Austin groused in silence, *not me.*

CHAPTER 2

"THAT'S A WRAP, Echo Platoon. Go home and enjoy your weekend."

With those words, Lieutenant Sam Sasseville put an end to a day that had started at zero-dark thirty that morning. It was 15:00 hours on a frigid Friday in February, and Chuck was still a free man. Standing at the door of the kill house with smoke still drifting from tear gas canisters tossed inside, Chuck faced the nearby Atlantic Ocean. A stiff breeze blew inland, penetrating the weave of his Navy working uniform and wicking away the sweat of a solid day's work.

My loyalty to Country and Team is beyond reproach. He could still say those words from creed and mean them.

And yet, the mere fact that he had passed intelligence to an enemy nation, however inaccurate and harmless to US interests, troubled him, as did his fear of reprisal. Given that he had ignored his last dead drop for six months to the day, Chuck's handler, Lee, was bound to have reported to the RGB that Chuck had "gone to ground," having essentially disappeared off Lee's radar.

"Use good judgment."

Sam's admonishment shook Chuck out of his reverie. He slung his M-4 series Carbine over one shoulder and fell into step with Austin as they marched back to the Team building together.

"Especially you, Bam-Bam," Sam shouted after them.

Austin whirled and snapped off a sharp salute. "Hooyah, sir!"

"Come on." Chuck grabbed his belt and pulled him around. "He might stop calling you that if you would stop punching people."

"Hey, Bam-Bam, wait up." Suddenly Sam was coming after them.

Chuck watched with interest as Austin's expression turned sullen. Sam drew a piece of paper from his pocket as he reached them. "Here's the name of that person I said I would find for you. She offers weekend and evening hours. Call today before she closes shop and set up an appointment."

Austin scowled as he took the written note. "It's a woman?"

Sam's face hardened. "You got a problem with that?"

Austin didn't look up. "No, sir. It's cool."

Chuck wondered what the name and number was about.

"Make sure he doesn't miss his appointments, Haiku."

Chuck nodded. "Yes, sir."

Sam started to turn away, then caught himself. "Oh, and Chuck?"

"Sir?"

"You should smile once in a while. Your long face is depressing me."

Dismayed that his private concerns were visible to outsiders, Chuck managed a "Hooyah, LT." Then he and Austin continued their way along the sandy track between the kill house, where they practiced insertions, and the armory, where they stowed their weapons.

Austin elbowed him as they left the armory minutes later, headed for the parking lot. "Smile, brother, it's Friday."

Chuck grunted. The wind and rain earlier that week had given way to clear skies and starkly colder temperatures. He used to revel in their weekend ritual of bar-hopping and indoor sports activities. Then, every Sunday morning, he would call home and spend hours talking to his family. Weekends hadn't been the same since he'd severed ties with them. Tonight, all he wanted to do was to go home and sleep.

Austin studied him over the top of Chuck's new Subaru. "You want to go to counseling with me?"

"Hah." A laugh escaped Chuck as he realized Austin had to go to *counseling* for punching that guy at the bar. His smile died. "Thanks, but I'm fine."

"Are you, though? You seem really preoccupied."

Chuck set his mouth into a firm line and unlocked the vehicle. Austin gave up with a sigh and got in.

They used to take turns carpooling to work, but Chuck had insisted he drive every day since it was his idea for them to move seven miles north of their old apartment. Just before moving day, he had traded in his Honda Civic for a silver Subaru BRZ—not so much for its horsepower as for its tinted windows. He didn't want Lee to spot him driving on and off the base.

"Call that counselor," he reminded Austin as they exited the main gate.

It took them twelve minutes to drive seven miles to their new apartment, giving Austin plenty of time to place his call.

With a resentful sigh, Austin took his and Chuck's cellphones out of the glove box where they stored them when it wasn't hot. Chuck eyed his mirrors while sticking his phone into his pocket. He'd seen nothing to indicate that Lee had picked up his trail. Then again, Lee, who'd never given him the rest of his name, was a professional case officer. He knew tricks and tactics that went far beyond what Sobo had taught Chuck.

"Yes, ma'am. Hi."

Austin's conversation caught Chuck's attention.

"My name's Austin Collins. My platoon leader gave me your number. He said I could see you for some counseling on weekends and evenings?"

Chuck's lips twitched at how humiliated Austin sounded. A tinny voice replied in the affirmative, then offered Austin several time slots.

Austin opted to see her that very Sunday, then hung up.

"She sounds sexy," he remarked, putting his phone away.

Shaking his head at the ridiculous statement, Chuck drove them over the scenic bridge that conveyed them to the downtown area. A moped, moving fast for its size, passed them on the right, snatching Chuck's attention from the ice-laced shore to the slim driver, encased all in leather. He had the slight build of Chuck's handler, but with a helmet over his head, it was impossible to tell. With a quick look back, the driver changed lanes right in front of them and sped on.

It's not Lee, Chuck assured himself.

Hotels and boutiques surrounded them, obscuring their view of the Atlantic Ocean's choppy waters two blocks east. For nine months out of the year, the oceanfront crawled with tourists and locals alike, but in winter it resembled a post-apocalyptic city for the lack of traffic and pedestrians. Chuck liked it better that way.

The moped was several blocks ahead of them when Chuck turned left at 18th Street, headed for their brand-new East Harbor Apartments. Austin had loved the idea of living only five blocks from the boardwalk.

As they turned between the last two buildings of the complex, Chuck noted an orange and white U-Haul backing into a parking space across from theirs. His gaze alighted on the woman at the wheel, and alarms went off in his head.

Austin spotted her, too. "Hey, isn't that Katy from Calypso last weekend? Is she moving in?"

She obviously was, into an apartment within throwing distance of their own. What the hell?

A thorn of suspicion shot beneath Chuck's skin. That fact that she spoke Korean had freaked him out last weekend—not to mention how bright and appealing she was. And now she was their newest neighbor. What were the odds of that?

"Let's go say hi!" Austin started taking off his seatbelt.

Chuck hadn't even finished parking before his roommate vaulted out of the Subaru. Through his side mirror, Chuck watched as Austin greeted Katy, who hopped out of the van to hug him. The look of astonishment on her face abated some of Chuck's suspicion.

Then Austin pointed at Chuck's car, prompting a groan from him. Great, now *he* had to get out and come over.

Uneasiness slithered through him as he approached the pair. While he didn't trust anyone who spoke Korean, Katy was every bit as appealing in jeans, a Georgetown University T-shirt and an open jean jacket as in a form-fitting dress. As she smiled over at him, the single dimple that appeared on one cheek nearly obliterated his suspicions. She was maybe five feet, three inches tall, with super long hair. How dangerous could she be? Still, appearances were deceiving, as any good SEAL knew.

"Lisa, guess what?" Katy called over the nearby redhead who'd been talking on her cellphone while waving the truck into position. The redhead ventured closer, putting her phone away.

"What?"

"I already know a couple of our neighbors. This is Austin." Katy gestured graciously. "And this is Chuck. Or do you already know each other?"

Chuck knew her all right. She had at least five guys visiting on a rotating basis.

Lisa's catlike eyes hadn't left Austin. "I've seen them around."

Austin ignored her. "You remember our names," he praised Katy.

The redhead wasn't deterred. "You're Navy SEALs, aren't you?"

"Well, he is." Austin jerked his head at Chuck. "But I'm not."

Lisa frowned. "What?"

"He's kidding." Katy pointed to their uniforms. "They have the same insignia, see? I didn't notice that the other night."

Chuck finally found his tongue. "Really? Why are you moving here?"

Austin turned on him for his rudeness. "Dude!"

Kelly's eyebrows rose. "Um, I'm going to graduate school nearby."

"Didn't the semester start already?"

"Well, of course, it has." Her super-sweet reply held a steely undertone. "But I'm sick of commuting all the way from Norfolk, so I'm moving closer to campus."

"Which one?"

"Virginia Wesleyan." She propped her hands on her hips as if to say, *Is that okay with you?*

Her defiant posture excited him for some reason. She was feisty. He liked that. "What are you studying?"

"Masters of Business Administration."

"Yeah, you said you were a student," Austin inserted, clearly desperate to keep things friendly.

"And since I just lost my roommate," Lisa chimed in, putting her arm through Katy's in a show of solidarity, "the timing worked out well for both of us."

Austin gestured to the small van. "Do you want help carrying all this stuff up?"

Chuck almost kicked him. But then he thought he might like to see what Katy had brought with her.

Know your enemy, Sobo used to tell him.

Thirty minutes later, Chuck had burned several hundred calories helping Austin carry up Katy's bed frame, a queen-sized mattress, and a dresser. The chill that hit him every time he went down for another item kept him from sweating under his Navy working uniform. Apart from the furniture, which was all gently used, there were two tall wardrobe boxes, a foot locker just for shoes, and six smaller boxes. Several of the latter were the only ones left.

Chuck hefted two of them and ran straight into Katy who was coming down the stairs. His awareness spiked as she blocked his assent.

Nervousness made him blurt, "You have a shoe fetish, don't you?"

She didn't step aside. "Can you tell? I left half my collection at my parents' house in Springfield. They're hoping I'll move back in with them after I get my MBA. You probably know what that's like."

"Why would I know?"

She frowned at him. "Asian culture? Wouldn't your parents just love it if you moved back in?"

She couldn't know he hadn't spoken to his parents since Christmas Day. "I'm fifth-generation Japanese," he retorted. "We stopped being Asian in the last century." Actually, his family revered the Asian culture, but she didn't need to know that.

Her eyes went wide, and she moved over, letting

him pass her. "Sorry I asked," he heard her mutter.

Chiding himself for being so hostile, Chuck continued his trek to her third-story apartment. The door had been propped open, sucking cold air into the warm apartment.

In the living area, which was a mirror layout of his own, but with a cathedral ceiling instead of a flat one, Lisa was talking Austin into fixing the blinds at the door leading to the balcony.

Chuck proceeded to Katy's bedroom which, incidentally, gave her a clear view across the narrow parking lot into his own second-story room. Finding himself alone, Chuck seized his chance to snoop. He lowered his boxes onto the bed and peeled back the tape on one of them. It was filled with textbooks on business management, which suggested she *was* telling the truth. But there were also spy novels by John le Carré. He taped it shut again.

The second box held a lovely wooden chest with a mother-of-pearl peacock inlay. He lifted the ornate lid then quickly shut it as a mechanical music box started chiming. The drawers he opened more cautiously, coming across delicate earrings, pendants, and tiny rings riding in a velvet tray. He didn't see any pistols or knives or mysterious spy gadgets.

"We're all done, folks. Time for happy hour!"

Katy's announcement startled Chuck into shutting the second box and sticking the tape back on as fast as he could. He turned toward the living room, barreling into Katy as he rounded the corner.

"Oh! Sorry."

A spicy sweet aroma filled his head—ginger and oranges—along with an impression of warm, supple limbs.

"Last box." She slid into the room with it and put it next to those he'd just opened. Chuck gulped as the tape he'd tamped down curled up suddenly. But Katy had turned away with a smile, not noticing.

"It's time to relax." She curled a small hand around his elbow and towed him toward the living room.

Her proprietary gesture made his heart trot.

"What's your preferred poison?" she inquired as she released him, stepping up to the boxes on the kitchen counter.

Chuck looked for Austin and Lisa and spotted them sitting out on the balcony, despite the cold. "I don't care," he said.

"Come on, that's not true. Bourbon, right? I've got that here somewhere." She pulled a bubble-wrapped bottle from the box and peeled back the wrapping. "Nope, vodka. I used to manage an ABC store," she added, explaining her stash. "Ah, here's the bourbon."

It was, in fact, his favorite brand. Suspicion speared Chuck anew. Why had she scrutinized which brand of bourbon he preferred if she wasn't going to see him again?

"What about you two?" she called as Austin and Lisa came running back inside, shuddering with cold. "Have a splash to warm you up?"

"Sure, I'll take some." Austin wedged himself between Chuck and the wall, clearly trying to avoid the redhead.

With an obvious pout, Lisa sat on a stool "Me, too."

Katy poured bourbon over four tumblers full of ice. She picked up her glass, then waited for them to do the same. "Here's to new friendships."

Austin cast a sly smile at Chuck as he raised his tumbler. "Here, here."

Chuck refused to toast, but he wouldn't let the bourbon go to waste. He wasn't going to be friends with their new neighbor. A woman that cute and interested in him had to be up to something.

Making excuses several minutes later, Chuck dragged Austin from Katy's apartment and back to their own. "She just moved in. Give her time to unpack."

"Dude," Austin said, dogging his footsteps, "I can tell you like her, and she's into you, too."

Horrified by his transparency, Chuck said nothing and picked up his pace.

"Hah," Austin called, chasing him up their own stairs. "Your invisibility cloak changes nothing. If you're too shy to ask her, I'll set you up on a date."

"No." Turning at his door, Chuck shot him a glare as he pulled his keyring from his pocket.

"What are you afraid of? She's a take-charge kind of woman. That's your type, isn't it? She'll tell you what she likes."

Oh, God. Chuck's face burned with humiliation. He shoved the door open. "Leave it alone. I'm not interested."

"All right, jeez." Austin followed him in and shut the door. "I just thought having a girlfriend would be the perfect antidote to this funk you're in."

"I'm not in a funk." Chuck went straight to the kitchen to forage for food. To his own ears, he could tell he was protesting too much. And, of course, Austin was right. Having a girlfriend *would* be a welcome distraction from the sense of isolation that had left him feeling adrift for two months now. But he needed to know first if he could trust Katy.

Did she want him in her bed, behind bars, or six feet underground?

CHAPTER 3

K ELLY ROLLED OUT of bed at eight the next morning and peeked through the dark blue curtains she had hung the night before. Her move-in had been . . . interesting. But now that she was in position, there was little more to do than to settle into her role as friendly neighbor. She couldn't report on Chuck's activities even if she wanted to. He had lowered his blinds the instant he'd returned to his apartment the previous evening, like he suspected her already.

She blew out a breath. "Way to go." Offering him his favorite bourbon had been over the top, hadn't it? At least he hadn't seen anything suspicious when he'd searched the boxes on her bed—nor would he ever.

Katy Tang, her undercover persona, was not a Special Agent. Nor did she possess a single object that might suggest otherwise. Her gun, her crypto pass, and handcuffs were all secured in her desk at the Norfolk Field Office. Her only communication with the Bu, as Special Agents called the Bureau, was through her cellphone, and even that been purchased under the name Katy Tang.

Still, the fact that Chuck had peeked at her things meant he already held her in suspicion, and that was not a good sign. On the other hand, it also suggested he had something to hide. But it wasn't Kelly's job to discover what, so much as to befriend him, gaining his confidence and his trust.

But that would take time. All she could do in the meantime was to keep up with her studies as her masters would be attributed to the real Kelly Yang by the time she earned it. She could also make herself at home in her new environs. One thing she intended to take full advantage of was her proximity to the ocean. Instead of running on the treadmill at the gym at the field office, she could now run outdoors on the boardwalk. Anticipating just that, Kelly spun from the window to search for her running attire.

CHUCK RAISED HIS blinds on a yawn and froze. There on the curb opposite his window was his suspicious new neighbor, stretching out her quads. Her workout wear, complete with a turquoise jog-bra peeking out over the zipper of her black windbreaker, suggested she was heading out on a run, heedless of the cold that turned her breath to vapor.

His gaze slid to her sleek thighs and firm, rounded bottom, and his interest in her deepened. Every tiny thing about her appealed to him, from her scent, to her slim but solid body, to the challenging glint in her alert brown eyes.

Where was she headed on this inhospitably cold morning? For a run, obviously, but might she be meeting up with someone? A terrible suspicion dropped into his head. What if she was working for Lee, his former handler? That meant Lee had discovered where Chuck now lived. What if he had sent Katy to persuade Chuck to pick up the drop he'd been ignoring and to complete whatever task was detailed therein?

An even worse suspicion followed on the heels of the first. Or what if Katy was a Special Agent, heading out to meet up with others like her so they could plot his downfall?

There was only one way to find out. Chuck whirled from the window and hastily dressed.

By the time he reached the parking lot, Katy was gone. Gone where? The boardwalk seemed the most likely destination. He didn't feel like chasing her on foot. The cold air nipped at his nose and ears. He charged back upstairs for his phone and his keyring.

A minute later, Chuck was cruising toward the oceanfront, passing a church, a strip mall, condos, and a bank. He spotted Katy by her dark ponytail swinging behind her as she dashed across Atlantic Avenue one intersection ahead of him. The wide, bricked alley on the other side divided a parking garage from a two-star hotel and conveyed pedestrians to the boardwalk.

By the time Chuck reached the second intersection, Katy had disappeared from view. The only way to keep an eye on her now was by foot. As he waited for the light to turn green, his attention went to the red moped bearing down on him through his rearview mirror. His pulse ticked upward. It was the same moped that had passed him yesterday.

The light turned green as it drew alongside him, squeezing between his Subaru and the curb. Chuck sped forward, eyes glued to his rearview. The moped turned right, mocking his fears. Lee had driven a yellow Toyota pickup, anyway, so why worry about a man on a moped?

Chuck zipped into the parking garage, relieved to see parking was free for the first two hours as he'd left his wallet at the apartment. He turned into the first empty space, jumped out, and hustled through a bricked plaza hoping to discover what Katy was up to.

By the time he arrived at the bird sculpture that distinguished 18th Street Plaza from the other cut-throughs, Katy was at least a quarter mile up the boardwalk. Wet air blew in off the fitful ocean, obscuring his view of her. Both of Chuck's knees twinged at the mere thought of giving chase. He had run on the beach in boots every day that week. He would wait to see if she came back in a timely manner.

He eyed the establishments along the boardwalk. Wasn't there a coffee shop in the lobby of the Fairfield

Inn and Suites? Yes, and it overlooked the boardwalk, which was exactly what he wanted.

Minutes later, he had paid for a donut and a coffee using the digital debit card on his cellphone. He sat by the window dunking the plain donut into his black coffee. That action made him think of the coffee shop across town where he'd met Lee on more than one occasion.

Lithe and likeable, Lee had sidled up to Chuck at a hardware store, of all places, claiming he knew of Chuck's relationship to Kim Chun-ja, Chuck's grandmother, who was also the great aunt of Kim Jong-un, himself. Lee also claimed distant kinship to North Korea's leader. That commonality made them cousins, Lee had insisted. The forty-something RGB agent worked at the Norfolk Naval Shipyard as a supposed South Korean immigrant with a green card. He had invited Chuck to a baseball game, to go deep-sea fishing, then to a wrestling match. Lee had seemed fun and easy-going until he talked about the fate of North Korea, at which point he got intense, reminding Chuck of his obligation to defend the hermit kingdom from invasion and conquest.

Chuck's chest filled with self-loathing for having cooperated with the RGB's demands. Merely communicating with Pyongyang was treachery enough to get him kicked off the Teams and sent to prison. Thank God he had quit before he'd dug him himself too deep a hole to get out of. Or was that the case already?

He dipped his donut, bit into the soggy treat, and stared out at the pounding surf. Growing bored, he checked the news on his cellphone, looking up every now and then to see if Katy had made her way back.

Half an hour passed. Draining his coffee, Chuck gave up waiting for her. She'd clearly met up with someone and now he would never know who. He dumped his trash on his way to the door. Salt-laced wind buffeted him as he stepped onto the boardwalk, then drew up short. There was Katy resting on a bench not a hundred yards away, staring out at the ocean.

Unwilling to return to the coffee shop, Chuck hastened in the direction of his car, hugging the facades of the buildings in the hope that she wouldn't get up and immediately see him. He was crossing under the sculpture of the birds in flight when something brushed his shoulder then struck one of the columns holding up the birds.

Thunk!

Chuck wheeled behind the tall sculpture before his brain even registered, *That was a bullet!* In disbelief, he peeked around his scant protection at the man bearing down on him, and his heart dropped to his feet.

No, no, no. Not this. Not now.

It was Lee, dressed in black leather and wearing

sunglasses, no helmet. The grim set of the man's mouth communicated his intent. Chuck cast about for better cover, but the hotel exit required a keycard. The entrance to the parking garage was too far away.

Heart pounding, Chuck assessed his nemesis. Was it too much to hope Lee's first shot had been a warning? Not with that hand hidden under his jacket.

Chuck wasn't entirely defenseless. From the ankle wrap he wore ever since his trip to Spain, he retrieved his three throwing stars, or *shuriken*.

He hurled the first one immediately. It struck Lee's leather jacket and bounced right off as if the jacket was lined with Kevlar.

Lee smirked, then fired in retaliation. The bullet sang past Chuck's ear, a near miss.

The ocean's roar drowned Lee's footsteps as he came closer. Chuck flung his second star, aiming lower this time. It imbedded in the man's thigh.

With a grunt of agony, Lee halted. Gritting his teeth, he tore the razor-edged weapon from his flesh. Blood gushed through the slit in his leather pants. Chuck's confidence rose. He readied himself to hurl his last *shuriken* directly at Lee's face.

"Hey!"

Chuck glanced over at a woman's cry. Lee did not. He took off, firing at Chuck as he ran past him.

The impact of the bullet knocked Chuck off his feet. He sprawled onto the sandy brick plaza, dropping his last *shuriken* as pain seared his chest. *This can't be happening.* He clapped a hand to the source of pain, felt blood well between his fingers, warm and slippery.

Lee had disappeared into the parking garage. With a groan of defeat, Chuck gave his attention to the woman skidding onto her knees next to him. Her expression was nothing short of stricken.

"Oh, my God. That man just shot you!" She produced a cellphone from her zippered pocket.

"Wh-what are you doing?" Chuck didn't want to explain to *anyone* what had just happened.

"You need an ambulance." Her voice quavered but it brooked no argument.

In the distance, Chuck heard the little engine of a moped roar to life. He craned his neck, just in time to see Lee zip out of the garage, headed for Atlantic Avenue. Damn it all. He should have heeded his foreboding.

"Yes." Katy's words recaptured his attention. "I need an ambulance, stat, at the 18th Street Plaza near the boardwalk. A man's been shot. The assailant just drove off on his moped."

The horror on Katy's face suggested Chuck might not make it. The pain corkscrewing into his chest confirmed it.

"Just let me die," he pleaded. If the police managed to catch his handler, Lee would drag Chuck down with him.

Katy ignored him, crying into the phone. "Yes, the plaza. Hurry!" She put her phone down. "The hell I am going to let you die," she added.

Her ferocity was beautiful. Chuck stared into her moist, determined gaze and realized he had only one regret—not getting to know her better.

"You're spectacular," he whispered. Why not tell the truth? He wasn't going to survive the shooting anyway. He could feel the bullet tracking toward his heart.

"Stop talking," she pleaded, while covering his hand with both of hers.

Chuck's gaze went up the columns of the sculpture to the three sea birds frozen in flight. Their golden patina caught and held the feeble sunlight. He wished he could take a photo of them. He wished he could start over with Katy and live a normal life. But he wasn't going to make it. Lee had seen to that.

WATCHING CHUCK GET triaged and then swept into an ambulance was nothing short of surreal. Kelly's knees jittered with shock. Who was the man who'd just tried to kill him? She hadn't seen more than a glimpse of his face, but she could tell he was Asian. Did that mean anything?

"Ma'am, I know this is a bad time, but can I ask

you some questions?"

As the doors of the ambulance clanged shut, Kelly turned toward the gruff voice and met the ocean-blue eyes of a craggy-faced man in his late forties, who held up a badge while chomping on a piece of gum.

"Detective Mike Scruggs."

Dressed in civilian clothing, Scruggs still carried himself like a cop. The badge gave way to a notepad and a pen, suggesting he was not a fan of technology.

"May I get your name?"

Kelly couldn't reveal her connection with the FBI, not even to a police officer. "Katy Tang," she said.

"Any relation to the victim?"

"I'm his neighbor. We live in the same apartments, East Harbor, just up the road."

Scruggs, who'd clearly had bad acne as an adolescent, stopped chewing on his gum and stared at her. "Okay, Katy Tang. Are you carrying any ID?"

"No. I was out running. I don't have it on me."

"But you have your phone." One corner of his mouth twitched, suggesting he found that ironic. "Tell me your address and phone number," he requested. Once he'd scribbled down the information, he said, "And the victim's name and address."

She had both of those memorized. "I don't know his phone number." But she *had* appropriated both Chuck's cellphone and his car keys after he passed out.

Scruggs gestured toward the cordoned-off area and

said, "Why don't you describe for me what happened here, Katy Tang?"

Kelly walked him away from the small crowd of onlookers toward the bird sculptures where Chuck had collapsed. The memory of him lying flat on his back made her stomach lurch. *You're spectacular*, he'd said. Traitor or not, she didn't want him dying right now. She wanted to get to know him—professionally, of course.

Hugging herself against sudden tremors, she indicated Chuck's location, the direction the shooter had come from, and where she was when she'd spotted the pair. "At first I didn't see the gun. I recognized Chuck, though, when I saw him hurl an object at the man approaching him."

"Object?"

"Here's one." Kelly pointed to the weapon Chuck had been clutching when he fell. She turned and walked to where the shooter had been standing when she came upon them. "And there's another." She pointed at the bloody *shuriken* lying near a bush. "That's the shooter's blood," she realized. Nausea roiled up suddenly.

Scruggs bent over to draw a circle of chalk around the weapon. Then he bagged it, sticking the evidence in the coat of his thick, brown jacket.

"Who attacked whom first?" he asked as he straightened.

Kelly thought back. "I couldn't tell you, but Chuck was clearly on the defensive. I'm sure you'll find several shell casings in this area. Yep, there's one there." She pointed to it.

"What did this shooter look like? Do you think you could identify him?" Scruggs squatted to examine a casing without touching it.

"I didn't get a good look at him, but I think he was Asian, average height, slender, with a short haircut. He took off running when I yelled, but he still got another shot off."

"And then what happened?"

"Chuck fell, and the shooter ran to the parking garage. Seconds later he roared out on a red moped and took off up Atlantic Avenue."

"Red, huh? I don't suppose you got a look at the plates?"

"He had Virginia tags," she recalled, "but he was too far away for me to read them. Maybe the parking garage has surveillance cameras."

The suggestion seemed to amuse him. "I'll look into that. Thank you."

Kelly bit her lip. Had she been too thorough? She dragged her ponytail out of her face. "Can I go now?"

"Just one more question. Any idea what the victim was up to this morning? What was he doing on the boardwalk this early?"

"I don't know. Taking a walk?" *Or maybe he'd been*

following me, she considered with a jolt of alarm.

The detective chomped his gum and narrowed his eyes. "Is there anything else you'd like to share with me, Miss Katy Tang?"

"I can't think of anything." Afraid her teeth might chatter if she said too much, Kelly said, "You got a business card? If I think of something else, I'll call you."

One corner of Scruggs' mouth curled as he reached into a pocket. "Stay in touch, Miss Katy Tang." He handed her the card, which she stowed inside her full pocket.

His repeated use of her cover name annoyed her. Without another word to him, Kelly hurried to the parking garage. At least, with Chuck's car here, she could return to the apartment quickly. Moreover, having Chuck's keys afforded her the chance to search his new car. Not right now, though. First, she needed to tell Hannah what had happened.

The sleek, silver Subaru was parked right inside the garage's entrance. Kelly thumbed the remote, then used one index finger to open the door. She sank onto the leather seat and used the same finger to pull the door shut. The new-car smell had her reaching for the travel-pack of tissues on the dash. She wiped off as much of the blood on her hands as she could, then speed-dialed Hannah.

"Good morning, Munchkin. What's up?"

Kelly hated to ruin Hannah's good mood. "The target was just shot near the boardwalk by an unidentified shooter." She spoke quickly, trying and failing to quell the tremor in her voice. "I was the first one to come across him. It's bad."

In the stunned silence that followed, Kelly could hear Hannah's three young sons chattering.

"Hang on." Hannah went silent as she presumably walked into a different room and shut the door. "Luther's going to be horrified," she continued on a hushed note, "but I can't tell him what happened without jeopardizing the investigation. Go back to the apartment and tell the roommate. He'll contact their platoon leader, and news will go up the chain of command from there."

"Okay. Headed to the apartment now." Kelly punched the ignition button. "Hey, you should know that a Virginia Beach detective is looking into the shooting. I've got his number. You want it?"

"Yes."

Kelly pulled the card from her pocket and relayed Mike Scruggs' name and number. "He might find the shooter before we do," Kelly warned.

"We'll take care of him," Hannah promised. "You just stick to your cover."

"One more thing." Kelly drew a breath. "I secured the target's new cellphone after he passed out."

"Oh, wow, that's great!"

"I know." The Bu's attempt to tap the target's old phone had come to naught when he'd stopped using that number back in December.

"Maybe Ernie can pick it up from you later today," Hannah suggested.

"I want to bring it in. Chuck will never know. I'm telling you he's in serious condition."

"Okay. If you can get away without raising suspicions."

"I think I can. I'll let you know."

"Sounds good. Are you okay, Munchkin? It's traumatic, I know, seeing someone get shot."

Kelly's eyes stung at the words. "I'm fine," she insisted. But her hands were still sticky with Chuck's blood. Belated shock left her queasy. She closed her eyes and gulped.

"I'll let you go, then. Keep in touch."

Kelly zipped her phone next to Chuck's, adjusted the seat so she could see over the steering wheel, then backed out of the parking spot using the back-up camera. She couldn't see out of any of the mirrors.

Two minutes later, she parked Chuck's car where it belonged, next to Austin's and returned Chuck's seat to its previous position. Taking the bloody tissues with her, she hurried up the stairs to the SEALs' apartment, where she released her grip on her tightly held emotions. Tears rushed into her eyes as she knocked on their door.

By the time a sleepy Austin stood before her looking like Adonis in plaid pajama pants, her cheeks were wet.

His eyes widened as he took in her appearance. "Katy, what's wrong?"

"Chuck was just shot." Her voice cracked as she delivered the news.

"What? Is that his blood on those tissues?"

"Yes. He's still alive, I think. But he was unconscious when the ambulance took him."

Austin pulled her into the apartment. Hands heavy on her shoulders, he asked in a suddenly calm voice what happened.

With her voice quaking, Kelly related how she'd been coming back from her run when she realized Chuck was trying to fend off a shooter dressed in black leather.

"I yelled at the man, who took off on a moped. Then I called 911 and the ambulance came. They took him to Sentara Princess Anne."

Austin released her to drag a hand through his hair. "I'll go there now. You want to come?"

"Yes, of course."

"I have to call my platoon leader. You can toss those tissues in the trash and wash your hands." He pointed at the kitchen sink as he headed for his bedroom.

Watching the pink water swill down the kitchen

sink, Kelly wondered what would happen if the target died. The Bu would never know to what lengths he'd been spying, and Chuck himself would certainly never look at her again as he had that morning. He'd be dead.

Austin was still in his bedroom. She ventured down the hall and called through his cracked door, "Hey, we need to bring Chuck's insurance information. He didn't have his wallet on him."

"I think it's on his dresser. Take out his military ID. That's all he needs."

Unexpected access to Chuck's bedroom made Kelly's heart trot. The space was a mirror-image of her own, with a window straight ahead and a private bathroom to her left. The sparse furnishings seemed to suit Chuck. A double bed with a teak headboard stood against the left wall. Its white down comforter had been tossed over itself, as if he'd left in a hurry.

A matching teak desk and dresser faced the bed, with the desk closer to the window. Drawn to an antique-looking sword mounted on the wall above it, Kelly approached the sword and recognized the lettering inscribed into the blade as a type of Japanese script. Was this a family heirloom from Chuck's paternal line? The sword seemed to be guarding his laptop.

She turned toward his dresser, where the framed photo of a lovely blue butterfly struck her as less ominous. Who would have guessed Chuck liked butterflies?

Austin's audible phone conversation in the room next door wrested Kelly's attention to the wallet and bowl of change lying atop the dresser. She rifled through Chuck's wallet, finding his military ID. It had a newer photo than the one in his personnel file. He carried two credit cards—she already knew that—plus a blood donor card, a library card, and thirty-two dollars in cash.

With Austin still on his call, Kelly helped herself to the military ID, put the wallet back, and looked around. The single drawer on his nightstand caught her eye. With a glance at the door, she crossed over to it and slowly slid the drawer open. A bag of cough drops and an unopened box of condoms.

"Gonna brush my teeth real quick." Austin pushed into his bathroom across the hall from Chuck's door.

With a guilty start, Kelly shut the nightstand. Had Austin noticed her snooping? She returned to the living room to wait.

The common area, like Chuck's room, was surprisingly neat for a pair of bachelors. Chuck had left his shoes by the front door, betraying a cultural practice Kelly also practiced. The black leather couch, positioned before a flatscreen TV, made it easy to imagine the roommates watching football together. With a pang, she wondered if Chuck would ever wear those shoes or watch another game again.

Austin reappeared in a gray sweatsuit that matched his distracted gaze. "Question," he said as he approached her. "Both you and Chuck were on the boardwalk. Did you go together?"

"No, I went for a run and he, apparently, drove there. I'm not sure why."

"Drove there. Where's his car now?"

"I brought it back so he wouldn't get it towed."

"Where are the keys?"

"I just put them in the drawer beside his bed," she lied, thinking fast. "Here's his ID." She handed it to Austin. "We should hurry. Would you like me to drive?"

"No. I'll take us."

Austin didn't speak again as he sped them down General Booth Boulevard headed for the hospital. "Tell me exactly what happened," he requested.

His focused tone made her nervous. He was clearly in Navy SEAL mode, which meant he could drive like a bat out of hell with precision that impressed her, all while asking clarifying questions and coping with the shock that his roommate had just been shot. Kelly told him what she'd told Detective Scruggs earlier.

Austin's jaw flexed as he listened. "Why would someone shoot him like that, in broad daylight?"

"I have no idea. I'm sure the police will find out, though." She found herself laying a reassuring hand on his upper arm. Hello, muscles. It was hard not to like Austin, who struck her as a cross between Captain America and a Golden Retriever. It would probably cripple him to find out his own roommate was a spy.

She cringed, looking out the window to hide her expression. If Chuck was, indeed, the SEAL spy reported by the CIA's North Korean source, then he had betrayed more than his country. He'd betrayed his SEAL brothers and the bond of trust they'd forged through shared ideology and experience.

That didn't stop Charles Suzuki from leading a double life, did it? His being shot that morning was proof that there was more to him than met the eye. The shooter being of Asian descent raised more questions than answers, however. Who was he, exactly, and what entity did he represent? The only question to which she had a clear answer was what did the shooter want? He wanted Chuck to die. But why? Her mind drew a blank.

CHAPTER 4

FORCED TO KEEP up with Austin's longer strides, Kelly broke into a jog as they hurried across the hospital's half-empty parking lot and through the sliding glass doors of the emergency room at Sentara Princess Anne.

The essence of diffused lavender greeted them as they stepped into a well-appointed waiting room. It would have been virtually empty if weren't for the knot of grim-faced, hard-bodied men sitting in the far corner, making the chairs look like doll furniture. Clearly, they lived closer to the hospital than Austin did.

Lieutenant Sam Sasseville looked up, and Kelly gulped, recalling the lie she'd told Austin at Calypso. The lieutenant had brought his wife with him, if Kelly's memory served. Kelly had researched every SEAL on the east coast, using information provided by the Naval Criminal Investigation Service.

Austin towed Kelly in his wake as her steps lagged. "How's he doing?" he demanded of the group.

Their tense expressions said it all. Lieutenant Sasseville answered for them. "We don't know. He's in emergency surgery. Who's this?" Kelly locked her knees as the lieutenant stood up, prompting the others to do likewise.

Austin threw a friendly arm over her shoulders. "This is Katy. She was on the boardwalk when Chuck got shot." But then he divided a puzzled glance between Sam and Kelly. "Wait, you met Katy at Calypso last week, when you told her that I speak Korean."

Jungle-green eyes narrowed with confusion on Kelly.

"That's right," she said with forced confidence, "the night Austin punched that bully in the nose. Good to see you again."

"You, too," Sam said, clearly mystified.

"This is Sam's wife, Maddie," Austin added.

Happy to move on, Kelly accepted the attractive blonde's handshake.

"These guys are Chief Adams, Jeremiah Bullfrog, Tristan Halliday, and Mitch Thoreau."

As the men inclined their heads at her, Kelly nodded back. She was already familiar with their names, but Bullfrog? That had to be a code name. Chief Adams's eyes were as blue as they'd been in his military mug shot. Tristan Halliday was the former NASCAR racer, and Mitch Thoreau was, according to his personnel file, related to the 19th century American author, Henry David Thoreau.

As they all resumed their seats, Austin pulled Kelly onto a settee across from them.

Sam was staring at her, clearly still trying to place her. "So, you were there when Chuck got shot? Tell us what happened." A faint Hispanic accent colored his vowels.

"Sam." His wife nudged him. "Don't grill her."

The man grimaced at Kelly. "Sorry. I'm protective of my men."

"I understand." Nervousness tangled Kelly's tongue. With Chuck's teammates hanging on her every word, she stammered that she'd gone for a jog that morning and, just as she was headed back toward her apartment, she'd run into a man with a gun targeting someone who was trying to conceal himself. "You know the bird sculptures at the 18th Street Plaza? Chuck was taking cover behind one of the pillars. I recognized him when he threw a star-shaped thingy at his attacker's leg."

Sam was scowling. "His *shuriken.*"

"I yelled, *Hey!* but the shooter ran off, firing again, and Chuck went down." She described how the man had peeled out of the parking garage on a moped and how she'd called 911 while trying to slow Chuck's bleeding. "Then the ambulance came and took him away. A police detective asked me a bunch of questions. After that, I found Chuck's car and drove it back to tell Austin what had happened."

The lieutenant's gaze hadn't left her face. "What do you do? You seem to have training of some kind."

"Oh." Kelly huffed nervously. "No training. I'm a graduate student."

To her relief, the blue-eyed chief interrupted, "Here comes Becca."

They all stood up again as a pretty brunette in pink scrubs approached them. Her pained expression did not bode well.

"Hey, everyone." Becca went straight up to Adams and leaned into him. Kelly spied their matching wedding rings as he put an arm around her.

"Well, the news isn't great but it's not terrible either," the nurse relayed. "Chuck made it through surgery. The bullet went into his chest, right under his armpit, bruising a rib and causing a large hemothorax which collapsed his left lung. The bullet is out, the blood in the pleural space is draining, but he is still hemodynamically unstable, so he's going to spend some time in ICU. Intake is asking for his insurance information. Does anyone have that?"

"Right here." Austin produced Chuck's ID and gave it to her.

"Thanks. I'll put it with his belongings when intake's done with it."

Jeremiah Winters—that was his real name Kelly recalled—had been standing very still with his eyes closed. He opened them suddenly and said, "Chuck's going to make it. He'll be all right."

To Kelly's bemusement, the SEALs heaved a collective sigh of relief at the tall man's prediction.

Lieutenant Sasseville pointed Kelly out to Becca. "This woman saw Chuck get shot and called the paramedics. Katy this Becca Adams."

Nurse Adams's expression softened as she took in Kelly's awkward smile. "So, you're the one that saved his life. You should know if Chuck had arrived ten minutes later than he did, the bullet would have killed him."

All six SEALs, including Austin, eyed Kelly with considerably more warmth.

"That makes you one of us now," Sam declared.

Kelly shrugged off her contribution. "Anybody would have done the same."

The nurse's husband asked her suddenly. "Can you describe the shooter for us?"

"Um, well, I didn't see his face at all, but he looked Asian from the back. He was slim, not very tall. He wore black leather from head to toe, and he drove a red moped, older model."

"Dang." Austin elbowed her. "You should go into law enforcement."

Kelly bit her lower lip.

"Bam-Bam," Lieutenant Sasseville said while looking at Austin, "Chuck's not involved with any gangs around here, is he?"

Bam-Bam? Kelly hadn't known Austin had a nick-name.

He scoffed at the idea. "Of course not. Chuck has no social life apart from the Team. You know that."

Adams said, "Maybe it was a case of mistaken identity."

"Hmph." Sam clearly didn't think so. He focused back on Kelly. "What do the police know? Anything?"

"They didn't tell me anything."

"What about the Chinese?" Adams asked.

The question elicited silence while the men all looked at each other. Kelly could only imagine what they were recollecting and why Adams would make such a suggestion.

Sam's wife, Maddie, took her husband's hand and murmured, "Honey, we need to get back to Melinda. Emma has a hair appointment at—what time, Jeremiah?"

"Noon, I think," the tall man replied.

It was apparent to Kelly that the tight-knit group watched each other's children now and then.

"There's no point to you all waiting here," Becca said to all of them. "Chuck will be in ICU until he's stable enough to be moved, and no one's allowed in ICU, so you can't visit him. I'm working until 8 PM tonight." She nodded toward her husband. "I'll keep Brant informed of Chuck's progress and he'll update the rest of you."

"Right," Brant Adams agreed. "Chuck will be safe in ICU."

"That's true," Becca agreed. "It takes a badge and a code to get in there."

"All right. We need to head out," Sam said. "You'll let us know if he's moved? I want to talk to him the minute he's cleared for visitors. I'm sure the XO and the CO will too."

"Of course." Becca focused on him. "I assume you're going to reach out to his family. They live in California, don't they?"

San Diego, Kelly almost volunteered, having researched Chuck's family extensively.

"Yeah." Sam blew out a breath, clearly not relishing the task. "I'll call them."

Maddie gave the nurse a quick hug. "Thanks, Becca."

Friends, Kelly deduced.

"Anytime." Becca held up Chuck's ID card. "I have to get this over to Intake. Bye, sweetie." She kissed her husband's cheek, then waved at the others as she hurried off.

As Sam prepared to leave with his wife, he jutted out his hand for Kelly to shake. "Now that you're one of us, Katy, we'll see you again, right?"

His hand completely engulfed her own. "I hope so." Kelly shared a smile with Maddie and Jeremiah. Then the threesome headed out together.

Tristan, the former NASCAR driver declared, with a southern drawl, "I'm hittin' up the cafeteria for coffee first. Who's comin' with me?"

"I'll go," Thoreau replied.

"Me, too." Chief Adams clamped a hand on Austin's shoulder as they started for the cafeteria. "Chuck's gonna be fine, buddy. They'll take good care of him here."

Austin simply nodded. He and Kelly were left standing by themselves.

"Should we go?" Kelly suggested. Her surveillance squad was waiting to get their hands on Chuck's cellphone.

Austin stared down at the carpet. "Just feels wrong to leave."

He sounded so forlorn she was moved to touch his arm again. "You heard what Jeremiah Bullfrog said. Chuck's going to be okay."

"True." Austin lifted his gaze. "Jeremiah's never wrong, either. He's got clairvoyant powers. Supposedly we all have them."

"So, he'll be fine," she insisted. In her mind, a clock had started ticking down the seconds. Who knew when Chuck was going to wake up and ask for his cellphone?

"All right. Let's leave, I guess."

Austin drove them back to their apartment, saying not a word. As they neared 18th Street, she broke the silence. "Can I give you my cell number so you can update me?"

"Yeah, yeah. Text my phone. That way I'll have it." He recited his number to her, and she sent him a text, *Katy Tang.*

"I'll be studying at the library this afternoon," she let him know as he zipped across the bridge at Rudee Inlet. Sunlight glanced off the water below them.

"You mean the Oceanfront Library right up the street?"

"No, the one on my campus. It takes like twenty minutes to get there, but they have all the resources I need. Would you text me the minute you hear anything?"

"Sure."

Curiosity got the better of her as they closed in on 18th Street. "How'd you get that nickname Bam-Bam?"

He managed a wan smile. "I collect Flintstone paraphernalia."

"Oh. So that's what your license plate says." The letters FLNSTN now made sense.

"I also tend to beat up bullies, but I'm working on that," he confessed with touching humility.

"Good for you." She smiled her approval as he turned into their apartment complex.

Austin parked his Clubman, then caught Kelly off-guard by giving her a swift, sincere hug. "Thanks for saving Chuck's life today." The next instant, he was stepping out of his car.

Kelly followed suit, feeling strangely guilty. "Listen, if Chuck—*when* Chuck recovers," she amended, over the top of the car, "I'd like to go with you if you plan to visit him."

Austin nodded. "Sure. He'd like that. I'll keep in touch." Patting the cellphone in his pocket, he turned and plodded toward the steps to his apartment.

Kelly dashed toward her own apartment where she texted both Hannah and Ernie. *I can meet you at the office in half an hour.* Then she took her phone into her bathroom and waited for a reply.

As anxious as she was for Chuck to pull through and as bizarre as the shooting had been, it had delivered her directly into Chuck's circle of friends. According to Sam, she was one of them now.

She had never imagined she would be part of the target's inner circle in less than a day. She even had his cellphone in her possession. Imagine finding proof of his clandestine connection to North Korea before the day was even over!

LESS THAN AN hour later, Kelly marched into the FBI field office, a sprawling modern building surrounded by a wrought iron fence. In a room known fondly as The Bull Pen, she took a seat at the conference table.

It was here in the Bull Pen where Kelly had filled her "coloring book," working year after year in one of the cubicles lining the walls, hoping to advance her way to undercover work.

At the table with Kelly were three of her closest colleagues, all willing to take time out of their Saturday in the hopes of discovering new evidence. Ernie Savowitz—balding, pudgy, and pushing forty—was responsible for all things technical. He had hurdled the security measures on Chuck's cellphone and gained complete access. Hannah—late thirties, redheaded, and six feet tall in her running shoes—sat catty-corner to Ernie tapping long fingers on the tabletop. In stark contrast to Hannah, their supervising agent, Rafael Valentino, sat across from her, as still and peaceful as a pond. Valentino also supervised the unarmed surveillance specialists known as the Gs, as well as their armed equivalents, the Special Operations Group Agents, or SOGs. A distinguished gentleman approximately fifty-five, Valentino bore a scar on his neck from a violent encounter that had damaged his vocal cords. If gargoyles could talk, Kelly imagined they would sound like Valentino did whenever he spoke.

Ernie sighed and turned his laptop around so everyone could see. "Well, I'm sorry to tell you this, but there's hardly anything on this phone or even in the iCloud account associated with it." The screen was a replica of Chuck's home screen.

Hannah's fingers stilled. Kelly's hopes plunged.

"What do you mean?" Valentino grated.

Ernie gestured at the actual phone, lying face up on the table in front of them. "I mean, that is a brand-new iPhone. Apple just came out with that model, and there are only a handful of apps on it. Also, when the target bought it, he linked it to a new, unused iCloud account. The tech wiz met Kelly's disappointed gaze and grimaced his apology. They had worked together often over the years. Kelly suspected Ernie had a crush on her, though he had never once crossed the line.

"Well, does it at least tell us where he's been lately?" Hannah asked.

"Unfortunately, no. His location services are all turned off. We have no history of where he's been, but that's about to change. I've turned location services on, only it still looks like they're off. From now on, we'll know where he is, provided he's got his phone with him. We'll also hear everything he says, even when his phone's turned *off*, as long as it's got battery life."

Kelly made a scoffing sound. "Could it be any more obvious that he's hiding something?"

"Or hiding himself," Valentino suggested.

Kelly looked at him, puzzled.

Valentino gestured. "Who do you think shot the target this morning?"

His answer met with silence, which Kelly broke.

"One of the men on Chuck's team suggested it might be the Chinese."

Valentino tipped his salt-and-pepper curls. "Allow me to make another suggestion. The target was shot by a North Korean, possibly even his own handler."

The astonishing thought made Kelly blink.

"Why?" Hannah demanded.

"Failure to cooperate?" Valentino shrugged. "Perhaps he's become a security risk."

Hannah rubbed her forehead. "This opens a whole new can of worms."

"There is one app on his phone that kind of ties in with that theory." Ernie touched the app and opened it for them to see.

Kelly recognized Chuck and Austin's living room and gasped. "He's got a security camera in his apartment!"

"Lots of people have security cameras," Hannah pointed out. "It doesn't mean they're expecting the worst or fearing reprisal."

Kelly interrupted. "Wait, is that the only camera?" If he had one in his bedroom, it would have filmed her snooping.

"It's the only one connected to the app," Ernie assured her. "This model requires Wi-Fi to work, so we'll just jam the Wi-Fi when we make our clandestine entry."

"And there goes everyone's Wi-Fi in the apartment

complex," Kelly pointed out.

Hannah waved aside her objection. "That's fine. Red only needs a couple of hours to install surveillance. Assuming the target has a laptop—"

"He does," Kelly affirmed.

"Then we'll send in a CART expert at the same time," Hannah decided, referring to the FBI's Computer Analysis Response Team. "Let's hope there's more on his laptop than there was on his phone."

Kelly remembered Chuck's keyring. "We don't even have to break in." She dug into her pocket for the item she'd been withholding until then. "I got the target's car fob and the key to his apartment." And she needed to return then both before Austin realized she had lied to him.

Hannah snatched them from her with a grin of approval. "Ernie, go and make two copies of the house key and see what you can do with the car fob. I think we should enter the apartment Monday, while the target's still in the hospital and the roommate is at work."

Kelly nodded. "I agree, but I have class in the morning, so it'll have to be afternoon."

Valentino interrupted, "I assume we have a FISA order to search his residence?" Per the Foreign Intelligence Surveillance Act of 1978, the order was required before they could pursue any sort of surveillance.

"It came in yesterday," Hannah assured him, "just in time. It covers his apartment, as well as his car and his new iPhone."

"The sooner the better, then," Valentino agreed.

As Ernie left the room to make copies, Kelly lunged for Chuck's phone which was still unlocked. "I want to see his photos and his contact list," she explained as she clicked on the camera icon and thumbed through his pictures. "Oh, wow."

Her colleagues could see on Ernie's laptop what Kelly was looking at. Valentino made a thoughtful sound.

Chuck had dozens of photos, nearly every one of them a work of art. There were trees shrouded in mist, a breathtaking sunrise, the moon reflected on the ocean. Kelly's thoughts flashed to the framed photo of the butterfly hanging over his dresser.

"He's a good photographer," Hannah commented. "Do you think he took all those?"

"I think so." Coming to the last photo, Kelly opened Chuck's list of contacts and perused them. Recognizing most of the names as those of the teammates she'd just met, she realized the list was exceptionally short. She scrolled through it again, and a thought occurred to her as she came to the letter S.

"There's only Sam Sasseville here," she stated. "Where is his family?"

Silence fell between the trio before Hannah suggested, "Maybe he has their numbers memorized?"

Kelly reviewed in her mind what she knew of Chuck's family. He had spent his entire childhood living in the same house in San Diego. His father and grandfather before him owned and operated Suzuki Enterprises, exporting goods to the Far East. Having investigated each member already, Kelly had found no evidence suggesting they were anything but upstanding US citizens—all except his mysterious grandmother whose records stated she'd been born in what was now North Korea.

Kelly shook her head. "Memorized or not, it makes no sense his family isn't among his contacts. I mean, maybe, if they communicated via Facebook or Instagram, but the man has no social media apps of any kind."

"SEALs are very private people," Valentino stated, "and with good reason."

"He has Gmail," Kelly discovered, scanning his Inbox, "but there's nothing in it except Junk mail, advertisements and such." Frustrated, she cleared the screen and zipped the phone back into her pocket. "Better get this back to the target. I'll go find Ernie on my way out."

Hannah glanced at her watch. "It's been four hours since you called me."

"Right." Kelly scooted her seat back. "Hey, did

you reach out to Detective Scruggs yet?"

"Not yet. I'll do that next—"

"Mike Scruggs?" Valentino divided a sharp look between them. "With the Virginia Beach PD?"

"Yes." Kelly and Hannah said at the same time.

"He's the one investigating the shooting?"

"Yes."

Valentino smiled and rubbed his palms together. "I've worked with Scruggs before, way back in '02 when we collaborated with local law enforcement to combat homegrown terrorism. I've never forgotten Scruggs. Still a detective, is he? Hah. I'm not surprised. I'll reach out to him myself, if you don't mind."

Hannah peeled a Post-it note off the paper in front of her. "I'd love that. Here's his number."

Kelly turned to Valentino. "Are you going to tell him that I'm working undercover?"

The supervisor nodded slowly. "I think it best to do so. That way he keeps us apprised of his investigation and we can make suggestions. If the shooter is North Korean, then it suits our interests to surveil the man, not arrest him."

Kelly stood and started for the door. "Bye, guys. I'll find Ernie on my way out."

"I'll have Scruggs call you after we talk," Valentino called.

"Great." Kelly grimaced, not relishing another round with the gruff detective. She reached for the door right as Ernie reentered.

"Here you go." He handed her back Chuck's keyring. "The car fob's going to take a day or two. I took a reading of its bit-code and put in an order for a copy."

Kelly pulled the door open. "Thanks, guys. Gotta run. I'll be in touch about Monday," she promised as she let herself out.

Striding across the parking lot, Kelly shot a glance at her actual vehicle, a white Nissan Rogue sitting under a tarp. She exited the gate, sharing a word with the guard and started on the long hike back to her cover car, a black Prius. As protocol demanded, she had parked three blocks from the FBI building, performing a circuitous walk both ways. The surveillance detection route, or SDR, was a precaution taken to discover whether someone might be following her.

Of course, nobody was. When she finally shut herself into her cover car, she took her cellphone from the compartment between the seats and checked it. Not a single message from Austin about Chuck's condition. Her concern rose. Did that mean he was dead? She nibbled her lower lip, worried Jeremiah Bullfrog might have been wrong.

You're spectacular. The memory of Chuck's last words to her brought on a visceral rush she'd been too overwrought to feel when he'd said it. She didn't want him to die—and not only because she suspected him to be the traitor they were looking for. Something brimming with potential would be cut short if Chuck didn't make it.

Nonsense. She shook off the ridiculous thought with a huff of annoyance. The military secrets that had found their way into Pyongyang had come from an east coast SEAL. Chuck Suzuki was the only SEAL with biological ties to the Korean peninsula. Kelly knew in her gut Chuck was the traitor they were looking for. His being shot at today was all the evidence she needed. Chuck Suzuki led a double life. Ergo, the only thing she ought to be feeling was contempt, not disappointment.

CHAPTER 5

EVERY BREATH CAUSED a knife-like stab of pain, rousing Chuck to awareness. *Am I dead?*

He cracked weighted eyelids to see what was crushing his chest, only to find his torso bare, apart from a neat bandage peeking out from under his left armpit, along with a tube, and a half-dozen disks stuck to his chest. Definitely not dead. A scan of his environs told him he was in a hospital, probably in ICU, given the quantity of medical instruments pressing in on him. The *blip, blip, blip* of his heartbeat accelerated as he thought, *What now?*

Memories flooded him. Lee had apparently been watching him for days, waiting for his chance. He'd targeted Chuck thinking no one was around to see. With his last *shuriken*, Chuck could have shredded Lee's face before that man fired again. Katy's unexpected intervention had made him hesitate. Not Lee, though. The man was a professional, delivering a near-lethal shot even as he fled the scene.

Then Katy had rushed to Chuck's aid, no doubt saving his life in the process. Or was she actually to blame, having distracted him at a critical moment?

Now, here he was, lying helpless in a hospital with an IV imbedded into his left hand and an oximeter clipped to his right index finger. He took it off so he could feel his face, tearing away the oxygen tubes stuck into his nostrils. He had to find a weapon. He had to find his phone.

A high-pitched alarm went off, ratcheting his distress up another notch. The door flew open and in walked a familiar face. *Thank God.*

"You're back!" Chief Adams's pretty wife hurried over to the blaring machines and silenced them before searching his expression with concerned brown eyes. "How do you feel, Chuck?"

He swallowed against a dry throat. "Dumbo is sitting on my chest."

"I bet it feels that way. The surgeon had to dig deep to get the bullet out. You had a huge hemothorax that collapsed your lung and pressed on your heart. Right now, you have a chest tube drawing out the blood and allowing your lung to re-expand. The tube was inserted between your ribs. You're really lucky to be alive."

He wasn't lucky; he was a big fat target. Avoiding Becca's searching gaze, Chuck envisioned the next few days. Once Lee discovered he'd failed in his first assassination attempt, the North Korean would target him a second time. Chuck couldn't possibly pull off a second disappearing act when the first one had failed.

The electro cardio monitor blared again. Becca silenced it a second time.

"It's okay." She laid a soothing hand on Chuck's bare forehead. "You need to relax, Haiku. You're in great hands. You're going to get past this, but you have to stay calm."

"I'm zen," he said. But in his head, he was realizing Sam was going to contact his family if he hadn't already. They would fly out to see him, undoing all the work he'd done to cut them from his life.

He shut his eyes. *Oh, God. Oh, no.*

"I'll be right back." Becca eased toward the door. He could tell by her tone that she was concerned. Hell, so was he. He couldn't just lie here. He had to tell Sam *not* to notify his family. They couldn't come here, pressuring him to take up his cross, so to speak.

Where's my cellphone?

Chuck searched the room for his clothing and spied a narrow armoire. His clothes were probably in there. Too bad he couldn't simply use the landline phone hanging on the wall next to him because he didn't have Sam's number memorized.

You stupid schmuck. You deserve to be killed.

He wiggled his toes and the sheet moved. Good, he wasn't paralyzed, but when he shifted, something alien rubbed along his thigh. With rising horror, he raised the sheet and groaned. They'd fucking catheterized him! Annoyance and chagrin emboldened him to reach down and pull out the offending tube.

Well, shit. That wasn't coming out.

He eyed the sensors on his chest next. One by one, he peeled them off, happy for once that he had no chest hair. His IV came from a bag that was hooked to an electronic IV pole plugged into the wall. Perfect, he would use the pole for support—otherwise, the IV would have to come out, too.

Ignoring the fierce, dull pressure in his chest, he raised the back of his bed until he was sitting straight up. It took a minute to figure out how to lower the rail and then some Houdini-like contortions to figure out how to actually release it. *Fucking contraption.* Whipping back his covers, he swung his feet off the side of the gurney and lowered them cautiously to the floor. Then he stood up, freezing at the dull pain that surged, then ebbed.

I'm good.

He eyed the length of tubing coming out of his chest, headed for a drain box—plenty of slack to move around. He unplugged the electronic IV pole, draped the power cord over one of the hooks, then wheeled it with him as he shuffled carefully toward the armoire. A glance out the window showed a mellowing sky. Was it evening already? God forbid it was a different day! Surely not. They'd taken his watch off. It had to be in the armoire with his clothes.

He had taken only a few shuffling steps when the

door flew open. Rebecca and the doctor drew up short with identical expressions of horror.

"Haiku!"

"What the hell are you doing?" The doctor bore down on him and seized his left elbow. "Let's get you back in the bed," he said, toning down his obvious alarm.

Chuck didn't budge. "I need my cellphone."

"Cellphone use is prohibited in this room." The doctor, whose badge read Dr. Steven Rogers, tugged at him. "There are critical systems in this room."

"One cellphone isn't going to interfere with anything. I need to make a call."

Becca spoke up. "Haiku, I catalogued your belongings when you came in, and you didn't have a cellphone on you."

Chuck thought back. "It's in the pocket of my jacket."

"I'll check," she promised. "If it's not there, you can borrow my phone."

Her cajoling prompted him to turn back to his bed. Lapsing into dark thoughts, Chuck scarcely paid attention as yet another nurse entered the room. His three attendants settled him back onto the mattress. The new nurse clucked with dismay to find the pulse sensors removed, his IV backed up with blood, and the oximeter knocked to the floor.

Chuck was certain his cellphone still was in his

jacket. Becca went to search the armoire. When she came back, he put out his hand, but she shook her head.

What? He drew a breath of consternation, wondering how he'd lost his phone. Had it fallen from his pocket when he fell. What if Katy had it?

His thoughts stilled. After all, her face was the last thing he'd seen before he blacked out. Suspicions bubbled to the surface only to evaporate at the recollection of her horror and her stubborn determination to save him. *Oh, no.* Hadn't he said something outlandish, thinking he had nothing to lose? What was it?

"Stop breathing for a moment." The doctor pressed the end of his stethoscope to Chuck's chest.

With a held breath, Chuck gauged his condition by the doctor's lessoning frown.

"Good strong heartbeat," the man declared. "All the same, I want to get a portable X-ray and see how his hemothorax is resolving."

"Right away, doctor," Becca affirmed, then sent her assistant to relay the test orders.

"Young man." The doctor bent over him until they were practically nose-to-nose. "You need to promise me you will not get out of this bed until cleared to do so. I will *not* have you dropping dead on my watch. Do you understand me?"

Chuck's thoughts flashed to his grandmother. She

and the doc were two of a kind.

"Roger, Rogers," he replied, causing the doctor to straighten and frown down his nose at him.

"That's Haiku's way of saying he understands," Becca interpreted.

"Well, I hope so. For his sake." Rogers turned and stalked to the door, tossing over his shoulder, "I'll assess him again when the tests are complete."

"Chuck." Becca now bent over him just as the doctor had. By contrast, her expression was full of compassion. "This isn't the time to be a SEAL. Getting up and getting going isn't the mission. The mission is to lie here and let your body heal from the inside out."

"How long am I being held hostage?"

"That depends on how well you follow instructions. Progress comes in steps. If you think you can use the urinal then I will take out your catheter."

"Take it out," Chuck begged through his teeth. "I need to find my cellphone." There was nothing incriminating on it; he'd made sure of that, but the sooner he called his platoon leader, the greater chance he could prevent his family from visiting him.

He thought he might die of mortification, but, in a matter of minutes, the offending tube was out and Becca was holding her personal cellphone, ready to assist him.

"Who do you want to call?"

"Sam."

She proceeded to dial the number for him. "He was here earlier, along with several of the guys, plus Austin and the woman that saved your life."

"Katy," he supplied, surprised to hear she'd visited the hospital.

"That's the one. If she hadn't acted as quickly as she did, you wouldn't be alive right now."

Wrong, he thought. If Katy hadn't interfered, Chuck would have been the one to leave the scene in a hurry, and Lee would have died on the plaza.

The door opened suddenly, forcing Becca to end her call as the doctor marched in, carrying an iPhone with a distinctive red case. "Is this what you were looking for? Someone from the police department left it up front for you."

Chuck held out his hand for it, but the doctor set the phone on the counter, well out of reach. "You can make your phone calls later. We're bringing in the Lodox. I don't want any electronic interference with that machine."

Thwarted, Chuck turned to Becca who went to lower the bar on the other side of Chuck's bed. "Can you get a message to Sam for me?"

She tucked the sheet around him. "Sure."

"Tell him not to call my family."

Her sharp upward glance was a blow to the gut. "Too late?" he guessed, only partially aware of a state-of-the-art imaging machine being rolled into the room.

"I think so." Becca backed away so specialists could get to work on him.

Chuck retreated into his thoughts, blocking out the medical personnel as they prepared the fancy machine to scan his torso. Sam had already called his family.

Fuck. Knowing Sobo, she was probably coming with them. Chuck shut his eyes to hide his deep dismay. Seeing any one of them right now would strain his resolution.

And then there was Katy. Given that she'd saved his life, she probably wasn't an assassin. But he couldn't rule out undercover agent. *God, I'm paranoid!* He would have to keep her far away from his family. She could speak Korean, too, and Sobo always spoke of tradecraft in that language.

He heaved a hopeless sigh. *It would have been better if I'd just died.*

KELLY LEFT THE hospital, relieved to have dropped off Chuck's phone without her story being questioned. Her stomach rumbled as she slipped back into her car, reminding her she hadn't eaten anything since breakfast. Nor had she showered or changed out of her running attire. She couldn't wait to take a long hot soak in her new bathtub and review the events of the day, trying to make sense of them.

She was about to pull away when her cellphone, intentionally not connected to her car's Bluetooth, rang. She put her car back in park and answered. "Hello?"

"Well, hello, Miss Katy Tang," rasped a familiar voice. "Or should I call you Kelly Yang?"

Valentino had obviously informed Detective Scruggs about the investigation. "Katy's fine for now," she retorted. "Are you calling me with an update?"

Scruggs chuckled, clearly amused by her terse tone. "Yes, I am, and I was told you'd be interested."

"Go ahead." She moved her phone to her left ear and scanned the darkening parking lot.

"I got my hands on surveillance footage from the parking garage and managed to make out the license plate of the moped. It's registered to a Ralph Emory of Virginia Beach."

That wasn't the kind of name she was expecting. "White guy?"

"Yep. He's got one DUI but no other criminal history and no more tickets in the last six years."

"I'd like his address," she requested.

A distinctive pause followed. "How about you meet me here at the station in an hour? We'll go to the address together," Scruggs offered.

In other words, Scruggs wanted to run his own criminal investigation. He had every right, of course, but the FBI wouldn't want the shooter arrested or lawyering up. They wanted to watch him at work so they could determine who he was.

Kelly glanced at the clock on her dash, then down at her yoga pants. She wasn't supposed to follow any leads unless Hannah or Valentino cleared it. On the other hand, Scruggs had Valentino's blessing, so she couldn't get into too much trouble working alongside the man. He'd given her just enough time to hurry home, shower, change, and eat.

"One hour," she repeated and then hung up on him.

Fifty-eight minutes later, with an organic pasta salad sitting heavily in her stomach and dressed in her ankle boots, black leggings, and a thick purple sweater that made a coat unnecessary, Kelly took in the monstrous dimensions of the brick municipal building as she approached it. The three-story, colonial replica touted a lawn of yellowed grass, all enclosed by a perimeter-fencing meant to ward off assaults.

She realized she missed wearing the 9mm pistol she had carried in a harness under her left arm for years. But since Katy Tang, the graduate student, wouldn't have a pistol, Kelly didn't have one either. It was locked in her desk in the Bull Pen, along with her crypto pass and handcuffs.

Once inside the drafty building, Kelly read a plaque for directions to Scruggs' office. Newly installed carpeting muffled her footfalls as she headed for the last door in the hall. She found it open, with Scruggs at his desk, still chewing gum while staring at one of three monitors. At her knock, he motioned her over without looking up from his screen.

Scruggs was rewinding a video. "Have a look." He clicked stop and then play.

Kelly recognized the inside of the parking garage at the18th Street Plaza. As a man dashed into the dark space, Scruggs froze the image and zoomed in on the blurry figure.

"That the shooter?"

Kelly took in the man's slim build, the cut of his hair, the black leather jacket. "Yes."

Scruggs hit the power button, and his monitor went dark. "Let's go meet him," he said, coming up out of his chair.

He still wore the same clothing he'd had on that morning, his shirt dusted with crumbs from whatever meal he'd recently eaten. She noted the Magnum holstered under his arm as he threaded his arms through the sleeves of his brown jacket. Spitting out his gum into a trashcan, he gestured for her to precede him.

Scruggs' car turned out to be an older model Pontiac, littered with coffee cups and discarded fast-food bags. He cleared off the passenger seat by tossing trash into the back. Night had fallen. Uneasiness turned

Kelly rigid as she buckled herself in and they took off.

She realized she would have liked having Hannah's reassuring voice in her ear. She ought to have advised the case agent of her actions, only Scruggs wouldn't have waited for Hannah's approval.

"Don't you think we should have backup?" she inquired.

Scruggs' blue eyes burned through the shadows as he slanted her a look. "Trust me, the moped doesn't belong to the perp. My hunch is he either stole it or borrowed it."

All the same, Kelly would have felt better if several squad cars accompanied them.

Scruggs sped them onto the highway, then glanced over at her. "Relax," he said, "I'm not going to kidnap you."

The word *kidnap* plucked her taut nerves. "Who says I'm tense?" she snapped.

He laughed, a warm chuckle that allayed her uneasiness. "Come on," he scoffed. "I take it this is your first undercover."

The words mortified her. "How would you know that?"

He looked at her again. "For one thing, you're the youngest Special Agent I've ever met—"

"I'm twenty-nine," she shot back.

"You're a baby." At her fulminating glare, he added, "Sorry if that offends you, but I tend to call things as I see them."

"I guess that explains why you never made chief," she muttered, remembering Valentino's comment about Scruggs still being a detective.

Scruggs' smile fled, but then he issued a reluctant laugh. "Yeah, I guess it does," he agreed. "I spoke with your supervisor this afternoon. Rafael Valentino. We worked together in '02."

"He told me."

"Did he also tell you we were both street cops in the 90s? He doesn't talk about it, but the mob murdered his entire family."

Kelly had heard that rumor and had hoped it wasn't true. "That's awful."

"That's the street for you. You know what happened to his voice?"

"He got shot?"

"Yeah, in the chest, only the bullet hit his Saint Christopher medal. The thing split in half, went up and sliced open his voice box."

Kelly winced.

"Saved his life, though. His dead wife had given him that medal. Do you think the dead look out for the living, Katy Tang?"

"Sure." She'd been raised to believe her ancestors protected her.

"Your supervisor didn't tell me why the perp went after a Navy SEAL," Scruggs added, clearly fishing for details.

Kelly kept her mouth shut.

"C'mon. Gimme something," Scruggs said as he felt inside his jacket and pulled out a stick of gum. "What's the shooter's relationship to the victim?"

"You know I can't say," she retorted.

Scruggs unwrapped the fresh stick of gum and stuck it in his mouth, chewing vigorously. He pulled into the right lane and signaled. "Curious that both the shooter and the victim are Asians, though, right?" he finally observed. "Are we talking gangs? Chinese mafia?"

Kelly firmed her lips and said nothing.

"That's fine. You don't have to tell me. You're an open book anyway. I can read your mind."

She turned her head to glare at him.

He laughed again, a rusty chuckle that cooled her ire. "Okay, that's a lie. If that were true, I wouldn't be asking so many questions."

Mollified, Kelly looked back at the road just as Scruggs exited the highway, popping his gum at the same time.

"I could teach you some tips, though," he offered unexpectedly, "if you're interested. I've learned a few things about intelligence gathering."

At the bottom of the ramp, he executed a smooth right turn, putting them on a narrow road dotted with derelict storefronts and abandoned lots. Kelly gulped, having never been to this side of town.

She moistened her dry lips. "Sure, why not?"

Scruggs' grin reflected the lights of his dash as he turned left this time, putting them on a street lined with tiny '50s-era houses, most of them rundown, with dim lighting and no driveways. Utilitarian vehicles were parked along the curb. The detective wedged his big car between two smaller ones, then killed the engine. He pointed to the cream-colored, one-and-a-half story structure across and up the street.

"That's it, 502 Lawson Lane. Lights are on. Let's pay Ralph Emory a visit."

Together they crossed the quiet street. A dog, penned in a nearby yard, barked stridently. Kelly's heart pattered. Her investigations up to this point had never been particularly exciting or dangerous. If Emory was the shooter, contrary to Scruggs' hunch, then he wasn't going to be happy to see them. *Something could definitely go south tonight.*

Glancing at her companion, she took reassurance from Scruggs' relaxed stance. He spat his gum into the bushes, then gave an assertive knock. The porch light came on. The door opened and an out-of-shape, red-cheeked Millennial stood there holding his tuxedo cat. The scent of something cooking wafted toward them.

Scruggs held up his badge. "Mr. Emory?"

"Yes."

"Detective Scruggs, Virginia Beach Police. We'd

like to talk to you about your moped. It was spotted at the scene of a crime early this morning."

The man looked at Kelly as if to see if Scruggs was joking. "It was?"

"Did you drive it to the oceanfront any time recently?"

Clearly baffled, Emory shook his head and clutched the cat harder. "No. It's been parked out back for years."

Kelly sensed he was telling the truth.

Scruggs pressed on. "Did you loan it to somebody else?"

"No."

"Anybody have access to the keys for the bike?"

"No . . ." Emory blinked. "Well, maybe my roommate."

Scruggs slanted Kelly a look that said *Bingo.* "You mind if we come inside? This is a sensitive matter."

"Um." Emory looked again at Kelly and decided they were harmless. "Sure." He stepped back and held the door open for them.

Kelly couldn't help but compare Austin and Chuck's neat apartment to the slovenly living room of the cramped little house. Light shone from the bright kitchen where the tantalizing aromas told her Emory was an accomplished cook.

Scruggs had slipped his hand inside of his jacket, hand on his Magnum, just in case their suspect sprang out of the dark hallway. "Is your roommate home?"

"I haven't seen him." Emory edged toward the front window and pulled aside the curtain. "His truck's not here."

"What about your moped?" Kelly asked him. "Is that still out back?"

Looking worried, Emory crossed into the adjoining dining room and peered outside the rear window. "Yeah, it's right against the back of the house where it always is."

So, the suspect had returned here after shooting Chuck.

Emory turned slowly from the window. "Am I in trouble?"

"Not at all. Tell us about your roommate," Scruggs requested.

The eyes of Emory's cat bulged as the man hugged him harder. "I hardly even know him," he insisted. "I've rented a room out to him about two years now. But he's Korean or something. He barely even speaks English, and he keeps to himself."

Kelly pounced on the information. "Did you have him sign a lease agreement?"

"Uh. Yes, actually."

"We'd like to see that," Scruggs stated, "plus his room. Chances are, he's not coming back to it."

Kelly took note of Scruggs' assertiveness. They didn't have a warrant, but Emory, who was eager to absolve himself of any role in the alleged crime, escorted them down the hallway, flipping on a light so they could see. He opened the first door on the right, groped for the light switch, then gaped with surprise.

"He's gone!"

Following Emory into the room, they found it stripped of all personal items. The room consisted of a twin bed, bare mattress, a dresser with empty drawers hanging open, and an empty closet. Not a trace of garbage, no forgotten shoelace, pencil, or gum wrapper had been left behind.

Scruggs turned a raised eyebrow at Kelly, a silent message that the shooter wasn't an amateur. Kelly guessed they'd be wasting their time looking for fingerprints.

"He didn't even pay me this month's rent yet," Emory lamented.

Kelly faced him. "I'd like to see that lease agreement."

"Sure." The dazed man left the room. As they listened to him rifle through a drawer in the next room, Scruggs stepped into the closet and came out with a shake of his head.

"Here it is." Emory reappeared, this time without the cat. He handed Kelly a single sheet of paper, with a simple do-it-yourself contract typed up.

Her eyes went straight to the renter's obviously Korean name, "Lee Soo-jin," she murmured. "Did he show you any kind of ID?"

"Yeah, a visa of some kind. He said was working at the shipyard."

Scruggs folded his arms across his chest. "Shipyard, huh? You said he drives a truck?"

"Yeah, an old Toyota SR5."

Scruggs pulled out the notebook Kelly had seen him use before. "Color?"

"Yellowish."

"What else can you tell us about him? Any habits you know of?"

Emory divided a worried gaze between them. "Um, well, sometimes he takes his guitar case with him when he goes out, so maybe he performs somewhere?"

"Hmm." Scruggs scribbled in his notebook.

"He killed somebody, didn't he? Is that why he took off?"

Kelly suspected Emory wouldn't ever rent out his room again. "Nobody's dead," she assured him.

Scruggs cut her off, handing Emory his business card as he put his pad away. "You've been very helpful, Mr. Emory. I'll be back tomorrow evening with a search warrant and a forensic team. Don't touch anything in this room. What time are you home from work?"

Emory stuttered out an answer.

"Should the suspect reach out to you, ask him

where he is, then call me."

"Yeah, sure."

"We'll see ourselves out." Scruggs pushed Kelly out of the room ahead of him and steered her to the door, which he then pulled open.

"Never volunteer details," he growled under his breath as they came off the stoop and headed for their vehicle. "Emory might seem completely innocent, but he could also be the shooter's best friend. You want the assassin to know his target is still alive?"

Kelly, who did not share Scruggs' assessment of Ralph's complicity, resisted the impulse to defend herself. "Of course not. But the newspaper will say the same thing."

"Not if I withhold it from the press release." He unlocked his car door.

Kelly eyed him from the other side. "Could you do that?"

"Sure, but you'd owe me."

As they shut themselves into the car, Scruggs met her uncertain stare. "Oh, don't look at me that way." He stuck his key into the ignition and started the engine. "I just want to know if the shooter's North Korean."

The man was quick at picking up details. "You'd better ask Valentino that question."

Scruggs chuckled at her reply. "You sure like to play hardball, Katy Tang. But I gotta say, I admire you for it." He leaned forward, flipping his glove box open.

"What's this?" Kelly asked as he handed her what looked like a sandwich bag with something in it.

"Two of the victim's throwing stars." He shut the glove box and sat back. "I kept the one with the blood on it for forensic reasons. Something tells me he's going to need these two back." With those words, Scruggs started up his car.

The weight of the deadly-sharp, stainless-steel stars drove home the frightening fact that Chuck wasn't just the FBI's target. Lee Soo-jin wanted Chuck dead, not alive as the FBI did. The question was why? What had Chuck done to deserve such a fate?

CHAPTER 6

KELLY SPILLED ACROSS her bed at 9 PM that night, exhausted. How could so much have happened in one day, after months of literally nothing?

She lay on her stomach, thinking of Chuck and what kind of relationship he'd had with the mysterious Lee Soo-jin. If that man was an assassin, who had sent him? If he was Chuck's handler, what could Chuck have done to deserve assassination?

Agitated by the lack of answers, Kelly reached for the cellphone charging on her bedside table. Had she missed a text from Austin updating her on Chuck's condition? No, she hadn't.

A shaft of concern had her sitting up. She lifted the edge of her curtain to peek outside. Chuck's room was still dark, the blinds still down from when he'd lowered them the night before. A sense of loss swept through her. What if he'd died, and Austin was too devastated to do anything? Or what if he'd realized she'd lied to him about putting Chuck's keys back? Dread pooled in her as she regarded the phone in her hand. Taking the cowardly way out, she decided to text him.

What's the news on Chuck?

When Austin didn't immediately respond, she looked outside again to see if Austin was even at home. His Clubman stood next to Chuck's Subaru. Their vehicles seemed emblematic of their differences. While Austin's Clubman was a friendly car, with big clear windows and plenty of legroom for extra passengers, Chuck's sleek sports car, on the other hand, was barely big enough for two. Its dark tinted windows made it impossible to see inside. It was inscrutable, just like Chuck.

The phone in her palm vibrated. Austin was calling instead of texting. She drew a bracing breath before answering, "Hello?"

"Hey, sorry. I just saw your text."

His cheerful tone informed her both that Chuck was okay and he hadn't checked her story about returning the keys. She closed her eyes in relief and asked, on an exhale, "What's the word?"

"He's doing pretty well, but they're keeping him in ICU until Monday or Tuesday."

"Oh, thank God. That's so good to hear." But then fear pricked her as she pictured Lee Soo-jin entering the hospital with his pistol in his jacket. Valentino would have to place a couple of SOGs at key chokepoints.

"He actually got out of the bed to look for his cellphone."

The words startled a "What?" out of her.

"Yeah, the doctor freaked and ordered more tests, but they came out all right, I guess."

"Did he ever find his cellphone?"

"Someone from the police station turned it in. Chuck recently texted me with it, actually."

"Oh? What did he say?"

"He wondered if you were okay."

"That's it?"

"Well, you know Chuck. He's not a big talker."

"True." But there were big thoughts happening in his head. She fished for more information. "Who did he need to call so badly that he got out of bed? He could've really hurt himself."

"Our platoon leader. Chuck didn't want his family knowing what happened."

Kelly's imagination caught fire. "Why not?"

"He said he doesn't want them flying out for no reason."

"No reason! He was shot and almost killed today."

"I know. And he's usually tight with his family. Not recently, though," Austin added on a thoughtful note.

"Did they have a falling out?" That would explain why they weren't in his contact list.

"I don't know. He used to call them all the time, but I haven't heard him do that lately."

"Huh." That gave her plenty to think about. "Did

he say anything about the guy who shot him?"

"Yeah, he said he never saw him before in his life."

"So weird." Questions clamored for articulation. She allowed herself just one more. "What did Chief Adams mean today when he brought up the Chinese?"

"Oh." Austin fell silent.

"I guess you can't talk about that" she added.

"I can, a little. We dropped in on one of their ships recently and snatched up all the weapons they were sending to Venezuela."

"Oh, wow."

"I don't know how they would've identified Chuck, though. Our faces were covered in camo paint. But don't worry. We won't let it happen again."

"What do you mean *we*?"

"The guys and I are going to set up a security detail once Chuck is out of ICU, just in case the shooter comes after him again."

"Oh, that's a good idea." Unless SEALs and SOGs started tripping over one another.

"I hope he's not out of ICU tomorrow, though 'cause I have to man the duty desk at the Team, starting at oh-dark thirty."

"On a Sunday? That stinks," she sympathized, though she was thinking that would be the perfect time to search Chuck's car. "You'd better get to bed then."

"Yup. Then in the afternoon, I have counseling.

I'm being punished for punching that guy out at the bar."

He sounded so annoyed Kelly had to smile. "Well, you know you can't keep doing that."

"I don't see why not."

"Hah! Then you should definitely go to counseling."

"The counselor is a woman with a sexy voice," Austin volunteered. "Evelyn Haskins. I like saying her name. It sounds so British. Evelyn Haskins." He said it with a British accent.

Kelly frowned. One of her sorority sisters at Georgetown had the same name. "What time is counseling?" she fished.

"Thirteen hundred."

"Well, I hope you benefit from it. You don't want to keep getting into trouble."

"I guess."

"Hey, thanks for the update, Austin. You'd better get to bed. It's been a long day for both of us."

"Sure has. Hey, Katy? Thanks again for saving Chuck's life today."

His neutral tone made her hesitate. "Of course."

"Most people run away from danger, not toward it," he added.

Was he trying to make a point? "Well, I'm not anything special," she assured him. "I'm just the girl next door."

"Hah. We'll see." In the next instant he hung up on her.

Kelly sat processing their conversation. Why did it feel like Austin was one step ahead of her? She knew from having read his military records he was MENSA material. Maybe that was the reason. Or—"Shit."— maybe he *had* checked Chuck's nightstand and knew she'd lied to him. The possibility disconcerted her.

Vowing to worry about it in the morning, Kelly went to brush her teeth in the adjoining bathroom. The good news was, Chuck was still alive. She would bring him his remaining two *shuriken* so he could protect himself should Lee get past both the SOGs and the SEALs. With Lee's blurry image now in the hands of the FBI, thanks to Scruggs' cooperation, perhaps they would have a motive soon.

Katy met her gaze in the bathroom mirror and raised an eyebrow. "Spectacular, huh? You should see me now." Her hair was mussed, dark circles rimmed her eyes.

At least he was attracted to her. That would make it easier to crawl into his head and maybe even sway his loyalties.

The framed butterfly print popped into her thoughts, followed by the memory of his other photos. A man with an eye for natural beauty couldn't be inherently evil, could he?

Tread carefully, she cautioned, snapping off the light.

You have no idea how this will play out.

✕

CHUCK LAY IN the dimly lit ICU, riding waves of agony. They rolled through him like tsunamis. He had no idea it could hurt so much just to breathe. He had to pee, and the restroom seemed a thousand miles away.

Perhaps if he could sleep, he would heal, but every time he drifted off, another tsunami crested inside of him, jarring him awake. He deliberated pushing the button for the nurse and begging for the pain meds he had refused earlier.

"Dumb ass," he muttered. He had stopped Megan from infusing morphine into his IV because he wanted to remain alert, to think of a plan.

What was he going to do about Lee, who would surely pursue him again once he learned his assassination had failed? More pressing still, what was Chuck going to do about his family? He had sent a text to his platoon leader the minute his battery of tests was complete. He'd told Sam he didn't want them seeing him in his condition.

Sorry, buddy. They've already been told, was Sam's reply.

Did you give them my new phone number? Chuck's intestines had knotted as he'd waited for Sam's reply.

Yes. I was surprised they didn't have it.

Chuck hadn't texted much after that, except to say, *So, you think they're coming?*

Yeah, man. They were really worried about you.

"I bet they were," Chuck muttered darkly. Sam's call to his parents would have been the first news they'd heard of Chuck in two months. Honestly, he was surprised his mother hadn't called his new number immediately, now that she had it. Probably Sobo had forbidden it, or the old crow had kept the number to herself—not that *she* would call him. Oh, no. Sobo preferred face-to-face correspondence—less chance of a message getting intercepted. After all, his grandmother was the ultimate deep-cover case officer. She had probably already reserved herself a flight.

With a groan of mixed pain and turmoil, Chuck cast about for a means of avoiding a visit. Sobo couldn't visit him in ICU. Maybe he should simply stay in *here* for as long as possible. Then Sobo would run out of funds and eventually leave.

Sure, like that would work. Sobo would never return to San Diego in defeat.

He could have saved her the headache of coming in the first place. He already knew what she would say. She would tell him he had deserved to die for his unfaithfulness to the Supreme Leader. She would say fate had given him one more chance to prove his loyalty. Then she would demand something enormous

of him, something that would make him a truly
pathetic human being, should he follow through.

Do I have a choice, though? Everything Chuck had
done to break ties with the past had failed. There was
no escaping his inheritance, even when he wanted no
part of it. In fact, he could think of only one way to
end his nightmare, but it came at an impossible
price—the arrest and condemnation of his entire
family, for aiding and abetting the spy in their midst.
Even his sweet mother who had done nothing but
turn a blind eye would face punishment. He couldn't
do that to her, to any of them.

I wish I had just died.

Dying for a noble cause was honorable, he assured
himself, like the ritual disembowelment performed by
Samurai warriors for reasons having to do with honor.
People died all the time in ICU. No one would think it
at all suspicious if Chuck kicked the bucket right here.
He raised the back of his bed to ninety degrees to
contemplate his options, and the pain in his chest
abruptly eased.

Hey, that's better.

Sitting in the semi-darkness, breathing hard, and
listening to the tube draining his chest gurgle quietly,
Chuck looked around the shadow-filled room. Surely,
in this space jam-packed with medical equipment there
was something he could use to end his life, preferably
painlessly. Alas, Megan had marched off with the

morphine he'd refused, leaving none lying around. Perhaps there something in that cabinet above the sink.

He bent forward, groping for the release that would enable him to lower his railing, when the door opened suddenly, and the lights blinked on. An as an older nurse—not Megan nor Becca, who'd gone home hours ago—drew up short at the site of his contortions.

"What do you think you're doing?" she cried. Without another word, she crossed to a button on the wall and slammed her hand on it, sending a signal to other health professionals. "I've heard about you, Mr. Navy SEAL. You're the hotshot who got out of bed earlier looking for his cellphone, the same tough guy who told Megan you didn't need any morphine."

"I need to use the restroom," he explained.

The running of feet heralded the arrival of two more personnel, including the infamous Dr. Rogers— Christ, did the man have no home life?

"What now, Petty Officer Suzuki?" Rogers marched into the room with young Megan on his heels.

"Special Officer," Chuck corrected through his teeth.

The old biddy answered for him. "He was getting out of bed so he could void his bladder."

"No one is getting out of bed." Rogers pointed at

the younger nurse. "Megan, put a condom catheter on him."

Chuck's eyes widened with horror. "What is that?"

Dr. Rogers met his gaze. "Relax, son. It goes on the outside like a condom."

"I need morphine." Chuck could only hope to fall asleep before Megan humiliated him.

Rogers frowned and consulted the computer on wheels. "When was your last dose?"

"He never got one," Megan said in a small voice.

"What?" Rogers leveled a glare at both nurses.

"He refused the morphine, sir," Megan insisted.

Chuck became the recipient of Rogers' glare. "Son, you have got to stop resisting us, or you'll never get out of ICU."

But that's the plan, Chuck thought as the doctor pointed to the older nurse.

"Nancy, give this man four milligrams of morphine so he can get comfortable."

Chuck could tell that four was more than the usual dose. It wouldn't be enough to kill him, though. Nancy stabbed a needle into the port on his IV, and the room went instantly out of focus. As the cold, alien substance spilled into his bloodstream, it weighted his eyelids, giving him hope of losing consciousness before Megan put that condom catheter on him.

Guess I'm not dying tonight.

A part of him breathed a sigh of relief. He didn't really want to die—not without discovering why Katy had rushed to his defense. Had she really been protecting him? Or had she given Lee the opening he needed to fire a lethal shot? It was hard to believe the latter might be true, not with the memory of her leaning over him, the very picture of concern.

AUSTIN'S ALARM WOKE him up at zero-five-thirty on Sunday morning. He lay there asking himself why the hell he'd made up that falsehood about having duty. He could actually sleep in if he wanted to, but he'd lied to Katy because he needed to know the reason why she'd lied to *him* about returning Chuck's keyring. Now he wished he'd just come out and asked.

He'd wracked his brain all day yesterday for a reason why she'd held on to them. Was she planning to use Chuck's car for something? He really didn't know her well enough to say what she was capable of. If she'd lied about the keys, might she have also lied about going to the library yesterday, following their visit to the hospital? Where else might she have gone? Was she in cahoots with the man who'd shot Chuck? Had she gone to tell the shooter Chuck was still alive?

The more questions that had run through his mind, the more Austin needed to have his suspicions either confirmed or denied. Hence his little white lie about having duty that morning.

"The truth will out," he murmured, quoting Shakespeare as he rolled out of bed.

Leaving the lights off, Austin donned his Navy working uniform in the dark. Chuck would hear nothing about this until Austin knew for sure whether Katy was a friend or a foe. With his health compromised, Chuck couldn't afford to get upset. Getting upset was Austin's job, and he excelled at it.

Their neighbor might be cute, but she might have nefarious plans, and not only with Chuck's car, Austin realized as he laced up his boots. Chuck had a key to their apartment on his keyring. Maybe Katy was plotting with the Chinese to break into their home and assassinate them both as they slept. Honestly, it was difficult to imagine that, given how stricken she had been delivering news of Chuck's shooting the previous morning. All the same, Austin needed to be sure.

He hummed the theme song to *007* as he prepared for his morning reconnaissance. "Dum-da-da-daah-da-da-da. Dum-da-da-daah-da-da-da."

In the kitchen, he fixed two peanut-butter-and-banana sandwiches on seeded bread, tearing into one of them while wrapping the other in tin foil. Next, he filled a lidded coffee cup with almond milk before draining the rest of the carton. Both the cup and the sandwich went into his camouflaged pack, along with a camera belonging to the Team, which he'd intentionally forgotten to turn in after his last op. The reconnaissance camera took pictures of objects up to 1000 feet away, in both daylight and in darkness.

Using his Android, Austin checked the weather. The high that morning wouldn't get past forty degrees. He shoved a warm blanket into the bag, then brushed his teeth and headed for the door.

It was still dark outside when he jogged down the steps to his vehicle. He made a big ordeal out of leaving, tossing his pack into his passenger seat and slamming that door before shutting himself behind the wheel.

He revved the engine. *I'm leaving now.*

Surely Katy could hear him from her room, even three stories up. He squealed out of his parking space for good measure and drove two blocks away, to a pay-as-you-stay parking lot tucked between two buildings.

With his pack over his shoulder, Austin started back toward the apartments. The sun was just starting to rise up out of the ocean, hidden from view by tall hotels. Buttery rays of sunlight fingered the tops of the buildings as he hurried past them. The cold, damp air heightened his awareness.

On 19th Street, he marched straight for the vantage point from which he knew he could watch Chuck's car. It was the roof of Old Port Brewing Company, a remodeled 19th-century warehouse, gutted and whitewashed. Austin had stood on its roof-top terrace last Fourth of July to watch the fireworks when he'd realized he could see his apartment from there.

With the front doors locked and not due to open until 4 PM, Austin helped himself to the rusty fire escape. One minute later, he had scaled the building and was crossing the puddle-covered cement roof toward the back of the building. He found the best vantage from which to keep an eye on the parking lot between his and Katy's buildings, wrapped himself in the blanket, and leaned against the waist-high wall to watch.

Not a single car, apart from his, had left the East Harbor Apartments since his departure. Austin sighed and looked toward the ocean, which he could now see. The emerging sun drenched the sky in tones of bronze, gold, and fiery orange.

It was seven thirty before someone stirred. An older neighbor, who lived four doors down from his and Chuck's place, got into his car and headed for church, given the tie he was wearing.

At zero-eight hundred, Austin got a text from Chuck.

There's talk of me getting out of ICU early.

Really? Austin was glad to hear it but didn't know if he could keep an eye on Katy and protect Chuck at the same time.

This afternoon, if I keep improving.

Let me know, Austin urged. *I have to see that counselor today at 13:00, but after that, I'll come see you.*

You don't have to babysit me.

I'll be there.

Chuck knew better than to argue with him. Austin looked back at the apartment and did a double take. He quickly traded his android for the camera, then zoomed in on the woman standing next to Chuck's Subaru. *Gotcha.* Katy looking casually around. Sure enough, she was up to something.

Click. Austin snapped her picture. He took several more closeups as she slipped into the driver's seat. He wondered wildly if she was going to drive away in Chuck's car. He would have to call the cops if she did.

The car didn't move. After several minutes inside, Katy got out, went around to the back, and opened the hatch. *Click. Click.* Austin took more pictures.

"What the hell is she looking for?" he murmured while admiring her trim figure sheathed in a form-fitting, gray jacket. Her silky hair spilled over one shoulder as she ducked her head into Chuck's trunk, probing it thoroughly. All Chuck had in there, Austin recalled, was a wetsuit, maybe a paint-ball gun, and reusable grocery bags.

With a carefully neutral expression, Katy straight-ened and shut the trunk. She looked discreetly around as if sensing eyes on her, then went back into her apartment.

Baffled, Austin blew out a breath and lowered the camera. He put his back against the low wall and reviewed the pictures he had taken.

The quality was excellent. Katy looked like a petite car model. The closeups of her face were just what he needed. He would share his images with the Team's terrorist expert, Stuart Rudolph, also known as Hack. Maybe Katy would show up in one of the many databases to which Hack had access.

For Chuck's sake, Austin hoped she wasn't a Chinese agent. But why would any honest, decent, all-American graduate student want to peek in Chuck's car? Nothing else made sense.

Confusion gripped him, followed by a cold determination to protect Chuck from whatever entity was after him. He remembered that night at Calypso when Katy had first introduced herself. She'd wanted to speak Korean—why? To avert the suspicion that she might be Chinese?

Something about Austin's theory didn't fit, he acknowledged, as he put away the camera and stuffed the blanket back into his pack. The MSS, China's equivalent of the CIA, would have had to plan their actions a while ago in order to position Katy in an apartment immediately across from his and Chuck's. Yet, the SEALs had boarded that Chinese ship only two weeks ago. No way could retaliation have come so quickly. Moreover, why would the Chinese have singled out Chuck for retribution and none of the other seven SEALs who'd boarded the vessel that night?

With a shrug of his shoulders, Austin headed for the fire escape. The only thing he was sure of was the need to stay vigilant. Something was happening—something big—and it was taking place right under his nose.

Good thing Chuck had people like Austin looking out for him. No one was going to catch Haiku, or any members of Echo Platoon, unaware again. That was for damn sure.

CHAPTER 7

EVELYN HASKINS, LICENSED Professional Counselor, tried not to stare at her client, but the young SEAL was riveting. He stood at just over six feet tall, according to his personnel file which, as a contractor working for the military, she'd had a right to request. His perfectly proportioned body swelled with muscles that strained the fabric of his long-sleeved gray polo and worn jeans. His hair was a golden-brown shade, wavy and slightly overgrown. His jaw was strong, his lips sensual.

And those eyes, she thought. Light gray and surrounded by eyelashes any woman would envy, they gave him an honest aspect. He looked like he belonged in a DC Comic Book, but what would his nickname be?

"Ricochet" to his fellow superheroes, she decided, because he never stopped moving.

While answering her questions about why he'd been referred for counseling, he'd picked up the small jade elephant on the end table, turning it over in hands that were the epitome of masculine grace.

"Do you agree with Lieutenant Sasseville that you

have a potential problem?" she inquired.

He shrugged, shoulders and lips moving in one unified gesture. "Not really."

"Tell me why you say that."

He shot her a wry glance, and her stomach lurched at the impact of his gaze.

"Operant conditioning. You know, B.F. Skinner? If a guy gets punched out for talking crap to his girlfriend, is he going to think twice before he does it again? I think so."

Intrigued by his reference to Skinner, Evelyn sneaked another glance at his file. High school education, that was it. But then she noted the scores he had received from the battery of the military aptitude tests he'd been given. His IQ made her eyebrows shoot up. Great, she had a flipping genius on her hands!

"Advocates of operant conditioning," she countered, pushing up the purple-framed glasses that had slipped down her nose, "claim it takes twenty-one repetitions to establish a new habit. Do you see what I'm saying?"

His handsome lips quirked. "You're saying I needed to punch that douchebag twenty more times."

She had to smile at his conclusion. "Not exactly."

He put the elephant back and let his gaze wander.

"So, why do you think it's your job to teach these douchebags a lesson?" Her use of his colorful word brought his attention back.

He flashed her a grin. "You've never said that word before, have you?"

She smiled back. "I asked you a question first."

He looked away again, seeming to catalogue every item in her office with his roving gaze. "I don't know why."

Evelyn groaned inwardly. This young man was going to be a hard nut to crack. Anyone forced into therapy wasn't going to benefit. He had to *want* to open up to her, which meant she needed to take a different tact.

"Hey, I have an idea." She put her notepad down and stood up, recapturing his attention as she crossed to a cabinet where she stored books and games. "Since you really don't want to be here, and since I have better things to do than to bang my head against your walls, what do you say we play a game to pass the time?" Opening both cabinet doors, she let him see inside. "Which game should we play? I have Parcheesi, Scrabble, Charades, Backgammon, Chess, Checkers, and Mancala." She usually played them with her younger clients. Austin was five years younger than she was. Did that count?

"Seriously?" His expression had turned wary.

"Well, I don't want to waste my time any more than you do, so let's do something else. I've got a deck of cards here, too." She lifted them out and riffled them with her thumb.

Austin cracked his knuckles and stared. "I'll talk to you. Sorry," he added. "I've never seen a counselor before."

Perplexed by his sudden cooperation, Evelyn shut the cabinet and returned to her chair. "You don't have to apologize. It was my suggestion."

He avoided eye contact. "It wouldn't be right. My platoon leader expects results. I couldn't only pretend to go to counseling and not do it."

"I see." *Powerful conscience*, she scribbled onto her notepad.

"Also, I'm having trouble focusing. My roommate's in the hospital and my new neighbor has been really weird."

Evelyn lowered her pen. "What happened to your roommate? Is he okay?"

"He was shot by some random guy."

"In action?"

"No, right on the boardwalk yesterday morning. Our new neighbor, Katy—she's this cute Korean chic, at least she says she's Korean. Anyway, she claims she surprised the shooter, who ran off, but now I'm wondering if she wasn't in on it."

Evelyn's eyebrows rose. "In on it?"

"Part of an assassination attempt." Austin ran a hand through his wavy hair. "It could have been the Chinese," he said with conviction. "They have good reason for hating us SEALs right now."

"What makes you think your neighbor is involved? You said she scared the shooter away."

Austin sat forward. "Because she drove Chuck's car back from the boardwalk, and then she lied to me about returning his car keys. I watched her searching his car this morning. What kind of person does that?"

"A cop?" Evelyn suggested.

"She's not a cop—" Austin cut himself off abruptly. "She says she's a graduate student." He went perfectly still, clearly reshuffling his assumptions.

"Tell me more about your roommate," Evelyn requested. At least the patient was talking now. "What's his name?"

"Chuck. But most of us call him Haiku because he's part Japanese and he uses a lot of metaphors. Some people find that habit annoying."

"Do you?"

"No. I like figuring out what he means."

"And the neighbor? What is she like?"

"Tiny but tough. I took pictures of her searching Chuck's car. The camera's in my car. Want to see them?"

Afraid he would drive off if he got into his car, she shook her head. "No, that's okay. Could Chuck be doing anything illegal?

Austin made a face. "Are you kidding? All he does is work, work out, and take pictures of nature. Thing is, he's hot for the new neighbor, and I don't want to have to tell him she's a spy or something."

Evelyn realized, given Austin's line of work, his suspicions might not be an exaggeration. "Can't you talk to someone about this?"

"I'm talking to you. No, I'm just messing with you," he added when all she could do was stare. "Yeah, I got a teammate with connections. I'm going to show him the photos I took."

"Good." She swallowed her relief and tried to keep the conversation going. "So, you and Chuck get along?"

"We do." Austin fiddled with a button on the front of his shirt. "Even though we're polar opposites."

"How so?"

"Hah. Well, he's calm—me, not so much. I jump first, ask questions later. Chuck thinks before he acts."

"What's his specialty? And what's yours?" This was working well.

"Chuck is our comms guy. In the field, he handles all communications between us and Southern Command. I'm the resident linguist. I talk to the locals for HUMINT purposes. That's—"

"Human Intelligence," she finished. "I know. I'm a Navy brat myself."

"Yeah?"

For the first time since he'd first slunk into her office, Austin Collins took the time to really *look* at her. His gaze traveled from her shoulder-length, ash-brown hair, to her blue eyes magnified by her lenses, before sliding leisurely toward her gray-and-white patterned, button-up blouse. To her chagrin, she felt her nipples pearl as he assessed her full breasts before taking in her gray snug-fitting slacks to her bare ankles, two-inch pumps, then back up again. Her pulse became erratic as he met her gaze again. The last time a man had looked her over that thoroughly, she'd been in high school in Italy, where her third stepfather had been stationed.

"Who's your dad?" Austin asked. "Would I know him?"

"No." She wouldn't even recognize her biological father, as it wasn't so much her father who'd made a career in the Navy as it was her mother, having had four husbands who were all sailors.

"Well, where was he stationed? Where did you live?"

"Japan, Spain, Italy and three different states. I would bore you if I listed them all."

"Aw, come on now," Austin chided her with a grin. "If I'm gonna tell you stuff about me, you should have to do the same thing."

She had to smile at his attempt to level the playing field. "Who's the therapist in this room?" She arched an eyebrow at him.

"Hey, I can give great advice."

"I'm sure you can. You're a smart guy according to your testing scores. How come you never went to college?"

She'd hoped the subject wasn't a sore one, but when he shot to his feet and moved to the chair with the little sand garden next to it, she kicked herself for asking it.

"I've heard about these sand gardens." Picking up the miniature rake, he began to shape and sculpt the sand with it. Then he traded the rake for a seashell.

Evelyn watched him make a border with the tiny seashells.

She ventured another question she hoped didn't touch a nerve. "Have you ever been diagnosed with ADHD?"

He abandoned his creative endeavor, throwing himself down in a different chair, this one closer to her. "What do you think?"

The wry expression on his face supplied an answer.

"Were you prescribed medication? Did you take it?"

"Yes and no. I found the perfect career for myself. Turns out having ADHD works great in Special Operations. I can multitask better than most."

"That's wonderful. But do you want to be a SEAL for the rest of your life? I hear it takes a toll on the body."

He looked down at his relaxed body as if inspecting it for damage. Evelyn seized his distraction to admire the swell of his muscle-hewn thighs encased in denim.

"What's wrong with my body?"

He caught her staring and she flushed. "Nothing. That's not what I meant."

"Do you have a boyfriend?"

Evelyn's jaw dropped. "That's not something you're supposed to ask your therapist!"

He looked away, chagrined. "Sorry. Sometimes my mouth says what I'm thinking before I can catch it. You're really pretty," he added. "Damn it, I did it again."

Evelyn's face heated. She had never been with a client who could fluster her without even trying. "Yes," she said, answering his first question. "I have a boyfriend."

"Ah." Austin had the grace to look disappointed. "Is he military?"

"He's the manager at the Post Exchange here on base."

"Bet I know him."

"Bet you don't."

"Try me."

"I'd rather not say his name. We're supposed to be talking about you."

Austin plucked at a thread coming out of the cuff of his long-sleeved polo. "Fine." He sighed with resignation. "What do you want to know?"

"I'd like to hear about your childhood."

"Yeah, because every flaw we have can be traced to some trauma from our past, right?"

She took her time answering. "Well, if that's true, then I must have a lot of flaws," she countered. Maybe honestly on her part would get him talking.

"You don't look flawed to me."

The line was offered so artlessly, she couldn't scold him for it. "Let's compare childhoods," she suggested.

Heck, why not? She had nothing to lose by showing him how her childhood had shaped her into who she was. Once he acknowledged the same was true for him, he would know why he went around punching out men who talked trash to women.

"Okaaay." The drawn-out word betrayed mistrust.

"I'll start. I was born in San Diego, my mother's first child. My father was a submariner. My mother met him at a bar and continued to frequent that bar whenever he was out at sea. They divorced when I was four."

"I'm sorry."

His sincerity made him likeable. "Now you say something."

"Um, I was born in Louisville, Kentucky. My mom was a Russian waitress working in the states on a J-1 visa. My dad was an Army Ranger. They were happy together. I had a great childhood until he died in

Operation Iraqi Freedom when I was only six."

"Oh, God, I'm so sorry." She regarded him in a new light, trying to fathom his loss. "Do you remember him?"

His gaze shifted down and to the right, letting her know he was tapping into memories. "Yeah." Given his warm tone, they were good memories.

"I'm glad. I don't remember my real father, but I was adopted by my last stepdad when my mother bailed on both of us. We were stationed in Italy at the time."

His attention had returned to her. "I'm happy to hear that," he said quite sincerely.

Evelyn cleared her throat and selected the next question. She'd never worked with a client like this, exposing herself in the process. It unsettled her, but it seemed to be working. "What's the next big moment from your childhood? It could be a bad memory or a good one."

He thought for a minute. "I got expelled from middle school for causing an explosion in science class." His lopsided smile suggested he was proud of himself. "What about you?"

"We moved from California to Washington DC, when my mom remarried."

Austin's eyes narrowed as he searched her face. "So, you had a stepdad."

"Three, to be exact."

"Whoa."

"Yep. My mom had a habit of catching men, using them, and dropping them. All Navy men," she added.

"You wouldn't do that," he said as if he knew her.

She wasn't so sure. The reason she was almost thirty and still not married was she was terrified she might turn into her mother. "What about you?" She cocked her and asked, "Did you ever have a stepdad?"

He nodded. "Yep. Just one. He's still my stepdad."

"You get along with him, then?"

"Not at first. He used to drink. Drank like a fish, every night of the week. And when he drank, he got mean. He'd come home and yell at us. Sometimes he got physical."

Evelyn's stomach tightened. "That sucks. I had a stepdad like that once."

"Yeah?"

"Wait, you said he *used* to drink. Did he get help for his habit?"

"Eventually."

Austin had gone back to using one-word sentences.

"You're going to have to give me more than that," she pleaded.

He reached for the swivel bar on the blinds at the window next to him and twisted it. *Open, close. Open, close.*

"What made your stepdad get help?" Evelyn prodded.

"Well." He created a strobe-light effect, entertaining himself, she supposed. "One night he came home drunk as usual, and he slapped my mom so hard she went flying. So, I punched his lights out."

Ah. Now they were getting somewhere. "Is that the first time you punched a guy out for mistreating a woman?"

"Yep."

"What happened after that? What were the consequences?"

"My stepdad realized he was screwing up. He quit drinking and became an upstanding guy."

"Seriously?"

"Cross my heart."

"Wow." Austin had clearly associated the use of his fists with positive outcomes. Now that she knew *that*, she could work with him more effectively.

The alarm on her phone gave a timely beep. She silenced it, amazed by how quickly their session had passed.

"Counseling's over?" Austin guessed.

"For now. Shall we schedule our next meeting?"

"Look at you, all business again."

She shot him a frown and ignored the comment. "How about next Sunday, same time slot?"

"No, I'm supposed to see you twice a week. How about Thursday right after work. I can get here by

4 PM."

Pleased by his enthusiasm, Evelyn consulted the calendar on her iPad. "I can actually make that work."

"Cool."

"It was nice to meet you, Austin." She stood up and crossed to the door.

Putting hands on his knees, he pushed to his feet and followed more slowly.

The door pulled inward. As she stepped to one side, Austin stopped in front of her. She tipped her head back, sending him a practiced smile. His gaze held hers, then dropped to her lips. He leaned toward her, causing her pulse to skip.

"I see you," he whispered.

His expression was so transparent that the words didn't creep her out. On the contrary, her body prickled as if she were standing there naked in front of him.

In the next instant, Austin was gone, walking down the hall with the loose-limbed stride of a confident male.

His words reverberated in her head, causing belated self-doubt.

Wait. What did he see, exactly? Uncertainty usurped her confidence.

Did he see her as an imposter? She had studied psychology and mental health so she could figure herself out. Six years of schooling and six more in the business hadn't brought her any closer to fixing herself. How was she supposed to fix other people?

With a whispered curse, Evelyn shut herself into her office. Too many brain cells and a wired nervous system made Austin Collins say things he ought not to say. She almost hoped he wouldn't come back, but then she hoped he would.

Snatching up her notepad, she jotted down her diagnosis, though she knew she wouldn't forget it. *Client associates physical retaliation with positive results.*

CHAPTER 8

K ELLY GNAWED ON a thumbnail, worried Austin would come home early, as she stood before her closed curtains, watching his apartment through a slight opening.

Even with Valentino's unarmed surveillance agents on the lookout for him, Kelly sensed Austin was fully capable of catching her squad in the middle of their clandestine entry, especially since they hadn't gotten started until her return from school. That had been at 1 o'clock and now it was approaching 4 PM. Last week, Austin and Chuck had been home from work by 4:15. With every passing minute, Kelly's tension rose. Holding her laptop in her left arm, she glanced at it every few seconds, waiting for the Internet to come back on, a sign that the work in Chuck's apartment was finally complete.

Ernie, who was parked down by the dumpster, had jammed the Wi-Fi three hours ago, allowing Kelly to slip into Chuck and Austin's apartment so she could return Chuck's car keys. When she'd exited, she had left the door unlocked for the Computer Analysis Response Team member and the electronic surveillance installer. Both men had pulled up in a van as she'd crossed the parking lot. Dressed in blue coveralls and carrying toolboxes, they'd looked exactly like the apartment maintenance personnel.

Kelly checked the time again and wondered how many of her neighbors were ranting at their internet provider. A flicker of movement brought her focus back outside. Finally! There were the men in coveralls coming briskly out of Chuck's building.

She didn't recognize the CART expert, but the shock of red hair on the taller of the two belonged to Red, one of the branch's best "Wires and Pliers," as the installers were called. As their van took off, the Wi-Fi signal reappeared on Kelly's Dell. Seconds later, Ernie drove off in his nondescript sedan.

Hannah's message to the group appeared on Kelly's cellphone. *We have eyes and ears. Good work, all. We'll talk tomorrow.*

In other words, not only had the Bu piggybacked on Chuck's security system, but they had a camera in Chuck's bedroom, as well. And thanks to the CART expert, the Bu had remote access to Chuck's laptop, allowing them to see not only what was in it, but any activity he might perform on it.

Kelly blew out a breath and rolled her tense shoulders. Their entry had gone off without a hitch. She ought to be able to focus on reading three chapters from the gargantuan textbook lying on her bed. She sat down next to it, shut her laptop, and dragged the book closer.

But her concern that Austin would notice something different about his apartment kept her from absorbing anything she read. She wondered if Hannah would grant her a favor, then decided it wouldn't hurt to ask.

"Hello?"

"Hey, I need a huge favor." Kelly cut right to the chase.

"What's that?" Hannah sounded like she was chopping vegetables in her kitchen.

"You know how you say your husband notices everything?"

Hannah's husband, who had no clue they were investigating a member of his own SEAL Team, was a former Dallas Cowboys tight end. Hannah had fretted more than once that Luther, who always knew when she threw him a surprise party, would somehow guess the Bu was investigating Haiku, whom he held in high esteem.

"What if Austin is like that, too? I didn't mention this earlier," Kelly added, revealing her cause for concern, "but he caught me looking in Chuck's nightstand, so I told him I left Chuck's keys in there when, in fact, I just did that today. What if he checked my story? He might be onto me."

Hannah stopped making noise. "God, I hope not."

"I'd feel a whole lot better," Kelly added before Hannah could take her to task, "if I could see Austin's reaction when he gets home today. Please, can I go to the Club and watch the ELSUR?"

A pot clanged as Hannah considered Kelly's request to review their recent video footage. "Fine," she said, at last, "as long as you're back in your apartment by the time the campus library closes."

Katy checked her watch. "It's a weekday. They don't close until ten."

"Then you have plenty of time for an SDR in both directions. I'll call ahead and clear you."

"Thank you!"

Abandoning her open textbook, Kelly snatched up her coat and purse and raced out of her apartment.

ON MONDAY AT the end of the day, Austin left the Team building calling good-byes to his colleagues as he crossed the damp parking lot. Without Chuck's oblique comments and mystifying metaphors to keep his teammates entertained, the workday had seemed endless. Loneliness ambushed him as slipped into his chilly Clubman. Good thing he didn't have to go straight home to his empty apartment. Hack had invited him over to help Austin identify Katy by her pictures. He had even tossed in a dinner invitation, but

Austin had figured Hack and his wife, Hilary, had their hands full caring for a newborn baby girl. He had promised to leave before dinnertime.

As he always did, Austin took his cellphone from the console and checked it before leaving work. A notification from his and Chuck's security system caught his eye. He clicked on it, half-expecting to see a video of Katy entering his and Chuck's apartment. Instead, he got an error message saying the Wi-Fi had been down for almost three hours that afternoon.

Austin's eyes narrowed. Coincidence or circumstance? Had Katy even noticed their security system, let alone been savvy enough to disable the Wi-Fi?

He would know the answer to that when he got back to his apartment. Since realizing she'd lied to him about Chuck's car keys, he'd taken to leaving a strand of his hair between the door and the door frame whenever he left. That way, if Katy let herself in, the hair would fall, and he would know. He had learned years ago never to rely on technology when simple physics sufficed.

"Hmm." He was tempted to return home to see what she'd been up to, but Hack was expecting him, so he laid his phone down and started driving.

Hack and Hilary lived not far from base, in the same established neighborhood as Sam and Maddie. Unlike the other SEALs in Echo Platoon, Hack, with the blessing of Special Operations Command, also worked for Ghost Security Group, a civilian counter-terrorism organization that took on terrorists in the digital world.

If anyone could help Austin identify Katy, it was Hack, whose real name was Chief Stuart Rudolph. Stu had access to dozens of databases. By this evening Austin might just know who Katy was—a cop like his therapist had suggested, or a Chinese assassin. Considering Chuck's interest in the woman, Austin would prefer she was a cop, though what had she been up to searching Chuck's car?

Minutes later, Austin stood in Hack's windowless basement skimming the framed newspaper articles hanging on the whitewashed walls. Each article documented the arrest and indictment of a terrorist or terrorist cell, both domestic and foreign. There were over a dozen framed clippings.

"Were you involved in all of these cases?" He turned back to Hack, who sat behind his massive, U-shaped desk. The glass surface was covered with at least ten monitors and laptops, while servers lining the wall behind him hummed and blinked as they crunched millions of megabytes of data.

Hack was focused on the photos of Katy, down-loaded from the camera's SD card. He snagged the clearest image of her face to run it through his databases.

"Most of 'em," he muttered, leaning down to extract the SD card, which he then handed back to Austin.

Tall and gangly, Hack's long arm was roped with muscle. As nerdy as he was, he could hold his own with the best of his SEAL brothers in the field.

"I need some basic facts about this woman," he requested as Austin popped the card back into the camera. Hack spoke with a thick Vermont accent that hadn't faded one iota since his transplant to Virginia a decade ago. "What's her name?"

"Katy Tang." He had been pleased when Katy included her last name in their first text exchange. "She's supposedly a US citizen whose grandparents came from Korea."

Hack stared at the picture of Katy he had captured and enlarged. "You got a social or a driver's license number, anything like that?"

"No. But I'll get one if you really need it."

"Probably. Let me see what I can find without it." Hack's long fingers fluttered over his keyboard, executing commands too fast for Austin to follow. In the next instant, a list of names populated his screen. "Where's she from? There are over two thousand Katy Tangs in the US."

Damn. Austin thought back. He'd never asked Katy where she was from. "I don't know. Sorry. She's getting her MBA at Virginia Wesleyan. Does that help?"

Stu cocked his head, thinking. "Student information is private. I can probably hack their server to check her records, but it might take a couple days."

"What've you got on the Chinese?"

The question caused Hack's head to swivel. His dark eyes searched Austin's face. "You just said she's Korean."

Austin shrugged. "It's only a theory. Can you search something like that?"

Hack turned back to his laptop, but his fingers didn't move. "I'll start with databases open to the public, like the FBI's most wanted. If she came into the US in the last five years, she ought to pop in TSA's database, along with a photo that could help identify her—that's assuming she hasn't altered her appearance."

Austin couldn't imagine Katy looking any different. "So, you don't have a database of Chinese spies you could check, huh?"

Hack gave a bark of laughter. "I wish. The Chinese secret service is one nut we haven't cracked. What makes you think she's one of them?"

Austin blew out a breath. "Because she was there when Chuck got shot. Did she lure him into the shooter's crosshairs? I don't know." He gestured at the pictures on one of Hack's screens. "Just like I don't know why she took Chuck's keys and searched his car. What the hell is she looking for?"

Hack gave Katy's pictures due consideration. "Maybe she's a cop."

Austin frowned. That was what his therapist had said. A vision of Evelyn Haskins short-wired his thoughts. "Why would a cop want to search Chuck's car? He hasn't done anything wrong."

Hack looked back at him. "Why did someone target him if he's done nothing wrong?"

Loyalty stiffened Austin's spine. "I don't know."

"He's been acting different lately," Hack gently pointed out.

Austin started to argue, only to realize Hack was right. Chuck had been depressed and detached since before they'd moved to their new apartment.

"Shit." He wheeled around and stalked to the far side of the long, cool chamber, his heart heavy with confusion. What could Chuck have done to merit police scrutiny? He was such a straight shooter. Nothing in the world could compel him to break the law.

"Listen," Stu called, "Let me work on this alone. It might take me a while, but I think I can identify this Katy Tang, especially if she is a cop."

Austin had walked the length of the room and back. "Thanks, man."

"If you can find me a driver's license number or a social, something like that, I can obviously do it faster."

"Sure. I'll work on that."

Stu swung around to face him. "How's Chuck doing?"

"Good. Better. He's says he's getting out of ICU tomorrow. Sam is setting up a security detail for when Chuck gets a regular room. You want to sign up for that?"

Hack nodded gravely. "Sure. You think the shooter's coming back?"

Austin shrugged. "He might. Hey, thanks for your help, Hack." He stuck his hand out. "Let me know as soon as you find out anything, doesn't matter how small."

Hack's grip was solid. "You got it, brother."

"I'll see myself out." Austin pivoted toward the vault-style door and pulled it open. A run of steps took him to the ground level, where he hit a button that caused the wall at the top to rotate inward, presenting him with a bookcase just like the others making up Hack's home office. Austin stepped through the opening, then watched the bookcase closed fluidly behind him. No one looking at it would suspect Hack had a basement, let alone a data center inside of it.

Without disturbing Hack's wife, Hilary, whom he could see through a door nursing their baby on a sofa, Austin left the Rudolph residence the same way he'd come in, through a door at the back of the library. It let him out into a garden, currently devoid of the roses Hilary loved to tend. A series of paving stones conveyed him to his car. Halfway down the street, a car took off from the curb, attracting his narrowed gaze. Hadn't he seen that car some time earlier that day?

Doubtful. Why would anyone be following him?

THE CLUB WAS a secure space in the Norfolk field office where the ELSUR, or electronic surveillance, from every ongoing investigation was fed, analyzed, translated, and prepared for the case agents. Kelly had never actually been inside it before, but her undercover op, or UCO, gave her excuse enough for access. Any inference or nuance could get lost in a report. She needed to see for herself how Austin behaved when he returned home to his apartment.

At the moment, it was the roommate and not the target who posed a real and present threat to her cover. For that reason, she followed procedure to the letter, parking three blocks from the field office and completing a surveillance detection route before ending up at the gate to the field office. She didn't want it to be her fault if Operation Snowball *snowballed*. Kelly snickered at the play on words. Oh, gosh, Chuck was rubbing off on her.

Two heads swiveled as she marched into the Club, having punched in her code at the door while a guard looked on. The two techs inside greeted her by name. She had met them when they were briefed on her undercover operation.

"I've got you set up over here." Thanks to Hannah's calling ahead, the female tech had set her up at a private console where she could view the recent feed from her op in isolation.

"Perfect." Kelly took a seat, and the woman toggled the equipment.

As the feed started up, the tech walked away. Kelly eyed the unlit interior of both Chuck's living room and bedroom. Red had installed their hidden camera to look down on Chuck's desk, she noted. Apart from that, only one corner of Chuck's bed was within the camera's field of site, showing respect for his privacy.

The larger camera in the living room with its convex lens, on the other hand, picked up everything. The place wasn't so tidy with Chuck in the hospital. She could see a duffel bag lying open on the area rug. For the first time, she noticed a Flintstone poster hanging over the pub table in their dining area. It featured Barney and the rest of the gang, even little Bam-Bam, with his bat. Honestly, Austin did resemble the kid.

Kelly wrested her attention to the time stamp of 17:45. According to the surveillance expert who had tailed Austin from Dam Neck Naval Annex to the home of a teammate, then finally to his apartment, he'd arrived home at 5:45. Kelly gulped. She was about to see what had happened half an hour earlier when Austin walked through the door.

Movement at the bottom of the screen made Kelly's breath hitch. The door swung slowly open. Light from the stairwell spilled across the dark vinyl planks inside. A shoulder appeared as Austin edged into the apartment. But he didn't turn on the lights.

Oh, shit, Kelly thought. Why was he just standing there in the dark like that?

She watched him close the door softly behind him. A shiver licked up her spine as he held perfectly still. Then with stealthy grace, he crossed to the island in the kitchen. A drawer opened and closed. As his silhouette turned, he was gripping a gun.

Kelly gasped. *Oh, good to know that's there.*

Weapon in hand, Austin moved to the living room, which he swiftly cleared before heading for the bedrooms. Kelly's attention jumped to the view of Chuck's bedroom. A light came on, but with the camera focused on Chuck's desk, she couldn't see what Austin was doing. Straining to listen, she thought she heard him open the drawer beside Chuck's bed. Thank God, she'd put the keys there earlier that day.

The room went dark. Kelly looked back at the first frame, where Austin now flicked on the kitchen light. She watched him put the gun away, then open the fridge. He took out a bottle of juice. Putting his back to the fridge, he sipped from the bottle while letting his gaze drift around the living space, as if searching for something.

Once the bottle was empty, he put it down and crossed toward the camera. Kelly held her breath as his face filled the screen. Her perspective tilted as he presumably examined the device. At last, he replaced it, then pulled his cellphone from his pocket and frowned at it. He couldn't possibly know the FBI was watching him.

Looking more relaxed, Austin crossed to the couch and flopped down to look at his phone. Kelly's concerns faded when he let out a laugh, a stress-free sound that allowed her to draw her first deep breath since that morning.

Her squad had hurdled the first big obstacle, getting eyes and ears into the target's apartment. While Austin had clearly suspected something, a fact that still worried Kelly, he hadn't found anything to corroborate his suspicions.

Placing her hands on her knees, she stood up, glad that she had come.

"Have a good night," she called as she made her way to the door. Neither of the techs responded.

A glance at her watch informed Kelly she had just enough of a window for a thorough SDR while still arriving at her apartment soon after the library on campus closed for the night. Working undercover required far more attention to detail than she'd ever imagined it would.

CHAPTER 9

T HE NURSE RIPPING the blood pressure cuff off Chuck's upper arm frowned at him. "Your blood pressure is elevated. I'll come back and check it in an hour."

Of course, it was elevated. He'd been transferred out of ICU and into this bright, private room without any advanced warning whatsoever, and the only weapon he'd managed to snag in case Lee came at him again was a pen. Austin had assured him SEALs in their platoon had signed up to stand guard outside his door, and Austin was the first name on that list. Only Austin wasn't here yet because Chuck hadn't known about his transfer until it happened.

As the nurse departed with a worried backward glance, Chuck's cellphone buzzed. Finally, Austin had replied to his SOS text to say he was on his way. Chuck heaved a sigh of relief and considered his environment.

His private room was spacious and painted a buttery yellow. It boasted a large window fronted by a padded bench that doubled as a cot for visitors. Now that his IV infusion had been converted to a saline lock, he was free to get up and use his very own bathroom any time he wanted—no more condom catheter for this man. The saline lock dangled at his wrist and allowed immediate access to his veins, should his recovery take a turn for the worse. But Chuck wasn't going to let that happen. There was too much to do to allow for any backsliding.

His cellphone buzzed, keeping his pulse elevated. Someone was calling him from an unfamiliar number. Chuck waited to see what happened. The vibrating stopped. Then a moment of silence. Then a notification informing him he had a voicemail message.

He tapped his phone to play the recording.

Hey, it's Seiko. His brother's strained voice made Chuck's heart drop like a rock down a well. *We're in the airport on our way to see you. Sobo wants you to know we'll be visiting in the morning. Make sure you're alone.*

Chuck deleted the message, then reached for his large mug of water and chugged a good portion of it. Looking on the positive side, Austin, who had met his family on two prior occasions, would not be guarding his room *tomorrow.* Hence, his family could visit without Austin ever knowing—a true reprieve, since Austin would immediately notice Chuck's reluctance to receive them.

Not for the first time, Chuck considered coming clean with his roommate. But would Austin understand and forgive him for betraying his country? He wasn't so sure. Austin could never understand what obligation to family entailed. He had never even met his own grandparents.

Heels scuffed the floor outside his door. Chuck tensed and seized his pen. The unexpected vision of Katy pushing into the room, followed immediately by Austin, filled him with mixed elation and consternation.

"He's awake!" Katy tossed behind her as she hurried toward him.

Searching her expression for the least suggestion that she'd conspired with Lee, all Chuck could see was concern and relief on her lovely face. His suspicions evaporated.

Austin came in behind her, grinning. "Surprise, bro! I brought you a visitor. I hope your lungs can take it."

Chuck was breathing fast but, for the first time in days, it didn't hurt at all.

AUSTIN WATCHED HIS best friend's response to Katy's visit. What he saw—a flush on Chuck's cheekbones and a spark in his eyes—affirmed what Austin already knew: Chuck found Katy irresistible.

Awesome. Having a cute, spunky woman in his life was exactly what Chuck needed right now to cheer him up. But there was more to Katy than met the eye, and Austin wasn't going to overlook that. She had searched Chuck's car and broken into their apartment yesterday to return the car keys she'd stolen. For the time being, Austin would let all that slide. Keeping Chuck alive and happy—that was his priority. But so was protecting his friend from whatever strange designs Katy had on him.

He watched her tip her head to one side as she inspected the invalid. "You look good," she said, taking frowning note of the tube still sticking out from under his covers and draining blood into a receptacle. "How do you feel?" Her gaze was warm, her tone concerned.

Chuck basked in her attention. "I've felt better. It hurts to take a deep breath."

"I'm so sorry." She placed a tiny, graceful hand on Chuck's shoulder. Her thumb stroked him through the fabric of his hospital gown.

Chuck cleared his throat. "You shouldn't apologize. You saved my life."

At those words, Katy's lips firmed, and she removed her hand to pull a small paper bag out of her coat pocket. "I brought you something. The police detective working on your case brought these by so I could give them back."

Oh? This was news to Austin. Since when were she and this detective chummy?

Chuck took the bag and peeked inside of it. "My *shuriken*," he said with relief. "Thank you. Where's the third one?"

"I guess the police kept it." Katy shrugged. "I think it had the shooter's blood on it, and they needed that for evidence."

Chuck blinked. "The police. Have they found anything?" He rolled down the top of the bag and stuck it under his sheet.

Katy lifted her shoulders in a shrug. "I don't know. I don't think they've found the guy who shot you yet. They'll want a better description from you, though, since I only saw the back of his head."

Chuck nodded and averted his gaze.

Interesting, Austin thought with a pinch of worry. Maybe Chuck *was* up to something illegal.

Katy put her hand on his shoulder again. "Don't worry. Austin and your teammates won't let anything happen to you."

Chuck looked to Austin for more information.

"That's right. There's a sitting area right down the hall. We'll take eight-hour rotations watching your door."

"Great," Chuck said, with no expression.

Austin tested the waters. "Unless you know who the guy was, and you can guarantee he won't try again."

"I don't know who he was," came the quick reply.

Austin cut his gaze to Katy, expecting her to quiz Chuck for details. Instead, she stood there, biting her lower lip and looking worried.

A brisk knock on the door preceded the entrance of a male orderly bearing a tray. "Cafeteria service," sang out the lanky carrot top. "I've brought your breakfast, and a menu," he added with effeminate flair.

Katy scuttled aside so the orderly could put the tray down.

"Be sure to place your lunch order by eleven," the orderly instructed as he wheeled the rolling table closer to Chuck and adjusted its height. "This morning, you've got scrambled eggs, toast, coffee and orange juice." He whipped the lid off the tray. "And there's your lunch menu and a pencil. Simply send it back with the tray when you're done. Enjoy!" Whirling away, he swept out of the room, leaving Katy, Austin, and Chuck all looking at each other.

Chuck reached for his silverware, and Katy signaled to Austin she had to get going.

"Okay, bro. Katy's got to get to the library, and I'm gonna park myself around the corner." Austin headed for the door.

"Oh." Chuck looked sad to see her leave. "Okay. Thank you for my *shuriken*, Katy," he said, staring at her.

"You're welcome." With the tray in the way, she couldn't hug or kiss him. She backed toward the door. "I hope you don't have to use them again."

Austin pulled the door. "You need me for anything, brother, just yell my name," Austin instructed. "Or maybe text me."

"Bye, Chuck." Katy raised a hand, then preceded Austin into the hallway.

Neither of them spoke as they entered the sitting area next to the elevators. Overstuffed chairs and live plants were backed by a wall of windows with a view of Gateway Park on the other side of the parking lot.

Katy faced him abruptly. "Are you going to be here all day?"

"Yep." He felt her out further. "You really think the shooter's still a threat?"

She lifted a worried gaze at him. "I sure hope not." Pulling her cellphone from her pocket, she rolled her eyes at the latest message. "My study buddy is waiting for me. See you." She hurried toward a closing elevator and disappeared.

Austin considered her slippery behavior. Maybe she was a cop, working undercover, but in full contact with the police working on Chuck's case, and that was how she'd gotten her hands on Chuck's *shuriken*. Or maybe the detective had her address and brought them by like she'd said, so she could give them back to Chuck. It was hard to tell if she was lying to them, or not.

Hopefully, Hack would soon have information that would clear up the mystery of Katy, once and for all.

✕

KELLY JUMPED INTO the Prius and punched the ignition button. She then speed-dialed Hannah, putting her phone on speaker and snapping it into the phone holder on her dash.

Hannah answered cheerily. "Good morning."

"Hah," Kelly said. "I can tell by your voice that it worked."

She didn't have to spell out what she meant. Red, the same Wires and Pliers that had given them eyes and ears in Chuck's apartment, had not only passed himself off as an orderly delivering breakfast, he had managed to stick a bugging device to the bottom of Chuck's tray table. Now the Bu had two ways of listening to Chuck while at the hospital: both through FISA order on his cellphone and the bug in his hospital room.

"Like a well-oiled engine," Hannah replied, "which is good news because we just got word that Granny and Junior are flying east, no doubt to visit Chuck tonight or tomorrow."

"I want to meet them," Kelly requested.

"No way in hell," her case manager retorted. "I don't want you going anywhere near Granny."

"Oh, didn't you say you doubted she was an actor in this play?"

"That was before she bought a plane ticket."

"Right." Kelly, who'd suspected Kim Chun-ja all along, smiled smugly. "She's eighty-six years old. Why fly all day to visit her grandson when she could make a phone call?"

"My thoughts exactly," Hannah replied. "For now, just settle into your role, Munchkin, and keep up with school."

Kelly rolled her eyes. "Yes, Mother. I'll check in later."

Thumbing the call to a close, she proceeded to drive toward the campus library, where several of her peers were meeting up to work on a group project.

She was nearing campus when her ringing phone cut into the classical music playing on her radio. Kelly recognized the name of the caller and reluctantly answered it. "Hello, detective."

"Hello, Miss Katy Tang."

"What's new?"

Scruggs chomped gum in her ear. "I almost caught the shooter, that's what."

Kelly shot a disbelieving look at her cellphone. "Really? What happened?"

"Well, we knew the man was injured, right? Figuring he may have needed stitches, I called every hospital and clinic in the area and gave his description. One of the clinics called me back. They said they had an Asian patient by the name of Sung who had an inflamed laceration on his thigh."

"That could've been him."

"Oh, it was him, Miss Tang. Problem is, he must've overheard the conversation because he slipped out the back entry, and he was gone by the time I got there."

Kelly moved into the right lane. "Good luck finding him now that he knows you're onto him."

"Don't underestimate me, Miss Tang."

"I wouldn't dare, detective. Listen, if you do find him, don't arrest him. We need him operationally."

"Yeah, yeah. Valentino already told me. Just wanted you to know the shooter's still around, and he's got fifteen stitches on his right thigh."

"Good to know. Thanks, detective."

"Any time, Miss Tang."

Kelly hung up with more to think about than ever. Chuck's shooter, who might also be his handler, was likely still gunning for him; and Chuck's family, whom he might have been trying to avoid, were on their way to pay him a visit.

It wasn't concern for her country that put a crease on Kelly's forehead. It was Chuck she was worried about.

✕

CHUCK SOUGHT TO distract himself from his family's dreaded visit by exercising. The previous evening, the

IV had been removed from his hand and the heart monitors from his chest, freeing him to move about. He'd quickly discovered that lifting his left arm higher than shoulder-height hurt the rib cracked by the bullet's intrusion. And elevating his heartbeat made his whole chest ache. Even so, he pushed himself through a series of modified exercises. With his future hanging in the balance, he could not afford to lose muscle nor agility.

Weakness washed over him as he finished his routine. He climbed back into his bed, dismayed by his lack of stamina. He was staring out the window at clouds scudding across the blue sky when a soft knock whipped his attention to the door. His voice failed him as the door swung inward. Seiko stepped into view, his gaze apologetic as he held the door open wordlessly. In shuffled Sobo. Chuck took in her slow gait, her pinched mouth, the bags under her deep-set eyes. Guilt pricked him, but only a little.

He held her hard stare as she came to stand at the foot of his bed. Seiko joined her there.

"Why didn't Mom and Dad come?" Chuck demanded.

Seiko looked to Sobo for permission to speak. "Dad just got his hip replaced. Mom's looking after him."

"Oh." Chuck hadn't even known about his father's surgery. He would send a card, now that Sobo had found him. "How's he doing?"

Seiko smiled weakly. "You know dad. He pokes fun at himself for being an invalid."

Taking in his younger brother's rigid posture, the strain on his face, Chuck's resentment toward his grandmother rose. She'd had no right to drag him away from his studies at USC.

"You've wasted your time coming here," he told both of them.

Sobo's chest swelled at his statement. Her blue-veined hand gripped the metal rail by his feet. She responded in Korean, in a feeble voice underlaid with steel.

"Wrong. We are saving your life, you thoughtless ingrate." She rounded the bed, her hissed words scarcely audible. "Word of your betrayal has reached my great nephew. Now you see the consequences of your impulsive behavior. This is your one and *only* chance to make amends. If you do not, the next time your mother sees you, you will be lying in a coffin."

The prediction filled Chuck with bleak hopelessness.

His brother spoke up suddenly, his voice cracking, "Please don't let that happen, Chuck."

Guilt bubbled up as Chuck held Seiko's pleading gaze. It didn't matter that Sobo had coached Seiko on what to say, he couldn't stand the thought of his brother, mother, or father suffering in any way because of him.

Sobo grubbed inside of her handbag.

Tense with suspicion, Chuck watched her with-draw first a greeting card and then a pen. With the steely-eyed glare of a general, she slapped them down onto his tray table, then rolled the table over his lap.

CONGRATULATIONS said the card, in Korean. Chuck opened it, but the card was blank.

"You will congratulate the Supreme Leader upon the tenth anniversary of his rule. You will swear your loyalty to him." Her voice emerged in a hushed growl.

Chuck raised the back of his bed farther then re-luctantly picked up the pen. He had been taught by Sobo to read and write in the Korean alphabet, but it had been years since he'd had to use that skill. Lee's messages, when decrypted, had always been in English.

"I will tell you what to say," Sobo assured him.

Numb acceptance stole over Chuck. He did *not* want to do this, but the consequences of non-compliance were too high. Lee remained an omnipres-ent threat. If not called off by his superiors, Lee would certainly end Chuck's life on his next attempt.

Strangely, Chuck's thoughts flashed to Katy, whose touch that morning had made his pain vanish. His suspicion of her had given way to something new and exciting. For the first time in months, he anticipated the days to come, the chance to know her better. That would only happen if he capitulated to Sobo's demands. Maybe later, when he could think more clearly, he would find a way to extricate himself from his familial obligation.

"Honorable and Supreme Leader," Sobo began to dictate.

With a tremor in his fingers, Chuck applied himself to shaping the intricate letters of *chosŏn muntcha*, the North Korean alphabet. Twice his memory failed him, but Sobo coached him on the forgotten forms. A bitter taste filled his mouth as he signed his code name, DAKEN, from the Marvel Comics he had read as a child, to a message of absolute obedience and submissiveness.

When he was done, Sobo snatched the card from him and slipped it into the complementary envelope. He knew, since she was the one who had taught him steganography, how she would take a digital picture of the card's contents, encrypt it, and then bury it in some seemingly innocent photograph before posting it on her Google Photos, monitored by the RGB, much the way Chuck's Instagram had been. The RGB, of course, knew what to look for.

This can't be all there is to it, he realized as Sobo slipped the envelope into her purse. "What else?" he demanded.

She managed a smile for him. "You must finish the task you left undone six months ago."

Chuck's thoughts flashed to the dead drop left

within the hollow of a tree at First Landing State Park, the same place where he'd recovered the tiny camera gifted to him five years ago by the RGB. Every fiber of his being resisted the idea.

"I'm in the hospital," he grated. "I need time to recover."

"From the day you leave the hospital, you will have two weeks to complete the tasking, and not a day more. You have gained this reprieve for the sole reason that you are my grandson." Her lips drew back as she hissed with warning, "Do not make a fool out of me."

Staring into Sobo's flinty eyes, it occurred to Chuck that, however hard she was being on him now, she had clearly gone toe-to-toe with the RGB, citing her kinship with the Glorious Leader to save his life. Grudging gratitude forced him to mutter, "Thank you, Sobo. I will do as you say."

His words seemed to smooth the wrinkles from her face. Only then could Chuck see any resemblance to the beautiful bride his grandfather had brought home from the Korean Conflict.

Sobo turned away tottering toward the window seat, where she sank down, visibly exhausted. Seiko took her place at Chuck's bedside. Resentment stirred anew in Chuck as he met his brother's fearful gaze.

"You'll follow through, right?" Seiko asked in voice too quiet for Sobo to hear.

Chuck swallowed. "I don't know yet." He couldn't lie to his brother. They were both victims caught up in a tradition they wanted no part of.

Seiko's hand stole from his side to cover Chuck's in a show of solidarity.

"How long are you staying?" Chuck asked him. "You shouldn't be missing school."

"I'll catch up," Seiko assured him. "We're flying back today." He checked his phone. "In three hours."

Chuck caught his brother's hand before he could pull it back. "Have you been pulled in yet?"

Their grandmother spoke up suddenly as she rose from her seat. "It is rude to whisper," she interrupted in Korean. "We must leave for the airport."

Chuck didn't imagine his brother, still a post-graduate student, was of use to Sobo yet. But once he earned his PhD and found a job as a robotics expert, all bets would be off. Chuck could only hope Sobo would be dead by then.

He released his brother's hand.

Seiko's gaze grew shiny as he stepped back. "You should get back on Instagram," he said.

Knowing the RGB expected information in his pictures, Chuck simply shook his head. "It was good to see you, brother."

He wished he could say the same to his grandmother as she edged Seiko aside and dropped a dutiful kiss on his cheek.

Under her breath she hissed, "Do not disappoint me."

Chuck couldn't bring himself to reassure her. He watched Seiko offer his arm to Sobo, then escort her to the door. On their way out, his brother cast one final look at him. The look burned the backs of Chuck's eyes long after Seiko and Sobo had disappeared.

He wondered if he would live to see his brother again.

CHAPTER 10

A T THE END class on Wednesday, Kelly hustled toward the nearest empty stairwell to check her phone for updates. Chuck's meeting with his family had taken place that very morning as she had sat in class, scarcely able to follow the lecture. Now that class was over, she could finally discover if the Bu's ELSUR of Chuck's hospital room had yielded any actionable intelligence.

Hannah had texted her. *Let's go out for ice cream— Bruster's, 5 PM.*

"Yes!" Kelly breathed, recognizing the coded message as an instruction to meet at the FBI's Peninsula Resident Agency, situated thirty miles to the north, in the opposite direction of the field office she'd already visited twice. First, Kelly had to stop in at the misdirected site, Bruster's Ice Cream, just in case someone was following her.

The extra precaution seemed a waste of time. Only Austin had any reason to suspect her, but that day, he was back at work and a different teammate guarded Chuck's door. All the same, Kelly followed protocol and left campus, headed for Bruster's.

It was a dreary Wednesday in late February, the last day anyone would want to go out for ice cream. By the time she entered Bruster's, used their restroom, and left the establishment, every sailor from Norfolk Naval Station and Little Creek Amphib Base seemed hellbent on joining her in crossing the Hampton Roads Bridge Tunnel.

A full hour later, Kelly arrived at her destination, parking her Prius in the lot of a deserted office park. The white-collar workers had all gone home for the day. Positive she was *not* being tailed, she skipped performing the last of her surveillance detection route and walked directly into the largest of the office buildings.

The food court on the ground floor was still open. Kelly bought a chicken sandwich and took the elevator to the 3rd floor, where Ernie answered her knock at Suite 312. Blushing with apparent pleasure, Ernie admitted her into a room resembling their Bull Pen at the Norfolk office, only smaller, with a wall of windows where the blinds remained perpetually drawn. Hannah, the only other agent present, glanced up from a monitor and waved her over.

Hannah's intent expression brought adrenaline rushing into Kelly's bloodstream. She shook off her jacket, left her sandwich for later, and dropped into the seat next to her case manager. Hannah had logged into their Trilogy platform, where Kelly could see the transcript forwarded by the linguists at the Club.

"What's it say?" She leaned in to read it.

"I want you to listen and read it at the same time." Hannah offered her a headset. "Not that I don't trust our linguists, but you're familiar with the target. Maybe you can tell by the sound of his voice what he's thinking."

With inexplicable foreboding, Kelly donned the headset, then nodded at Hannah, who clicked play on the conversation between Chuck and his family members.

Ears pricked to every word, every nuance, Kelly read the transcript as she listened to his meeting with Granny and the brother. Chuck spoke in Korean with the former, in English with the latter. The bug installed by Red had picked up every sound, including the steely undertone in the old woman's voice. It sent a chill skating up Kelly's spine.

I will tell you what to say.

Kelly leaned in, eyes intent on the transcript, discovering it to be perfectly accurate. Chuck's grandmother was dictating a letter from Chuck to Kim Jong-un, himself.

Honorable and Supreme Leader. Please accept my felicitations upon the tenth anniversary of your rule. Under your guidance, the People of the great Democratic Republic are secure and happy.

"Bullshit," Kelly murmured.

Please forgive your humble servant for shirking my duties these past months. You will soon find no fault in me as, with humility, I swear my continued allegiance to you and to the Republic.

The words hit Kelly like a punch to the stomach. She had sensed Chuck's nefarious activities since the start of her investigation. She had also intuited his grandmother was involved, if not the reason for Chuck's connection with the hostile country. And yet, she still felt betrayed.

She continued to listen, filling in gaps with the same suppositions provided by the analysts in their report.

You must finish the task you left undone six months ago.

He'd left a task undone. What was it? How had it been communicated—verbally? Through a secret message? Dead drop? And why hadn't he carried out the task to begin with? Perhaps he'd had second thoughts about betraying his country, or was that only wishful thinking? It made sense, considering he'd moved to a new apartment, bought a new car, a new phone.

Kelly's scalp tightened. My God, yes! He'd been avoiding his handler also! That was the reason Lee Soo-jin had attempted to kill Chuck. After six months of silence from his asset, the case officer had feared the Navy SEAL was going to ground or, worse yet, confessing to US authorities what he'd done.

Poor Chuck. Pity welled in Kelly unexpectedly. She struggled for detachment. As the recording came to an end, she pulled off the headset, swiveled slowly in her seat, and met Hannah and Ernie's grave regard.

"Holy shit," she commented.

"My thoughts exactly. We've alerted the San Diego division to the likelihood that Kim Chun-ja has been running a spy ring for decades there, without anyone the wiser."

Kelly nodded her agreement. "Chuck may simply be her minion, and a reluctant one at that. That's why Lee tried to finish him. We have a motive for the shooting," she pointed out.

"Possibly," Hannah conceded, clearly having reached the same conclusion.

"What's more, Lee is still a threat until he gets orders to stand down, and those might take a while to reach him," Kelly added. "Detective Scruggs nearly caught him. Did you hear about that?"

"Yes." Hannah rolled her eyes. "Valentino shared that news with me this afternoon. Unfortunately, that just means Lee Soo-jin is going to take greater pains to conceal himself."

Chuck's untenable situation gripped Kelly with sudden fear.

"I need a minute," she requested, standing up and crossing toward the small private restroom near the entrance.

Locking the door behind her, she met her wide-eyed gaze and wondered why she felt so panicked. Her suspicions of Charles Suzuki had proven a hundred percent correct. What she hadn't guessed was his reluctance to be a spy in the first place. Chuck was being *made* to spy on his country. Knowing that it wasn't money, ideology, ego that drove him seem nobler, in her eyes.

"It's all good," she whispered. Chuck's being coerced meant the FBI stood a really good chance of flipping him when the time was right. Chuck could avoid jail time by agreeing to become a double agent. Sure, he would continue to "work" for the RGB, but the Bu would know exactly what the enemy wanted, and they would funnel, through Chuck, just enough intelligence to keep the RGB content.

"It's all good," she repeated. But she still felt conflicted, and the reason was obvious. Charles Suzuki wasn't the bad guy she had initially believed him to be. He was a man who'd tried to do the right thing only to face lethal consequences.

Her role in the unfolding drama was suddenly less appealing, if not repellent. She was to get as close to the target as possible, not only to report on his words and actions, but to gather personal data that Hannah could use as leverage when it came time to flip him. In other words, she was supposed to *pretend* to be his friend.

Pretending had been easier when she'd considered him a traitor.

EVELYN HASKINS JUGGLED the shopping bags in her arms so she could slip her key into the lock on the door of her condominium. To her surprise, she found it unlocked, though it was already dark outside, the light on the stoop unlit.

Well, of course—she had forgotten Jeff was here. His SUV was parked in the garage, contributing to her memory lapse. Jeff, a manager at the post exchange on Little Creek, had moved in with her only last week, promising to make a host of improvements to her condo during his one-week vacation from work. They had picked out a new glass-tile backsplash for the kitchen. She couldn't wait to see what he might have accomplished on his first free day.

"I'm home, honey," she called as she managed to twist open the door, then step into the unlit foyer. She could hear the sound of gunfire from a video game coming from the family room at the back of the unit. "Can I get some help with the groceries?" She used her shoulder to shut the door behind her.

"I'm in the middle of a game."

His retort lacked even a hint of contrition. *Wow.*

Evelyn powered forward with her load, making it

up the short hall to the kitchen on her right. Over the breakfast bar, she took in the view of Jeff sitting on her sofa in the dark family room, staring intently at the television while toggling controls. The video game cast an ever-changing light on his intent, almost maniacal expression.

He was of average height, with straight sandy hair and brown eyes. Pleasant and articulate, he had appealed to her for being the antithesis of a military male. Here was the steady, beta type she was looking for, the reliable soul with whom she would build a strong foundation for a lasting relationship.

None of her original impressions were being affirmed at that moment, however.

As she put away the groceries, she reassessed the man sitting on her sofa sectional cursing and vociferating in his fight to stay alive in a virtual war. She waited for his game to finish, waited for him to drop what he was doing and come lend a hand. He would take her into his arms, gaze into her eyes, and say, "Sorry, darling. How was your day?"

Only he didn't. As she folded her reusable grocery bags, Evelyn asked herself whether she was going to put up with being ignored. A relationship should begin with clearly stated expectations. His ignoring her, even acting like her arrival at home was a nuisance, was unacceptable. As difficult as it was for her to bring up a potential conflict, she knew she had to say something, or her resentment would grow.

But Jeff spoke up first. "Turn off that light in there," he requested on an impatient note. "It's putting a glare on the screen."

Evelyn turned rigid. All the same, she flipped the light switch next to her and stood there in the shadows, her disillusionment growing.

This was *not* how she'd envisioned their relationship evolving. Had he done anything on his first day of vacation to make up for his behavior now? She inspected the dark kitchen and saw no evidence that he had.

Walking out of it, she went to stand behind the couch where she observed his game for a moment, trying to step into his shoes so she could understand why *Sniper Elite*, a game he'd brought with him, along with his X-Box and fifty other video games, had taken precedence to the plans they'd discussed.

When her gaze fell upon the bottle of tequila standing on the coffee table next to his socked feet, she rocked back on her heels. The bottle had been sitting in her liquor cabinet for months, unopened, and now it was two-thirds empty. Drawing a dismayed breath, she inhaled the distinct tang of alcohol emanating from Jeff's skin.

Evelyn gulped and turned blindly toward her first-floor bedroom.

"Hey," Jeff protested as she flipped on the light.

She immediately shut the door between them, not at all to appease him but to give herself time to analyze what was happening.

She had been dating him for three months. He had just moved into her condo to avoid renewing his lease on a ridiculously expensive apartment. She had been quite certain she was going to end up marrying him. Still, she'd wanted to be smart and not to rush into something she might one day regret. She never would have guessed that would happen their first week of living together!

Fist pressed to her churning stomach, Evelyn caught a glimpse of her reflection in her dresser mirror. She immediately turned away from it. It was the same look she'd worn as a teenager listening to her mother verbally assault whatever husband she happened to be married to.

I am not going to turn into her. Those words had become a litany she repeated over and over to herself, year after year. Still, the fear that she would become like her mother had kept her single longer than most.

She drew a shaky breath. She didn't want to stay single forever. Maybe she could still salvage things with Jeff. After all, she was a therapist. She ought to be able to patch up any relationship. Tomorrow, when he was sober, they would discuss what he'd done.

All at once the door flew open, bouncing off the rubber stop on the wall behind it. Jeff filled the doorframe, unsteady on his feet, a scowl on his forehead. "I lost," he stated with disgust. Marching past her without making eye contact, he went into the bathroom and unzipped his fly. Urine streamed into the toilet as he peed with the door wide open.

Repulsed, Evelyn exited the bedroom and returned to the kitchen, turning on lights as she went. She hadn't eaten since noon, and it was pushing 6 PM. She would fix their dinner and say nothing about Jeff's actions.

But the memory of conversations between her mother and whatever hapless stepfather happened to be around fueled a similar conversation in Evelyn's head.

Would have been nice if Jeff had fixed dinner for the both of us, instead of playing Sniper Elite all day long.

You don't know for certain he's been playing all day.

Oh, yeah? I don't see anything else done around here. He couldn't even put his plate from lunch into the dishwasher.

Chill, you're getting too worked up over this. Don't blow up your relationship over a simple evening of indiscretion.

Whirling toward the refrigerator, Evelyn drew back, surprised to find Jeff standing at the refrigerator, about to dispense more ice into his glass.

"What's for dinner?" he asked, the words slurred.

He did not just say that.

She counted to five while the ice dropped into his

glass. "It's been a long day and I'm tired," she said, modulating her voice to keep from yelling. "We're having omelets."

His head swiveled. For the first time since she'd come home, he actually *looked* at her. "I can make them. You go put your feet up." He gestured to the living room.

She forced a smile. That was better. "Thank you, but I don't mind. Do you want cheese in yours?"

Jeff was lactose intolerant. "No."

No, thank you, she corrected silently as she rummaged through the refrigerator. Three days of living together and he'd already forgotten how to be polite. That did not bode well. Fighting to keep her expression neutral, she laid a pepper, mushrooms, tomato, and green onion on the counter. She turned to the pantry to fetch olive oil, and Jeff blocked her path.

"You're mad at me," he accused. Tequila-laced breath fanned her cheek.

Evelyn edged around him.

He grabbed her arm and pulled her back. "Don't ignore me."

Jeff was only a couple inches taller than she was. Nor was he trained in any fighting techniques like a certain Navy SEAL she knew, but she sensed he could hurt her if he wanted to.

"Sorry." She sought to diffuse the anger she could feel rolling off him. "I'm not ignoring you, and I'm not mad at you. I'm just tired, is all."

"You're mad at me for not working all day on your damn kitchen."

Alarm tightened Evelyn's muscles. He wasn't calming down at all. He was working himself into a snit. "Of course not," she soothed. "This is your first day off in six months."

His right hand came up without warning, closing around her throat, cutting off her air. "You're lying to me," he accused. "Don't fucking lie to me. If you're pissed at me, then say it."

She couldn't have spoken if she'd wanted to. He had a death grip on her larynx. Seizing his wrist with both hands and fueled with adrenaline, she managed to pull his arm down, then wheeled away, coughing and sputtering even as she crossed straight to the knife rack.

Common sense urged her not to pull out the biggest knife and defend herself with it. Things would go from bad to worse if she did that. She turned her back on the blades.

The words *Get out* formed in her mouth, but she didn't say them, mostly because she still couldn't speak, but also because those were the words her mother used to say. Besides, Jeff was standing in silent horror, staring at the hand he'd just choked her with.

He slowly lifted his gaze to her. "Evelyn, I'm so sorry."

He stepped toward her, and it was all she could do not to shrink away. His hands were gentle as he clasped her shoulders and pulled her stiff body closer. Then his arms went round her, and finally he was holding her the way she'd thought he would hold her when she first got home.

"I'm so sorry," he repeated in her ear. "I don't know why I did that. It won't happen again."

A sob wracked her bruised larynx. As much as she wanted to believe him, as much as she wanted to pretend this evening had never happened and would never happen again, she wasn't *that* naïve. Jeff had a drinking problem she hadn't noticed before. Drinking made him dangerous, and she didn't want to spend the rest of her life afraid of him.

"It's okay," she whispered, even though it wasn't. She was going to have to shake free of him, somehow.

A vision of Austin Collins formed suddenly in her mind, along with the irrational hope that maybe he could help her.

She thrust the ridiculous thought aside. Her job was to teach Austin how to resolve his issues *without* using his fists.

"We'll talk about this tomorrow," she told him, in a hoarse voice. "Just forget it happened."

To her relief, Jeff set her away from him and nodded. "I'll slice up the vegetables," he offered.

CHAPTER 11

WITH A WHISPERED curse, Chuck rubbed the grit from his eyes and looked around. Dismay shot through him to realize a breakfast tray had been left by his bed without his even realizing it. Perturbed to think someone other than the flamboyant orderly could have waltzed into his room and shot him as he slept, Chuck swung his feet off the side of his bed. No, that wouldn't have happened, he reminded himself—not with one of his teammates posting guard near the elevator.

He put his feet to the floor and stood, encouraged to note that the pain in his chest had diminished. A tube still drained blood from the hemothorax in his chest, but so little was draining, they'd replaced the collection box with a one-way valve and a small cylinder, taped to his side. It was likely his pain was being masked by the Percocet he'd been given like clockwork now that he was weaned off morphine; still, he could tell he was improving. At this rate, he might actually be well enough to complete the task that awaited him.

Repugnance curled his lips at the reminder. He had

stayed awake late into the night, brainstorming some way, *any* way, to get out of fulfilling his obligation. Reporting both himself and Sobo to the authorities would bring dishonor on his family. Yet, even if the rest of his family members were acquitted of wrongdoing, his parents and his brother would suffer slander and the disdain of their neighbors, their clients. Their shipping business would flounder. They would have to sell it and relocate.

Weighing the cost of their pain against his own, Chuck knew there was never a question. He would do what needed to be done.

That being the case, he needed to get released so he could clear his drop and discover what the RGB had tasked him to do. In all likelihood, he would need every one of the fourteen-days Sobo had won for him. Reaching under the blanket for his *shuriken*, he took them with him into the adjoining bathroom, where a fresh gown lay folded atop the counter.

He reached behind himself with his good arm, managing with persistence to undo the knots keeping the laces tied. As the old gown dropped to his feet, Chuck turned to regard the bandage under his arm marking the entry point for Lee's bullet. An impressive bruise surrounded it, an outward indication of the rib that had cracked. Beneath the bandage, a short drain tube protruded from his ribcage, capped by a one-way valve and the collection cylinder.

With instructions not to get his chest wet, Chuck gave up on the idea of a shower. He scrubbed his body with a soapy, wet washcloth, instead. But seeing his hair still greasy, he turned the shower on anyway, took the wand down, and leaned into the shower stall to wash his hair.

That wasn't so easy, he discovered, when the only arm he could raise above his head was holding the shower wand. He turned the water off to add shampoo, then turned it back on to rinse out the suds. Toweling his hair dry proved equally awkward. With his hair still dripping, he funneled his way into the fresh gown, pulling the laces to one side to tie them.

Who did they make these gowns for? he marveled. *And why the hell hadn't anyone designed a gown yet that didn't hang open in the back?*

He was about to emerge from the bathroom when he heard a light knock followed by a faint groan as his door opened. Chuck's pulse spiked. Lee would not have gotten word to stand down yet. Chuck shook his *shuriken* out of the bag into his palm, then tucked himself into the tiled shower and waited, prepared to hit the panic button on the wall if Lee barged in on him.

"Chuck?" Katy's voice sounded just outside the door. "Are you okay?"

"Yeah." He expelled a slow breath and added calmly, "Be right out."

Leaving the two *shuriken* on the sink, he emerged self-consciously. Her smile hit him like a sunrise, keeping his heartbeat elevated.

"Did you shower?" Her gaze flickered over him, making him realize that the thin gown was now molded to his damp body.

"Cat bath."

"How do you feel?"

"Right as rain," he said, soaking up her attention. "I could join the circus right now." He pretended to walk a tight rope.

"Don't overdo it." With a chiding look, she caught his hand and guided him toward his bed. "Here, sit down."

As with the last time she'd touched him, all traces of his pain disappeared. He sat, disappointed when she let go.

She clicked her tongue. "Your hair is still wet."

"Yeah, I can only raise one arm."

"Here, I got you."

She disappeared into the bathroom and came out with a dry towel. Standing on her tiptoes, with her body pressed against him, she towel-dried his hair. The sensual onslaught was almost too much. Not only were her hip and bosom pressed against him, but she was rubbing his head with slow, thorough motions that made him think of sex. Breathing through his nose filled his head with the essence of ginger, oranges, and woman.

"There." She removed the towel, leaned away, and combed her finger through his hair to style it.

It was the most erotic thing Chuck had ever experienced. He was grateful to be sitting down.

"All better." She moved away to hang up the towel, then sat down next to him, mere inches away. "You're not feeling any pain today, are you?"

Not with her around. "A smidge," he said.

"Good. You know you're going to have to take it easy for a while. Tell me you won't have to go back to work right away."

"Shouldn't have to. Commander Montgomery makes that call after seeing the hospital's recommendation."

"You must be chafing to get out of here."

Unable to explain his mixed feelings about that, he just grunted.

Katy jumped off the bed to lift the rounded cover off his breakfast tray. "Oh, pancakes, yum. Here," she wheeled the food closer. "Eat up. You gotta get your strength back. Do you want to sit there and eat, or do you want to lie back down?"

"I'm a clam, right here."

For a split second her eyebrows pulled together. "Oh, happy as a clam. I get it," she said, wheeling the tray table up to him.

Chuck reached for the rolled utensils with his left

hand, only to and wince with discomfort.

"I'll get that." Kelly took the silverware from him, handed him the napkin, which he put on his lap, then took it upon herself to cut his pancakes into bite-sized morsels.

"Thanks."

It was a novel experience for Chuck, being fussed over by an attentive and attractive woman. He'd lived a monk-like existence since becoming a SEAL—not that women weren't constantly throwing themselves at him. He'd simply warded them off by refusing to engage. Caught up in his double life, he hadn't relaxed long enough with a woman to actually get to know her.

Katy didn't give him any choice. "Say when." She drizzled the syrup from the ramekin.

"Then."

"That's cheating." But she stopped pouring at once.

Instead of handing him the fork, she stabbed it into his pancakes and carried the food to his mouth. *I can feed myself.* He kept those words to himself as being fed this way was not unlike foreplay. As he closed his lips around each bite, he imagined her kissing him, tasting maple syrup on his lips and tongue.

"Thirsty?" She handed him the glass of orange juice.

He was draining it when a commanding knock

sounded at the door. Stiffening, Chuck spared a regretful thought for the two *shuriken* in the bathroom. But the man who stepped inside wasn't Lee. It was a stocky, middle-aged man with acne scars not entirely concealed by several days' growth of facial hair.

"Charles Suzuki?"

"Yes, sir."

The man held a badge up. "Detective Scruggs, VBPD."

Caught off guard at coming face-to-face with law enforcement, Chuck put his cup down and pushed the tray away so he could stand, but the man waved him down, while pointing at Katy in recognition.

"Katy Tang," he said, apparently recalling her name from some previous encounter.

"Yes. Hello, again. We met the morning you were shot," she explained to Chuck.

Scruggs looked back at him. "It's good to see you up and moving around," he said. "You looked half-dead last time I saw you."

Chuck acknowledged the raw words with a simple nod. The breakfast he'd swallowed sat heavily in his stomach. Caught up in his failure to escape the RGB, he hadn't resolved yet how to deal with law enforcement.

"Please, don't let me interrupt your breakfast." Scruggs produced a notepad and pen from the lining of his jacket. "I just have a couple of questions, and then I'll be on my way."

Chuck shoved the tray table away from him. "Go ahead. I'm done."

Scruggs glanced pointedly at Katy. "You don't mind if she listens?"

"I can leave." Katy started to move away.

Chuck caught her wrist. "I don't mind. I mean, you saved my life, from what I hear."

"There's no doubt about that," the detective drawled.

With a warm smile, Katy returned to Chuck's side, standing close enough that their legs touched. He took comfort from her presence, though Scruggs' first question flustered him.

"What were you doing on the boardwalk so early on the morning of the incident?"

"Uh." Chuck thought fast. "I went for coffee at my favorite coffee shop."

"The one in the lobby of the Fairfield Hotel?" Scruggs sounded dubious.

"Yes."

"And you go there every weekend?"

"About once a month."

"Okay. And then what happened?"

Chuck shrugged. "I finished my coffee, and I was headed back to my apartment when I realized someone was shooting at me."

"And where was that?"

"Right at the 18th Street Plaza."

"Did you recognize the shooter?"

"No, sir." The lie made Chuck feel physically ill. God, he hated this cloak-and-dagger shit, despised the fact that he'd been sucked right back into it after working so hard to distance himself.

Scruggs scribbled in his notepad, then pulled out a cellphone and showed Chuck an image on it. "Is this the man who shot you?"

It was a closeup shot of Lee, grainy and obviously taken from video footage in the parking garage, but Chuck recognized him anyway.

"Yes, sir." Sweat breached his hairline. "Have you identified him?"

"Not yet."

The words eased Chuck's immediate fears. Lee was too clever to let himself get caught. Scruggs asked him several more questions which he answered automatically—whom did he work for? The name of his commander. Did he wish to press charges?

"Of course." Chuck mustered a look of indignation.

"And you have no idea why the suspect targeted you."

Chuck shook his head. "None at all." He was suddenly conscious of Katy watching him. Cutting his eyes to her, he caught a strangely detached expression on her face before she smiled encouragingly.

My imagination. She knew nothing about his relationship with Lee. If she did, she wouldn't even speak to him.

ANSWERING SCRUGGS' QUESTIONS, Chuck resembled a worm squirming in hot ashes, Kelly reflected, but that was only because she knew the true story. And so did Scruggs, who hid his cynicism behind a veneer of interested concern. The detective was right. She could learn a thing or two from him.

Scruggs finished up the interview with a perfunctory smile and put away his notepad. "Thank you for your time, Mr. Suzuki. We'll do our best to bring your shooter to justice."

Chuck's Adam's apple bobbed. "Thanks."

It was obvious to Kelly he fervently hoped Lee would *not* be caught.

"You just concentrate on getting well," Scruggs said to the patient. He tipped an imaginary hat at Kelly. "Miss Tang." Swiveling on his scuffed shoes, he let himself out of the room.

An awkward silence fell between her and Chuck. "You want any more of your breakfast?" She went to draw the tray table back over, but he put up a hand to wave it off.

"I think I'll get back in bed."

It was obvious to her he wanted to be alone so he could brood over the situation he was in. She couldn't blame him. "That's probably a good idea. I have to get to the library anyway."

She watched him recline onto the hospital bed, caught a glimpse of his muscle-hewn thighs as he bent his knees to get his legs under the blankets. Wanting to help, she straightened out the blanket where it had bunched up.

"There." She stepped back, waiting for him to look at her. "I hope you get to go home soon."

"Thanks." He'd retreated into the shell he'd been hiding in when they first met.

"I'll check on you later," she added as she backed to the door.

"Hey, which of my teammates is standing watch right now?"

The question told he was considering his next move.

"It's Chief Adams. He thinks the Chinese are responsible for what happened to you."

Chuck blinked at the statement. "Could you send him in here on your way out?"

She smiled at him warmly. "Of course."

Her hand was on the door handle when he added, "Hey, Katy?"

"Yeah?"

"Thanks for the TLC."

Her face heated. "My pleasure." She left his room marveling that it really had been a pleasure. She liked touching Chuck Suzuki—liked it a hell of a lot more than she ought to. What would her grandparents think of her fawning over a North Korean spy, considering they'd fled the tide of communism spreading there?

Caught up in her self-censure, Kelly remembered at the last instant to tell Chief Adams that Chuck was asking for him.

Blue Eyes turned from the big window he'd been staring out of when she called his name. Looking relieved to have something to do, he bid her good day and headed for Chuck's room with the confident stride of a SEAL.

She found herself envying the ER nurse, Becca, for her and her husband's loving relationship. Clearly some couples made it work, despite the long separations and the dangers SEALs encountered on a constant basis.

"Don't even think about it," Kelly muttered as she punched the button for the elevator.

Chuck wasn't your average, everyday SEAL, if such a thing even existed. He was currently an enemy of the federal government, and even if the Bu managed to flip him, Chuck could never learn that Katy Tang was actually Kelly Yang. His knowing the CIA had a source within Kim Jong-un's inner circle put that insider at risk. In the world of espionage, the source was protected at all costs. That man was the sole fount of information coming out of Pyongyang. A single rumor could put his life in jeopardy.

So, no. To Chuck, Katy would always be Katy. And she wasn't about to spend the rest of her life pretending she was somebody she wasn't. Relationships weren't meant to be built on lies. Their chemistry was merely a resource for her to exploit so she could crawl into his mind. She needed to realize and accept that.

The stupidest thing she could do was to develop feelings for him.

AUSTIN SAT IN the chair he had occupied during his first therapy session. The sun shining through the window behind him cast a warm mantle over his shoulders. He smiled at Evelyn as she dropped into the seat across from him, crossed her slim legs encased in black leggings that day, and smoothed her hands over her lap in what struck him as a nervous gesture. Over the leggings, she wore a mauve sweater with a mock turtle neck. It accentuated her generous breasts before tapering to her thighs.

"You look pretty in that color," Austin observed.

She eyed him dryly through the glasses that made her blue eyes huge. "Thank you." Her cool tone was meant to keep him at a distance. She had put her ash-brown hair into a bun to complete the look. The bloom he had brought to her cheeks during their last session was conspicuously absent. In fact, Austin thought, the longer he stared, the more she struck him as reserved and troubled, which suggested she hadn't been looking forward to their second session as much as he had.

Well, damn.

"How is your roommate doing, the one that was shot?" she asked with professional concern.

"He's good, thanks. He might be released from the hospital soon."

"That's great." Her countenance brightened as if the news truly pleased her. "I hope he's given plenty of time to recover at home."

"Oh, yeah. Our command takes good care of us," Austin assured her.

"And the snooping neighbor? Any more on her?"

"Well, she returned Chuck's car keys, which means she let herself into our apartment."

Evelyn's baby blues narrowed. "Interesting."

"Isn't it, though? I still haven't figured out her agenda."

"Why don't you just ask her?"

"Nah. I like knowing something she doesn't know."

"Hmm." Evelyn blinked thoughtfully behind her glasses. "What about you? How's your week been so far?"

Austin shrugged. "I haven't punched anyone if that's what you're asking."

Her eyebrows rose. "I wasn't. But thank you for sharing. Let's get to work, shall we? I've got a questionnaire I need you to fill out so I can help you better." She picked up the clipboard sitting next to her and extended it across the space between them.

Austin's gaze dropped automatically toward her cleavage, but given the high neckline of her sweater, all he saw was the length of her neck. Her long, slender, *bruised* neck.

He took the clipboard automatically, stunned by what he'd seen. His mind supplied a short list of means by which she could have come by such bruises. One, she could have been jogging and run into a clothesline. Two, she'd had a procedure done on her thyroid. Neither seemed likely.

Shifting his attention to the paperwork in his hand, he took the pen from under the clip and scratched his name and date of birth into the first two blanks. But his thoughts returned to the bruises he'd just glimpsed, keeping him from making sense of the questions.

"Having trouble there?" his therapist asked.

Austin lifted his gaze to her. "I'd like to ask you that question."

She looked baffled. "What do you mean?"

"How'd you get those bruises on your neck?"

Her eyes flared, filling the lenses of her glasses

before she quickly looked away. "Oh, that's nothing. I, uh, I hurt myself."

"Did you really?" His dubious statement brought her attention back to him.

"Austin, I need you to focus on the questionnaire," she said sternly.

Her assertive tone of voice would have amused him if he weren't so unamused by her discolored neck. "Your boyfriend tried to choke you," he gently guessed.

The tide of color that suffused her porcelain face was all the confirmation he needed. "What the hell?" he breathed, taking her silence for assent. "He *did.*"

A protective tide rolled through him. He set aside the clipboard, scooted his chair closer to hers, and grabbed her hands in his. "Hey, look at me," he requested.

MORTIFICATION PINCHED EVELYN'S cheeks as she met Austin's searching gaze. His gentle grasp only confirmed that she'd lost control of this session in a manner she never could have predicted. She wanted the floor beneath her to open up and swallow her whole. In Spain, they had the perfect expression for this, Trágame, Tierra—swallow me, Earth.

"Don't be embarrassed," he ordered, reading her like a book. "You're still a professional and I'm still the guy that needs my head examined, but you gotta know, this is unacceptable. Can I look?"

He was already pulling down the neckline of her sweater and assessing the damage. "Christ, I can see his fingerprints!"

His indignation alarmed her. "Keep calm," she pleaded. After all, he was the one who'd been sent to her for punching people.

"I am calm." His tone was soft, once more self-controlled. He released her and sat back. "Question is, why are you calm? You should be spitting mad. Did you get him arrested?"

"No, I didn't get him arrested."

Evelyn stood up to distance herself. She crossed to the window where she crossed her arms and stared out at the parking lot. "Listen, I really don't think my personal life should be a topic for discussion." Over her shoulder, she took in Austin's reaction. He had pushed his chair back where it belonged and was sitting there with his arms folded.

"That's not exactly fair, is it?" he pointed out. "You get to pry into my life, and I'm not supposed to show any concern for yours?"

"This is therapy, not a support group."

"But it could be." He propped his right calf onto his left knee assuming a casual stance. "I won't tell," he tacked on. "We'll help each other."

His hopeful expression was her undoing. God help the woman who ended up falling in love with this man! She heaved a sigh and shook her head. "Okay. Fine, if that's the only way to get you to work on yourself, then I'll do it. We'll give each other advice." The words coming out of her mouth appalled her.

His slow grin made it all worthwhile. "Cool. You start first." He waited for her to resume her seat across from him. "What happened? I thought you were happy with this guy."

She found herself opening up to him as she might to a close female confidante. She told him how Jeff's lease had come due and how she'd suggested they move in together; how they'd decided he would work on the updates to her kitchen during his vacation; how she'd come home the night before and found him playing *Sniper Elite* in the dark.

"That is a cool game," Austin interjected.

"I'm not even sure what set him off, but he'd been drinking, which is something he should never do. It turned him mean as a snake. I said I wasn't mad, and he called me a liar. Next thing I knew, his hand was crushing my windpipe."

Austin's jaw hardened. "Fucker," he muttered. "Excuse me. Go on."

"I was terrified. I managed to tear his hand from my throat. I turned away and . . . " Her thoughts about pulling a knife on Jeff would make her sound crazy so she omitted that part. "Suddenly, he apologized, and he was fine after that."

Austin's clenched jaw made his opinion of Jeff very clear. His gaze cut down at the carpet and he thought for a moment. Then he pushed to his feet and gestured for her to do likewise. "First thing I'm going to do is teach you how to get out of a one-handed choke hold."

Evelyn looked around. "Right here?" But she started to stand up.

He grabbed her arm and drew her closer to the windows. "There's more room over here."

He was serious. "If somebody outside sees us, they'll call the MPs," she warned.

"So, we close the blinds." He went to both windows and swiveled the sticks, blotting out the rays of the setting sun.

All at once, her office felt terribly private. Evelyn gave a thought to the other counselors, all of whom had likely left for the day. Her heart began to trot.

Austin seemed oblivious to her heightened awareness. He put both hands on her shoulders and positioned her. "Stand right here. Now, I'm going to pretend to be Jeff, not that I would *ever* use force on a woman. I take it he's right-handed?"

"Yes."

Austin gently encircled her neck. Even with her sweater protecting her bruised flesh, she could tell his hand was larger than Jeff's, and probably much more lethal. "Now, bring up your right hand," Austin instructed, "and pin my wrist in place. I know it seems counterintuitive, but you don't want his hand to leave your neck yet."

"Okay." Puzzled, she obliged.

"Harder. I shouldn't be able to pull my hand back. Yes, better. Good, get feisty."

Warmth pooled in her core at the word *feisty*.

"Now, plant your left hand on my elbow so I can't bend it. Good, now push my arm forward and down. And when I lean over with it," he added as she followed his instructions, "you can knee me right in the chest or the face."

She pretended to raise her knee then released him.

"Again." He resumed his light hold on her neck. "Tell me if I hurt you."

"You're not hurting me." On the contrary, his touch electrified her.

"Good."

His gaze dropped to her lips, and Evelyn's mouth went dry. The hope that he would kiss her blew through her mind, sent on its way by a kick of her conscience.

"Ready?" he prompted.

Wordlessly, she trapped his hand against her neck, clapped her other hand to the back of his elbow, forced his arm down and forward, and pretended to knee him.

"Awesome. You're a quick study. Last time." He

grabbed her neck again.

She got him off her within a second.

"Excellent. Have you taken self-defense classes?"

"My stepfather, Andrew, taught me a few things when we were in Italy. The males there are super persistent."

"Good for him. Andrew, huh? What did he do in the Navy?"

"He was the base commander. Now he works as a defense contractor."

"No way. Are you still close to him?"

"Yeah." So close, in fact, that when her mother divorced Andrew for an Italian billionaire, Evelyn had opted to stay with her stepdad. But Austin didn't need to know all that.

He had returned to his chair, leaving Evelyn to follow his example, privately disappointed that their sparring was over.

Maybe the chemistry she'd felt was all in her head. Or maybe he had more self-control than she had. She dropped into her chair wondering how they'd veered so far from a normal client/counselor exchange.

"So that was it?" Austin propped his elbows on his splayed knees and waited for her to finish her story. "No repercussions?"

"Not yet."

"Not yet," he repeated. "Tell me you're not going to stay with him and hope this never happens again."

Feeling exposed to his penetrating gaze, she drew a breath. "Here's the thing." She forced herself to say it. "I can't keep banishing boyfriends because they're not perfect."

Austin's eyebrows climbed toward his hairline. "Did he acknowledge he has a drinking problem?"

"No," she admitted.

"Well, then you must really love him to risk being killed by him one day."

There was no mistaking Austin's sarcasm for anything else. Evelyn shook her head. "I don't. It's just that—" If she ditched Jeff, he would be the fourth boyfriend she'd banished since college. She sighed, unwilling to explain her reluctance to break things off.

"You don't want to end up like your mother?"

Evelyn's mouth fell open. How was it she was so transparent to this man? "Something like that," she admitted, her face growing hot.

"What if you didn't kick him out? What if I do it for you?"

"What?" The offer astonished her, even though it had occurred to her already. "Oh, no, no, no. I'm not going to encourage the very behavior we're trying to eradicate."

"I won't punch him, I promise. I'll use my words. I'll be completely reasonable."

Evelyn rolled her eyes. "You're mollifying me. I know you're planning to beat him up."

"As appealing as sounds, ma'am, I just gave you my word. And my word is my bond."

His dead-serious tone had her reassessing him. Maybe Austin wasn't as boyish as she'd pegged him to be. He had a mature side, too. An honorable side. Considering his suggestion, it occurred to her providing him with a real-life opportunity to practice the skills she intended to teach him, instead of using his fists, might actually be the best therapy for him.

"Well, okay then," she agreed, cottoning on to the notion. "You have my permission to befriend him and to get him out of my life, but I have one condition."

Austin quirked a smile at her. "For you the world."

She steeled herself against his charm. "Just like you taught me to defend myself, I'm going to teach you how to keep from pounding people you don't like into the ground."

His grin widened. "Sounds fun. When do we start?"

She glanced at her watch, amazed to find that, as with their first session, the time had flown by. She didn't care. She would stay late. Before unleashing Austin on her hopefully-soon-to-be-ex boyfriend, she needed to arm him with skills in self-restraint.

CHAPTER 12

CHUCK SAT IN the passenger seat of Lieutenant Commander Gabe Renault's Jaguar XF, eyes peeled for any indication that Lee was watching his release from the hospital.

It had been two days since Sobo and Seiko took off with Chuck's ass-kissing letter to Kim Jong-un. He wasn't at all certain his letter had been read by the Supreme Leader yet, let alone that Lee had been ordered to stand down. That circumstance kept Chuck's pulse elevated and his mind vigilant—as vigilant as he could be with narcotics still in his bloodstream.

No quantity of painkillers could numb the humiliation of being taken down to the XO's Jaguar in a wheelchair, however. In the absence of available family members, and with Austin training on a coastal patrol boat with their platoon that day, it had fallen to Chuck's command to expedite his release. Commander Montgomery, Executive Officer Gabe Renault, and Senior Chief Solomon McGuire had all drawn straws to determine who would deliver Chuck to his home. The XO had pulled the shortest straw.

Embarrassment heated Chuck's face. If it wasn't bad enough that he'd shared military information with the enemy—albeit harmless information—now he was imposing on a man who was a living legend in the Teams. Seventeen years ago, when Gabe Renault was just a lieutenant, he'd been found by North Koreans during an op gone bad. Having found him unconscious, they'd taken him hostage. For a year he'd been tortured and detained until he'd finally managed to escape, making his way back to his Team and to his family.

The legendary SEAL slipped behind the wheel next to Chuck and sent him a pitying look. The XO's yellow-green eyes must have given him his old code name, Jaguar—or had he always driven a vehicle like this one?

"Trust me, son, I know exactly how you feel," Renault stated as he pulled away from the hospital doors.

Hah. Chuck almost scoffed out loud. Renault had never betrayed his country, not even when he'd been tortured in captivity. The man exemplified pure heroism. "Thank you, sir."

As the XO sped him toward his apartment, Chuck tried to determine whether Lee might be trailing them, but the mirror next to him showed only the back seat. Nor did he wish to crane his neck, making his paranoia apparent. He stared dead ahead and tried calming his fast-beating heart. At least it was a clear day, warm for March 1st. The bright sun hinted of an early spring.

"You're going to have to tell me where to go," Renault reminded him.

"Yes, sir. 18th Street, not far from the boardwalk." *Where I was shot and nearly killed.*

Chuck's thoughts returned to his unenviable situation. He'd been ordered not to drive, not just because of the pain meds which he intended to toss the minute he got home, but also because the cylinder was still taped to his chest, collecting whatever drained from the tube sticking out of him, which wasn't much. Once the tube was taken out and he was off his meds, he could drive again, but that could be another week. How else was he supposed to get to the dead drop and then to the signal site to acknowledge to Lee that the drop had been cleared? Both actions required transportation.

Renault seemed to read his mind. "Make sure you follow your doctor's orders to the letter, Haiku. If you need a ride anywhere, I'm happy to take you."

The tips of Chuck's ears burned. "Thank you, sir. I've got a roommate for that." Plus Katy. That realization cheered him a little.

At last, Renault swung into East Harbor Apartments and slowed to a stop between Chuck's Subaru and Katy's parked Prius. She was at home.

"Thank you for the ride, sir."

"Don't forget your bag."

Chuck reached for the sack by his feet. It contained the pain meds he would no longer take, the big plastic mug he'd been drinking out of, his *shuriken*, and paperwork on how to care for his wound. He opened the door with his good hand and went to step out. Only, it wasn't that easy. He had to put both feet on the ground first, then use the frame of the door to push himself up. To his relief, Renault didn't help.

As the XO drove away, Chuck lifted his gaze to Katy's third story window. Had her curtain just twitched? It sure would be nice if she came over and coddled him again.

Annoyed with himself, he turned and plodded to his apartment, taking the steps slowly and carefully to the second floor. A pang in his chest accompanied each beat of his heart. It wasn't until he reached his door that he realized he didn't have his keys to get in.

Too exhausted to curse, Chuck rested his forehead against the cold vinyl and thought. Austin, who was out on the Chesapeake Bay somewhere, could not be reached. Chuck would have to walk clear to the office management building and request help. Or he could call them.

He was pulling his phone from his pocket when the flurry of footfalls heralded a visitor. He glanced up in time to see Katy's smile morph into a look of concern.

"Hey, are you okay?" She rushed up to him, touching him like he was hers to touch, not that he minded.

"I'm locked out of my apartment," he explained.

"Oh." Thoughts flowed behind her almond-brown eyes.

"I thought I'd call management."

"Why don't you come over to my place? I'll make you some miso soup and spicy Korean noodles called *japchae*."

He knew exactly what *japchae* was. His stomach rumbled, reminding him that he'd hardly eaten any breakfast. "Don't you have to get to class?"

"Friday's a study day. Classes are Mondays and Wednesdays."

"I don't want to impose," he protested, but she was reaching for his bag.

"Here, give me this so you can hold the railing."

Before Chuck knew it, he was crossing the parking lot to get to her building. He must have groaned out loud as he eyed the two flights of stairs awaiting him because she linked arms with him and said, "Don't worry. I'll help you."

They climbed the stairs together, slowly and steadily.

"This is embarrassing," Chuck huffed, having to pause and catch his breath.

She scowled up at him. "Oh, cut yourself a break. You almost died six days ago. Are you lightheaded?"

"No, just weak."

"We'll rest here, then," she decided. She faced him, stepping one riser up so they stood at eye-level. Chuck's gaze fell helplessly to her mouth.

"I'm so glad you didn't die." She leaned into him and dropped the gentlest of kisses on his lips. Chuck felt it all the way to his toes. He let go of the railing, pinning her against him and catching her mouth before it got away. Pleasure streaked along his neural pathways as he kissed her more deeply. Passion fueled his heart into a trot.

Ten seconds later . . . or maybe it was twenty, they both broke off for air.

"Wow," Katy breathed, looking a little alarmed.

Wow was right. He'd heard of drug users experiencing instant euphoria. Their kiss had been exactly like that, completely consuming. Now all he could think about was when he would get his next fix. He went in for another, but she stopped him, putting a hand on his chest.

"Save your strength."

Was that her way of saying no thank you? Or would he get another kiss if he made it up one more flight of stairs?

"I'm ready," he said, properly motivated.

Before he knew it, they had reached the third floor.

"Where's your roommate?" Chuck asked as Katy bent and produced a hidden key from behind a bit of lifted siding.

"Working, supposedly." She unlocked the door and put the key back.

Chuck wasn't so drugged up that he missed the sarcasm in Katy's tone, nor the fact that she hid a key outside her door. "You two don't get along?"

"Oh, we're civil." She escorted him into the apartment and straight toward the cream-colored sectional that took up most of the room. "We're just very different people. Here, have a seat."

As he sank gingerly onto one end of the sofa, she placed his bag at his feet. "I'll be right back with some water, and then I'll make lunch. Do you need anything?"

"I'm good, thanks." He needed another kiss—badly—but apparently it was up to her whether that would happen again, and when.

I AM IN deep kimchi, Kelly thought, heading to the kitchen to dispense a tall class of water. The splendor of their kiss broke over her anew, giving rise to goosebumps. Sure, she had sensed chemistry between them from the get-go, but that kiss had been next level.

No part of her job description entailed getting intimate with the target. The most she was supposed to do was become a confidante. *So, forget it. No more kisses.* But that wasn't a satisfying solution. Wouldn't it be smarter to use their attraction as a tool? Chuck might tell her more if he believed they were on their way to intimacy.

With oddly clumsy fingers, she prepared their lunch while keeping one eye on Chuck, whose chin sank repeatedly toward his chest only to jerk upright.

"Why don't you stretch out on the couch?" she called. "There's a throw right behind you."

"I feel better sitting up."

She shrugged. "Suit yourself."

Apparently, he could sleep fine that way, for soon the sound of his soft snores merged with the bubbling of water on her stove. Twenty minutes later, she carried his food out to him on a tray. As she bent to place the tray on the coffee table, Chuck's eyes snapped open, and his head came up. Exhaustion had given way to an alert glow. He looked ready to take on the world.

She couldn't stop herself from brushing back the dark brown lock of hair that had fallen over his forehead. "Now that's what I call a power nap."

"Rest is a fine medicine." His gaze traveled from her face to the food. "Wow, that looks amazing!"

"Thanks. How long has it been since you had a home-cooked meal?" She stepped away to hand him his bowl of *japchae*.

"Not since Christmas."

Over Christmas, he had flown to San Diego to see

his family, she recalled. "Fork or chopsticks?" She'd brought both.

"Chopsticks."

She handed him the chopsticks, then picked up her own bowl and sat down cross-legged on the cushion next to him. "The miso's cooling off. Dig in."

Twirling her noodles with her fork, Kelly watched Chuck ply his chopsticks expertly, then slurp down a big helping of *japchae*.

"Mmm." His eyes closed as he chewed, the muscles of his strong jaw flexing. "So good."

The low rasp of his voice flooded her with desire. She couldn't wait to kiss him again. "Do you ever cook for yourself?"

"Nope, I wasn't allowed in the kitchen."

"Cooking probably isn't your passion. What is?"

He glanced over, smiling at a private thought.

"What's your passion?" she repeated.

"Photography."

She feigned astonishment. "I never would have guessed. Show me some photos. Do you have some?"

He hesitated, making her worry she was pushing too hard. But then he dug into his pocket, pulling out his cellphone.

Kelly took one look at the phone and remembered—*oh, crap*—the Bu was listening to everything they said. Of course, conversations not directly bearing on the investigation never got past the techs at the

Club, but a talk between the target and the undercover agent was likely to get scrutinized. Had they overheard the kiss? What would Hannah think of Kelly schmoozing with the target?

She hid her sudden consternation behind the curtain of her hair as she leaned in to view Chuck's photos.

"Oh, that's beautiful!" she said of the full-moon-reflected-on-the-ocean pic. "Wow," she added, as he thumbed through the collection she had marveled over already. "You are really talented," she avowed as he put his phone away. "You should frame some of those. Seriously."

"I have framed a few," he admitted. "What about you. What are your hobbies?"

"Um . . . " She probably shouldn't mention target practice or jujitsu. "Well, besides running and cooking, I don't have many hobbies right now, not with school going on."

His mouth worked as if he wanted to articulate a question.

"What?" she prompted.

"I was thinking, I could use some fresh air. You know, to get my strength back and stuff. It's supposed to rain all weekend, but the weather looks good on Monday. Maybe we could go for a walk together, like at a park or something, and I could take some pictures."

She had never heard him say so much at once, without throwing in a single metaphor.

"Um, sure. But I have school on Monday. Maybe in the afternoon? Or Tuesday? I'm completely free on Tuesday."

Chuck hesitated. He had to be thinking about the time constraint he was under.

"Tuesday works."

"Are you sure?"

"Yeah, I'm supposed to take it easy anyway. I've still got a tube sticking out of my chest."

She had felt something attached to him when they were coming up the stairs.

"But that that should be gone by Tuesday," he added.

"I hope so. Does it hurt you?"

"Only when I bump it."

She cringed. "Which park?"

"First Landing State Park. That's where I take most of my pictures."

Parks were ideal places for dead drops. What were the odds he would clear his dead drop with her tagging along?

"First Landing." She cocked her head. "I think I went there when I first moved to the area."

"When was that?"

"Six years ago, when I moved down to Norfolk to manage an ABC store." That was according to her legend, anyway.

"Oh, yeah? How does it feel to be a student again?"

She blew out a breath. "It's rough." It felt good to vent her frustrations. "I haven't been in school in eight years. I'm having to reteach myself *everything*, and it feels like all I do is study." She took a stab at using a metaphor like he would do. "All work and no play makes Katy a dull girl."

"Hah." His teeth flashed in a rare smile. "You're not dull." He bent his head over his bowl to conceal the heightened color in his face.

He was flirting with her. The realization both thrilled and terrified her. "What about you?" she inquired, though she knew the answer. "Did you go to college?"

"Just radio communication training through the military. I've had to master all available frequencies—AM, FM, high frequency, and ultra-high frequency electromagnetic waves, even Morse code."

"I bet you know some super-secret stuff," she commented casually.

Chuck scraped at the last noodle in his bowl and kept quiet.

"I'm sorry there's no more *japchae*." Kicking herself for her comment, Kelly held out a hand for his empty bowl and stood up. "But I bet the miso has cooled off."

Back in the kitchen, she counseled herself to slow down. No need to force information out of him.

"Here you go," she said returning to the couch and passing Chuck the larger serving of miso.

"Thank you."

As their fingers brushed, his gaze jumped to hers. It couldn't be more apparent that he felt, as she did, the awareness leaping between them. Their chemistry added another layer of complexity to an already nuanced situation.

Silence fell between them as she sat back down. They sipped their broth, both of them suddenly contemplative.

"I feel like I'm imposing on you," he said once his cup was empty. "You should be studying."

She grimaced. "Probably." She took his empty cup, then stood and watched helplessly as he came painstakingly to his feet.

"Now that I know you can cook, I might start showing up at your door, wanting more."

The statement was too loaded for Kelly to handle. She fled to the kitchen. "Let me call the building manager."

Minutes later, they were headed back to Chuck's apartment.

"I can probably make it on my own," he protested. But then belied his words by throwing an arm around her and leaning on her for support.

Kelly told herself to squirm away. His helplessness was a ploy to keep them touching, but she found she didn't mind it, not even a little. Under the weight of his arm, she felt protected, not put upon.

But then, as they crossed the parking lot, she caught Chuck scanning the area and realized he could be using her as a deterrent to keep Lee from shooting him. *Great, I'm a human shield now.* Not even that thought made her want to step away.

As they mounted the stairs in lockstep to his apartment door, they came upon the building manager waiting for them.

"You're all set." He unlocked the door, not bothering to ask for Chuck's ID. "You two have a great day." He winked at them as he left.

Oh, God. Was Chuck going to invite her in. *Please don't*, Kelly pleaded in silence, not because she didn't want to but because she did.

Chuck removed his arm from around her.

"I'd invite you in," he said, looking at her lips, "but then I'd probably end up right back in the hospital."

His inference that they'd end up having gymnastic sex brought her to her senses. What was she thinking, leading him on as she had? "Well, I wouldn't want you to hurt yourself again." She backed away, only to realize she was still carrying his bag. "Oh, this is yours."

She thrust it at him, whirled, and fled down the

stairs. "Call me about Tuesday."

"I don't even have your number."

Kelly didn't slow down. "Austin gave me yours. I'll text you!" she shouted over her shoulder.

His silence conveyed perplexity.

Kelly hurried back to her own place, filled with remorse and trepidation. It couldn't be more obvious she and Chuck had chemistry like she'd only ever dreamed about. But now he had expectations of getting to know her intimately, and that wouldn't do. They were headed at a hundred miles an hour into a hot-and-heavy love affair.

Oh, no, no. She could not, would not let that happen. She wasn't going to sleep with a suspected North Korean spy, for one thing. For another, it wouldn't be fair to Chuck to imply that they had a future together. Once the Bu had what they needed to leverage Chuck into telling them everything, Katy Tang would cease to exist. It would be cruel of her to let him think otherwise.

She had to walk a fine line the next time they were together—tease him, keep him coming for the bait, but don't hook him to the point that he couldn't swim away. She was a professional investigator, not a woman who was free to act on her impulses. She'd better remember that the next time Chuck kissed her.

CHAPTER 13

O N SATURDAY, CHUCK resisted reaching for the Percocet. He gritted his teeth and rode out the pain, miserable and unable to sleep. He wished Katy would call him. The mere sound of her voice would ease his discomfort, as it had before. But she didn't call, and Chuck refused to get her number from Austin in order to call her first. He didn't need to look that desperate.

On Sunday, he slept most of the day, lulled by the rain that fell in a steady downpour between his and Katy's apartments. He woke up feeling better. Katy still hadn't called him, but his family did, catching him off guard.

"Mom."

Chuck spoke at length with his mother, loving the sound of her voice, catching up on all the news he'd missed these past two months. He hoped he would never have to go without hearing her voice again, but his future remained as clear as mud.

"How's Dad's new hip?" he asked.

"Why don't you ask him yourself. Here he is."

"My son."

Within seconds his father had Chuck laughing, wiping away tears that were part mirth, part heartache. It was like he'd never broken ties in the first place.

The thought filled him with panic. How could he have found himself in the exact same position he'd been in before Christmas?

Neither his mother nor his father mentioned a word about Sobo and Seiko's visit. They asked no questions about the shooting. They didn't want to discuss, any more than Chuck did, what was at stake— their future as well as his.

"I'll call you next Sunday," he promised, loath to speak to Sobo or listen to her repeat her threats. He knew what was expected of him. He knew it, and he abhorred it.

On Monday, despite earlier forecasts, the sky was spitting a cold rain that bordered on sleet. A home health aide visited Chuck at his apartment to check on the collection cylinder. When it proved to be dry, the aide pulled the tube out of him, applied pressure, and left a bandage below the bandage covering his bullet wound.

Chuck was standing near the balcony door, alone in the wake of the aide's departure and sipping hot tea, when he saw Katy dash through the rain with her computer bag slung over one shoulder.

"Headed for school," he murmured, mocking himself for ever thinking her an assassin or a Special

Agent. She was just an assertive young woman moving up in the world. He admired her ambition.

But why hadn't she called and talked to him since their amazing kiss the other day? She could have at least texted. Hadn't she felt that magnetic tug between them? He had dreamed more than once of them getting carried away, taking their clothes off.

She'd said, *Wow*. That had to mean something.

He looked up at the sky, more yellow than gray. The rain was abating. He felt his left side. Without a tube snaking out of his chest, he felt almost normal. He could most certainly drive himself. Why not collect his dead drop alone today, instead of violating a huge rule in tradecraft and bringing someone with him?

Because he didn't relish hiking in a rain-soaked forest along a slippery, muddy path, for one thing. The drop had waited six months; it could wait one more day; at which time, Katy would accompany him, taking his mind off the RGB's expectations and his worrisome deadline.

Only ten days remained before they considered him once more a deserter.

On Tuesday morning, Chuck cracked his eyes and smiled. Sunlight slanted through his blinds. The weather was perfect for a visit to the park—his and Katy's first date. He rolled out of bed, then realized he had yet to get Katy's number from Austin. Thank goodness her car was parked outside, reassuring him that she was home. He would hike to her door and knock if he had to. He couldn't go another day without seeing her sparkly eyes and adorable dimple.

Chuck headed straight for the shower. He was finally able to get his bullet wound wet. The stitches were being absorbed into his skin. The bruise around his cracked rib was fading. The hole where the tube had drained his hemothorax was almost closed. He flexed before his mirror, wondering what Katy would think of his body. He had lost some muscle definition, but he would get that back in no time.

He dressed in jeans, a long-sleeved Celtics T-shirt, and sturdy hiking shoes. Anticipation cycled through his veins. He'd never thought he would be taking a date to First Landing State Park, of all places.

He was spooning down a bowl of granola cereal when Katy actually texted him.

When are we going?

Relieved she'd lived up to her word and still wanted to go with him, he texted back, *Is 10 AM too soon?*

No, I'm ready.

Me, too. See you in the parking lot in ten minutes.

He beat her to her car. Katy, looking as pretty as a daisy in a yellow jacket, stepped casually out of the stairwell. Her dimple appeared, and her eyes locked onto his. His heart pounded with joy and without so much as a twinge of pain.

"Hi," she said, showing him the hippie-style bag

hanging by her hip. "I brought water for us. How're you feeling?"

"Great."

"Super. I assume I'm driving?"

"If that's okay." Her driving them decreased the odds of Lee spotting Chuck's car, which of course he would recognize now that he'd found him.

"Of course." Katy unlocked her doors and they both climbed in.

Minutes later, they were speeding north on quiet city streets. Most adults were already well into their workday. Kids were at school. Chuck glanced surreptitiously about, ever on the lookout for Lee.

Surely Lee had gotten orders from his superiors by now to stand down. But it was possible he hadn't yet. Katy, in her bright yellow jacket, would make them easy to spot, even from a distance.

She glanced over at him. "You're awfully quiet. You sure you're okay?"

"Fit as a fiddle. I like just looking at you."

His excuse made her flush beneath her creamy, almond-milk complexion. She wouldn't respond that way if she weren't as hot for him as he was for her. Pretty soon she would admit it.

By the time they turned off of Shore Drive into the state park, Chuck had convinced himself everything would be okay. Considering it was the off season, only half a dozen vehicles dotted the parking area. With three thousand acres of wilderness and nineteen miles of trails, he and Katy might not come across another living soul here, let alone Lee. That would suit Chuck just fine.

They left her car parked in the shade and headed toward the Trail Center, finding it closed until April. Chuck pointed at the trail map carved into a wooden placard.

"This is the best hike here, Long Creek Trail. It follows the edge of a saltwater marsh and takes us past a lake. We should see plenty of waterfowl."

"But it's four miles long, and then you have to hike back. Are you sure you're up for that?"

Chuck smiled ruefully. Before getting shot, he could run four miles with a sixty-pound rucksack. "We can always turn around if I get tired." With one more glance at the quiet lot behind them, he led the way.

Katy caught up to him and slipped her hand into his. As their fingers twined, Chuck's contentment pushed aside any doubts about Lee. He wanted to back Katy against a tree and ravish her. All in good time, he comforted himself. Setting an easy, deliberate pace, he tried getting lost in the moment.

The scent of wet leaves and the tang of the saltwater marsh hung in the cool air. Apart from birds twittering and an airplane taking off out of Norfolk International Airport, he and Katy seemed utterly isolated. Their footsteps, cushioned by the damp, sandy earth, scarcely disturbed the peaceful quiet. Sunlight slivered through the stunted pines and slender maples, infusing warmth into the brisk air.

"I love the forest in winter," Katy declared, her tone serene. "I like how you can see so deep into the woods."

"Yeah." Chuck liked that, too. It made it easier to see people sneaking up on them.

A pair of squirrels scampered across their path, plucking his nerves taut before they scrabbled up a nearby tree.

"I never knew this part of the park existed," Katy mused. "The last time I came here, I went to the beach."

The hum of traffic grew indistinct from the wind blowing inland from the Bay. They could have been lost in the wilderness for the sense of isolation and peace.

"I took my moon shot on that beach," Chuck told her.

"Really? I love that photo. Why don't you have a big, fancy camera like most photographers?" She cast him a sidelong glance.

"Because you never have that camera on you when you need it. Besides, I'm an amateur, not a professional."

About a mile into their walk, the trees thinned, and they arrived at an expanse of marsh grass, carved up by muddy streams and studded with tall dead trees.

"This is the saltwater marsh," Chuck said unnecessarily.

"Cool!" Kelly tugged him toward the raised walkway that would carry them over it. "This is awesome."

Chuck knew, if he bothered looking for it, he could see the beech tree on the opposite shore where his dead drop awaited him. Instead, he admired the way Katy's hair lifted in the breeze that stirred up the smell of brackish water.

She peered over the walkway's edge at the muddy water snaking beneath them. "Hey, we should go kayaking one day when you're all healed up. Do you like to kayak?"

"Of course."

She followed the curve of the stream with her eyes, then gasped.

Tensing, Chuck followed her pointing finger to the great blue heron poised at the edge of a mudflat.

"There's your next picture," she whispered.

Chuck teased his phone from his pocket. He made a big to-do about zooming in on the bird, then adjusting the amount of sunlight entering his lens. Then he took a series of shots, changing the angle each time. In the back of his head, he heard a clock ticking. He thrust his phone at Katy and said, "Here you take some. I need to water a tree. I'll be right back."

With a quizzical smile, she took his phone. "Okay." Then she turned her back on him.

✕

LEE SOO-JIN TURNED into First Landing State Park after driving past it a minute earlier.

With his swing shift not starting until 4 PM, he had gone that morning to Daken's apartment, just in time to see him take off with the woman who had interfered in Lee's first attempt to terminate the rogue agent. Who was *she*? Was Daken involved with her? Had he told her all about his North Korean connection?

Lee scratched the itchy growth of beard on his chin. Why would Daken be coming here if not to clear the drop he'd ignored for over six months? And why now, after months of avoiding his handler? Had it taken a close brush with death to motivate him?

By the time Lee parked not far from the woman's black Prius, his target had disappeared. He glanced toward the security vehicle parked by the Trail Center—empty. Good. The last thing Lee needed was more trouble with law enforcement. Ever since the fiasco at the boardwalk, he had been dodging a Virginia Beach detective. That had entailed growing facial hair, exchanging his pickup for a red Volkswagen, and hopping from one safe house to the next. It took more out of Lee than he cared to admit.

His failure to silence Daken was stressful enough. It made him look incompetent in the eyes of his superiors. If Daken were to confess his spying to the authorities, everyone in the North Korean Mission to the UN, from the Ambassador on down, would get tossed out of the country. Either Lee killed Daken before that happened, or Lee himself would be taken out.

Retrieving his guitar case from the back seat of his Volkswagen Beetle, he looped the strap over his head then limped as quickly as he could down the trail that ran parallel to Long Creek. Cape Henry Trail put Lee on higher ground and within range of his target. He had mapped every inch of this park before choosing his drop site.

By the time he reached the vantage point that was his destination, Lee was gasping for breath.

He sagged against a tree trunk while peering down the sloping forested terrain toward the marsh. A flash of yellow caught his eye. There, about a hundred yards below him, stood the woman, alone on the raised footbridge. If Daken had left her there, he had to be clearing his dead drop.

Confused and uncertain of Daken's allegiance, Lee dropped with a grimace to his knees and opened his guitar case. With speed born of practice, he assembled the scoped Winchester, Model 70, long-range sniper rifle, in mere seconds. Then he dropped to his stomach and elbow-crawled for a clearer view of the elevated walkway, waiting for Daken to return to the woman.

Moisture seeped into his clothing as he waited, making adjustments to account for the wind. His cellphone vibrated once, deep within his pocket, shattering his concentration.

With Daken still out of sight, Lee lowered his rifle and pulled his phone out. It took an iris scan and a PIN to access his messaging app. A high-priority message awaited him.

Torn between wanting to finish off his target and following orders to the letter, Lee copied and pasted the message into his decryption app, all the while keeping tabs on the yellow jacket.

The software finished crunching. It spit out a single message: *Daken has ten days in which to prove his loyalty. You will terminate if he fails. Details to follow.*

Lee stared at the instructions, incredulous. Clearly, it paid to have friends in high places. Daken's distant kinship with the Supreme Leader had gained him a reprieve.

Ten days to prove his loyalty, eh? That explained why Daken was clearing his drop. But would he complete his tasking? Lee, who'd been stood up by him too many times to count, gave a dubious snort.

No matter, he decided, as he squirmed backward,

out of sight of the SEAL's keen eyes. Whether Daken proved his worth remained to be seen. But Lee, whose loyalty never wavered, would be ready to finish him should he fail.

SHE DOESN'T SUSPECT *a thing*, Chuck assured himself as he returned to the bridge, having secured the contents of the dead drop.

He had left Katy concentrating on her photos of the heron. The breeze, rustling the marsh grass, had concealed the crunch of leaves beneath his feet when he'd left the path to climb to the speckled tree with a hollow on one side.

Pretending to unzip his fly, Chuck had delved a hand into the well of rotting leaves, groping for Lee's drop. He'd finally felt the plastic 35mm film canister and freed the single strip of paper coiled like a snake inside.

He pushed the paper deep into the front pocket of his jeans, dropped the canister into the pocket of his jacket to be discarded farther away from the drop. A feeling like doom accompanied him back to the path.

By the time he rejoined Kelly, she was taking pictures with her own phone. She caught sight of him, put her phone away, and held his out with a proud look on her face.

"Look, I caught him eating a fish!"

Chuck regarded the close-ups she had taken on his

phone. "They're good," he praised, but nothing mattered anymore save the encrypted message in his pocket. It had robbed him of his contentment and filled him with bitter determination to do whatever the RGB had asked of him. Maybe, then, by some miracle, he would be relieved of any further obligations. Hah, like that would ever happen.

"Hey, I think we should head back," he suggested, his voice tired, like an old man's. "I'm running out of steam, all of a sudden."

"Oh?" Katy searched his face with a worried expression. "Are you lightheaded? Do you need to rest?"

"No, just wiped out. We should turn around."

"Of course. Come on, let's get you home." She looped her arm through his and turned them back the way they'd come.

With his free hand, Chuck teased the film canister out of his jacket. The first time Katy turned her head to look at something, he dropped it into the marsh. Unfortunately, it hit water and not mud, landing with a distinct *plop*.

Katy peered behind him. "What was that?"

Chuck didn't break his stride. "Turtle, probably."

They were stepping off the raised walkway when the crack of a branch on the ridge above them made him freeze and listen.

"What's wrong?" Katy asked.

Chuck strained his ears. He could hear debris

crunching as someone made their way along the path parallel to this one. *Lee?* he guessed, his heart pounding.

"I hear deer," he said. Glancing at Katy, he found her eyes wide with trepidation. "You're not afraid of deer, are you?"

She made a face. "Pfft, no."

He squeezed her hand. "Don't worry. I'll protect you." *But who will protect me?* Lee must have been making sure he collected the drop. He would undoubtedly keep an eye on Chuck until the task—whatever it might be—was done.

Hastening his step, Chuck kept his eyes peeled for signs of his former handler. As they reached the parking lot, a bright red Volkswagen Beetle exited onto Shore Drive. What were the odds that Lee had traded in his Toyota for a car like that?

As they got into Katy's car, she handed him a bottle of water.

"Here, drink up. Maybe you're dehydrated."

"Thanks."

She started up her car. "How do you feel now?"

"Not bad. Need to rest is all."

"Would you like to come to my place for lunch? I make a really juicy burger."

"Sounds like heaven," he admitted, regretting the need to turn her down. "But I need to sleep."

With a searching look, she replied, "Better get you

home, then."

IT WAS ALL Kelly could do to act like nothing had just happened. When Chuck had abandoned her on the bridge, the certainty that he'd gone to clear his dead drop had her pulling out her own phone. She'd used it to capture the relative positioning of the drop site.

Hannah, who had rejected the idea of a surveillance specialist following them on foot into the woods, would probably kick herself.

Chuck was gone for approximately seven minutes, plenty of time in which to clear his drop. Moreover, he'd seemed like a different man when he'd come back, tense, even morose. Her suspicion had solidified when he cited sudden fatigue.

Then, as they'd retraced their steps across the bridge, he'd dropped something into the water. *Turtle, my ass.*

It wasn't until the sound of someone hustling through the woods not far from them drove home the dangers inherent to Kelly's situation. My God, was Chuck being watched to make sure he lived up to his pledge of loyalty? Of course he was. Why would his handler suddenly trust him again?

Her heart would not stop racing. She couldn't wait to update Hannah on what had happened. Chuck *cleared* his drop. Moreover, his sudden need to "rest" suggested he had picked up a message and now needed to decrypt it.

With more pity than contempt, Kelly sped them back to East Harbor Apartments. Thanks to the Wires and Pliers, the Bu would be watching Chuck do just that, assuming he sat at his desk to get the job done.

Her head spun. What had started as a pleasant outing had turned into a critical event, advancing Chuck's career as a spy as well as Operation Snowball's efforts to incriminate him.

By the time she parked in her reserved space at the apartments, Chuck had lapsed into sullen silence. Kelly made one more attempt to keeping him online and communicating. She caught his arm as he reached for the door. "Hey, text me if you change your mind about lunch." Leaning into him, she planted a soft, inviting kiss on the corner of his lips.

For a full two seconds, she had his undivided attention, but then he blinked and pushed his door open. "Thanks."

In the next instant, he was hastening up the steps toward his apartment without a single look back.

Kelly faced front and swiftly texted her case manager. *You won't believe what's happening.*

CHAPTER 14

ONCE ALONE IN his apartment, Chuck turned the deadbolt, keeping everyone but Austin out, and even he wouldn't be home for several more hours.

Chuck went straight to his bedroom. The memory of Katy's kiss taunted him. Hell, if he weren't under a time constraint to complete his task, he'd have taken her up on the offer of lunch. Juicy burgers? If that wasn't an invitation to more, he didn't know what was. God damn the RGB for interfering in the natural course of his and Katy's relationship!

He crossed to his window and snapped shut his blinds. Sobo had taught him to decrypt messages in as little light as possible. The room abruptly filled with shadows, the way his life was filled with secrets.

He hated living this way. Why couldn't he lead a normal existence—meet a girl, fall in love, get married? Would that ever happen? How could it? Either he would have to lie to Katy for the rest of his life or tell her the truth and risk repelling her—or worse, causing her to turn him in. Neither option appealed to him. Even now, with a critical task awaiting him, he couldn't wait to be with her again.

Standing in the filaments of sunlight shooting
through the cracks in his blinds, Chuck withdrew the
message from his pocket and looked at it. For now, it
was just a meaningless sequence of numbers, but it
held the power to change the course of his future.
Sweat beaded his brow.

He turned toward his slim, teak desk and flipped
the switch on his little ten-watt lamp, but nothing
happened. He verified that it was plugged in, tightened
the little bulb, and flipped the switch again. Still
nothing.

Heaving a tedious sigh, Chuck unscrewed the bulb
and went in search of another. There were regular
sized bulbs in the hallway closet, but no little bulbs
that fit his lamp. Chuck tossed the bulb, went back
into his room and decided there was sufficient daylight
coming through his blinds. He picked up one end of
his desk and dragged it into the filaments of sunlight.
Then he moved his chair over, blew out a breath, and
sat down.

To begin, he took a spiral notebook, pencil, and
swingline stapler from his desk drawer. From his
pocket, he retrieved a dime. He then applied the dime
to the screws on the bottom of the stapler, using it to
remove the baseplate.

Two tiny pads, both merely a square inch in size
fell out, one into his hand, the other rolling across his
desk. These pads and his memorized phrase, known

only to Chuck and to the RGB, were indispensable to their communication. He'd have thrown the pads away if he'd remembered they were still in his stapler.

Chuck recovered the runaway pad. Its red font identified it as the decryption pad.

He flipped open his lined notebook, then copied the encrypted message, two numbers at a time, leaving space between each set of two. Once the numbers were transcribed, he consulted the red pad. For every number on his worksheet, he wrote one from the pad beneath it, two digits at a time. Continuing in this vein, he filled a second row, then performed the subtraction sequence taught him by Sobo, to create the third row of numbers: 85 82 92 91 84 95 . . . Each pair would identify a row and column on his phrase table, the next step.

The work was tedious. It required concentration, which he fought to maintain as his thoughts drifted to Katy and her soft, sweet kiss. Rigorous training under Sobo and similar training within his chosen field gave Chuck both speed and accuracy, even with his focus under attack. He could sense his task taking shape, like a figure emerging from the fog. A bead of sweat trickled down his jaw.

With his third line complete, Chuck tore the page from his notebook. On a fresh sheet he wrote his memorized phrase, DON'T LOOK BACK IN ANGER, deleting any repeated letters then adding letters from the alphabet that had not been used yet, then numbers, then punctuation to fill in a seven-column alpha-numeric table that would turn each two consecutive numbers from line three of his previous page into clear text. The first two numbers from line three were 85. On the phrase table, Chuck found where Row 8 intersected with Column 5. The letter L from his personal phrase became the first letter of his message. He wrote it at the bottom, then identified the next letter in the same manner.

Twenty minutes later, Chuck could read the entirety of his task: LOCATE AND ELIMINATE THE TRAITOR KYONG WON-HA, AKA KEN W HARRIS, LAST KNOWN RESIDENCE SOUTH-EAST VA. Expelling a harsh breath, Chuck shoved his seat away from his desk, as if that could distance himself from the grim directive.

He remembered reading about Kyong Won-ha in the newspaper a year ago. At one of the Six-Party Talks happening in Geneva, an "interpreter" had approached a US diplomat, claiming he was, in fact, the senior physicist in charge of North Korea's weapons program. Kyong's identity had been kept a secret, even to members of his own delegation, to keep foreign intelligence from targeting him. In the end, it was Kyong Won-ha who had approached a US diplomat begging for asylum.

The US had immediately complied, of course.

They'd flown the physicist straight to the United States, where he was no doubt debriefed by all the alphabet agencies, given an American name and somewhere safe to live. With a little digging, Chuck could certainly find the defector's exact address. His training, of course, made killing the man a simple feat.

He dragged a hand over his face. "Fuck me."

The sound of someone knocking at his door startled him. His heart pounded. He jumped from his seat to regard his littered desk in horror. There wasn't time to put away his one-time pads, let alone burn the original message and the worksheets. He opened his desk drawer and swept everything into it. He would clean up later.

"Who is it?" He called as he left his darkened room into a sunlit hallway.

"It's Katy."

The announcement both perturbed and cheered him. Clearly, she hadn't gotten the hint when he'd told her he should rest for the remainder of the day. But with his message now decrypted, he realized he wanted to forget about it for a while. Katy's visit was a welcome distraction. So long as he kept her away from his bedroom, what was the harm in having her over?

"I brought you some food," she sang out enticingly.

A peak through his peephole showed her wearing a red sweater and holding a basket in her arms. A rush of anticipation swamped him as he opened the door and grinned at her. "Hello, Little Red Riding Hood."

Her eyes widened. "Oh. Does that make you the big, bad wolf?"

"Most certainly. But I promise to eat whatever's in that basket and not you."

She flushed beneath her dusky skin. "Good, because this basket's heavy."

He took the cue to relieve her of it. A delicious, meaty aroma wafted into his nostrils, turning him ravenous, and no wonder, as it was nearly two in the afternoon. Austin wouldn't be home for another few hours. Pleased to have something—anything—other than his terrible task to think about, Chuck ushered Katy inside.

WITH NERVOUSNESS FIZZING in her veins, Kelly slipped her shoes off by the door, then followed Chuck to the kitchen.

Honestly, she hadn't been sure he would invite her in. Not an hour ago, he'd made his desire to be alone quite clear. But Kelly had stewed with concern as she'd grilled the patties she had shaped and left marinating overnight. Solitude wasn't what Chuck needed, in her opinion.

He had reached a critical juncture in his career as a spy. If he believed in what he was doing, he could push through the unpleasantness. But he didn't believe in it. He played the game because it was expected of him and to avoid being assassinated. With both Granny and the RGB bearing down on him, what would stop Chuck from deciding suicide was his only means of escape? The more time he spent alone, the higher the odds suicide might cross his mind. Growing increasingly alarmed, Kelly had wrapped up the lunch she'd meant for them and packed her picnic basket hoping, once he smelled what she had cooked, he would lack the willpower to send her away.

Sure enough, he'd let her in.

"Feeling better?" she asked, as she trailed him into his kitchen.

"I am, thanks." Chuck put her basket on the counter and cracked the lid. "Are these the juicy burgers you were bragging about?"

"Um, I don't brag," she explained sweetly. "I state facts. Yes, those are my amazing, juicy burgers. They are so good, I thought it would be criminal to eat them both without sharing."

"Wine, too?" He lifted out the bottle and raised an eyebrow at her.

Kelly bit her lip. The wine had been an impulse. She'd pictured him breaking down and confessing to everything after consuming several glasses. That was naïve, of course. Chuck had more backbone than that.

"We don't have to drink it," she assured him. "It's a little early for wine."

"No, I'd love some. Burgers and wine. What could be better?" He took two wine glasses from the cupboard and set them next to the bottle.

Watching him, Kelly wondered at the change in Chuck's demeanor. His preoccupation was gone. He'd wanted to be alone an hour ago, and now he seemed content to while away the afternoon drinking wine with her. What had changed?

Taking over the basket, Kelly set out the plates she had wrapped in aluminum foil.

"Voilà," she said, uncovering them and showing Chuck the plump, homemade patties, the toasted buns, the slices of tomato and onion, one leaf of lettuce each.

"I also brought condiments, just in case you didn't have everything."

"You're like a catering service," he stated, sweeping the plates and then the condiments onto his pub-style table. "And relish, too. Who doesn't *relish* relish?" he added, making a pun as he fetched two knives and napkins.

Kelly twisted the screw top off the wine and filled the wine glasses. *Don't drink too much*, she cautioned herself. The idea was to lower Chuck's inhibitions, not hers.

She handed him the fuller of two glasses.

"To our friendship," he said, catching her off guard.

Kelly's smile wobbled as she touched her glass to his. God forbid he ever discovered who she really was. Her motives would seem so self-serving, when they were anything but. She only wanted to protect him.

"Let's eat," Chuck declared, waving her over to the table.

Kelly followed with the wine bottle. As she put it down, he pulled out one of the tall chairs for her.

"Up you go, Munchkin."

Kelly froze.

"I'm sorry. Was that insensitive?"

"No, that's. . . " He seemed sincere in his apology. "That's just what my colleagues used to call me. I hadn't heard it in a while."

He pushed her chair in. "At the liquor store?"

"Yes."

"So, you don't mind if I call you Munchkin?"

"Not at all." He wouldn't catch her off guard the next time.

He smiled as he sat across from her, shaking out his napkin and tucking it into the neckline of his shirt. "This is special." With gusto, he began doctoring his burger with mayo and relish.

Kelly assessed him surreptitiously. Chuck's upbeat behavior struck her as forced. He wasn't really feeling better, was he?

The insight made her glad she'd foisted herself on him, even though he'd pushed her away. Talking to another human being, even about matters that had nothing to do with his connection to North Korea, was the best thing for him.

"I enjoyed the park this morning," she stated as she spread relish on her bun. "Let's go again sometime."

"Sure." His face hardened as he no doubt thought of the dead drop site. "We'll go to the beach next time. They have camp sites there. Do you like camping?"

She pictured camping with him, knowing it would never happen. "I love it. Tenting in the woods or on the beach is the best. I haven't done it in years, though."

"Let's do it together," he suggested. "Soon."

The determined, almost desperate look in his eyes confirmed her earlier impression. Chuck was trying to forget whatever the RGB had tasked him to do. He didn't want to do it. He was looking for a way out.

Unaware of her thoughts, Chuck bit into his burger, then moaned with appreciation. "Oh, man," he said, talking out the side of his mouth. "First *japchae* and miso, now burgers. Where'd you learn to cook like this?"

"My mother taught me." It felt nice to say something true for a change.

"Good mother," Chuck said, still chewing.

"She is. What about your mom?"

Chuck's forced cheeriness slipped, but he answered the question, surprising her. "Would you believe she's an Amish girl from Ohio?"

He proceeded to tell her how Diane had left her tight-knit community to attend college in LA. "That's where she met my father. Both of them were accounting majors."

Kelly gasped. "I was an accounting major!"

"You'd have lots to talk about." The downward sweep of his eyes betrayed regret. His break with his family still panged him, apparently.

"What about siblings?" she gently probed.

"I have a brother named Seiko," he admitted. "He came to visit me at the hospital."

"He did? I didn't know your family came to see you." It pleased her that he'd admitted as much.

"Just him." Chuck kept his gaze averted. "My father recently got his hip replaced, so he and my mom couldn't make it."

"Oh, gosh, I hope your dad's okay." *No mention of Granny*, Kelly noted, tipping more wine into Chuck's glass. Something was getting him to talk. "Tell me more about Seiko. How old is he?"

"Twenty-three. He's studying robotics at UCLA."

"Oh, so he got all the brains," Kelly teased, wanting to see Chuck smile again.

He shrugged. "Possibly. But I got all the brawn." He waggled his eyebrows suggestively.

Laughter spilled out of Kelly spontaneously.

"Good one," she praised him, wiping a tear of mirth from one eye. She realized Chuck was staring at her.

"Your laughter could heal me," he stated quietly.

The touching words, his sudden gravity, brought a lump to Kelly's throat. She swallowed down her compassion and directed their conversation to a lighter topic.

"I wish I had siblings." She did, in fact, have a brother named Cameron, but not according to her legend. If she mentioned Cameron, she would want to mention her kidnapping, an event that had shaped her career choice, and Chuck couldn't know anything about that.

Her chiming cellphone kept her from elaborating. "I'm sorry," she apologized. "I need to check this message."

"Go ahead."

Kelly read Hannah's message to her and Ernie with a queasy lurch in her stomach.

Bingo. Ice Cream, 6 o'clock.

Bingo meant Chuck had decrypted a message. *Ice cream* meant Hannah wanted to share what it said at the Peninsula Residence Agency. Fighting for a neutral expression, Kelly put her phone away.

"Bad news?"

Her eyes widened. Could Chuck read her that easily? "Oh, no. I just forgot I'm supposed to meet with my group at the campus library this evening.

We're working on a project."

"Oh." Disappointment colored his voice.

Kelly could sense dark thoughts rushing at him. "But not until 5 PM," she heard herself add. That still left her an hour to get to the Peninsula RA.

He checked his watch and managed a smile for her. "What should we do in the meantime?"

"I don't know. What do you want to do?"

"Did you know the way we spend our time defines who we are?" he said, instead of answering.

She raised an eyebrow at him. "Did you just make that up?"

"No, I'm a parrot more than anything." He stretched a hand across the table, like a drowning man reaching for help. "I don't remember who said it first."

Without a second thought, Kelly linked hands with him. As their palms connected and their fingers twined, the desire to protect him solidified inside her. Chuck wasn't a traitor. He was a man caught between two nations, between two ideologies.

At the same time, her awareness of his smooth, warm palm, the latent power in his hand, summoned an overwhelming desire to know him better.

She could think of a very specific way to pass the time, only she might never get another undercover job again if anyone at the Bu found out. Then again, maybe she could argue that Chuck was in danger of taking his own life. She had no empirical evidence to support that frightening thought. All she knew was Chuck needed her, right now, desperately.

✖

AUSTIN HAD WAITED days for Evelyn's abusive boyfriend to go back to work at the Post Exchange on Little Creek Amphibious Base.

The fact that his own work had him zipping in and out of the port on the amphib base struck him as providential. While he'd enjoyed every moment of slamming across ocean waves in the new Mark VI, a boat that bristled with firepower and screamed along at 40 knots, he'd been looking forward to his day to end so he could put his newfound skills to the test.

By the time Echo Platoon idled back into port on Tuesday afternoon, Austin's uniform was damp with sea spray and his mood was confident. Invigorated, he saluted Sam with a cheery farewell and headed for his car.

With the sky starting to mellow, cold air filled the rising shadows. The first thing Austin did when he jumped into his car was to crank on the heat. The second was to check his cellphone. A message from Hack awaited him.

Katy Tang is a registered graduate student at VWU. Found a picture of her driver's license and shot record. She looks legit to me.

"Huh." Austin rubbed his five o'clock shadow and thought for a moment. Maybe Katy was exactly who she'd said she was. Maybe she'd lost something in Chuck's car that was too embarrassing or personal to admit, so she'd held onto the keys to search it. Why would she search the trunk though?

With a shrug, Austin put his phone in his pocket and focused on his immediate objective. He drove straight to the Post Exchange. The time had come to fulfill his promise to his therapist. Once the abusive boyfriend left, Evelyn Haskins would be single.

As he drove, Austin checked his reflection in the rearview mirror and wondered if Evelyn would consider dating a client who had behavioral issues, who was several years younger than she was. Hell, it wouldn't hurt to ask. The more he contemplated asking, the more confident he became that she would say yes.

The PX, of course, was packed at the end of the workday. Austin visited the PX often, just to see what they had. If he saw something he liked, he usually bought it. The post exchange sold everything from clothing to engine oil, even gift cards, and the best part was paying zero sales tax. But tonight, Austin wasn't shopping.

He got out of his car, aware that adrenaline was cycling through his bloodstream, lending him a ton of energy. He caught himself cracking his knuckles and shoved his fingers into his pockets.

He had promised Evelyn he wouldn't punch Jeff's lights out. On their third session this past Sunday, she had taught him numerous verbal techniques—tools for his toolbox, she'd called them. Austin had promised he would put them to use.

It took him several false starts to locate Jeff. He had to ask three different salesclerks where to find their manager. He finally ran into a man who fit Jeff's description, emerging from the staff lounge. One look at the skinny, rather pasty-faced boyfriend, Austin's first thought was *Evelyn can do better.*

"Hey, you're the manager, right?" Austin checked Jeff's name tag and made a positive ID.

"Yeah, that me." Jeff's gaze went to the patch on Austin's uniform. He immediately perked up, recognizing the SEAL trident. "How can I help you?"

Austin said the first thing that popped into his head. "So, I was over in the electronics section looking for the latest version of *Sniper Elite.* Do you not have it here?"

"Oh, no." Jeff's tone turned apologetic. "I'm so sorry. We're all sold out."

"Aw, no way." Austin feigned dismay. "Are you getting a new shipment anytime soon?"

"Not for another week. But I'll save one when it comes in."

Austin blew out a breath. "Thing is, I need something for tonight. My buddies are coming over, and all I have is the same version we've played a dozen times plus some really old games for my NES."

Jeff's face lit up. "You've got a Nintendo Entertainment System?"

Austin noted the man's excitement. Evelyn had told him he was an avid collector of video games. "Yep. Still works great."

"You said you have games for it?"

Austin mentioned the games he'd held onto, ticking them off on his fingers. "Oh, plus, the best one, a Flintstones game called Surprise at Dinosaur Peak."

"No way!" Jeff's small eyes rounded. "Dude, do you realize how much that's worth?"

"No, is it valuable?" This was good. They were talking. Evelyn had drilled the importance of connection through communication.

Jeff pulled out his cellphone to perform a search. "Check it out." He showed Austin the price tag for the same game being sold on eBay.

Austin's eyebrows shot up. He'd had no idea the game he'd played as a child was worth so much money now. "Cool."

"Hey, I'll buy it from you," Jeff offered unexpectedly. "I'll give you the same price as this person's asking for online."

Austin took note of the offer and wondered if they might make a swap. "Do you even have an NES to play it on?"

Jeff's face fell. "Not anymore. It broke. Hey, do you want to sell yours? I'll pay good money for it."

Ah. All at once, Austin knew how he was going to word his ultimatum. "Well." He folded his arms across his chest, aware that his stance swelled the breadth of his chest. "How about I make you an offer you can't refuse."

Jeff looked puzzled. "Like what?"

"Hear me out." Austin's tone went hard and quiet. He bored holes into Jeff's head with his coldest stare. "I'm willing to give you the Nintendo Entertainment System, the Flintstone game, and about eight more games that I have, all for free. But there's something you gotta do for me first."

Jeff regarded him with his mouth hanging open.

"You're going to find a place of your own to live, pack up your possessions, and leave the woman you're living with."

"What?!" The man roused from his astonishment. "What are you talking about. Who are you?" A hint of panic colored his tone.

Austin tipped his head thoughtfully. "Let's just say I'm a friend of Evelyn's, and I've seen the bruises you left on her neck."

He watched with satisfaction as his words bleached the pink hue from Jeff's cheeks.

"Now, normally," Austin continued, "I would beat

the living shit out of someone who laid a hand on a woman. However, I'm turning over a new leaf." He realized as he said the words, he was committed to his transformation. "So, if I were you, I would take the deal I'm offering. All you have to do is leave her, buddy. Once I hear you're gone, I'll deliver the NES and all the games in a box, right here, with your name on it."

Jeff's Adam's apple bobbed. A sheen of sweat now glimmered on his narrow forehead. "How. . . how do I know you'll keep your word?"

Austin sensed a win forthcoming. One side of his mouth kicked upward. "Well, you can take my word for it," he replied, in a voice so cold it prickled his own nape. "Or," he shrugged, "you can wait and see what happens if you don't move out. It's entirely up to you." He nodded to reinforce how reasonable he was being.

Jeff had frozen in a posture of indecision. He spoke, at last, at a little over a whisper. "How long do I have to think about it?"

"Well, let's see." Austin consulted his mental calendar. His next appointment with Evelyn was on Thursday evening. "Better move out by Thursday morning."

"Thursday morning?" Jeff's voice had climbed an octave. "How am I supposed to find a place in only two days?"

Austin cuffed the man's arm in a playful gesture that nearly sent Jeff sprawling. "I have total confidence in you, good man. Remember, you will be rewarded for your actions. By the way, my stepdad used to drink, too. Made him mean as hell until he quit for good. You might want to consider that option."

With a sympathetic grimace, Austin swiveled on his scuffed boots and headed for the exit. He had a really good feeling about what had just transpired. Jeff was afraid of him. Jeff felt guilty. Jeff would get rewarded for doing the right thing.

What Austin hadn't realized was how good it would feel to teach a bully a lesson without breaking his nose. He also didn't realize how exhilarating it would be to liberate Evelyn from an unwanted relationship. Now she could go out with *him*. If she would have him.

He left the PX with a bounce in his step. He couldn't wait for his next therapy session later that week.

CHAPTER 15

THE WINE BOTTLE was nearly empty. Kelly, conscious of the fact she would soon have to drive forty-five minutes—maybe longer if there was traffic—drained the remainder of the wine into Chuck's glass, leaving hers empty. The burgers were long gone, their plates were washed and stowed in her basket, and the condiments were keeping cool in Chuck's refrigerator.

"I should have brought something for dessert," Kelly lamented as she looked around his kitchen for something else to do.

Chuck's gaze drifting over her betrayed his thoughts. She considered her options. While she dared not go all the way with him, would it hurt to give him something to look forward to—just in case suicide *had* crossed his mind?

Grabbing his hand, she led him over to the black, leather couch. With his security camera filming their every move, she couldn't get too carried away, she assured herself. Pulling him down next to her, she snuggled closer, completely and illogically at ease. As they sank into yielding cushions, her shoulder went under his armpit, her free arm looped around his lean waist. Her head rested on his shoulder.

"This is nice," she sighed, eyes closing involuntarily. *More like paradise*, said a wistful voice in her head.

Hugging her back, Chuck released a huge, unconscious sigh. She sensed she was the only thing keeping his dark thoughts at bay.

"Thanks for letting me come over," she murmured.

"I wish you didn't have to leave."

She didn't *want* to leave. His heart thudded swiftly and steadily under her ear. His scent—fabric softener and clean skin—drew her nose to his neck where she breathed it in.

"You don't have to bribe me with food, you know."

She lifted her chin to look at him. The banked flames in his eyes whipped her heart into a trot.

"Oh?" Her voice came out in a husky whisper. "Is there something else I could bribe you with?"

"That's not what I meant, but I'll take whatever you're offering."

In the next instant, he was kissing her. Or maybe she kissed him first. Either way, their mouths fused, and the kiss was every bit as amazing as that first kiss on the stairs. Desire flooded her veins like Niagara Falls, sweeping away all reason, flinging her off a precipice, plunging her into a pool of sensation. There was only her and Chuck and this magical interface.

Hello, people are watching! shouted Kelly's conscience.

With a groan of deprivation, she tore her lips from Chuck's and pointed. "Is that camera there filming us right now?"

Chuck followed her finger and frowned. "Yeah, but no one's watching . . . unless Austin has nothing better to do."

"But it records, right? Like you could watch it later."

One corner of his mouth tipped suggestively "That's a good idea. We'd make one hell of a video."

Her toes curled at the naughty thought. "Right, but then your future wife might find it and come hunt me down."

The haze filming Chuck's heavy-lidded eyes seemed to clear. "What if I'm looking at my future wife?" he countered. "Then you'd have nothing to worry about."

The veiled proposal sobered Kelly to what she was doing—acting on impulses that violated the Bu's methodical and ethical investigative style. She needed to *leave*. Instead, she whispered into his ear, "Please unplug it."

Chuck wordlessly released her, stood up and walked over to the camera. Watching him remove it from its power source, Kelly told herself, *Last chance. Get up and go. Right now!*

It could cost her dearly to stay, in more ways than she cared to think about. But the memory of Chuck stretching out a hand across the table, like a man reaching out for help, kept her where she was. If she got up right now and walked away, the despair she sensed hovering in the room might possess him. She would blame herself if he did something drastic.

And then it was too late. He was holding out a hand to her. "Want to go to my bedroom?"

She thought about the camera in his bedroom. It might be pointing down at the desk, but the techs at the Club would hear her voice and recognize it. They might also hear Chuck say her name.

"Let's stay right here." She shocked herself by reaching for the button on his jeans. Chuck watched her work it free, like he couldn't believe what was happening.

"What if Austin comes home early?"

"When has he ever done that?"

He stopped her from unzipping his jeans. "I need to get something. Be right back." He strode off toward his bedroom.

Kelly watched him disappear, then looked at the door. *Go. Last chance.* Leaving now would be rude, she told herself. She couldn't do that to Chuck. She didn't want to.

He returned, held up a condom sheepishly, and Kelly smiled, knowing exactly where he'd found it.

Clamping the condom between his teeth, he reached over his head with his good arm and pulled off his long-sleeved T-shirt. She had never seen him bare-chested before, but she had known, having felt his solid torso, he would look incredible. Six-pack abs, dusky-colored skin, and no chest hair—yep, perfect.

"Wow," she breathed.

"Now you." Self-conscious of her ordinary figure, Kelly pulled her sweater off.

Chuck stared at her black lace bra and visibly swallowed. "Wow," he repeated. He unzipped his jeans and shucked them off, leaving on his gray boxer briefs and black crew socks. He gestured for Kelly to follow suit.

Without standing up, she unbuttoned her jeans and wriggled them off. By some marvelous stroke of luck, the black panties she'd put on that morning matched her bra.

"Nice," Chuck said, staring. At last, he looked down at himself, then pulled his socks off.

Kelly laughed. "That's cheating."

With a grin, Chuck went down on his knees. He shuffled closer. Kelly held her breath as he reached for her, stroking a reverent hand up the outside of her thigh.

"So soft."

Freed to do likewise, she put her hand on his smooth chest. All swells and valleys, it was virtually a playground. "So hard," she countered.

He chuckled. Catching one of her hands, he drew it toward the shaft peeking through the slit of his boxer briefs. "No, *this* is hard."

Kelly sucked in a breath of appreciation as she cupped him through the cotton-spandex blend of his underwear. *I can't believe I'm doing this*, she thought.

Chuck tore into the condom. Skimming off his boxer briefs, he covered himself hastily. Then, without warning, he caught both of her ankles and tugged her hips to the edge of the couch.

Kelly let out a squeak. Her toes touched the floor on either side of him. He ducked his head and lightly bit the inside of her thigh. She broke into laughter as he nibbled, licked, and kissed his way higher.

"Ticklish?"

"Yes!" she gasped. The air seemed to lack oxygen.

Her panties offered scant protection as he reached the apex of her thighs and laved her through the satin fabric. She arched her hips, enjoying the tease, but cooperating fully when he peeled her panties off.

"Oh!" He cupped her fanny and sluiced his tongue along her sensitive folds.

Whimpers followed and then sounds of encouragement as his ministrations grew more focused. She gripped the thick hair on his head. Teetering at the edge of climax, she slit her eyes to watch his tender lashing. Over the twin peaks of her breasts, their gazes locked.

The climax that had been building in her broke with force. Kelly gripped the leather cushions on either side of her, holding on for dear life as ecstasy wrung her body for timeless moments before tapering away. She went limp, catching back a sob.

Nothing in her limited experience had prepared her for *that*.

Chuck rose. Putting a knee on the couch, he hooked her waist with his good arm and turned her to lie the length of the cushions. Then he crawled over her, holding his weight above her as he bent his nose to her breasts.

"You smell so good to me."

Kelly shivered. He kissed her collarbones lightly, drawing goosebumps in his wake as he moved lower. As circled her nipples with his tongue, she spared a thought for Hannah's message and wondered what time it was now.

Hannah could wait. All the same, Kelly tugged on Chuck's ears, encouraging his mouth to return to hers. They kissed deeply, desperately. He lowered his weight atop her. The feel of their naked bodies touching was a delight in itself. Kelly pulled him closer, spread her thighs, and wrapped her legs around him. He probed her gently, seeking entry, finding it. She gasped as he filled her, adjusting, softening. He surged with more confidence. She welcomed him, digging her fingernails into his back. It was both too much and not enough.

They moved together—lips fused, skin damp with ecstasy. Each slow thrust sent Kelly to a higher tier of fulfillment.

"I'm close," Chuck whispered apologetically.

The thought of him on the brink spurred her own release. It unfurled, expanding outward, colliding with the storm that broke over Chuck. They weathered the tempest together, holding each other as if their very lives depended on it.

As her pleasure ebbed, Kelly closed her eyes and sighed. Chuck slid an arm beneath her back and flipped her onto her side so he could squeeze himself between her and the back of the couch.

With her head on his shoulder, his warmth and scent lulling her, Kelly pondered her discovery of paradise with belated concern.

She couldn't stay like this much longer—and not just because Austin might waltz through the door at any moment. It was a weekday, and traffic headed for the Peninsula would be awful. *Drats.*

"I'm so sorry. I have to run."

She eased away from him, shocked by the sudden cold as she extracted herself from his embrace. Snatching up her clothing, Kelly hurried down the hall for Austin's bathroom.

Flicking on the light, she locked the door, then hastily dressed, grimacing at the necessity of donning damp underwear before stepping into her jeans. She avoided looking into the mirror. She would have plenty of time on the drive north to think about what she'd done.

A light knock startled her. She hadn't heard his approach. "You good in there? Need a towel or anything?"

She strove for levity. "No, I'm going to run home and change. Thanks, though."

She could tell he remained nearby as she latched her bra and tunneled into her sweater. Exiting, she came face-to-face with him. Her heart gave a happy leap as their eyes met. Kissing his lips felt as natural as blinking. "I had a really good time," she stated truthfully.

He pinned her a moment to his naked chest. "Drive safely." Then he released her. "I'll see you later, when I bring your basket back."

"Oh, yeah. Okay." She eased past him, hurrying to collect her phone from the table. She wriggled her feet into her flats as she opened the door. A backward glance showed Chuck standing in naked splendor at the end of the hallway. Her heart seemed to flutter.

"Bye," she called, stepping into chilly evening air.

CHUCK RAISED A hand then let it drop as the door closed behind Katy. He had just experienced the best sex in his life, but something about her fixation with

the camera and then her hasty departure jarred his
contentment.

He turned toward his dark bedroom, flipped on
the light, and immediately remembered his decoded
message was sitting right there in the drawer for
anyone to read. Christ, what a terrible spy he made!
Good thing Katy wasn't the secret agent he'd suspected her of being. She could have slipped him a roofie
and rendered him unconscious, giving her the chance
to search his room. He swiped a hand over his eyes,
belatedly grateful she'd wanted to have sex on the
couch.

And what an experience that had been! Their late
lunch had also been amazing. So why the nagging
sense that he was overlooking something?

Chuck went into his own bathroom and cleaned
up. He needed to dress before Austin came home, put
away his one-time pads, and destroy his worksheets.
Memories of his and Katy's incredible coupling played
over and over in his head, keeping the horror of his
task for the RGB at bay. It had been so good he didn't
even regret that remark about him looking at his future
wife. Katy had let it pass without comment, though.

Did she not feel the way he did? What if she'd
been hurt and was fearful of commitment? Damn it,
why even torture himself with these questions? He
couldn't *be* in a relationship or even think about a
future with Katy until he found a way out of his

predicament.

The RGB wanted their former lead physicist dead. If Chuck obliged them, would they cut him free? He doubted it. After this job, there would be another, then another after that. He could either give them what they wanted—or pretend to, as he had done previously. But if he were caught lying or shirking his duties, he knew from experience, he would be killed faster than he could say *My loyalty to Country and Team is beyond reproach.*

KELLY ARRIVED AT the Peninsula Resident Agency twelve minutes late, even when she'd skipped the SDR by not driving to Bruster's first. Nobody was following her, she was certain. Unwilling to wait for the elevator, she tore up the stairs to the third floor. She knocked on the door of room 312, out of breath.

Ernie opened the door as he had on her previous visit. His greeting gave way to a searching frown. Kelly touched a self-conscious hand to her disheveled hair. Ernie couldn't possibly guess what she'd been up to. She stepped into a room lit with artificial lighting. The blinds were backed by a dark sky. Hannah glanced up from the same console where Kelly had listened to Granny dictate Chuck's card to the Glorious Leader.

"Hey," the redhead called.

Hot in the face, Kelly shook off the jacket she'd donned when she'd quickly changed clothing in her apartment and spritzed on perfume to disguise what she'd been up to.

Hannah patted the seat next to her.

Kelly dropped into the chair. The monitor showed Chuck's room lit by rays of light slipping through his blinds.

"Wait," she protested. "Why can't we see all of his desk? Did he move it?

"Apparently," Hannah said, not sounding pleased, "he was out of lightbulbs. He couldn't turn on his desk light, so he moved the desk closer to the window."

"Watch this," Ernie said, having come to stand behind them.

Chuck's hand came into view. He was holding a stapler. They watched him manipulate it off screen, with only his elbow showing. All at once, a tiny pad tumbled into view.

Kelly gasped. "That's a one-time pad. He keeps them in his stapler?"

"Yep," Hannah said, "and that's our confirmation of his intel operation."

Chuck picked up the pad and took it out of view. The edge of a notebook appeared, the rest of it off camera.

"He's copying the original message," Kelly deduced, picturing a long string of numbers in groups of five, which he would later transpose in pairs.

"Yes, only we don't get to see it." Hannah's disappointment kept her tone flat.

With Chuck's knuckles occasionally sliding into view, they watched him, presumably consult the one-time pad to write a second row of numbers. His knuckles appeared again, a little lower on the page.

"Wow, he's fast," Kelly observed, when it became apparent he was working on his third line, performing false subtraction based on the numbers on the two lines above.

"Plenty of practice," Ernie murmured.

Glued to the video, Kelly watched Chuck tear out the page he was working on. To her frustration, he did not set it within their view. He proceeded to work on the second page.

"He's making his phrase table," Kelly guessed, as she recognized the sound of lines being drawn. The process of decryption and encryption had been drilled into her at the FBI Academy. "I can't believe we can't see any of this."

"Just wait," Ernie urged.

For ten more minutes, they watched in frustration as Chuck worked off-camera, consulting his first page while decrypting his message on the second. At last, he set his pen down, within their view.

"He's done," Kelly concluded.

"Watch what happens now," Hannah said.

All at once, a knocking sounded in the background, startling Chuck, who leapt to his feet. He jerked open his desk drawer and swiped his paperwork into it. Ernie reached over Katy's shoulder and stopped the video, rewinding briefly, he froze it again.

"Have a look." He zoomed in on the spiral notebook, lying in the drawer with its binding against the front edge. The first word of Chuck's decrypted message was partially visible to them: LOCAT

Kelly's thoughts raced. "Locate? Location?"

Hannah nodded. "We think it's Locate. He's supposed to find someone."

"Who?" Kelly considered the limitless possibilities. "Where?"

"We don't know," Hannah answered, clearly irritated. "I take it that was you, knocking on his door?"

Kelly found herself the focus of Hannah's bright green gaze. "Um, yeah, I took him some food." She broke out in a cold sweat wondering how much video footage the Club had shared.

"Is that all the footage we have?" Kelly flicked an anxious glance up at Ernie. Surely if he knew what she'd done, his disappointment would be evident.

He shrugged easily. "According to the techs that's all that's relevant. They let us know a short while ago that he burned the worksheet, as expected."

"And moved his desk back under the sword," Hannah added, with a sigh. "Well, we know more than we did this morning, anyway." She looked back at Kelly. "Did he say anything to indicate what his tasking might be?"

Kelly shook her head. "No. I could tell he was upset and trying to forget about it. But, no. He didn't drop any clues."

"He likes you, though," Hannah replied, without judgment. "That's good. He might open up to you eventually."

Kelly grappled with unwieldy emotions.

"Who wouldn't like Kelly?" Ernie inserted.

She sent him a grateful smile. Her colleagues wouldn't be so complimentary if they knew she'd had sex with the target, who might also be picturing her as his future wife.

Which was worse? she asked herself. Stringing a man along with no hope for a future or implicating a good man of a crime he didn't want to commit in the first place?

AUSTIN STOOD BEHIND a tree that shielded him from the many mirrored windows of the building Katy had hurried into. Forty-five minutes ago, when there was still some light in the sky, he'd been sitting at an intersection waiting for a green arrow and savoring his victory with Jeff, when he'd noticed Katy at the wheel of her Prius, turning off the road he was about to turn onto.

Hack's recent text about Katy Tang being legit had flashed through Austin's mind. As much as he wanted to believe Hack, his instinct whispered otherwise. Normal people didn't search other people's cars. In that instant, Austin had made up his mind to follow Katy, if only to see where she went.

His work as a SEAL had taught him a thing or two about clandestine activity. He'd waited patiently for his own light to turn green, then switched lanes and went straight, instead of left. Hanging half a mile behind Katy, he followed her distinct taillights.

When she swooped onto highway 264, he'd figured she was taking the fastest route to the campus library. The twenty-minute trip required a quick jaunt on Interstate 64, but instead of getting off the exit that would take her to Virginia Wesleyan, Katy kept going.

Austin's suspicion had sharply escalated at that point. He'd followed her through the Hampton Roads Bridge Tunnel, and he was thinking she would never stop driving when she finally exited the interstate and made her way into an empty office park. Following at a snail's pace, Austin had arrived just in time to see Katy hoofing it into one of the many buildings. He'd parked on the opposite side of the complex, then made his way back to the four-storied, mirrored building.

Standing in the cold shadows some distance from the door, Austin strained his eyes to read the names on the plaque posted in the foyer. There were several businesses that might attract an MBA student, but scarcely any cars in the parking lot.

Perplexed, Austin moved behind a Douglass fir, using its lush boughs to block the light of his cellphone. He sent Hack a pin citing his location and appended the text, *Why is Katy Tang in this building? What is here?*

Then he shoved his phone into his pocket and hugged himself against the sharply colder air. His Navy working uniform didn't provide much warmth. It might take Hack, who was working in DC with Ghost Security Group, ages to get back to him. Moreover, Chuck had texted moments before saying they needed breakfast items from the store.

With a shrug, Austin headed for his car. His victory over Jeff earlier that evening had given way to a nagging certainty that Katy Tang was up to something she didn't want him or Chuck knowing about. What could it be, and should he share his suspicions with his roommate?

✕

AT ALMOST NINE o'clock that night, Chuck slipped into his apartment hoping to find Austin fast asleep in his bed. Instead, he was sitting on the sofa playing a Flintstone's video game with hokey background music.

"Where have you been?" Austin broke his concentration to look over at him.

Chuck held up the groceries he'd picked up on his way back from the drop. "Went to the store since I never heard back from you."

"I got your message, bro. You didn't need to do that."

"Oh, I didn't know." Plus, he'd needed an excuse to leave the apartment.

"I thought you weren't supposed to drive."

"No, I was cleared the other day when the nurse took the tube out." How else would he have gotten to the mailbox belonging to a lonely church and scratched his crayon through Lee's faded, original mark? The mark was important, letting Lee know that he was compliant to the RGB's directive.

Chuck took his purchases to the kitchen and put them away, all while keeping one eye on Austin's video game.

Fred and Barney were jumping up a series of cliffs and over a lava flow, trying to get to Pebbles and Bam-Bam, who'd gotten themselves into trouble. The circus-like background music lent itself to the urgent and almost-impossible mission.

All at once, Fred, who wasn't a good jumper, took a nosedive that brought Austin's quest to an abrupt end. He sighed, then used his controller to turn the game off.

"Why were you playing that?" Chuck asked him.

Austin crossed to the NES and ejected the cartridge. "Just playing my old games one last time."

"What do you mean, one last time?"

"I'm giving them away." Without looking at him, Austin reached for a cardboard box Chuck hadn't noticed until then. He proceeded to unplug his gaming system.

"You're giving away everything?"

"Yep."

"Why? Aren't they worth something?"

Austin smiled tightly, but he still didn't look at Chuck. "To make my therapist happy."

Chuck processed the statement and came up with the only logical conclusion. "She thinks you're addicted to video games?"

Austin gave a bark of laughter and finally made eye contact. "No, man. It's more complicated than that."

Chuck waited, expecting a lengthy explanation, but Austin didn't give him one. Instead, he lowered the NES into one side of his box, then stacked game cartridges on the other side.

"Whose picnic basket is next to the sink?" Austin asked, changing the subject.

Chuck looked over at it. "Katy's. She brought over a meal this afternoon." Memories of their lovemaking filled him with contentment.

Austin, who was staring at him, straightened abruptly. "You slept with her," he guessed. It sounded like an accusation.

Chuck wanted to deny it, but he could feel his face turning red.

"You did!"

"So?"

"So, how was it?"

Chuck shook his head, not about to answer, but he couldn't keep from smiling.

"That good, huh?"

Chuck turned back to the refrigerator.

"When was she here?" Austin asked. "How long did she stay?"

"Not too long." Chuck came out of the refrigerator with a bottle of berry-flavored Kombucha. "She had to get to her school library to work on a group project." He twisted off the cap and took a swig.

"School library, huh?" Austin didn't sound like he believed it. "She goes there a lot."

Puzzled, Chuck searched his roommate's expression. "Yeah, she's a student."

Austin stared at him. "So, you really like her," he finally said.

Chuck queried his feelings and took another sip of his drink. "Yeah," he admitted. "I think—I don't know—I think this might be the real deal. I think she's the one for me."

To his confusion, Austin looked more concerned than happy for him. "You barely even know her."

Chuck chugged his drink. "You said having a girl-friend would be good for me," he reminded Austin. "Don't you like Katy?"

"Sure, I do. It's just. . . maybe you should get to know her better before saying she's the one."

Chuck drained the bottle then tossed it into the recycle bin. "You're right. And I intend to." He would spend time with her next day, when he brought back her basket. She'd been in such a hurry to join her classmates, she had left it behind, even though she'd gone to her apartment first to change.

Austin turned away and finished packing up his games. Chuck still didn't know why his friend was giving away his NES collection. That had to be the reason he was acting grumpy and cautioning Chuck to take his time. With an inward shrug, Chuck headed for his bedroom to shower and prepare for bed.

With the deadline looming over his head, he would need to wake up as early as Austin to get started on his task. It would take diligent research to discover where Ken W. Harris worked and lived. The sooner he discovered that, the sooner he got his task over with, the sooner he might get to live a normal life.

Right. Like that would ever happen.

CHAPTER 16

KELLY BLINKED DOWN at the textbook in her lap and realized she'd read an entire page of her assignment without taking in a single point. How was she supposed to focus when she'd seen Chuck slip into his car last evening and drive away? A text to Hannah had been answered two hours later. Apparently, a surveillance specialist had followed Chuck from his apartment to a lonely church off Bell Road, where he had left a mark on the mailbox, signaling to his handler that he'd cleared his drop.

If that news wasn't enough to fragment Kelly's concentration, memories of her and Chuck's lovemaking the previous afternoon plagued her conscience. Her intentions had been good, truly they had, but bottom line was she'd slept with the target! How could she have behaved so unprofessionally? If Chuck had suicidal thoughts, it wasn't up to her to prevent them. Her job was to gain his trust, not sleep with him! Whatever it took, she had to resist the temptation to sleep with him again.

"Ugh." Thrusting the textbook off her lap, Kelly unfolded her legs, and scooted off the bed where she'd been studying. As she stretched the kinks in her back, her gaze went toward Chuck's apartment.

According to the surveillance specialist who'd watched his vehicle while Kelly went to class, he'd cloistered himself in his apartment all morning. She sought movement beyond the glass door of his balcony and past the blinds of his bedroom window, but everything looked still in there. According to Ernie, Chuck was on his laptop performing searches.

Heaving a tedious sigh, Kelly returned to her bed and plopped down on it, pulling her textbook closer and summoning her concentration. She had to pass her classes with a respectable grade. That was easier said than done with Operation Snowball distracting her.

For three hours, Kelly made inroads into her assignment. As evening approached, and with her focus fragmenting, she left her bedroom in search of food. Her footfalls sounded loud in the quiet apartment. Lisa had left perhaps ten minutes earlier, on a date with a fireman, this time. Or was it the body builder? Kelly stood at the counter eating what remained of the *bibimbap* she'd made right after school.

She was washing it down with carbonated water when a light knock sounded at the door. Her pulse spiked. She set down the can and crossed to the door where she stood on her tiptoes to peer through the peephole.

The sight of Chuck wearing workout wear and carrying the basket she'd brought over the afternoon before flooded Kelly with awareness. Every nerve in her body tingled. *I am not sleeping with him again*, she reminded herself, even as she hurriedly unlocked the door and pulled it open.

"Hi." She found herself grinning at him.

"I brought your stuff back." He made no move to hand it to her, however. "Have you visited the recreation center for residents here? There's a gym."

"No. Is the gym any good?"

"Not bad. You want to work out there with me?"

She looked down at the sweater she was wearing. "Um, sure. I'll have to change first. Do you want to come in?"

She waved him into the kitchen where he set her basket down on the counter. Fraught with nervous energy, Kelly emptied it, putting away the condiments and the washed plates.

"How'd your group work go last night?"

Kelly looked up at him blankly. "Oh, good," she replied as she realized what he was asking. She dragged the basket off the counter and stuck it inside her pantry, on the floor. "We didn't finish the project, though. We're going to have to work on it again sometime soon."

"Nothing worthwhile comes easily."

She straightened and faced him. "That's true."

Especially in her case, with regards to Operation Snowball.

The air seemed to thicken the longer their eyes remained locked. "Where's your roommate?"

The low timber of his voice made her pulse accelerate. "Out." Kelly swallowed hard. She told herself to go change for the gym, but Chuck's intent expression kept her attention glued to him.

"Good."

Whether Chuck moved first, or Kelly did, she couldn't say. Suddenly she was in his arms, being lifted against him as their mouths locked. Passion exploded between them even more potent than the last time. Kelly coiled her legs around Chuck's thighs and literally climbed him in her quest to get closer.

His hands delved beneath the black sweater she was wearing, hot and hungry.

"My room," she gasped against his lips. A muted voice in her head chastened her for her weakness, but she could scarcely hear it over the blood rushing past her eardrums.

Chuck headed straight for her sunlit bedroom. As he spilled her across the bed, he knocked her textbook to the floor. He stepped briefly to the window to jerk her curtains closed. Sunlight shone through the fabric, washing her room in a blue glow as Chuck stripped in front of her, a wrapped condom in one hand.

Just one more time, she told herself as she shrugged

out of her sweater. Before Chuck could tear into the condom, she slid off the bed onto her knees. With an upward glance at him, she encircled his rearing sex and closed her lips over the smooth tip.

Chuck hissed an indrawn breath and gently stroked her hair.

"You don't have to . . ." His words trailed off as she proceeded to do as she pleased.

After a minute, he caught her under her arms and lifted her. Kelly found herself on her back on the bed. As Chuck worked to cover himself with the condom, she shimmied out of her remaining clothing. In seconds, both of them were naked—no game-playing, no shyness, this time. He crawled over her, eyes burning, his breath flowing quickly. Kelly pulled him down onto her. No need for overtures. She needed him *now*.

Threading his fingers through hers, he pinned them to the mattress while, at the same time, pushing into her slippery heat. Their gazes caught and held. As they moved together, something flowed between them, a feeling like wonder; a sense of having discovered something bigger than the both of them, something life changing. It terrified her.

But then all she could think about was her pleasure as it built to awesome proportions. Just as it had happened the last time, they climaxed at the same moment, muffling their cries of bliss against each other's lips.

With his breath still gusting, Chuck rolled his weigh off her, taking her with him, so that she sprawled atop him. "Don't run away this time."

She didn't want to talk about the last time they'd had sex. That hadn't been part of the plan any more than this time was. Sheltered in his embrace and surrounded by the scent of their lovemaking, it felt like . . . *Don't think it!* But it was too late. The word *home* resonated in her head. It felt like home, like a place she would want to come back to again and again.

Regret coiled tentacles around her heart and squeezed. That could never happen. As long as the source in North Korea needed protecting, Kelly's true purpose could not be exposed. Even if Hannah managed to flip Chuck, getting him to work as a double agent, he could never be told Kelly worked for the FBI—not unless the source resigned or died. By then it would be too late. Chuck would be appalled to discover that Katy was really Kelly, a Special Agent. He would assume she'd fallen into bed with him for intelligence-related reasons only.

That sobering thought had her pushing out of his arms. "Shall we go to the rec center now?" From that moment on, she would spend time with Chuck, completing her duties to the Bu while ceasing all intimacy with the target. No more sleeping with him. It was simply too dangerous, not only to the investigation but to her heart, and especially to his.

Chuck blinked at her, clearly jarred by her haste to leave the bed. "Sure."

Her attention slid to the healing scar peeping out from under his arm. "Oh, I forgot, you're injured. How are you supposed to work out?"

He shrugged off his limitations. "I get two more weeks to recuperate, then it's back to jumping out of airplanes, so I'd better start getting in shape now."

"Well, let's go then, lazy." She scooped his shirt off the floor and tossed it at him. "What's the saying in the Teams? 'The only easy day was yesterday?'"

"Where did you learn that, Munchkin?"

Kelly walked into her bathroom where he couldn't see her face. "I've read a few autobiographies."

Hah, if he realized how much research she had done on Navy SEALs while hunting for the SEAL spy mentioned by the North Korean source, Chuck would never speak to her again. The realization pained her.

Just imagine, if he weren't a spy and if she weren't a Special Agent, they could have had something truly special. But they were who they were; hence, their romance was doomed. She laced up her shoes, deeply saddened.

MANY HOURS LATER, in the darkest part of night, Kelly jerked awake. Her heart pounded. Her breath sawed in the cool, still air. She felt the bed for Chuck, who had fallen asleep while holding her in his arms.

Gone. With her nightmare still fresh in her head, Kelly groped for the lamp and turned the switch to see.

Chuck must have slipped away while she was sleeping. And, yes, they'd had sex again, after their fun at the gym. But with the dream still enveloping her in horror, she couldn't summon an ounce of remorse.

The nightmare... she'd endured it many times before. This one had begun the same way, with the coarseness of the rope rousing her to consciousness. *Kelly awakened on her right side, lying on a dank-smelling mattress, wide-eyed, staring into the darkness, gasping for oxygen past the foul-tasting gag that kept her tongue useless.*

This was where the dream differed. *Light shone through a crack in the floorboards above her. It illumined her trussed body in a thin light. She looked down at herself. Horror crept over her like a tide of scuttling spiders as she recognized her clothing. She was still wearing the same floral top and capris she'd worn the day the older boys had pulled her into their car. Only now, both the blouse and the capris were ragged and filthy. They strained to contain her woman's body.*

Oh, my God. Realization had struck with a bolt of horror.

I was never rescued.

I've been lying on this ratty mattress seventeen years!

Impossible. What does this mean? It means that I was never rescued after three days by the FBI. My years in college, my career in the FBI—all a product of my imagination. Self-delusion. I am still a prisoner in a dark, dank basement in Chicago!

It was only a dream. A sob of relief filled Kelly's lungs. "Thank you. Thank you," she breathed. Imagine the horror of being held for years in the dark! She would never have finished school, never gone to college, or made it through FBI training at Quantico. She would never have met Chuck and known what it felt like to truly connect with someone.

Reaching out, she traced the indent left by his head on the pillow next to her.

Real.

Chuck was *real*, and her feelings for him were *real*, not that it made any difference to the Bu. She replayed their evening in her mind. As much as she beat herself up for having sex with Chuck a third time, she would *never* regret their runaway desire for each other.

Nothing, she suspected, would ever surpass it.

It wasn't just the sex, either, that felt so right. Their conversations, their wordplay, their workout in the recreation room—the memories brought a smile to her lips. The gym in the recreation building had been empty when they got there. Tackling the weight machines together, they had moved from one to the next, challenging and cheering each other to finish each set. Chuck had suggested they spread out the mats to do some core exercises. They wound up wrestling, him with one good arm, her with two. Chuck had let her win, she was certain. At one point they had laughed so hard their stomachs hurt.

Kelly's eyes misted with nostalgia. She had known, even in her giddiness, that their relationship had gotten too serious. She was falling in love with a spy, a traitor—albeit a reluctant one. Meanwhile, Chuck was crazy about Katy, a woman who didn't exist.

She had to end their affair before it ruined her career, before it hurt them even more than it already would. Kelly fell back against her pillows and let her tears of regret flow.

ON THURSDAY, AUSTIN showed up five minutes early to his 4 PM appointment with Evelyn. Unlike his three previous sessions, the door to the building wouldn't open. He stood on the front stoop, wishing he had brought a coat. The sun was obscured by a heavy layer of clouds. A wet breeze blowing off the ocean had driven the sea gulls, like those huddled in the parking lot, inland. Austin scrutinized the cars there. Notably absent was the old blue Volvo Austin now guessed belonged to Evelyn.

Concern burrowed into him. Had she forgotten about their appointment? Wouldn't she have been in the building all day with clients coming in before him?

He checked his phone for a cancelation notice. Nope, nothing.

He waited five more minutes, two on the stoop and three in his car because his fingers started turning numb. When she didn't make an appearance, the concern that Jeff had left her in the ugliest manner possible prompted him to call the same number he had called to make his original appointment.

To his relief, she answered on the third ring, in a strained voice. "Oh, my God. Austin. What time is it?"

"It's ten after four. What's wrong? Are you okay?"

"Um. Sure. Yes, I'm fine. I'm so sorry. My neighbors called me about an emergency, and I had to run home. I thought I'd be back right away."

"Emergency. What do you mean?"

"Jeff left."

She didn't sound relieved about it. "Isn't that what you wanted?"

She hesitated. "Yes, but I didn't expect him to destroy my house first."

"He *what?*" Austin went rigid. "Now I'm definitely going to break his nose."

"No, you're not. I called the police. He's going to face charges and he'll probably have to pay restitution for the damage."

"What did he break?"

"All the ceramic for my new backsplash. My neighbors, who are nosy, overheard it and they called me. By the time I got home, Jeff was gone."

"Huh." Austin didn't articulate what he was thinking—that Jeff didn't deserve his box of gaming stuff, after all.

"So, I'm sorry, but can we skip today's session, and pick up again on Sunday?"

"Sure, but first I want to help you clean up."

"No, you don't have to—"

"Plus, I want to show you something. It's about Jeff."

She heaved a sigh. "Okay. I guess I could use some help."

"What's your address?"

She peeled off an address which he quickly memorized. "See you in a couple minutes." He hung up. Plugging the address into Google Maps, he discovered she lived only two miles outside of the amphibious base.

Four minutes later, Austin pulled up in front of a contemporary condominium unit. The blue Volvo parked in the short driveway at 303 assured him he'd found the right place. He parked next to it, then carried the box for Jeff up to Evelyn's door. He was about to ring the doorbell when it swung open. Evelyn stood there in a pale blue blouse, black slacks, and a messy bun. Her red-rimmed eyes let him know she'd been crying.

"Hello." She eyed the box curiously and stepped

aside. "Come on in."

Austin joined her in a foyer with a cathedral ceiling and an open staircase leading to a loft.

Enjoying his glimpse into Evelyn's world, he trailed her down a hallway to a kitchen covered in ceramic shards. The half-painted wall and new granite countertop made it apparent she was in the midst of an update, which Jeff had set back by at least a week.

Austin left the box in the hall and headed for the broom propped against a tall cabinet. "I got this." He located the trash can and the dustpan. "Why don't you pour yourself a glass of wine or something and put your feet up?"

She tsked her tongue and wrung her hands together as he proceeded to sweep up the far-flung shards. "I feel terrible," she lamented.

"Are you kidding? This is easy work. We'll have this cleaned up and behind you in no time. How much did this material cost you?"

"Close to four hundred. Why?" She cut him a suspicious glance.

"No reason. Just curious."

Nope. Jeff wasn't getting his Nintendo, nor any of the games, for that matter.

With Evelyn looking on, Austin made short work of picking up the mess. He double bagged the heavy material and carried it out to Evelyn's tidy garage to put it in her trash bin.

"There," he said, dusting off his hands as he stepped back into the house. "Better?"

She managed a small smile for him. "Thank you. That would have taken me a lot longer. Can I get you a drink?"

"Glass of water would be nice."

As she fetched him a drink, Austin hefted the box he'd left in the hall.

"Have a seat," she invited, waving him into her living area at the back of the house.

The soaring ceiling and plush couch appealed to Austin. Evelyn's penchant for pinks and grays carried into her interior decorating. Her walls and furniture were decorated with floral art and lots of pictures of people.

He sat on the sofa, placing the box at his feet. Through an open door to what was clearly her master bedroom, he spotted her bed, stripped of its sheets.

"I'm sorry I missed your appointment," she said, using her professional voice as she sat catty-corner to him in an armchair.

Her vulnerability made Austin want to hug her. "Don't worry about it. This way I get to see where you live." His gaze swept the pleasing space. "It's nice."

"What's in the box?"

Her inquiry brought his attention back. He leaned forward, pulled the cardboard flaps back, then slid it across the carpet so she could see inside.

"Old video games and a way to play them?"

"That's a Nintendo Entertainment System. I grew up playing it. And I promised Jeff he could have all this if he left you."

Austin braced himself for Evelyn's reaction.

Her blue eyes seemed to fill her lenses. "He agreed to that?" She looked down at the box. "He traded me for a box of old video games?"

"Yes." Austin forbore to mention there would be grave consequences for Jeff if he didn't take the offer.

Tears pooled in her eyes as she grappled with her emotions. But then she blinked them back and looked abruptly up at Austin. "But . . . this is your personal collection. You were going to give it away, for me?"

He allowed himself a crooked smile. "Well, I couldn't punch him in the nose, so I had to persuade him somehow."

"But . . . why would you do that?"

Now that the time had come to tell her, Austin hesitated, suddenly nervous. "I mean, there's only one possible reason if you think about it." He waited for her to put it together.

But she just sat there looking mystified. "I don't . . . understand."

Austin cleared his throat and took a leap of faith. "I like you," he stated. "And I'd like to take you out myself, if you'd let me."

Her lips parted as her jaw went slack. She closed

her mouth and swallowed. "Wow, I did not see that coming."

He laughed with sudden self-doubt. "Really? You couldn't tell that we've got something between us?"

Her cheeks flushed, relieving him immensely. "Well, yes, but . . . " She twisted her hands in her lap. "I mean, I assumed any woman would be flustered with you around."

He grinned at her rationalization. "I fluster you?"

"Of course." She gestured. "Just look at you."

"I can't really see myself," he pointed out. "But I see you. And I like what I see. I think we'd be really good together."

She drew a deep breath and shook her head. "Austin, I'm your therapist. Ah—" She held up a hand as he started to protest. "I am also five years older than you are."

"What difference does that make?" he protested.

"A big difference." She put a hand over her heart. "I turn thirty years old this year. I'm ready to settle down and start a family. Plus, I don't do military men, and you're a SEAL. It would never work out."

Austin stared at her, nonplussed by her certain tone. "You don't know that."

"Well, I'm pretty sure."

"No. You're making assumptions about me, based on past experiences that have nothing to do with me. Give it a try. That's all I'm asking. Go out with me. I promise you won't be disappointed." He sent her his most winning smile.

He could tell she was tempted. The tip of her tongue sluiced across her lush upper lip.

He stood up suddenly and pulled her to her feet. "Just try. You might like it." He put his arms around her and planted a gentle but intentional kiss on her mouth. Evelyn stiffened but did not resist. Austin hummed his satisfaction. The chemistry he'd intuited flared like a hundred-watt lightbulb. He kissed her more deeply.

The tentative parting of her lips sent a spark of lust through him. *Oh, yeah.* She melted into him, like butter on a griddle. Within seconds, her arms were locked around his neck, her body flush against his, their tongues twining.

It was Austin who ended the kiss abruptly. "See?"

She released him as if jarred from a dream and edged away, smoothing hands on her slacks and blushing furiously.

"You should probably leave."

Austin's hopes went into freefall. Her tone didn't sound very convincing, but her words were all that mattered. He looked down at the box wondering what he might possibly say to change her mind.

She followed his gaze. "Don't give away your games for me," she added. "I should have kicked Jeff out of my house myself. That's on me."

With a heavy heart, Austin bent to collect the box. As his eyes came level with the coffee table, he found himself looking at a framed photograph of several handsome young women. One face in particular made him pick up the frame and show it to Evelyn. "Are these friends of yours?"

"Sorority sisters," Evelyn replied quizzically. "We still keep in touch."

He showed her the face he recognized. "Is this Katy Tang?"

Evelyn frowned. "No. That's Kelly Yang. She majored in accounting."

"Kelly Yang." Austin held the photo closer and studied it. She looked identical to Katy, only several years younger, which she would have been when the picture was taken. "She looks exactly like my neighbor."

Evelyn stepped closer. "You mean the neighbor who searched your roommate's car?"

"Yes. The one you suggested was a cop." Suspicion simmered anew. If only Austin would hear back from Stu, who was still off working with Ghost Security Group. "What does this Kelly do now?"

"Um, I don't know. I haven't really kept up with her."

"Can you find out for me?"

"Sure." She stepped back as if suddenly realizing how close they were standing.

Austin placed the frame back on the table and hefted the box. Disappointment weighted his footsteps as he followed a silent Evelyn to her front door. She pulled it open and stepped back.

"Thank you, Austin, for helping me clean up the mess." She was back to using her therapist's voice.

Austin nodded. "Any time. If he bothers you again, you just let me know." He turned to leave.

"Austin."

He paused on the first step, hoping she would relent and agree to a date.

"I don't think I can be your counselor anymore."

His hope plummeted, then spread wings. He started to smile. "Then you can date me, right? No conflict of interest?"

"No, that's not what I meant."

The wings folded and hope went into a nosedive.

"I meant, I don't think I should see you anymore, professionally or otherwise."

Austin's stubbornness kicked into overdrive. "Do you?"

"Yes," she whispered.

"Hmm." He watched the pink fade from her cheeks. "Then you'll send a glowing report to my platoon leader?"

"Of course."

"And you'll let me know what Kelly Yang does for a living?"

Evelyn nodded. "Yes."

"Okay then. If you change your mind, you know how to find me." With a final look at her stricken expression, Austin strode off Evelyn's stoop toward his car. No way in hell was he giving up that easily.

He stowed his box in the back seat and got behind the wheel, all while shutting his car doors gently. No need to storm off like a petulant loser, as Jeff had undoubtedly done. Evelyn was going to change her mind, he assured himself.

But first he was going to find Jeff and torture him for making that mess in Evelyn's kitchen.

Ten minutes later, Austin strode into the post exchange with the box under one arm. This time it didn't take him long to spot the whey-faced loser, who was hanging ties in the men's clothing section.

Austin made a beeline in Jeff's direction, scattering several patrons who took one look at his expression and got quickly out of his way.

Jeff sensed him coming and looked up. His eyes widened. He looked around as if hunting for the closest exit.

"There you are," Austin called, preventing Jeff from slipping away. "I brought you something."

Jeff's gaze dropped to the box. A hopeful expression started to replace his worried one.

"Here you go." Austin thrust the box at him with slightly more force than necessary. "A deal is a deal, right?" He had closed the box, so Jeff couldn't see inside it.

"Yeah. Of course. Thanks."

You're not welcome. Without another word, Austin swiveled on the soles of his scuffed boots and strode out of the exchange with his chin held high. He didn't need to look back to sense the dismay Jeff was feeling upon pulling back the flaps of the box.

As much as it had pained him to do so, Austin had smashed every single game and even his old NES, stomping on it in the alley behind the PX, rendering all of it completely useless. The irony, he was sure, would not be lost on Jeff, who'd shattered Evelyn's lovely ceramic tiles.

"Payback is a bitch," Austin muttered under his breath, but he didn't feel better for his revenge. That night, he and Jeff were both losers.

CHAPTER 17

DETECTIVE MIKE SCRUGGS was dressed in a Virginia Tech sweatshirt, jeans, and a hard hat. With a fake ID hanging on a lanyard around his neck, and carrying a clipboard in his hand, he figured he looked like an inspector of some sort, taking a break against the wall.

In reality, he was scoping out the workers in one of the many warehouses at the Norfolk Naval shipyard in a stubborn quest to locate Lee Soo-jin—not that he could arrest the man. The FBI had forbidden that, but Mike had the green light to find the perp, so they could monitor Lee's activities themselves.

"Making me do their dirty work."

Mike had muttered that litany half a dozen times in the past two weeks.

Unfortunately, thanks to his close call at the clinic, Lee Soo-jin suspected the law was looking for him. For that reason, he never stayed in one place for very long. Tracking Lee to this warehouse had been a feat more suited to a bloodhound than a detective. In the last week alone, the man had switched jobs three times, forcing Mike to get clever. He had shucked his uniform and coerced the pass office into supplying him with a fake badge.

In the beginning, he hadn't been so smart. He'd asked random employees if they recognized Lee's photo. Apparently, Lee was well liked, as Mike never got an honest answer. It was through a chance conversation overheard in the men's restroom, that Mike had discovered Lee now drove a forklift in Warehouse B.

Mike would outwit the crafty Korean this time. Lee would either punch out in a matter of minutes, or punch in, walking through a particular set of doors mere yards away from where Mike had concealed himself.

At last, a buzzer sounded, announcing the shift change. Workers headed in droves for the punch-out station. Chewing a fresh stick of gum, Mike scanned their faces, seeking anyone resembling the man in the grainy photo from the parking garage.

Men and women of all ages filed out the door calling their good-byes. Mike was just about to accept defeat when his gaze alighted on a slightly built man walking in the shadow of his larger colleague. They chatted amiably as they punched in their codes, then they both walked out the door.

Mike left his hiding spot and followed. Shading his eyes against the sun's glare, he spotted Lee slipping into a red Volkswagen Beetle. It was the dead-last car

Mike expected a spy to drive. Before Lee could see him, he turned his back and walked in the opposite direction, smirking his victory.

That same time tomorrow, Lee Soo-jin would be driving a car with a tracking device stuck to its underbelly.

Patting himself on the back, Mike spat out his gum as he got to his Pontiac. Once inside his warmed car, he took out his cellphone to look up Rafael Valentino's number. Envy stung him as he considered, for the hundredth time, how he and Valentino had both started out as beat cops. Yet, here Mike was, a lowly detective still hunting down petty thugs and criminals, while Valentino was a Supervisory Special Agent in America's most prestigious law enforcement agency.

"Hmph." Mike eyed his phone, deliberating.

Maybe he wouldn't tell Valentino just yet how close he was to knowing where Lee Soo-jin lived. If he did that, Valentino would take over, assigning one of his SOGs to watch the spy, and Mike would have to go back to his humble job with little more than a thank-you from the Bureau for locating their naughty North Korean. He would much rather play in the big leagues for a while.

Making up his mind, Mike set his phone in the cupholder and started up his car. He could have been a Supervisory Special Agent, too, if only he had learned to keep his mouth shut.

✕

ON FRIDAY EVENING, one day after expelling Austin from her life, Evelyn parked her Volvo in her driveway feeling blue. *It's from seasonal affective disorder*, she told herself, but the sunlight skimming the rooftop of her townhome belied that diagnosis. The arrival of spring ought to be chasing her blues away.

She got out of her car, pulling her purse and briefcase out behind her. *I miss Jeff*, she thought. But Jeff's face wasn't the one she was picturing. It was Austin's. And she wouldn't be seeing him this Sunday because she had sent a glowing report to his platoon leader explaining why Austin Collins no longer needed counseling.

Now, she had nothing to look forward to but more work in her kitchen. She needed to replace the backsplash Jeff had smashed and get started tiling it.

As she plodded toward her door, dreading the quiet days ahead, a white envelope protruding from under the doormat caught her attention. While bending to retrieve it, she realized a shiny brass door handle had replaced the dingy doorknob that used to be there. Figuring an explanation lay within the weighty envelope, she broke the seal and pulled out the written note tucked inside, along with a set of shiny new keys.

Hi, Evelyn. I hope I didn't overstep, but I figured Jeff still had a key to your place, so I got you a different set of locks. Here are the keys. Miss you, Austin.

Warmth and longing flooded her. Evelyn reread the note, written in calligraphy, no less! Who'd have guessed Austin Collins could write like this? Practicing calligraphy required concentration.

Bemused, she let herself into her home using a brand new key, then went straight to the back door to inspect the new lock there. Oh, my gosh, how sweet of Austin to see to her safety—unless he'd made a copy of the new keys for himself?

She shrugged, unconcerned. Austin was a good guy.

"Ricochet," she murmured, recalling her early impression of him.

The desire to thank him had her taking her cellphone from her purse, only to pause. What he wanted—to date her—was impossible. Honestly, it was ludicrous. She would need to get her head examined if she let a man five years her junior sweep her off her feet. She didn't have time for another failed relationship. All her life, she had dreamed of raising four kids. With only five years left in which to safely make babies, she couldn't afford a distraction.

So, no. No phone call. No lovely chat with a sweet, insightful, gorgeous Navy SEAL. Just a terse text that left no crack in her veneer for him to exploit. *Thank you for the new locks and keys.*

Sticking her phone into her rear pocket, she plodded to her kitchen to stick a Lean Cuisine into the microwave. The bare walls above her new granite countertop required attention. She would visit the brand-new kitchen and bath shop down the street this weekend to select more backsplash, something completely different from what Jeff had helped her pick out. She hadn't loved it anyway.

I bet Austin would pick out something you liked.

"Oh, hush." Evelyn squashed the wistful voice within and pulled open the microwave.

AUSTIN STEPPED OUT of his bathroom early Saturday afternoon. Chuck, whom he could see through his partially open door, was still sitting at his computer, plugging away. Annoyed by his roommate's hours-long session with his laptop, Austin pushed the door further ajar, which caused Chuck to start and turn his head.

If that wasn't a guilty expression, Austin would eat his own sock. "Are you looking at porn?"

"What? No."

Chuck's disgust was convincing. All the same, he closed several screens as Austin advanced toward him.

"You're looking at houses?" The photo of a beach house along with a full description caught Austin's eye.

He came closer.

"So what?"

Over Chuck's shoulder, Austin peered at the details. The house was a rental. "Dude, we can't afford that."

"Not to live in. For vacation."

"Oh." Austin straightened. "Like a vacation with Katy, or all the guys?"

"With Katy." Chuck minimized the screen.

"I see. So where is this future bride of yours? At the library?"

"She has a big paper due on Monday."

"Right."

Chuck swung around with a scowl on his face. "Why the sarcasm? Do you know something I don't know?"

And here it was, the opportunity to state his suspicions. Austin thought fast. Should he warn his friend there was more to Katy than met the eye? Where were his facts? He had none.

"No, man. I'm sorry." He dragged a hand through his wavy hair. "I'm just edgy right now. I thought I would've gotten more than a thank you for changing Evelyn's locks. I wish she'd give me a chance. I mean, am I that bad of a catch?"

"Dude, you're uglier than a hyena," Chuck said with a straight face. He shut his laptop and stood up. "Come on. Let's go shooting."

The prospect of punching holes in a human-shaped target cheered Austin immensely.

"Cool. Let me put some shoes on." He left Chuck's room to find his favorite cowboy boots. Wearing them always made him feel better.

As he tugged them on, Austin reflected not even a woman like Katy could get in the way of his and Chuck's friendship. So what if Chuck actually ended up with her? Austin would be happy for him because *nothing* could ever get in the way of their bond. They were teammates, forged in the same fire called Basic Underwater Demolition and SEALs training. They would always have each other's backs. *Always.*

With that cheering thought, Austin stood and rubbed his hands in glee. He was going to picture Jeff's face when he emptied the contents of his magazine, one bullet right after the other, into the black paper silhouette.

HIDING UP ON the second floor of her campus library, at a table in the corner farthest from the elevator, Kelly typed away on a paper that was due the next day. The window by her elbow framed an amber sky. It was Sunday evening, and the library would close at 7 PM, forcing her to write as quickly as possible. Racing the clock, she churned out paragraphs, inserting charts that supported her thesis and citing sources as she went.

The second floor of the library could have been a tomb for the hush that surrounded her. Nothing had intruded on her work for hours, except for thoughts of Chuck which stole her concentration regularly. She thrust them aside, dreading what she knew she had to do.

Hiding here at the library, instead of her apartment where Chuck might show up at her door, she was putting off the inevitable. Then, too, Chuck was preoccupied with the task the RGB had given him. According to Ernie, he spent hours every day on his laptop. So much for Kelly's fear that Chuck might choose suicide as a means of escaping his situation. Apparently, he had made the decision to do what the RGB wanted.

That realization hardened her heart toward him. He wasn't as noble or tormented as she'd thought. Nor did he require her intervention to save him from himself. She would channel her disappointment when she finally got around to pushing him away. That would make lying to him easier.

"Shit!"

Realizing her mind had wandered off task, Kelly reread the lines on her laptop, hoping to regain her stream of thought. All at once the elevator, invisible from where she sat, gave a *ding*, and the doors swooshed open. Kelly pricked her ears to the heavy footfalls padding toward her on the vinyl tiles. Her heart beat a little faster at the realization of her isolation.

When the stocky frame of Ernie Savowitz cleared the tall bookshelf in front of her, Kelly heaved a sigh of relief.

"There you are." He smiled pleasantly and helped himself to the seat across the table. "You said you'd be at the library, not hiding in the farthest corner of the second floor.

"Sorry. It's the only place quiet enough."

Ernie nodded at her laptop. "How's it going?"

She grimaced. "It's like a fulltime job."

"On top of the job you already have."

"Exactly." She searched his sympathetic expression. "I didn't know you wanted to talk to me. I could've come to you."

"No, no. I've got more time on my hands than you do. We've got updates." He pitched his voice lower, resting his beefy arms on the tabletop and leaning toward her to impart the latest intelligence. "The target has been going crazy performing internet searches, both on his phone and his laptop. He was looking at Asian Studies Departments at local universities, personnel at the Surry Power Plant, freelancers for a technical writing service, guest speakers at the World Affairs Council—you get the picture. All the disparate data points threw us off until we realized he was searching for one person in particular: Ken W. Harris."

"Who is Ken W. Harris?"

"We had no idea until Valentino drove up to Langley to meet with our CIA liaison." Ernie glanced around to make sure they were alone. "Do you remember reading about a lead physicist in North Korea's weapons program defecting last year?"

"It rings a bell."

"He was attending the Six-Party Talks in Geneva, acting as an interpreter to keep foreign intelligence from approaching him. That's ironic, since *he* was the one to approach an American diplomat and ask for asylum. He's been living in this area for the past year under the alias of Ken W. Harris."

Kelly pictured the tiny portion of the decrypted message they had glimpsed before Chuck shut it in his desk drawer. "Oh, no."

"Oh, yes," Ernie countered. "We believe the RGB wants Harris found and executed."

Goosebumps sprouted on Kelly's forearms.

Ernie sat back. "The CIA placed Harris in Sandbridge."

"Sandbridge. Where's that?"

"Right down the coast from here. The back gate of Dam Neck Naval Annex leads right to it. Lots of top brass live there, including Chuck's XO."

Kelly rubbed her stinging eyes. She couldn't picture Chuck killing a man in cold blood. Then again, he didn't have much choice if he didn't want the RGB hunting him down.

When Ernie didn't say anything, she dropped her hand to find him staring at her.

"You like him, don't you?"

She pretended to scoff at the idea. "Who, Chuck? He's traitor to his country. Why would I like him?"

Ernie looked like he was going to say something she really didn't want to hear. Oh, God. Did he know about her and Chuck?

"Just be careful, Kelly. Protect yourself. We're putting a plan in place to protect Harris's life and to rig his home with ELSUR."

"You need a ringer," Kelly said, referring to someone with training who would take Harris's place. She swallowed hard. The end was near.

"The Agency is looking for one right now. He won't have the science background, of course. All we really need is a SOG of Korean descent gutsy enough to pit himself against a Navy SEAL."

Such a man might be hard to find, Kelly imagined. "How can I help?"

Ernie leaned back in. "By monitoring the target's activity and gauging his moods. We can't predict when he's going to make his move solely on the basis of how frequently he recons the house in Sandbridge. So far, he's only looked at it on Google maps. Given your, uh, friendship with him, you'd probably have a better sense of where he is in his planning."

Kelly swallowed. "Okay." She would have to spend time with Chuck to get a feel for that. "I know he's still on medical leave for two more weeks."

"Good to know." Ernie pushed his chair back and stood. He stared at her for an extra second, broke eye contact, and turned away, leaving her wallowing in shame.

He knew about her and Chuck. Oh, God.

Kelly dropped her face into her hands, mortified. It was her own fault she'd gotten intimate with the target. She'd never intended to get involved with him—certainly not on a sexual level, even less so on an emotional level. Yet, in just a matter of days, he'd gone from being alluring to being irresistible. Her protective nature had gotten the better of her. But that was no excuse. It was time to clip the wings of their relationship while hopefully preserving their friendship. Operation Snowball depended on the latter.

Looking back at her laptop, Kelly threw up her hands in defeat. No way could she craft a concluding paragraph with her thoughts on Chuck and his horrific task—my God, murder? How could he bring himself to kill a man in cold blood? The Chuck she'd come to know would never do such a thing—in defense of his country, certainly, but not in support of an enemy nation.

Giving up on her paper, Kelly saved the document, put her laptop to sleep, and stowed it in her laptop bag. Tomorrow, before class, she would type up a swift conclusion.

She was about to stand when a shadow fell over the table. Her head came up and a gasp filled her lungs to find Chuck, of all people, standing at her table. He wore a black peacoat and a crooked smile that kept her from involuntarily screaming.

"Chuck. Oh, my God. Where did you come from?"

He gestured behind him. "The stairs. I've been searching the whole library for you."

His manner was friendly, his gaze hopeful. Kelly got no sense that he had overheard any part of her and Ernie's conversation. "You have? But this place is a twenty-minute drive from the apartment. And I'm about to leave."

He held out a full plastic sack. "I brought you some food. Figured it was my turn to feed you, for a change. You've been working yourself to death."

"Aw. That was sweet of you." Touched by his gesture, she had to think of his tasking to keep from jumping up and kissing him. She peeked inside the bag. He'd brought her a can of vegetable juice and a ciabatta sandwich from Panera. Her mouth instantly watered. "I am starving," she admitted. "But I'm not supposed to eat in the library."

"They'll never know." He glanced up at the ceiling. "I don't see any cameras."

Kelly's heart skipped a beat. Maybe he *had* overheard what Ernie said, and now he would murder her with no one around to bear witness.

"I've missed you, Munchkin."

The gruff confession, paired with her nickname, put her fears to rest, especially when he stepped closer and smoothed his thumb along her cheek, before letting his hand drop.

Relief and regret pushed tears into her eyes. "I've missed you, too." It was the most honest thing she'd ever said to him.

"So, you're not hiding from me?"

The question underscored his vulnerability. As compelled as she was to put his worries to rest, she couldn't. It was long past the time for her to push him away. She gestured at the empty chair across from her. "Will you sit down? I need to tell you something."

Chuck sank into the chair with a furrow on his forehead. The sight of it confirmed to Kelly she wasn't the only one feeling emotionally invested. How could she have let this happen to either of them? She cleared her throat. What she would say next would shock and confuse him. It was the only way she could think of to keep him out of her bed but still in her life.

She clasped her hands together. "You remember

how I said I was an only child? That wasn't exactly true."

Chuck listened, giving no outward indication of his surprise.

"I have a brother, Cameron. He's five years older. When we were growing up, our parents had a dry-cleaning business in Chicago. We weren't wealthy, but we had a nice house in a decent neighborhood. I attended an inner-city charter school, K through 6, while my brother went to a public high school. It was rough, and he got caught up in a gang."

Chuck was hanging on her every word.

"The teens in the gangs weren't really thugs, but they were headed in that direction. Whenever rival gangs clashed, there were always black eyes and broken noses. Then someone in Cameron's gang, the Creds, found a gun and shot a member of a rival gang. They, in turn, devised a way to get revenge."

She blew out a breath. *Just say it and get it over with.* "When I was twelve, I was walking home from school, a short walk of two blocks, when members of the rival gang pulled up in an old Dodge. They jumped out of the car and pulled me into it."

Chuck's dusky complexion seemed to pale. She remembered wanting to share this life-changing experience with him, but not like this, with the facts twisted.

"They hid me down in the basement of one of

their parents' houses. I was there for three days. My parents, of course, were overwrought. They called the police. My brother, thinking he was responsible, tried to overdose on pills. While he was in the hospital, I was kept in a basement, gagged so no adults could hear me scream." Here came the lie, which would keep Chuck from touching her again. "I was raped by the older boys."

Chuck drew a sharp breath. He tried to conceal his horror, but she could tell he was envisioning what had happened as his gaze skittered over her. "Oh, Katy." He stretched a hand across the table.

Guilt made her stomach hurt. She locked her hands in her lap to resist his offer of comfort. He slowly pulled his hand back.

"Since then . . ." She forced herself to build on the lie, "I've tried to be in relationships. At first, I'm okay, and I can enjoy myself. But then, as time goes on . . . I feel . . . repulsed, and I don't want to be close anymore."

Disbelief registered on Chuck's face, followed immediately by confusion. He shook his head. "Are you telling me you didn't enjoy yourself when we . . . "

"No, I did," she rushed to assure him. She couldn't destroy the beauty of what they'd shared. "I just know that . . . I won't . . . for much longer."

It took every ounce of determination merely to hold his gaze.

He eyed her with confoundment.

Kelly broke eye contact, dropping her chin to her chest to stare at her fisted hands.

"Hey, hey." Suddenly, Chuck was out of his chair, on his knees on the floor beside her. He enfolded her into the most tentative embrace imaginable. "It's okay. It's good that you told me. I had no idea."

Kelly had to question her sanity. This traitor who was planning to kill a defector on behalf of Pyongyang was the sweetest guy she'd ever met.

With a sharp sniff she sat up straighter. Chuck immediately released her. His gaze was somber and sincere. "I'm so sorry. I didn't know. I . . . I thought it was the same for you as it was for me."

Kelly wanted to kill herself. "It was," she assured him. "It just . . . it won't be. I'm so sorry," she added in a shaky voice.

He reached for her again, only to pull his hand back. "This is why you've been avoiding me."

She swallowed the lump in her throat and nodded.

Five seconds of silence elapsed. "Well, you don't have to hide anymore." He pushed to his feet.

With a pang in her chest, Kelly noted his closed expression, his distracted gaze.

"I'm going to need a little while to think about things." He finally met her gaze. "You're amazing, Katy, beautiful and smart and incredibly brave. I need some time to reset my thoughts."

"Of course." She nodded, relieved by his civility, sick at heart for her deception.

"You want me to walk you out?" He consulted his watch. "The library's about to close."

"No, that's okay." She couldn't bear another parting word from him.

He regarded her one last time, gave a slight shake of his head, then turned and disappeared as stealthily as he'd come.

When she was sure that he was finally gone, Kelly dropped her forehead onto the tabletop. The lie had exhausted her. It had emptied her of all anticipation, all the pleasure she'd been getting out of working undercover, everything. Her joy was gone.

FROM WITHIN HIS parked car, Chuck watched Katy exit the library and head for her car. Though it wasn't quite dark, he wanted to make sure she got safely to her vehicle. Virginia Beach wasn't Chicago, but it had its fair share of crime, even on a college campus. And though he'd discovered during their play-wrestling at the gym she knew some excellent defensive moves, you would never know it to look at her, especially with her eyes downcast and her shoulders slumped.

He tried to imagine how she felt, but he had trouble getting past his disillusionment. Just when he'd started thinking there was hope for his future—that once he dealt with his tasking, he might get to lead a normal life, one with a wife and kids, the whole nine yards—this had to happen.

Katy's story had dealt his hopes a fatal blow. She didn't want to have sex anymore. He shook his head, enraged with the youths who had kidnapped and raped her. Twelve years old, my God. Who could blame her for having intimacy issues? Not him. Poor little Katy would never be the same.

But neither would he. She had touched him in a way he'd thought he would never be touched. What they'd shared defied definition. To him, it had bordered on holy. But to Katy, it was one step away from abhorrent. He would never have guessed that by her behavior.

Finding his hands in his hair, Chuck lowered them and struck his steering wheel with his palm. Katy's car door closed. Her lights flared and she proceeded to pull away.

Chuck waited a minute, then peeled out of the parking spot he had backed into. He pointed his Subaru straight for Calypso Bar and Grille, hoping to find comfort in a tumbler, or two, of top-shelf bourbon.

CHAPTER 18

I T WAS ONLY 7 PM on a Sunday evening, yet Evelyn was ready to climb into her pajamas. Why not? Without an appointment that afternoon with Austin, there hadn't been much point to her even getting dressed in the first place. She'd worked on her kitchen in the morning starting on the new backsplash she had bought, then called every girlfriend she knew to see who wanted to go to a movie with her. None of them could. They were either tied up with their husbands or reluctant to leave their babies *with* their husbands. Evelyn had pictured Austin blowing raspberries on a giggling baby's belly. She would have no such reservations if he were the father of her child.

Her ringing cellphone cut into that errant thought. Recognizing the caller as her adoptive father, who called her every Sunday evening, she answered, "Hello," while considering the contents of her refrigerator. She could not remember the last time she had eaten.

"Hey, Ev. How's it going?"

Retired Rear Admiral Andrew Gault was the only military man Evelyn had ever liked—until she'd met

Austin. Mostly she admired Andrew for his sense of duty, his total commitment to being an upstanding father to a teenage girl who surely reminded him of the worst mistake he'd ever made—marrying the girl's mother.

"Um, I'm making progress on the kitchen." She closed the refrigerator and opened the freezer, taking out a Lean Cuisine. She stared at the cover on the box, trying to decide if she could stomach chicken alfredo.

"You sound depressed. Are you missing Jeff?"

Andrew didn't beat around the bush. She liked that trait, as well. "No." She put the Lean Cuisine back in the freezer and crossed to her pantry. "I'm missing a twenty-five-year-old Navy SEAL. Tell me I'm stupid."

"Oh, you don't want a relationship with a Navy SEAL."

Andrew's certain tone was exactly what Evelyn needed. She studied her selection of cereals. "I know," she said.

"SEALs are arrogant. They're gone all the time. They have expectations of their women that no one could live up to except another SEAL."

"Right," she agreed, pulling out a box of instant oatmeal. "I know. I'll forget about him eventually."

"That's my girl. Listen, I gotta cut this call short and gird myself for work tomorrow."

"Life as a civilian's not as easy as you thought it would be, huh?"

"Let's just say this world's a dangerous place and too many people are sticking their heads into the sand."

"Oh, dear. Well, if anyone can convince them to wise up, it's you."

"Thank you, sweetheart. We'll see. You keep your chin up. The right fella will come along eventually. Good night, Ev."

"'Night, Dad." She called him that from time to time. She suspected he liked it, though he never reacted one way or the other.

Putting her phone down, Evelyn shook a packet of oatmeal into a bowl. She was reaching for milk when her doorbell chimed. The sound made her freeze. She glanced out her window at the dark sky and shut her refrigerator door. Edging into the hallway, she peered toward the door. Through the narrow pane on one side, she could tell her porchlight wasn't on.

Whoever was there rang her doorbell again. They could see *her* perfectly.

Evelyn channeled Andrew's commanding voice as she neared the door. "Who's there?"

"It's Door Dash. I brought your dinner," said a woman.

Evelyn flicked on the porchlight and looked outside. A middle-aged woman stood there holding two bags full of food, presumably. Evelyn cracked the door open. "Um. I didn't order any Door Dash."

The delivery woman frowned and checked the receipt taped to one of the bags. "Are you Evelyn Haskins?"

"Well, yes, but I …"

"Look, just take the food," the woman pleaded. "I've got two more orders sitting in the car getting cold."

"Oh. Well, okay. I don't have any cash for a tip, though."

"Don't worry about it." The woman transferred both bags to Evelyn and strode to her idling car.

Evelyn relocked the door and carried the bags into the kitchen, putting them down on her small table. She peered into one bag and then the other, her eyes widening as she took in the veritable feast from a local steakhouse.

This had to be someone's order, and they were still waiting for their dinner to show up, but her name and her address were printed on the order slip. Who had paid for all this? Had Jeff suddenly developed a romantic streak or . . . Could it have been Austin? Her breath hitched and her heart beath faster.

She picked up her phone and realized he had texted her.

Missed you today.

The words brought a sound like a whimper up her throat. Recalling Andrew's advice, she sought to rouse her indignation. She had told Austin *no*. He should not be stalking her like this.

You shouldn't spend your money on me, Austin. I'm not going to change my mind.

She waited for him to say something back. When he didn't, she emptied one of the bags, feeling depleted. The sirloin steak he had purchased smelled delicious, but she wasn't hungry enough to eat it. As she emptied the second bag, she realized he had purchased two complete dinners—two side salads, two sirloin steaks, and two baked potatoes with little containers of chives and sour cream.

She rolled her eyes, upset but secretly pleased with his refusal to be pushed away. While common sense told her Andrew had encountered more SEALs in his life than she ever had, her traitorous heart lobbied for a practical use of Austin's hard-earned money. She picked up her phone and texted, *You could at least come help me eat all of this.* There. She still had the upper hand.

She knew even before he texted back with an emoji of The Road Runner that she was going to regret caving to his manipulations. What would she say to Andrew the next time he called to check on her?

"God, I'm pathetic!" Evelyn lamented.

Forget helping other patients lead full and happy lives. She was the one who needed extensive counseling. But first she was going to change her clothes and put on makeup. *Why?* She didn't want to answer that question. Austin had told her once that she was pretty. She figured she'd better live up to that.

"LISTEN." ACROSS THEIR half-empty plates and the tea light glowing in the small salt lamp on the kitchen table between them, Austin caught Evelyn's gaze. For the past half hour, he'd been reading mixed signals of wariness, regret, desire, and resignation. "You don't have to beat yourself up for inviting me over. I mean, I practically invited myself by buying two dinners. Hmm?"

She poked at her salad, saying nothing.

Austin tried again. "I missed you this week. Like, a lot. And I get that you don't want to date me because I'm younger, my job is dangerous, but those are crappy reasons."

"Really?" She lifted a dry gaze at him.

"You've got the wrong idea about me. I'm not into casual dating. I want the whole package. Between the two of us, we've got that. We could make it. We could beat the odds. Heck, I've been doing that my whole life."

Her lips pursed as if she were considering his words.

He smiled, sensing an eventual win. "Plus, we would be really good in bed together."

The words had her reaching for her water and draining it.

Austin's phone chimed. He cursed its timing. "Sorry, I gotta check my texts." God forbid it was an all-call to rally up at the Team building for an emergency operation. "Oh, it's Hack."

"Who?"

Austin didn't answer, he was too busy processing Stu's answer to the last text Austin had sent asking about the building Katy had entered the night he'd followed her.

That's where the Peninsula Residence Agency for the FBI is located. I've been there myself a few times.

"Oh, my God."

"What?"

Austin looked up at Evelyn. "Did you ever hear back from any sorority sisters about Kelly and what she does now?

"Um. I haven't checked my email since Friday. Do you want me to check it now?"

Austin hesitated. He'd been making progress convincing Evelyn to date him. "No, no, it can wait." He put his phone back into his pocket. "We were talking about our future."

Evelyn wet her lips in a nervous gesture. "Who is Hack?" she asked again.

Austin gave in. "He's a teammate with amazing computer skills. I asked him to identify the building

Katy went into last Tuesday night, I think it was, after I followed her through the tunnel, all the way to Hampton. She told Chuck she was going to the library."

"Ah, your mysterious neighbor. And what did Hack say?"

"He said the FBI has a residence agency in that building."

"The FBI?" Evelyn's eyebrows winged above her glasses. "Isn't that interesting! Hey, didn't I guess your neighbor was a cop?"

"Yes, you did," Austin recalled.

"Well, now I'm dying to find out if anyone got back to me." She produced her own phone and accessed her email.

Austin watched her scan one message and then another.

"Oh." With that telling exclamation, she looked up at him, blue eyes huge behind her lenses. "Rachel says Kelly is an analyst for the FBI."

The unpleasant but not-unexpected news robbed Austin of his appetite. *Holy hell*, he thought.

"Wait," Evelyn continued, "so if Kelly calls herself Katy and claims to be graduate student when she's really in the FBI, is she working undercover?"

Austin sat back as worry dropped like a rock to the well of his stomach.

"Who is she investigating?" Evelyn pressed. "Your

roommate?"

"I mean . . . " Austin searched for plausible reasons. "I'm the first person she talked to, and my mother is Russian," he reminded Evelyn, "but I have nothing to hide."

"Of course, it's not you." Evelyn dismissed the notion with a wave of her hand. "She was searching your roommate's car, Austin. Not yours."

"Right." But he couldn't imagine strait-laced Chuck doing anything illegal.

"What are you going to do?" Evelyn asked him gently. "Are you going to tell Chuck?"

He stared hard at the saltshaker, thinking. "No," he finally decided. "I'm going to talk to Katy—Kelly," he amended, "And if she won't tell me what's going on, then I'll tell Chuck."

"You don't want to blow an undercover operation," Evelyn cautioned.

"No, but . . . Chuck? There has to be a mistake." Or was there? Like Hack had said, Chuck had been acting different lately. Austin looked down at his plate, thinking. The attempt on Chuck's life two weeks ago had to figure in somehow, only he couldn't connect the dots quite yet.

Catching Evelyn studying him, he gave himself a mental shake. "I'm sorry. I tend to fixate on certain topics. It's my ADHD."

Evelyn's expression softened. "Don't apologize.

It's late anyway. I'll clean up. You should probably head home. Don't you have to wake up at the crack of dawn tomorrow?"

He did, but he'd been hoping he could spend the night here, with her. Apparently not. Despite their lovely dinner together, he clearly had yet to convince her to give them a try. He extended a hand across the table, palm side up, hoping she would take it.

Evelyn eyed it, visibly braced herself, then placed her slender hand over his. With his thumb, Austin stroked the velvety rise and fall of her knuckles. Her breasts rose with her indrawn breath. She was clearly not impervious to his touch. The subtle sign encouraged him.

"Don't shut me out of your life, Evelyn," he pleaded. "If you do, you'll miss out. You'll never know how good I can make you feel. How happy I'll make you."

Her throat worked to swallow. "I need to think about it," she said, barely above a whisper.

It wasn't a yes, but then it wasn't a no, either. Austin sent her an encouraging smile. "Fair enough." He pushed his chair back, then leaned across the table and kissed her stunned lips until they softened and parted. Just as she began to kiss him back, he pulled away. "Don't forget to turn the deadbolt."

He cast those words over his shoulder as he strode with more confidence than he was feeling out of her kitchen toward the exit. "See you soon, beautiful." He twisted the lock on the new doorhandle and shut the door behind him. A sliver of doubt sank into his consciousness as he headed for his car. His evening with Evelyn wasn't a win, was it? He shouldn't have allowed himself to get distracted.

As he peeled away in his Clubman, he kicked himself for leaving Evelyn with such haste. It was too late to confront Katy tonight anyway, especially since Chuck was at home. Austin didn't want his roommate wondering what he was up to, slipping in and out of Katy's apartment, not until he could explain himself with facts.

Then there was Chuck himself. What the hell was he involved in? There had to be a mistake.

And even if Chuck *had* done something illegal, unless he'd dishonored his Trident, which Austin knew he would never do, their friendship would survive. Their bond of brotherhood had been forged by mutual sacrifice and sweat. *Nothing* could break the bond they shared.

AT THE SOUND of a car leaving the apartment complex, Kelly froze in a plank position on her bedroom floor, a bead of sweat sliding down one cheek. The familiar hum of Chuck's Subaru BRZ had her popping to her feet and running to her window.

"Oh, so now he goes out."

All day long, Chuck had remained in his apartment, making no effort to reach out to her. He had been home when she'd left for class that morning, leaving early so that she had time to type up her concluding paragraph. When she'd come home again, Chuck was still up in his apartment. Having promised Ernie she would monitor Chuck's movement and moods, Kelly had studied in her room, then exercised on her carpet, popping up occasionally to check on Chuck's car. Given the enormous gulf that now separated them because of her awful lie, she couldn't tell what his mood might be. He was driving off in his car, and she had no idea why.

Kelly snatched up the cellphone charging by her bed.

Heads up. Target has left his apartment, she reported.

Interesting, Ernie replied. *He left his phone behind.*

Of course, Ernie could tell that by the stationary GPS of Chuck's cellphone. His leaving it behind suggested one thing: He didn't want his destination recorded—not that he necessarily suspected he being watched. That was simply standard tradecraft and no problem for Katy's squad. At least three of Valentino's unarmed surveillance agents were positioned at strategic choke points around the immediate area. One of them was bound to spot Chuck, then tail him.

Kelly swallowed against a dry throat. *It had begun.*

Up until that afternoon, Chuck's response to his tasking had been limited to web searches. Using only the Internet, Chuck had found his target, located the man's place of work, his residence, even the church he attended. But, tonight, Chuck might be transitioning to the next step: physical reconnaissance. That made sense, of course. The deadline given by the RGB and conveyed by Granny left Chuck only five more days, including today, to carry out his execution.

Kelly tried and failed to picture Chuck as an assassin. Perhaps she was in denial. It was hard enough to accept she'd developed feelings for a traitor spy, let alone a would-be assassin. She closed her eyes, hating herself for her crossing the line with Chuck, while at the same time holding tight to every passionate and perfect moment. How could the man who had felt like home to her morph into a conscienceless killer?

Waiting for updates, Kelly headed for the kitchen. Lisa, thank God, had just left with plans to eat out with friends. With her workout wear sticking to her sweaty back, Kelly blended herself a banana-and-peanut-butter milkshake. She carried her frothing drink out onto the balcony, letting the cold March air wick away her sweat while the smoothie chilled her from the inside out. The pink horizon drew a veil of darkness behind it.

I'm going to need a little while to think about things.

Chuck's final words to her cut across her memory like a razor. She had known her lie would push him away; that had been her goal. But for him to give up that easily on what they had discovered in each other? That hurt, regardless of who he was, what his intentions were.

Realizing she was shivering, Kelly pushed back into her apartment to the sound of her phone buzzing. She hurried over to it.

Target is headed toward Sandbridge.

The news was expected. The former North Korean physicist lived in Sandbridge. Chuck would likely spend the next few days acquainting himself with Ken W. Harris's routine. Her surveillance squad needed all the time they could get setting the stage before Chuck made his move.

According to Ernie's report that morning, the CIA had finally found a volunteer to play the ringer: a ballsy CIA case officer of Korean descent. Unfortunately, he didn't speak Korean, beyond a few words, and he couldn't fly into Virginia Beach until Wednesday morning. Ernie would pick him up from the airport.

At that same time, Ken W. Harris would be spirited away to safety. While all this was going on, the Wires and Pliers would be hard at work in Harris's home installing ELSUR, and Valentino's SOGs would be drilling on how to protect the ringer from Chuck's lethal intentions. If Chuck went for the kill before they were ready, things could get messy.

Kelly channeled her nervous energy into cleaning up the kitchen. With no more texts coming in, she carried her phone back to her bedroom, stripped, and jumped into the shower. While lathering herself with soap, the memory of Chuck's hot mouth on her body made her both sick and sorry—sick that she'd believed him a nobler person than he apparently was. Sorry that she would never be held by him again.

At last, a text arrived as she was toweling off.

Slow drive by of the residence.

Kelly reached for the comb to steady her nerves. A sudden imperative occurred to her as she drew the comb through her long, wet hair.

"I have to be there when it happens," she said to her reflection.

The only way to stop having feelings for Chuck was to watch him attempt to kill the man he believed to be Kyong Won-ha. To do that, she had to be watching the Bu's surveillance with Ernie, Valentino, and whomever else needed to be there. Hannah would be down the street in her own vehicle, ready to intercept Chuck when he emerged.

Kelly set her comb aside and picked up her phone, sending Ernie a private text.

You're going to need a translator if the target addresses the ringer in his native language. Let me do it.

Ernie did not immediately text her back.

Carrying her phone into her bedroom, Kelly laid it on her dresser. It was too early in the evening to jump into her pajamas. She compromised by donning a soft pair of jeans and the same Georgetown University T-shirt she had worn the day she moved in.

The textbook lying open on her bed reminded her she still had one more chapter to read before Wednesday's class. It was hard to muster her enthusiasm. To delay, she wriggled socks onto her feet and looked at her phone, wishing the surveillance specialist who was following Chuck would give detailed updates.

In her mind's eye, she pictured Chuck parked somewhere within eyesight of Harris's oceanfront home. For days, he would observe patterns and brainstorm methods of attack. His military experience and skillset made him the perfect man for the job.

Kelly jerked her admiring thoughts up short. Chuck wasn't a hero, for God's sake. A true hero would have balked at being coerced in the first place. He would have taken his own life first or gone to the Feds and confessed to everything, even if that meant throwing his grandmother under the bus. Instead, it was increasingly apparent Chuck intended to fulfill the RGB's orders, safeguarding his family's ties to the hermit kingdom while ensuring the RGB let him live.

"Coward." Disappointment brought tears to Kelly's eyes.

A loud knock at her front door startled her head up. Telling herself one of Lisa's suitors was looking for her, she crossed her apartment to see who it was.

A peek through the peephole showed Austin standing at her door still in his uniform. When had he come home?

Kelly opened the door with a ready smile. "Hey, what's up?"

His grim expression made her own smile fade.

"Can I come in?"

"Sure." As he strode into her living space, her mind raced for reasons why he would want a private audience.

"Is everything okay?" She closed the door, wary of the tension rolling off him.

He swung around. "Why don't you tell me?"

His SEAL voice, as she thought of it, raised warning flags. "What do you mean?"

"I think you do, Kelly."

The sound of her real name rocked her back on her heels. For a full three seconds, Kelly couldn't think at all. Then her survival instincts kicked in. "Why are you calling me that?"

"It's your name, isn't it, Kelly Yang? Funny how it rhymes with Katy Tang."

"What are you talking about?" She raised her chin, fighting to regain control. His knowing who she was could ruin everything.

"I recognized you from a photo taken with your sorority sisters. One of them is Evelyn Haskins. Ring any bells?"

Oh, no. What a small world. "Your therapist?"

Her mystified tone made Austin hesitate. "You went to Georgetown University together. You're wearing the T-shirt!" He gestured at it. "Are you going to deny that you went there?"

"Of course not. But GU has tens of thousands of alumni. Perhaps I look like one of them."

Austin's jaw tightened. "All right. Let's go back to the morning Chuck got shot. You said you put Chuck's car keys in the drawer beside his bed. But you didn't. What did you do with those keys, *Katy*?"

She could tell by his tone he knew exactly what she'd done. Better to come clean and offer up a valid reason. "Is that what this is about? Oh, gosh. Okay. Yes, I held onto Chuck's car keys for a couple of days. I'm sorry I lied to you about that. It's just . . . I needed to know if Chuck was as single as he claimed to be. I've been two-timed before, and I've learned it's better to verify than be blind-sided. So, yes, I held onto the keys and searched Chuck's car for any evidence of a woman in his life. And his bedroom, too," she tossed in. "Finding nothing, I returned the keys as soon as you went back to work."

Austin processed her confession with a frown.

"Wait," she added, "you weren't around when I

did that. You had duty that day."

"Not really." His gaze narrowed. "I was watching you from a rooftop bar two blocks from the apartment, Old Port Brewing Company. I even took pictures in case I needed to show them to Chuck."

She could sense him backing her into a corner. My God, what else had he realized without her knowledge?

"I followed you last Tuesday evening when you told Chuck you were going to the library. You drove all the way to Hampton, to a building that houses an FBI residence agency."

Shocked into momentary silence, Katy then counterattacked, desperate to subdue his suspicions. "There are lots of offices in that building, Austin, including an independent consulting group which my team at school is analyzing."

Holding Austin's disbelieving stare, Kelly could tell he didn't believe a word she was saying. This wasn't good. If her UCO was blown, the entire investigation would be left in shambles.

Austin took a step in her direction. Kelly locked her knees to keep from backing up. Austin stared at her through his absurdly long eyelashes. "You're still prevaricating, and I want to know why."

Kelly's heart pounded. It was time to lay down the law before he single-handedly destroyed all that had been accomplished.

"Listen to me, Austin." She drew herself to her full height and said in her firmest voice, "Don't interrupt and don't repeat any of this to anyone."

His stare became unblinking.

"I will neither confirm nor deny my identity to you. You know me as Katy Tang, a graduate student at Virginia Wesleyan University and as your neighbor. What you do *not* know are any details of what may be a highly sensitive undertaking of *significant* national importance." She put her hands on her hips. "You do *not* know the subject of the undertaking nor the location of any persons party to this undertaking. All you have are suspicions. But you are a Navy SEAL and holder of a top-secret security clearance. As such, you have sworn *never* to disclose classified material to anyone without a specific and identifiable need-to-know, and that includes *everyone* in your social and professional circles. You will treat and protect what I have just said in accordance with existing guidelines on the protection of classified National Security Information. Do I make myself perfectly clear?"

Instead of answering, he asked, "What do I tell Evelyn?"

"Tell her," Kelly said through her teeth, "that you were wrong. You know what white people say about Asians. We all look the same. You mistook me for someone else."

"Well, that's racially insensitive." Austin's lips

curled into a familiar smile, but his gaze remained hard. "My turn to talk. Chuck is more than my roommate. He's more than my best friend. He is my brother. If you slept with him for the sole purpose of extorting him for information, I will never forgive you."

The unexpectedly personal attack threw Kelly off her soap box. Tears stung her eyes without warning. "That wasn't supposed to happen," she admitted. "I was trying to protect him."

"From whom?"

"From himself," she answered honestly.

"You've messed with his heart, Katy. That is not cool."

Her eyes grew damp. They weren't talking about Chuck the spy anymore. "I never meant to hurt him. I've pulled away for professional reasons, but I still love him."

As Austin's accusatory expression softened, Kelly spun away, shocked by the words that had come out of her. Until that very moment, she'd blamed her behavior on Chuck's allure, her concern for him, and her inability to see the spy in him. But the emotion gripping her heart wasn't that complicated. *I do love him.*

"Have you told Chuck how you feel?"

Austin spoke with considerably less aggression.

She shook her head no. She had sullied their connection with a lie, not that it mattered now, given his commitment to his tasking.

Drawing on her desperation, Kelly turned and grabbed Austin's camouflage jacket. "You have to swear to me, on your Trident, that you won't mention a single word about our conversation here."

Austin laughed humorlessly and brushed her off.

"Austin, you swore to protect your country," she reminded him. "This is a matter of national security."

He held up his hands in a gesture for her to stop. "Fine," he agreed. "I swear on my Trident." He pointed a finger at her. "But you need to make things right with Chuck when this is over. And you need to tell him how you feel. He's crazy about you, Katy. Don't you dare break his heart."

The words thrilled and then crippled her. "Fine," Kelly echoed, though she had no intention of ever speaking to Chuck if he attempted what she thought he would. Once Hannah flipped him, assuming Chuck agreed to become a double agent, Katy would disappear from his life. Hannah, who would become Chuck's handler, would take over the job of keeping a close watch on him.

Austin stuck out a hand for her to shake. "Then we have an agreement."

Kelly put a cautious hand in his. He squeezed it with a forceful but painless grip. Bending, he said in her ear, "Don't make me regret trusting you."

In the next instant, her hand was free, and he was shutting the apartment door quietly behind him. Kelly tottered toward the closest chair and collapsed on it.

She had sensed from the moment she'd read Austin Collins' files that the junior SEAL might prove to be a problem. Behind his youthful visage lurked a man with a shrewd mind and a loyal heart. To think he had followed her without her noticing!

Hannah had to be told what had recently transpired. Maybe there was something Hannah could do to ensure Austin's cooperation, to tone down his suspicions. Austin could never be told what Chuck had done. And that was a good thing. Just imagine Austin's disillusionment if he found out that Chuck had betrayed the very country they risked their lives to protect!

Kelly had to accept the ugly truth, though. Chuck wasn't the reluctant villain she'd thought he was. He was the perfect tool for the RGB. And the only way she would ever fall out of love with him was to watch him try to kill Kyong Won-ha.

AUSTIN UNLOCKED HIS apartment door, reminded of the day he'd found the hair missing between the door and the lintel, indicating Katy had broken in to return Chuck's keys. That same sense that his sanctuary had been violated hit him as silence greeted him. Chuck was gone—where? And why had he left his cellphone behind, sitting forgotten on the kitchen island?

Austin picked it up and turned it over. With a shrug, he put it down again.

Intending to change out of his uniform, he turned toward the hall and spotted Chuck's door left partially ajar. Austin pushed the door open.

The tidy room looked the same way it always did. The sword over Chuck's desk held his attention. Austin crossed the room to study it intently. Words from the Samurai code of conduct were etched onto both sides of the blade. Chuck had translated them once: *Strike when it is just to strike* was etched onto one side. On the other: *Die when it is just to die.*

Chuck seemed to live by those words, making him something of a modern-day Samurai. That thought teased Austin's imagination. Was it possible Chuck still had connections to the far East? How well did Austin know his best friend anyway?

He searched his memory for indications that Chuck led a secret, double life. In every vignette that surfaced, Chuck emerged as a warrior of integrity, the first to extend a helping hand. Sure, he was contemplative, and his analogies were often mystifying, but he would be the last guy in the world to betray his oath, to tarnish his Trident.

The only explanation was the FBI was investigating someone else. Could they be after Chuck's shooter and not Chuck? Maybe they'd known Chuck's life was in danger, and they'd placed an undercover agent in the unit across from his to protect him. Katy could be keeping an eye on Chuck, not investigating him. Austin liked that theory better.

The buzzing of his cellphone broke into his thoughts. Recognizing the special ring tone ascribed to his command, he withdrew his phone and read the text as he walked out of Chuck's bedroom. *Team Building STAT.*

The call to arms never failed to jack up Austin's heart rate. It was all the warning SEALs often got before they were trundled into a helicopter, headed into danger.

So much for changing out of his uniform. On his way to the door, Austin grabbed an apple from the fridge. It might be the only food he got for hours. A glance at Chuck's forgotten cellphone made him pick it up to check if Chuck had received the same message. He had not.

"Oh, medical leave," Austin reminded himself, putting the phone back down.

With a thought for Evelyn, he locked the apartment behind himself and hurried to his car. He would call her once the briefing was over. That way, he could inform her, more or less, of what was going on.

He couldn't lie to himself, though. Evelyn's reservations about dating him made him anxious. When they spent time together, it was easy to believe he could win her affections. All he had to do was see the bloom in her cheeks to know she wanted him. Things weren't so obvious when they were apart.

He had a sinking feeling they were about to be *very* far apart in the days to come.

✕

"DON'T CALL HIM."

Evelyn had repeated those words to herself all day long. And up until she reclined on her bed to read, she had heeded the imperative, but curiosity had begun to erode her common sense. Austin had texted her the previous night to say he would put off confronting his mysterious neighbor until today.

Well, the day was nearly over, and still no word. Calling herself weak and self-sabotaging, Evelyn laid her book aside, sat up, and dialed Austin's number.

He picked it up on third ring. "Hello, beautiful. I was just about to call you." The words reassured her, but his business-like tone did not. She could tell by the quality of their connection he was likely driving somewhere, talking over Bluetooth.

"Hello, you were supposed to tell me what your neighbor Katy had to say."

"Oh, yeah, Katy. Sorry, I've had a really busy day

and it's not over yet."

"So, you haven't spoken to her yet?"

"Um . . . yeah, we spoke. I guess I jumped to conclusions. She's not who we thought she was."

"Really?" That was not what Evelyn had been expecting. "What did she say about searching Chuck's car?"

"She was looking for proof that he already had a girlfriend. Apparently, she's been two-timed before, and she figured she could search his car and his room and know if he was lying to her."

Evelyn frowned. "Do you believe that? What about the building she went into the night you followed her to Hampton?"

"There are lots of business in that building, including an independent consulting group which she and her classmates are evaluating."

"Huh." Evelyn tugged on her hair, wondering if the woman's explanations merited belief. "Maybe I could see her for myself. I would know if she's really Kelly."

"No."

Austin's answer made her frown. "Why not?"

"We're going to leave this one alone, Ev."

Andrew was the only other person who shortened her name like that. It made Austin even more appealing than he already was. "Are you okay?" she asked him. "You sound angry."

He blew out a breath. "I'm sorry. I just got word I'm leaving in the morning, and I'm upset about walking away from you right now."

Her stomach went into freefall. "Oh? Where are you going?"

"My translation services are needed. That's about all I can tell you."

"Which language?"

He hesitated, then apparently decided he could say that much. "Korean."

He was traveling all the way to *Korea*? "I see. Any idea when you'll be back?"

"Two weeks, maybe? I really don't know. But I *will* be back."

The reassurance in his tone did nothing for her. "No," she said, "it's better this way."

A beat of silence followed her words. Then, "What do you mean it's better?"

Now he sounded alarmed. She didn't want to distract him as he set out on some dangerous mission. Wait, South Korea was an ally nation. Good lord, was he going to *North* Korea? She didn't want to know. "Never mind. Be safe. Take care of yourself."

"Evelyn, don't do this."

How could he always tell what she was thinking?

"I'll be back soon," he added on an upbeat note. "Just go about your business, thinking happy thoughts, and when I get back, I'll help you put up that new backsplash."

Or, better yet, she would finish it herself and not sit around pining for him. "Okay," she said, letting him think that was the plan.

"I'll miss you."

The low rasp of his voice rippled through her raising goosebumps. "I'll miss you, too," she said, but she meant for the rest of her life, not only while he was away. "Be safe, Austin."

"Always. Good night, beautiful."

"Good night." Thumbing the call to a close, she dropped the phone on her aching chest and gave into the urge to cry.

The Universe was doing her a favor, clearly. Getting involved with a SEAL five years her junior was a study in stupidity. The statistics could not be overlooked, and Andrew had never been wrong. As a couple, she and Austin would never make it. And she refused to follow in her mother's footsteps by falling madly in love with a man in uniform, only to be caught off guard by the sacrifices required of a military spouse. Next thing she knew, she'd be cheating on him whenever he left—not that she could begin to picture that. Still, this wasn't the kind of relationship she wanted.

So, no. No matter how appealing and smart and intuitive Austin Collins was, heedless of the fact that he sometimes seemed to know her better than she knew herself, she was going to take advantage of his absence to steer her ship in a different direction.

Evelyn dropped her face into her hands and sobbed.

✕

AUSTIN SAT AT one end of the sofa in the dark, sipping on a bottle of Gatorade and waiting for Chuck to get home. He probably ought to go to bed. He had to report to the airfield at zero-four hundred hours to hop on a military flight that would take him straight to Coronado. Then again, he could catch up on sleep during the long flight.

At the sound of Chuck's Subaru zipping into its space downstairs, Austin put his bottle down. Chuck's headlights brightened their living room briefly, then went out, plunging the apartment back into darkness. Austin waited, his blood pumping faster.

Chuck could move with the stealth of the Japanese warriors he so admired. The key sliding into their door was the next sound Austin detected. The door opened quietly, and Chuck slipped inside, clearly unwilling to disturb Austin, whom he thought was sleeping. Austin stood up, switching on the lamp as he came to his feet. He caught a startled, almost guilty, look on his best friend's face.

"Where've you been?" His tone sounded more

accusative than he'd meant it to.

Chuck drew an audible breath. "Out with Katy."

The reply threw Austin off his game. Wait, was that true or a lie? Austin hadn't been home the whole evening. Chuck could've picked her up after he went back to base for his briefing. "Oh, yeah? Where'd you go?"

"For a walk on the beach. Then to dinner."

"Sounds nice. You left your phone here."

"Yeah, guess she distracted me. Why are you still up?" Chuck moved to the kitchen, turning away to get a glass out of the cupboard.

"Wanted to tell you SEAL Team 3 needs a Korean translator, and they chose me."

Chuck turned his head to look at him, betraying surprise as he pressed his glass to the water dispenser. "Oh, yeah? Did they say what for?"

"One of Kim Jong-un's cabinet members wants to defect."

Chuck slowly turned around, his expression inscrutable. "No shit."

"Apparently, the Supreme Ruler suspects a traitor among his closest advisors. He's been killing them off, one at a time. This guy figures his luck's about to run out."

Chuck took a quick sip of his drink. "How'd he get word to the US?"

"Think about it," Austin suggested.

Chuck cocked his head thinking, but he didn't have an answer.

"The guy we're going to extract *is* the traitor Jong-un's looking for. He's been talking to the CIA all along. Why else would the Agency bother saving his ass?"

Chuck hummed his agreement.

"Anyway, I'll be gone by the time you wake up tomorrow." Austin padded toward him. "Just wanted to say good-bye, in case something happens."

Chuck put his drink down and held out a hand. "Wish I could go with you," he said on a sincere note.

"You should be. Your Korean is better than mine."

"But I'm still on leave."

Chuck's firm, sincere handshake was all the confirmation Austin needed that his friend was everything he'd always believed him to be.

"All in, all the time," Chuck stated.

The SEAL motto was a reminder of that level of commitment required by all SEALs. Chuck might be temporarily sidelined, but he would be with Austin in spirit.

"Hooyah," Austin said, letting go.

"Good night, amigo," Chuck called as he turned away.

"Good night." Zero-four hundred hours would be here before Austin knew it. At least, now he could fall asleep with the private reassurance that, regardless of what the FBI was up to, Charles Suzuki was a mensch, to use a Yiddish word: someone of noble character, to be admired and emulated.

CHAPTER 19

C HUCK SAT IN his car in the dark parking lot of Sandbridge Seaside Market, the only grocery store in the coastal community, now closed. With his engine turned off, the lights of his dash extinguished, his car looked unoccupied.

A coy moon peeked now and again through the thin layer of clouds skating above him. The roar of the ocean came through his closed windows as a slow drumbeat followed by a hiss. His heartbeat was just as audible, spurred by the adrenaline flowing through him. Tonight, his inheritance collided with free will. He would carve his own destiny.

From where he sat in the deepening chill of his vehicle, Chuck could see Harris's driveway through a break in the scrubby hedge in front of him. Throughout his week-long reconnaissance, he had familiarized himself with the physicist's routine.

On weekdays, Harris worked as a consultant at Huntington Ingalls Industries, Inc., a fact Chuck had uncovered in his extensive online research. Every night between 6:00 and 6:30 PM, Harris returned home, likely stopping for dinner along the way, as his work ended at 5:00. Ten minutes after his arrival at home, blue light flickered in the man's lower-level windows as he watched television, except for Wednesday night when he attended Bible study at the Seaside Chapel. Even then, he was home by 9 PM sharp, at which time the lights on the lower level went out, and Harris retired to his bedroom on the second story. He probably read for a while in bed. His lights went out promptly at 10.

Chuck had spotted a utility van parked two days in a row in Harris's carport. The logo on the side of the van suggested repairs were being made to Harris's heating unit. Chuck looked up Beach's Best Heating and Air to verify it was a legitimate business, apparently so trustworthy that Harris let the company do repairs while he was away at work.

What Chuck could not find online was a single picture of the defector-physicist. Having glimpsed the man's face behind the wheel of his car and once, using binoculars, on the elevated deck of his home, Chuck had only a vague idea of what he looked like: average stature, graying hair, and glasses.

In the stygian darkness of his car, Chuck pulled back the sleeve of his wool coat. The time on the watch Seiko had given him at Christmas was 6:12 PM. Unless Harris broke with his routine on Fridays, he ought to be arriving home any moment.

Chuck gave a thought to his week-long reconnaissance. Austin's absence had proven to be a blessing in disguise, making it easier for Chuck to drive to Sandbridge sometimes twice in one day, but mostly in the evenings. All the while, uneasiness sat in his stomach like a heavy, greasy meal.

No one seemed to be following him, but he couldn't shake the feeling he was not alone. Perhaps it was only his guilt keeping him company, especially where Katy was concerned. He had not spoken to her, or even texted her, since the prior weekend at the library. No doubt she thought him, at best a coward, at worst unconcerned. He wasn't a coward. And he fully intended to preserve their friendship—more, if he could help her to work through her intimacy issues. He would happily visit a therapist with her. But not quite yet; not right now.

First, he had to complete the task he'd been given. Then he had to minimize the RGB's expectations of him while keeping them from sending Lee or another like him to tie off loose ends. If Chuck could do that much, then maybe, *just maybe*, he could lead a quasi-normal life with Katy as his best friend or, better yet, his wife, who may or may not ever be told his connection to North Korea.

Caught up in his thoughts, Chuck nearly over-looked Harris's maroon Buick as it passed right in front of him, cruising the only road leading in and out of Sandbridge.

His pulse ticked upward. *Time to roll.* Patting his pocket to ascertain he had his keys, he stepped out of his car, locked it with a swipe of his thumb and started following Harris's taillights.

The oceanfront community lost half its population during winter months. It was unlikely anyone noticed him melting in and out of shadows as he made his way down the unlit street closest to the ocean. An inhospitable breeze whipped the edges of his wool coat and chapped his cheeks, but his black boots, black cap, and gloves, kept him comfortable.

The Atlantic Ocean's surge and retreat mirrored Chuck's uncertainty about the future. He was exactly where he'd been six months earlier when he'd found his deception unacceptable. How was he supposed to live with it now?

The memory of his and Austin's final handshake speared his consciousness. It symbolized their bond of trust which, unbeknownst to Austin, unbeknownst to SOCOM, Chuck had violated. How would he live with *himself,* while sharing his future with an oblivious Katy?

Lights blinked on in Harris's home. Unlike the empty summer mansions on either side, Harris's modest home consisted of only two levels built atop thick pilings. A weathered deck wrapped around its shingled siding. The whimsical architectural details of the newer homes were lacking, save for the smaller deck off the master bedroom. Sand dunes encroached at the rear, and scraggly grass grew in the sandy yard out front. The maroon Buick was sitting in the carport beneath the home, engine ticking as it cooled.

Sand crunched beneath Chuck's boots as bypassed the car, headed for the flight of stairs to the main level. Sensing an alien presence, Chuck paused and listened. The absolute silence, broken only by the pounding of waves, encouraged him to proceed with caution. He scanned the pockets of darkness for signs that he was being watched. Arriving at the solid wooden door, he took a bracing breath, and rang the doorbell.

THE DOORBELL'S CHIME, audible through Kelly's headset, dumped adrenaline into her veins. She was thankful she was sitting down in the van's dark interior, along with Ernie, Valentino, and Red. All four of them were glued to the video feed being displayed on two separate monitors. One showed a view of the defector's front door, deck, and driveway, the other a view of his living room.

"Here we go." Ernie breathed.

The CIA imposter's footsteps betrayed wariness as he answered the summons. Kelly wondered if he was being compensated for his role. Surely he knew what he was up against—a Navy SEAL on a mission to assassinate him.

"Steady." Valentino's raspy instructions were directed to two members of his special operations group, one lying on the small deck off the master bedroom, with a rifle pointed down at the door. A second SOG was tucked inside the home.

Chuck lifted a hand, and Kelly's heart lodged itself in her throat. But all he did was pull the cap from his head, take his gloves off his hands and stuff all three into the pocket of his coat. Her gaze shifted to the ringer as he turned the lock on the door. *Imagine how he feels.* Younger than Harris by at least ten years, the volunteer had dyed his hair gray and wore glasses to better look the part.

Would Chuck try to shoot him where he stood? Kelly forced herself to watch.

The safety chain prevented the door from opening all the way. Lee's stand-in peered through the opening. "Yes?"

Chuck bowed respectfully. *"Annyeohngha seyo, sun saeng nim."*

Kelly, whose job it was to translate, spoke up quickly. "Good evening, sir." Her voice sounded in the ringer's ear through a tiny speaker, the same kind Kelly had worn into Calypso the night she'd met Austin and Chuck.

"Good evening," the ringer responded in English, while affecting an accent he didn't have. "Who are you?" He didn't have to fake his nervousness.

Chuck spoke slowly, in a tense voice Kelly had never heard him use before. "Forgive the intrusion, sir. I'm not here to hurt you. But others will come if you don't hear me out. Please, may I have a word inside?"

Kelly gulped. Was Chuck telling the truth? Or were his words just a ploy to get him out of sight of potential witnesses?

The ringer fumbled with the chain and pulled the door open. "May I take your coat?"

"No, thank you. I won't be long."

Would he be so polite if he meant to kill the man? Kelly watched Chuck step inside. His alert gaze went immediately to the expansive windows overlooking a dark ocean. He plumbed the state-of-the art kitchen, took in the high, raftered ceiling and, finally, the dark loft where, unbeknownst to him, Valentino's second SOG stood behind a bookcase with a bead on him.

With a queasy pitch of her stomach, Kelly realized she might have to watch Chuck die for real this time.

"Do you know what that is?" the ringer asked.

Chuck's attention had settled on the framed photo hanging on the wall below the loft. "A galaxy?"

"Atomic fusion." The man's faked accent was good. He must have picked it up from his elders. "Beautiful, don't you think?"

"Yes."

"Would you like to sit?" The ringer gestured to the recliner that would put Chuck in direct sight of the sniper on the loft, while he himself occupied the sofa opposite him. "You don't look Korean," he noted.

"No. My connection to your homeland is complicated. My grandmother is North Korean, like you."

The ringer feigned dismay. "How do you know where I am from?"

"I must explain myself to gain your forgiveness."

The word *forgiveness* sent a chill down Kelly's spine. Why would he need forgiveness unless he was going to go through with it?

"My grandfather was a Japanese American. He was a fighter pilot in the Korean Conflict, and his plane was shot down. But he did not become a prisoner-of-war. Instead, he was brought into Kim Il-sung's compound and treated as a guest. Can you understand my English?"

"Yes, yes, I understand."

"He was indoctrinated—you know, brainwashed?"

The ringer nodded.

"When the war ended, my grandfather was sent home with a North Korean bride. She was Kim Il-sung's sister."

In the dark van, Kelly exchanged a startled look with Ernie. Neither of them had realized Granny's close kinship to the ruling family. The ringer was likewise astonished.

Chuck wasn't done. "My grandmother has been a spy for North Korea for almost seven decades. My father was raised to assist her. Then me."

Chuck's flat tone brought Kelly's pity surging back.

"Sobo encouraged me to join the military. I suspected her motives, but I honestly hoped, once I was in the service, she would understand my loyalty was to my country. I should have known better. Now, she's grooming my brother to become a traitor, also." Chuck's voice grew harder. He looked directly at the man braced on the sofa. "I'm sure you can guess why I was sent here."

The ringer tensed. "You wouldn't," he stated in an uncertain voice.

"Ready," Valentino said to his sniper.

Kelly dug her nails into her palms to steady herself.

A thumping noise, possibly from the loft, brought Chuck abruptly to his feet. "What was that?"

"My cat." The ringer also stood. "Just my cat," he said, covering for the sniper who must have nudged the bookcase and caused a book to fall over.

"Please." The ringer spread his hands in an appeasing gesture. "I can see that you're an honorable man. If you meant to kill me, you would have done so by now."

"It's not that simple."

At those words, the hope fluttering in Kelly's chest became an ice pick of fear.

"Your location is known to the RGB," Chuck continued. "My handler has tried to kill me once for ignoring the RGB's directives. He will come for me again if your obituary fails to show up in the newspaper."

Chuck, no! Don't do it!

"Aim," murmured Valentino.

On the loft, Kelly pictured the sniper crooking his finger over the trigger. She covered her mouth to keep from screaming.

"Contact your keeper, your nanny, whatever you call him," Chuck continued, his words low and urgent. "Tell him you *must* be relocated, your death faked. Your obituary *must* appear in this Sunday's paper and online. Get out of here as fast as possible."

The words turned Kelly limp with relief.

Valentino recanted his last order. "Hold."

On the monitor, Chuck bowed solemnly and reverently to his would-be target. "Thank you for your time, *sun saeng nim*. I'll see myself out."

Leaving the ringer gaping at him, Chuck made his way to the door he had recently entered. With a hand on the knob, he looked up at the ceiling as if picturing someone in the loft directly above the foyer. Then he opened the door and stepped through it.

"Target is leaving the building," Ernie said into his headset. "Ringer is unharmed. Hannah, you're on."

"I'm coming. Listen, I just noticed there's a Volkswagen Beetle parked under the rental unit behind me. I haven't seen it before. Someone run the tags: XKY 9743."

"I'm on it." Ernie reached for a keyboard and started tapping on it.

Kelly sat in stunned relief. Chuck had totally re-deemed himself. Tears of joy, relief and love for him, slid down her face. *I knew he wasn't a killer.*

Hannah said in Kelly's headset. "Intercepting the target now. Wish me luck."

Kelly imagined Chuck was about to get the shock of his lifetime. But, given what he had just confessed to, how he'd been coerced into spying, Hannah would have no trouble persuading him to work for the Bureau.

How would such an outcome impact her and Chuck's relationship? That depended on Hannah who found herself in a difficult situation. On one hand, she was obligated to safeguard the existence of the source in North Korea, the same source that had warned the CIA of a traitor in the Teams. Admitting to Chuck that Katy had been sent undercover to investigate him wouldn't simply upset Chuck; it would betray the existence of the source, which had to be kept classi-fied. On the other hand, Katy had been forced to tell Hannah about Austin guessing her affiliation with the FBI. He didn't know exactly what Katy was investigat-ing. And he had sworn his discretion, but could he really be trusted not to tell his best friend?

Ernie pulled off his headset. He looked over at

Kelly and grinned. "That went better than expected."

Kelly hid her unwieldy emotions from him. "Did you run those tags?"

"Yep. The vehicle belongs to someone named Albert Sievers. He's probably renting."

"We should get Detective Scruggs to verify that, just in case."

"I'll tell Scruggs," Ernie promised, while giving her a searching look. "Are you okay? I thought you'd be pleased about the outcome."

"I am. I'm just . . . exhausted."

He studied her a moment longer. "Yeah, I get it. Why don't you go home and rest? I've got it from here."

"Thanks, Ernie."

"No problem, Munchkin." He got up and pulled open the van's door. "Drive safely."

"Good night." Kelly stepped out onto a dark street one block over from Harris's house. As she hurried toward her Prius, parked under an empty beach house, she caught a glimpse of Hannah's green family van braking on the next street over.

Chuck was getting picked up now.

HEARING A VEHICLE zipping up the road behind him, Chuck lengthened his stride. A glance back had him stepping off the road, prepared to bolt toward the shadowy carport of the nearest home, when he recognized the driver by the interior light she clicked on.

In that instant, the suspicion he was being watched congealed into ice-cold certainty.

Hannah Lindstrom, the wife of Chuck's operations officer, leaned her red head out of her lowered driver's window and called to him, "Haiku."

He stopped in his tracks.

The door behind the driver's seat slid open and out stepped a very large, casually dressed man with a hard face. His twin brother had rounded the front of the van from the passenger seat.

"Hop in," Hannah suggested.

Only an idiot would try to make a run for it. Resignation edged aside Chuck's shock as he stepped numbly toward the van, then submitted to a quick frisking.

"No weapons." The first man shoved him into the van's open door.

"You didn't check inside his sock," Hannah drawled as Chuck dropped into the far seat. The oversized twins got back in, shutting their respective doors, and Hannah started driving. "That's okay," she said to Chuck. "I'll let you keep your *shuriken*. You're a patriot at heart. Aren't you, Haiku?"

"Yes, ma'am." Armed with hindsight, Chuck realized he'd been under observation, probably for days. Bullfrog would have rebuked him for not heeding his intuition. Moreover, there'd been at least one other person in that house besides Harris—if that man was even the real physicist. There'd probably been cameras, as well, and microphones. "Did you hear what I told him?"

"Yes, we did."

The van sped up, headed for the Seaside Market and Chuck's car. One block over, a black Prius exactly like Kelly's car turned right, heading away from Sandbridge. Chuck squinted at the license plate. Lots of people drove Priuses. He made out UGS on the tag before it got too far away to see the rest.

Instead of leaving Sandbridge, Hannah continued straight at the intersection, driving down the coast. Perplexed as to their destination, Chuck kept one eye on the buildings as they sped past them—beach houses, a souvenir shop, a local restaurant, a church—his other eye on the vehicle's occupants. The large twins seemed fairly relaxed, like they didn't expect him to resist but were prepared if he did. Hannah herself looked unconcerned, even though she drove well past the speed limit.

Chuck, still reeling from the unexpected turn of events, relived the past few weeks, then months, seeking clues to his sudden revelation that the FBI had been watching him! He'd been so intent on avoiding Lee, it hadn't occurred to him to worry about anyone else. Apart from Lee's attempt on his life, there'd been nothing unusual, no one new, except for Katy, but she had nothing to do with this, unless that Prius . . . ?

The suspicion that had shot under his skin at their first two encounters sprouted new roots.

Chuck's gaze alighted on a large wooden sign as they neared it. The words illumined by the van's headlights read, BACK BAY WILDLIFE REFUGE.

The sign also said, CLOSED AT DUSK, but the gate preventing entrance was raised. And beyond the gate, in a parking area fronting a visitors' center, a couple of cars were parked. Light poured from the windows of a modest, rustic building. They had brought him here to interrogate him.

Chuck expected panic to hijack him, but it never came. All he could feel was numb acceptance, even a little relief. He wasn't a traitor anymore, not if the FBI had overheard his confession. It was done and he was glad for that. Honestly, he would rather face years in prison than continue giving up secrets to the enemy.

THREE HOURS LATER, Chuck parked at his apartment, feeling lighter than he had in years. In the visitors' center, he had confessed to Hannah everything he'd showed the RGB, along with his attempts to get around their demands. Their conversation had been nonconfrontational—just him and her in the lonely building, while the large twins kept watch from a car parked outside. He had no idea what the fallout of his actions would be. Hannah hadn't explained anything, only that they would meet all weekend long to continue their "discussion."

Even now, she was nosing her van into Austin's empty parking space. She had followed him home to pick up his one-time pads—not that she believed he would pen a harried message to the RGB letting them know he'd been compromised. It was standard procedure, she'd assured him.

Stepping out of his car, Chuck sent an uncomfortable glance up at Katy's window. Thank God, she appeared to be sleeping, her room dark, her curtains pulled. He didn't want her seeing a strange woman heading up to his apartment with him and jumping to the wrong conclusion.

Remembering to check her license plate, he dropped his gaze to the back of her car. The letters UGS hit him like a knee to the groin. It couldn't be . . . It had to be a coincidence . . . But how many black Priuses of a similar year had the same first three letters?

"Haiku, it's getting late."

Tamping his suspicions under a tight lid, Chuck led Hannah up the steps to his apartment. He let them both in, flicking on lights as he went. His heart could not accept what his mind was telling him: Katy Tang was working for the FBI, after all.

Moments of their time spent together panned through his mind. She had approached him and Austin at Calypso. Then she'd moved in right across the way, touching him, flirting with him—but not because she was attracted to him. My God, had she wormed her way into his heart for the sole purpose of discovering his secrets, his weaknesses? He had brought her with him to his dead drop site, for God's sake! They'd made love while his directive from the RGB was lying in plain English in his desk drawer!

"Wow, how old is that sword?"

Hannah's question pulled Chuck back to his immediate purpose. "It's from the 15th century," he replied, crossing to his desk to take out the stapler. He took a dime from the top of his dresser and worked loose the screws on the baseplate. Seconds later, he shook the two little one-time pads into his hand and surrendered them to Hannah.

"My passcode is memorized: *Don't look back in anger.* That's the only phrase I've ever used."

"Fair enough." Hannah slipped the two little pads into the pocket of her trench coat, then checked her watch. "I'll be picking you up at 9 AM sharp tomorrow. It'll be a long day. Get a good night's sleep and eat a big breakfast."

Nervousness assailed Chuck as he wondered what the weekend would entail. It wouldn't be as laidback as this evening's confrontation, that was for sure. "Yes, ma'am."

Hannah started for the door.

"Katy works for you, doesn't she?" Chuck blurted.

Without the least hint of a reaction, Hannah swung back to look at him. "Who's Katy?"

Chuck almost brought himself to believe she didn't know. "That's a good question," he replied, holding Hannah's green gaze.

She was the first to look away. "Hmm. I'll see you in the morning, Haiku."

Before Chuck could get to the main door to see her out, Hannah had left his apartment. He threw the deadbolt in her wake, then put his back to the door. A long, worried sigh escaped him. His conscience felt lighter, yet his heart sat like a sack of potatoes in his chest.

Maybe he was wrong. There had to be at least a few black Priuses in the area with the same first letters on the license plate.

No, he wasn't wrong. The evidence was glaring. She had pushed him away with that cock-and-bull story about being kidnapped and raped because they'd gotten too close. She'd started having feelings for him . . . God, he hoped that was the reason! If not, then her seduction had been coldly calculated, designed to get him to open up to her. Did the FBI operate that way or was that only in the movies?

Either way, the woman he'd started picturing as his wife was only a beautiful mirage, a product of his wishful thinking.

Heartbroken, he pulled out his cellphone and sent her a message: *I know you were in Sandbridge tonight. You've lied to me this whole time.*

Let her reply to that as she wished. He was done playing the naïve fool who'd let an undercover agent pass through his defensive walls into the secret tower no one else had ever seen.

CHAPTER 20

IN HER SUNLIT kitchen, Kelly fixed herself a cup of coffee while still digesting the shocking text she had received while she was sleeping. It had awakened her, then kept her sleepless, tossing and turning: *I know you were in Sandbridge tonight. You've lied to me this whole time.*

Chuck must have somehow spotted her in Sandbridge, as Hannah would never have divulged Kelly's participation in the surveillance effort. His choice of words—*lied to me*—conveyed utter disillusionment and disgust. With a queasy stomach, Kelly had stared at the message wondering what on earth she could say back. Lying to him was out of the question at this point. And there was simply no way to explain herself when she was obligated to protect the existence of the Source, whose identity was sacrosanct.

Not bothering with cream or sugar, Kelly carried her mug to the sliding glass door and stared numbly at Chuck's empty apartment. It ought to be a relief that her UC work was done, that Hannah had taken over. Chuck would spend the entire day with the case manager. She had picked him up that morning in her family van and would do so again tomorrow and the next day. In fact, Chuck would be kept busy the entire week.

Kelly was aware of the process involved in flipping him. He would be questioned, cross-questioned and questioned again in different ways to identify any lack-of-candor issues. Was he being completely transparent? Was he telling them everything he knew? The ELSUR of his apartment would not be disclosed to him, as the Bu would continue to monitor him for signs of being a runner. Kelly knew for certain he would not run. Chuck hadn't wanted to work for the RGB in the first place.

At some point, probably on Monday, with Chuck completely broken down, Hannah would give him the pitch: Do you want to be a double agent? She would sweeten the deal by adding that neither Chuck's command nor his teammates would ever know the details of his previous life, though they might one day be apprised of his double-agent status and encouraged to participate on joint operations.

Chuck would seize the deal, she was certain. What Kelly doubted was his ability to believe her remorse if she attempted an apology—even if she confessed to falling in love with him. Why bother? Her time in this apartment was dwindling. In six weeks, when the semester ended, Katy Tang would move out, citing difficulties getting along with her roommate. Chuck would never see her again, whether he forgave her or not.

Their love affair was over.

Kelly looked down at her mug of foul-tasting coffee, returned to the kitchen with it, and dumped it in the sink. She was going back to bed.

✕

"LET'S TALK ABOUT the attempt on your life," Hannah suggested.

Chuck adjusted his seat. Did that mean they were finally done picking apart every tiny detail associated with his work as a North Korean agent? For over six hours, Hannah had asked him to review every act he had ever committed for the RGB, including who had ordered it, how the order was communicated, and why it was ordered, if he knew. Striving for utter transparency, Chuck had given her every detail he could remember.

He had described the tiny camera he'd been ordered to smuggle into work with directions to photograph top-secret communications, installations, and any new technology. Too paranoid to carry the camera into secured areas, Chuck had brought home unclassified nonsense to which he attached classification markings and took pictures of those. He also smuggled out unclassified maps and even images he found online of cutting-edge technology, snapping off pictures of those items—anything to placate the RGB. In minute detail, he explained his methodology for hiding information in his nature photographs and uploading them to Instagram.

All the while, Hannah merely sat there listening, sometimes asking clarifying questions. She had announced up front that the entire debriefing process would be recorded.

It wasn't until mid-afternoon, after a lunch eaten in isolation and delivered from the cafeteria, that Chuck got to describe his attempt to break with the past, his angst and inner conflict, how he had smashed the little camera the day he'd made up his mind to vanish off Lee's radar.

He rubbed his aching eyes. "That obviously didn't work."

"No, it didn't, did it? Do you think Lee is still a threat?"

Chuck dropped his hands and looked up. "Depends on whether he believes Harris is really dead."

"Well," Hannah rolled her shoulders which were obviously stiff from sitting still so long, "we've come up with a body, arranged for a funeral, and written a convincing obituary. Let's hope, once you leave your mission accomplished signal, Lee is sold on your success and eager to report it to his superiors at the mission to the UN."

Chuck had described, as best he could, who Lee took his orders from. "Hope is the last thing ever lost," he murmured.

Hannah grunted. "I've heard about the way you talk. Most people talk too much and say too little, but that's not the case with you, is it?"

He cracked a smile for her. "No ma'am."

"Just Hannah," she corrected, pulling her elbows back in a stretch. "Well, let's do this again tomorrow, shall we? I'm going to want you to describe your grandmother's operations, if you can remember them, so a little reflection tonight might be in order. After that, you'll need to take a polygraph to prove you've been completely honest, as I'm sure you have been. I appreciate your cooperation, Haiku. I know this is a lengthy and tedious process."

"The donuts helped," he admitted. "What's the polygraph like?"

"It's about two hours long, but most of that time is taken up by the examiner, who'll explain the questions in advance to ensure you completely understand them. There will be no surprise or trick questions. Your responses will be limited to a simple yes or no. If, after a run, the examiner needs clarification, he'll ask you."

Chuck shrugged. Having withheld not a shred of information, he suffered no qualms about being polygraphed. "I'm an open window."

"Okay." Hannah checked her watch. "My oldest

has a soccer game at five, so I'd better get you back to your apartment." She pushed back her chair and stood.

Chuck followed suit, grabbing up his jacket. Thoughts of Katy immediately assailed him, along with the bitter taste of disillusionment. Because of her, he had been happy, even in the prison of his double life. Realizing that happiness had been built on a foundation of lies was a bitter pill to swallow.

KELLY SET OUT slowly. A good, hard run was exactly what she needed to exorcise her agitation, but her knees felt stiff after hours sitting cross-legged on her bed while typing up a paper—this time for her other class. With thoughts of Chuck chipping at her concentration, it had taken until mid-afternoon just to complete a five-page comparison of two business models. She'd saved the document and put away her laptop. Tomorrow, Sunday, she would do nothing but relax—if such a thing were possible, knowing Chuck felt utterly used by her.

I'm so sorry. She had contemplated texting him those words, then chickened out as it invited a rebuttal she might not want to read.

Minutes later, Kelly trotted toward the oceanfront with the sun warming her back. She hadn't run this same route since that fateful morning three weeks ago. The realization that fruit trees had bloomed in the intermittent weeks, dropping pink petals on the cement sidewalk, was a reminder that rebirth was possible, even after the coldest of winters.

But it wasn't technically spring yet, as the salt-laced breeze reminded her. The closer she got to the ocean, the more it whipped at her jacket and played with her ponytail.

When she reached the spot where Chuck had been struck by Lee's bullet, Kelly slowed to a stop. Traces of his blood still stained the brick where he'd lain. A vision of how he had looked with his complexion turning ashen, blood welling through his fingers, returned to her with gut-wrenching clarity.

You're spectacular, he had said.

The memory knifed across her heart. He didn't feel that way anymore, she imagined. But, yes, they'd be spectacular together. Closing her eyes, she savored that sense of completion she had known with him and only him. Tears rushed into her eyes, only to dry in the wind the instant she opened them.

Shaking off her blues, she took off running again, one of several people venturing out in the slightly warmer weather. White-capped waves threw themselves ashore. *Boom, shh, boom, shh, boom!* The fitful ocean gave voice to Kelly's turmoil.

Chuck was never going to forgive her. Even if he

did, eventually, and decided to come looking for her, he wouldn't be able to find her. Katy Tang would simply vanish off the face of the earth. Of course, if he became a double agent, he might visit the Norfolk Field Office on occasion and run into her. She reached for that thread of hope and clung to it.

Weighed down by her thoughts, it took Kelly longer than usual to arrive at the end of the Boardwalk. She was just turning around, about to make her way back, when the cellphone in her pocket vibrated.

Relieved for an excuse to catch her breath, she retrieved it. Scruggs was calling her.

"Hello, Detective."

"Hello, Miss Katy Tang. Sounds like you're in a wind tunnel."

She turned her back on the sea and cupped a hand around her mouth. "I am. What's up?"

"I wanted you to be the first to know I've found Lee Soo-jin."

"For real? You actually found him. Where?"

"Hunted him down at the Naval Shipyard, where I put a tracer on his vehicle. He's driving a red Volkswagen Beetle these days."

A million pinpricks stabbed at Katy's extremities. "What? Are you sure? Wait, did Ernie Savowitz get hold of you yet?"

"'Bout what?"

"About a Volkswagen Beetle registered to,

um . . . " she searched her memory for the name, "Albert Sievers."

"No, he didn't. But that is the name Lee used to register the car."

"Sievers is Lee? Shit!" The implications splintered her thoughts. Lee had been there in Sandbridge watching the whole thing? Oh, no, had he seen Chuck getting picked up by Hannah? What about the SOGs leaving Harris's home, or the Wires and Pliers disassembling the ELSUR?

"Oh, my God." All the work the Bu had done to that point, including the placement of Harris's obituary online and in tomorrow's newspaper, made no difference if Lee reported to the RGB that Chuck had failed to carry out his tasking.

"I have to go, Detective. Stay . . . Don't do anything. Someone's going to call you back!"

She hung up on Scruggs as she started walking and dialing Ernie. Bless his heart for answering on the first ring.

"Kelly."

"You never checked with Scruggs on the owner of the red Volkswagen!" she accused. "Scruggs just told me Albert Sievers is a cover name for Lee Soo-jin. He was there last night, Ernie. He probably saw everything."

Her words shocked Ernie into silence. "Oh, that's not good," he finally said.

"No shit! We have to tell Hannah not to bring Chuck back to his apartment. Lee is going to be gunning for him, and if he's told *his* handlers, we can kiss the DA option good-bye." She dared not say the words "double agent" out loud.

"I'll call Hannah right now. Don't worry, Kelly. We'll protect Chuck."

He hung up on her, his assurance proof that he knew of her feelings for the target. Kelly envisioned him calling Hannah and alerting Valentino. Hopefully, a battalion of SOGs would surround Chuck before he ever left the Norfolk Field office. Better yet, they should spirit him away to a safehouse where Lee couldn't find him. She liked that idea better.

She broke into a run, impelled by a nameless fear to return to her apartment, to warn Chuck in person if she had to. Fueled with adrenaline, she had nearly reached 18th Street Plaza when her phone buzzed a second time. She slowed to see who it was, stopping by the sculpture of the birds to answer. It was Scruggs again.

"What is it?"

"You didn't let me finish. I meant to tell you Lee's on his way to a microbrewery not far from your place. I think he plays guitar there. He's been going every evening when he works the day shift. It's called Old Port Brewing Company."

The name echoed in Kelly's head. *Old Port Brewing*

Company. Why did that sound so familiar?

"I'm headed there now." Scruggs sounded edgier than usual. "I'll be there in ten minutes, and I'll arrest him if you want me to."

"Yes! I mean, no! Jesus, I can't make that call! Hold tight, I'll have Hannah call you."

Glancing in both directions at the oncoming traffic on Atlantic Avenue, Kelly sprinted across the busy street, narrowly missing getting struck by a woman in a Lexus who blared her horn in fright. The sun shone directly in Kelly's eyes, blinding her view of the road up ahead. She slowed long enough to access Hannah's number, then ran with her phone pressed to one ear.

The endless shrill of Hannah's phone suggested Ernie was still talking to their case manager. Kelly forced herself to slow down before her heart exploded. She walked swiftly, catching her breath, and pressing the heel of her palm against a stitch in her side. *Everything is going to be okay.*

The sound of music drew her gaze to a building one block over, a three-story brick building with a flat roof. A string of Edison lights atop the roof, and the music floating out of an open window suggested the building was likely a bar. Oh, okay, that had to be the bar Lee frequented, according to Scruggs, Old Port Brewing Company. Wow, was Lee really that close to her? The memory that had evaded her earlier jumped front and center. Wait a minute. *Hadn't Austin said he'd taken pictures of her searching Chuck's car from a rooftop bar nearby?*

Kelly's horrified gaze swung from the tall building to her apartment complex. If Austin could take pictures of her in the parking lot between her and Chuck's buildings, then Lee Soo-jin, armed with a long-range rifle, had a straight shot at Chuck from that same vantage point.

"No!" She broke into a run while dialing Hannah's phone again.

THE CHURNING IN Mike Scruggs' stomach was a telltale sign that the shit was about to hit the fan, and it would be his fault if it did.

He switched lanes, speeding past a car that was going too slow. Damn it, he should have told Valentino a week ago about Lee Soo-jin driving a red Beetle. But, oh, no, he'd let ego get in the way of common sense and kept that information to himself, thinking he would keep tabs on Lee, then catch him when the FBI most needed him. Anything to make himself look good.

Truth was, Lee was hard to keep an eye on 24/7, most especially when he worked the day shift. After work, Lee went out until 3 AM, prowling the streets. Old Port Brewing Company was his latest haunt. The first time Lee had carried his guitar case into that bar with him, Mike had followed, only to watch him for hours, sitting at the bar, tossing back beers. Tired and bored, Mike had left before Lee ever took his guitar out. The second, third, and fourth time Lee headed for the bar, Mike drove off in search of his dinner, leaving Lee to party on his own.

Now he had a sinking suspicion Lee didn't even own a guitar, but, rather, a high-powered sniper rifle, which he intended to use on the man he'd tried killing once already. After all, Charles Suzuki lived only two blocks away.

Parking directly in front of a fire hydrant with one tire on the curb, Mike killed his engine. He checked the status of his Magnum. Full cartridge, first round in the chamber.

His intestines coiled with deep concern. *Please let this end well.* All he wanted was to look good in the eyes of Rafael Valentino, who'd so drastically surpassed him in his law enforcement career. Was that asking too much?

✕

"GOT IT."

Whatever Hannah Lindstrom was listening to via the phone pressed to her ear, Chuck could tell it wasn't good news. Her tone was terse, her knuckles on the steering wheel white.

Her cellphone had started ringing right as the Nor-folk Virginia Beach Expressway turned into 21st Street. Even riding shotgun, Chuck had been too drained to pay much attention to her conversation. Despite the donuts and the frequent breaks, the emotional toll of his confessions, coupled with the concern that Sobo, his parents, and Seiko would be made to pay a terrible price, had left him disquieted. Hannah had promised to tell him at some later date what would happen to them.

"Will do." She hung up as she turned off 21st Street toward 18th Street. "Change of plans," she informed. "An issue has come up, forcing us to move you to a safe house. We're going to wait in the van for a couple of Valentino's men to get here. Then they're going to escort you into your apartment to pack a bag of clothing, your toothbrush . . . " Her eyes raked the roofs and the balconies as she turned into the parking lot between his and Katy's buildings. What was she spooked about? ". . . whatever you need to spend several nights elsewhere."

She swung carefully into Austin's empty parking space.

Chuck frowned at her. Whatever the call was about, it had changed her from a friendly, if persistent, interrogator into warrior princess.

"What's going on?" he demanded. "You know I'm

committed to this. I'm not about to run."

Her green eyes met his. She seemed to consider him a moment. "It's not you, it's Lee. Apparently, he was in Sandbridge last night, renting a house not far from Harris's. I'm sure he was only making sure you followed through with your task, but he may have seen me pick you up afterwards."

Chuck dropped his head back against the seat. Fuck, not Lee again! The North Korean illegal had been an omnipresent pain in his ass since Chuck moved to the area.

The squeal of tires over asphalt made them both jump, as a car peeled into the parking lot.

"It's the SOGs," Hannah said, sounding relieved, as it barreled down on them.

Three men were in the car. Two popped out, dressed in loose shirts to disguise the pistols they were packing. Glancing casually about, they approached Chuck's vehicle.

"Go and get your stuff," Hannah urged.

Chuck stepped out of her van, somewhat flattered by their protection but also annoyed that a Navy SEAL should require bodyguards in the first place.

"Chuck!"

The familiar voice crying his name stopped him in his tracks as he shut the van door behind him. He turned toward a vision of Katy, ponytail streaming like a black pennant, as she sprinted toward him, all the while gesturing frantically.

"Take cover! Take cover!"

From what?

The SOGs, who seemed to recognize Katy, drew their weapons in wary confusion. Chuck, who couldn't get past the fact that Katy had lied to him all this time, just stood there wondering how he hadn't seen through her from the beginning.

Crack!

The middle window of Hannah's van exploded right next to him. He turned and gaped at the inch-wide hole and the crackled glass. His sluggish mind registered he'd been shot at. From where? He whipped back around only to be tackled onto the asphalt by a woman who was all limbs and hair.

"Get down, I said!"

More glass popped and crackled above them as the unseen shooter fired again.

Chuck couldn't get any lower than he was, flat on his back with his head on the curb, the wind knocked out of him. Katy kneeled over him, out of breath, white-faced.

"Are you okay? Are you hit?"

Chuck struggled to inflate his lungs. She was smoothing her tiny, but efficient hands all over him, searching for a wound.

One of the SOGs shouted from within the stair-well of the apartment building, where he'd taken cover. "Kelly, where is he? Where's the shooter?"

The man had gotten Katy's name wrong. Unless . . .

"On the roof of a building two blocks away," she shouted back. "Old Port Brewing Company. Detective Scruggs just told me."

"Well, where the hell is Scruggs now?" the SOG railed.

They were pinned by a sniper shooting from a distance too far away and too protected to defend themselves. Anyone who stood up or moved would get their brains blown out.

"Hannah!" Katy craned her neck to peer under the belly of the car. "Are you there? Are you okay?"

"I'm fine, damn it." Hannah's voice came from the tire well on the driver's side. "It never fails," she added, muttering to herself about missed soccer games.

Chuck stared at the woman hovering over him, morphing into a stranger who knew Hannah by name, who had rattled off news suggesting she was in contact with the detective who'd come to the hospital to see him. One of the SOGs had called her Kelly.

His Katy was gone. The gift of their lovemaking was nothing but a gag gift. *My God, had she faked everything? Was that the reason why their timing in bed had been so impeccable?*

"Get off me," he said, sitting up.

Her eyes flared at his surly tone, but she scrambled
back, all the same, saying only. "Keep your head
down."

No shit. He bit back the words, having never spoken to a woman like that in his life. But his glare must
have conveyed the same thing because she seemed to
wilt like a flower under excessive heat. The life went
out of her eyes.

"I'm so sorry," she murmured.

Certainly, the words eased his disillusionment, but
they changed nothing. He turned away from her, rising
to his knees, then into a low crouch, prepared to run if
need be.

✖

MIKE SCRUGGS PUSHED into Old Port Brewery
Company with his badge in one hand and his Magnum
in the other. The lower level was a museum of sorts,
empty but for big black-and-white pictures of what the
building, once a barrel shop, had looked like at the
turn of the last century.

He charged up the stairs to the second story, now
a bottle shop. Every kind of brew from German lagers
to Belgian whites lined the shelves, as well as peanuts,
cocktail mixers, and drinking steins. A couple was
browsing the selection. Mike flashed his badge at the
employee helping them.

"People, I need you to move to a rear exit, but do *not* go outside unless I tell you to clear the building. There's a potential shooter upstairs. Go."

The employee's eyes darted toward the cash register, but then she gestured for the couple to follow her behind the sales counter toward a rear door.

Scruggs charged up the staircase he had climbed only once before. The ancient treads creaked beneath his feet as he hurried up them, moving as fast as his desk-jockey body permitted. A murmuring of voices and the velvety notes of a saxophone greeted him. Barely a dozen people were getting an early start on their evening, but none of them were Lee.

"Folks," Mike yelled, gaining instant silence as he held up his badge. "Detective Scruggs, VBPD. I need you to put your drinks down and walk quickly and quietly to the lower level. Proceed to the rear exit but do *not* leave the building. There's a potential shooter on the roof. Take your possessions with you. Let's go!" he added when the customers failed to respond. His bellow got them moving. He waved them toward the stairs, "Faster. Step on it. This is not a drill."

"Should I call the police?" asked a server wearing an Old Port Brewery apron.

"I *am* the police."

Mike had wasted enough time. The only place Lee could be was up on the roof with his guitar case, waiting for his target to return home. Mike hastened toward the third flight of stairs, finding it cordoned off, with a sign that read ROOFTOP CLOSED. A sliver of soft light shone through the door at the top, however, indicating Lee had propped the door open.

With his heart throbbing in his throat, Mike stepped over the cord and swiftly ascended.

All of a sudden, the door flew open. Lee, guitar case hanging down his back by a strap, drew up short at the sight of a burly man blocking his path, pointing a gun at him. Recognition flared in his dark eyes.

"Leaving already?"

Lee had either killed his target or lost sight of him. Either way, he hoped to slip away before any police showed up. *Well, too late, buddy. I've got you now.*

"Sorry." Lee's right hand started sliding into his pocket. "No speak English."

Mike, highly conscious of the North Korean's superior training, didn't wait for Lee to produce a weapon. He squeezed the trigger.

The report was deafening. The impact of the close-range shot flung Lee and his guitar case back against the metal door. Lee dropped, blood shiny on his black windbreaker as he slid, dragging the guitar case behind him, *bumpity, bumpity, bumpity, bump*, in Mike's direction. Mike stepped to one side, ready to put a bullet in Lee's head at the least sign of life. Lee slid to a stop at his feet, mouth agape, eyes staring.

Mike sucked in a breath, gulped down his shock,

and bent over to feel for a pulse. It had been years since he'd actually killed a perp. In this case, he hoped he'd done the right thing, and that he'd done it in time.

With a shaky hand, he reached into his jacket for his cellphone, wanting to assure Katy Tang the threat had been contained.

✕

AT THE DISTANT crack of a gun, Kelly came to her knees, peering over Chuck's car at the rooftop clearly visible from her present vantage. The sniper's shots had ceased. Was it too much to hope Scruggs had caught up to Lee and dispatched him?

Her phone vibrated. Aware that Chuck was watching her, she took it from her pocket, noted the caller ID, and answered. "Tell me."

"Lee is dead. Hope you don't mind that I killed him."

She closed her eyes in relief. She could hear Scruggs unwrapping a stick of gum. "I don't." She couldn't speak for Hannah or Valentino.

"I'll call your boss now," Scruggs added, as he chewed. "Wanted you to be the first to know."

"Thank you. Hey, Mike?" she added before he hung up on her. "I've learned a lot."

"Hah. Thanks, kid."

The phone beeped twice as he hung up on her.

Kelly met Chuck's watchful gaze. "Lee's dead." She said it loud enough for Hannah and the SOGs to hear. She pushed to her feet, aware that her knees were bruised, her thigh muscles screaming.

"All right, guys . . ."

Whatever Hannah was saying to the SOGs, Kelly paid no heed. The resentment that had flared in Chuck's eyes when he'd told her to get off him still seared her. And now he was looking at her like he'd never seen her before.

She licked her chapped lips. "Chuck, I . . . "

He turned his back on her and walked away, headed for his apartment.

Kelly pressed a hand to her stomach as her heartstrings seemed to unravel. No good-byes, even. He had shunned her without a word. A wave of grief crested inside her. Tears pressured the backs of her eyes. She couldn't release them here with others playing witness. But they would flow, she knew, as soon as she found herself alone, and for a long time to come.

Chapter 21

AUSTIN SNATCHED HIS duffel bag off the tarmac, slinging it over one shoulder as he walked away from the C-17 cargo airplane. He'd been the only passenger to squeeze in with a shipment of military uniforms on a nonstop flight from San Diego.

Happy to get off the plane and even happier to be back at home, Austin loped toward the terminal building, taking in deep breaths of salt-laced air. In the three weeks he'd been gone, winter had given way to spring. The air was as warm here as it had been in California, and blooming forsythia waved their delicate yellow blossoms at him as he neared the glassed-in departure area.

Someone was watching him. The silhouette of a woman caused his hopes to leap and his stride to quicken. Had Evelyn decided to surprise him after ignoring all his texts?

But then the woman's features became apparent as he approached the entrance. Hope collided with reality as he recognized the tall, redheaded figure of Luther Lindstrom's wife. What was she doing here?

She opened the heavy glass door for him. "Hello,

Austin."

Confused, noting the lobby of the terminal was empty save for an employee stocking the vending machine, Austin nodded. "Hello, ma'am."

"Hannah," she corrected him. "Ma'am makes me sound old. Can I walk you to your car?"

"Um, sure." Concern dominated his confusion. Had someone died? No, Luther's wife wouldn't be sent to deliver the grim news like that. Wait, wasn't she in the FBI?

He shot her several sidelong glances as they pushed out of the main entrance and into the parking lot. They were headed toward his car when she said, "Kelly Yang is one of my most talented Special Agents."

Oh, this was about the oath he'd taken not to reveal Katy Tang's true name or purpose. "I haven't told anyone about her," he quickly avowed.

"No, I know that. I have complete confidence in your discretion, Austin. The thing is, it's not necessary anymore. The North Korean cabinet member you just helped to kidnap—" She painted air quotes for the last word—"was a source for the CIA for many years."

Austin smirked, having guessed as much already.

"In fact, he warned the CIA that a Navy SEAL was going to be targeted by a North Korean assassin. That SEAL was Chuck Suzuki, your roommate."

"Whoa." Austin stopped walking and stared at her

in consternation. "How did the source know Chuck was a Navy SEAL?"

"Through Chuck's grandmother, who still has kin in North Korea. When she boasted about her grandson's accomplishments online, the RGB—you know that acronym?"

"Yes, ma'am."

She sighed over his respectful form of address. "The RGB elected to target him. Long story short, the CIA informed the FBI that Chuck's life was in danger. We were a little late in saving him, as evidenced by the shooting in February. We had just placed Kelly Yang into East Harbor Apartments to protect Chuck and to teach him proper tradecraft when the shooting happened. Chuck has since communicated to the RGB that he's interested in saving his neck in exchange for secret information."

"What?" Austin halted by the bumper of his car. "Chuck would never give up military secrets!"

Hannah merely smiled at him and waited.

"Oh." Austin quickly put two and two together. "He's not really giving them what they want."

"No, of course not." She pitched her voice lower, even though no one was around to hear them. "He's going to act as a double agent so that we can learn what the RGB wants to know and how they play their spy games."

"Awesome!" Getting over his astonishment, Austin blew out a breath of relief. "I knew there had to be a reason for him to act so strange. Man, I feel bad for thinking he might have sold his soul to the devil."

"You're talking like him now," Hannah pointed out.

"It's contagious."

"I know. So, about Kelly Yang . . . " Hannah narrowed her green eyes against the sun's bright rays. "Chuck has known who she really is from the moment she introduced herself."

"Really?" Austin searched his memory and couldn't come up with a single instance to indicate that he had. "Wow, he really hid that well."

"Well, he is a quick study. Now, Austin." She put her hands on her hips and leveled a firm look at him. "Katy Tang is moving out of her apartment at the end of this month. Until then, her cover remains in effect as far as anyone in East Harbor Apartments is concerned."

"Okay." Austin frowned, thinking Chuck probably wasn't too happy about her leaving. "But Chuck can see her again, right, like the real Kelly? Can he date her, or is there some kind conduct code, since he's sort of an agent, too?"

"Shhh." Hannah looked over her shoulder. "Never say that out loud again."

"Yes, ma'am."

"Hannah, not ma'am," she reminded him. "Is

Chuck interested in dating her?"

She sounded a little surprised to hear it.

"Oh, yeah." Austin laughed about his earliest suspicions of Katy. "He's head over heels for her. Talked about marriage and everything."

Hannah's russet eyebrows shot up. "Really?"

Why so surprised, Austin wondered. Had neither Chuck nor Kelly mentioned their love affair?

"Well, I hope everything works out for them. Anyway, I thought I'd explain a few things that might have been troubling you. Welcome home and carry on." She clapped him on the arm and walked past him toward her own vehicle.

Austin admired her leggy stride and the way her red hair caught fire in the sunlight. He thought about his own lovely lady and pulled his phone from his pocket as well as his car keys.

With his duffel tossed into the back and his motor warming up, he rolled down the windows of his car to let the invigorating breeze replace the stale air. Then he called Evelyn's number again, anticipating the sound of her voice. As with the last two times he'd called, he heard a single ring before his call went to her voicemail.

"Hey, it's me. I'm back at the Beach. I'd like to see you soon. Call me. Please?"

He was starting to doubt she would. He had left Evelyn two previous voicemails, neither of which she had prompted her to call him back. Was it possible he would never see her again?

No. His heart refused to accept the possibility, but then the memory of their last conversation came back to him, and worry leeched into his bones.

She was all he had thought about the whole time he was gone: her baby blue eyes and the way he could tell exactly what she was thinking by the tone of her voice. Her clean cotton scent and the way her mother's actions had left her leery of love. She needed him, only she didn't realize he was the prince she was looking for.

Gritting his teeth with determination, Austin started up his car and accelerated out of the empty space in front of him.

If Evelyn Haskins thought she could get rid of him that easily, she was about to discover that a Navy SEAL *never* gave up.

✕

CHUCK MADE OUT the familiar purr of Austin's Clubman and double-checked the pizza in the oven. Almost done. Austin's favorite food was Greek pizza with feta, spinach, and olives. This one had come from a box but, hey, not everybody could cook like Katy . . . he swung a sword in his mind, severing the thought.

There *was* no Katy—only Kelly Yang who looked

like her and went to school like her, while apparently working fulltime for the FBI. In just a few weeks, Kelly's cover would cease to exist. She would move out of Lisa's apartment and back into her own place in Chesapeake, not far from the FBI building where Chuck had endured a weekend of interrogations only to be asked unexpectedly if he would work *against* the RGB as a double agent.

Of course, he'd jumped at the offer, wanting nothing more than to redeem himself. Only then had he been told what he'd already guessed—that Katy Tang was actually Kelly Yang, an undercover agent whose job it was to befriend him. He'd also been told his roommate, Austin, had guessed the truth about her right before leaving on his assignment. No surprise there, considering Austin was a genius, not to mention Austin hadn't been wearing the rose-colored lenses of infatuation.

The resentment that had been gnawing at Chuck's heart for the past three weeks had faded slowly into acceptance. He had no one to blame but himself for believing a cute-as-hell firecracker like Katy would ever have feelings for him. She might have been physically attracted to him, and she might have felt so bad about sleeping with him that she'd made up a story to keep him at a more professional distance. God, he hoped it was a story. Bottom line was she hadn't wanted to pursue a relationship with him.

Keeping tabs on Chuck the spy was all she'd really cared about.

At the sound of a key in the lock, Chuck set the timer for five more minutes, then turned with a welcoming smile and a pinch of concern. Hannah had assured him Austin would be briefed the instant he touched down at Oceana Naval Air Base. She had promised she would paint Chuck in the best possible light, while also explaining Kelly's undercover role. All Chuck had to do was to go along with the story that Katy had been placed across the street to protect him and to show him the ropes.

The door swung open. "Honey, I'm home!" Austin grinned at him as he kicked the door shut behind him and dropped his bag.

Shaking his head at Austin's joke, Chuck came toward him with his hand out. "Welcome home, *asshole*." He said the last word in Korean.

"Sir." Ignoring the slur, Austin pumped his hand heartily. "It is an honor and a privilege to serve with a patriot of your caliber."

Hannah had done her part well. And even though it was Sobo who was to blame for coercing her family into protecting the hermit kingdom, shame still burned the bottom of Chuck's soles. Sobo had taken her guilt to the grave, having consumed a cyanide pill at the very moment of her arrest. Chuck's mother and father, on the other hand, had submitted with grace, and even relief, to the penalties imposed on them. As part of their plea agreement, they had held onto their shipping business while surrendering all tradecraft, communication schedules, ongoing tasking requirements and any other items related to their work for the RGB. The Bureau would monitor them for intelligence purposes and offer personal security, if required. Seiko had been left alone to finish his schooling, though he, too, would be watched for years to come. Chuck was free to call any one of them every Sunday.

"How was the op?" he asked, looking Austin over. His hair had grown at least an inch. He hadn't shaved in days, and his Navy working uniform could use a thorough washing.

"Fantastic! I wish you could have been there." Austin's eyes lit up. "The cabinet member was in Wonsan, staying at one of the guest houses on Kim Jong-un's private compound. The place is a new tourist resort, right on the Sea of Japan. He was there inspecting the resort, and his wife and kid got to come as a perk, so we nabbed the entire family right off the beach south of the yacht harbor. Then, just to fuck with Kim Jong-un, we even left a ransom note in Chinese that read: Wire a million yen to the Peoples Bank of China Headquarters if you want Moon Min-yun returned."

"Brilliant. How'd the translating go?"

Austin cringed. "Rough at first but I got used to

his dialect, and then it was easy. Hey, didn't I tell you the cabinet member was a CIA informant? But you already knew that, didn't you?"

"Yeah." He hadn't really, but he'd been told so shortly after accepting Hannah's offer to become a double agent. The cabinet member, Moon Min-yun, had told the CIA about a Navy SEAL spy. If word of Chuck's espionage had never reached the FBI, and if Hannah hadn't found a way to flip him, Chuck might have remained a puppet of the RGB indefinitely. He owed Moon Min-yun a huge debt of gratitude.

Austin stepped toward a cabinet and pulled out a drinking glass. "You'll never guess who met me at the airfield and told me everything."

"Luther's wife."

"Right. Don't ever call her ma'am. She doesn't like it." Austin stuck his glass into the dispenser on the refrigerator and sniffed the air. "Do I smell pizza? I'm starving!"

Chuck cracked the oven. "Hunger is felt by slave and king alike."

"Well, this king is going to wash his hands. Be back in two minutes." Austin drained his glass as he walked away.

Three minutes later, the two SEALs sat at their pub table with the entire pizza lying between them, no plates.

Austin helped himself to the first slice. "So, Hannah told me," he said, picking up their conversation where they'd left off. "She told me *everything*," he added with a significant lift of his eyebrows.

"Yeah, she said she would." Hannah's version allowed Chuck to save face, and he was eternally grateful to her for that.

"Mmm." Austin stopped talking and demolished the food in his hands. "I can't believe you're a . . . " Austin looked around the room as if suspicious of cameras and bugs.

Chuck had recently learned his own surveillance system had been used by the FBI against him, making Katy—*Kelly's* request that he unplug the camera from its power source suddenly comprehensible. They'd even had a camera pointed down at his desk!

"A you-know-what," Austin finished.

"Right?" Chuck agreed. By sheer good fortune, it appeared Lee was so eager to prevent Chuck from spilling his guts to the FBI that he hadn't gotten off a message to his handlers that Daken had been compromised. With a simple explanation to the RGB, hidden in a picture and uploaded to his recreated Instagram, Chuck had established contact with Lee's handlers, explaining how the police had shot and killed Lee. The proof was in the newspapers.

"And I can't believe," Austin added, talking around a mouthful of pizza, "you knew Katy was working for the Feds. You hid that so well. Why'd you pretend to hate her so much?"

Chuck cautioned himself to be careful of Austin's intellect. "I guess I didn't like the idea of a woman protecting me. Stupid macho stuff."

"Hey, she could have done a better job. You still got shot," Austin pointed out, defending him, "though if she wasn't on the boardwalk that morning, you would have died. So, how are things going between you two? You still want to marry her?"

Chuck averted his hot face. "Um, I mean, she's pretty irresistible and all, but she's got her career and I've got mine." He shrugged to indicate they'd decided not to get serious.

Austin lowered the pizza he was about to take a bite of. "Wait, you're not going to see her anymore?"

"I don't think so. No, it wouldn't work out." Chuck forced himself to look squarely into Austin's eyes.

"But she's crazy about you."

"No, she's not." The words carved a deeper hole in him.

"Yes, she totally is," Austin insisted, putting his pizza down. "Listen, when I figured out that she was lying to us—well, to me—about who she really was, I confronted her."

Chuck had heard the story 3rd hand through Hannah. "What did you say to her?"

"Well, basically, I chewed her out for sleeping with

you and making you think about marriage and stuff."

Chuck sucked in a breath. He would marry her in a heartbeat if she loved him. "And what'd she say?"

"She choked up. She said what happened between you two wasn't supposed to happen, that she was trying to protect you, but she had to pull away because it was unprofessional of her. She told me that she loved you, man."

"She doesn't love me." Protect him how? From Lee or from himself?

"Dude, she totally does! You know I can read people. She's as crazy about you as you are about her."

The block sitting in Chuck's chest shifted. A freshwater spring bubbled up in its place. "She said she loves me?"

"Yeah. She was trying not to cry and everything. I mean, obviously she wanted to be a professional and do the right thing, but you guys have everything it takes to make this work. You can't just give up. . ."

His words faded off and Chuck could tell he was thinking about his own situation.

"I think Evelyn has blocked my number," Austin confessed, going off on a tangent. "She doesn't want to give me a chance. She doesn't date military guys, and she thinks I'm too young for her."

"Age is a state of mind."

Austin looked up at him and blinked. "I see what you're doing. We're talking about you and Kelly right now. Tell me you're going to talk to her. I want you to be happy."

Austin's pleading gaze was all the persuasion Chuck needed. "I promise," he agreed.

"Right now. Do it tonight."

"Tomorrow after work," Chuck insisted. He had met Katy on a Friday. He would meet Kelly on Friday, two months later, and start all over. Anticipation licked over him.

"Fair enough."

Austin's expression turned serious as he helped himself to a third slice.

"So, what are you going to do about Evelyn?" Chuck pressed.

"I don't know yet. I mean, I'm not the stalker type, so I can't simply show up at her house and let myself in." He bit the end off his pizza slice.

"Do you even have a key?"

Austin held up a finger and chewed. "Actually, I do," he finally said, "but I'm not going to use it until I'm invited. I think she needs something drastic to happen. Then I could rush in and save her, and she would see me for who I really am, not for how much younger I am, or the fact that I'm in the military."

"Something drastic," Chuck repeated. "Like what?"

"If I knew that, I wouldn't be sitting here in my odiferous uniform, stuffing my face with pizza."

Chuck took in the determined frown on Austin's face. "You'll think of something." He had total confidence in his roommate to win Evelyn over.

It was himself he wasn't so sure of. What if he approached Kelly, aiming to start anew, and she rebuffed him?

Well, then, you'll be no worse off than you are right now, answered his hopeful heart.

He was going to do it. He was going to put his heart on the line the next time he saw her. All at once, the future didn't look so grim.

✕

KELLY LEFT HER apartment in her running attire, trying to whip up her enthusiasm for a five-mile run.

It was a gorgeous evening in late April. The sunset had turned the inland sky a surreal shade of pink, blending into mandarin orange. Mouth-watering aromas released by local restaurants floated on the breeze blowing in from the ocean. The weather was cooler than the day before. The brisk air would keep her from breaking into a sweat on her run, though it was nowhere near as cold as when she'd first tackled the boardwalk the morning Chuck had been shot.

Plodding down the steps, Kelly wished she had a new assignment, just *something* to look forward to besides the semester being over. She was sick of

mulling over the past, imagining what might have
happened if only she'd kept things platonic between
her and Chuck.

Maybe then he'd have been able to accept who she
really was, why she'd deceived him about her real
name, her true purpose. Instead, she had crossed the
line, letting her desire and concern for him overrule
reason. That, in turn, had necessitated she lie to him in
an attempt to regain her professional footing. In short,
she had mucked up a relationship that had all the
hallmarks of lasting the test of time.

Stepping out of the stairwell, Kelly's gaze went
automatically to Chuck's empty parking space. She
could guess where he was—at Calypso Bar and Grille,
sipping on his second tumbler of bourbon. According
to the special surveillance member who still monitored
Chuck's movements, Chuck and Austin had gone to
Calypso's every Friday night since she'd first approached him there, save his first night home from the
hospital.

Kelly checked her watch. Any moment, the two
SEALs would return home together.

Hah, was that why she had finally dragged herself
out of her apartment? Was she hoping to cross paths
with him?

"God, just give it up," she muttered to herself.

They hadn't exchanged a single word since that
horrible day that she'd tackled him to the curb and

he'd said, *Get off me.* A month had passed since then, and she was still reliving the delight of getting to know him, their laughter, making love, the feeling of having found *home* in his embrace.

Using the streetlamp for balance, Kelly stood on one leg and grabbed her foot behind her, stretching out her left quadricep. A breeze lifted and lowered her ponytail. The familiar purr of Chuck's Subaru pricked her ears as it turned into the parking lot. She pretended not to hear it, directing her gaze above the roof of Chuck's building to admire the cotton candy clouds.

She switched legs, standing on her left foot to stretch out her other quad. When she moved out of Lisa's apartment in only a few weeks, she would surely miss the oceanfront. Running on the treadmill back at the field office gym wouldn't be the same. Living far away from the man she loved was going to suck, even worse than it did now.

Chuck's motor died. Out of the corner of her eye, she saw his brake lights dim. His car doors opened. Austin, who had returned from his assignment to North Korea last evening, popped out of one door, Chuck out of the other.

"Hey, Katy," Austin called.

She smiled at him and raised a hand. She could feel Chuck looking at her, but she turned her shoulder on him. The two SEALs would head up to their apartment together and maybe watch a soccer game.

Loneliness assailed her.

She released the lamp pole and stretched her hamstring by bending one knee, keeping the other leg out straight in front of her.

Hinged at the hip, hands planted on her thighs, she overheard the soft tread of boots crossing asphalt. Was someone walking toward her? Turning her head, she realized Chuck was stepping up onto the curb right next to her.

Kelly straightened abruptly. Her senses sharpened. She drank in the sight of him, still dressed in his Navy working uniform, his hair recently cut, looking incredibly virile, achingly familiar.

Their gazes caught and held. Her heart thumped. Neither of them spoke.

"Hi." He broke the silence and held out a hand to her. "My name's Chuck. I live across the street from you." Without looking away, he pointed behind him just as the lights blinked on in his apartment.

Hope swamped Kelly. Meeting his eyes again, she offered him her hand and nearly wept as his fingers closed around hers, forgiving and firm.

"I'm Kelly," she said around the lump swelling in her throat. "Though I go by Katy for now. I work for the FBI," she added. "What do you do?"

"I'm a Navy SEAL and a patriot," he tacked on.

Tears of relief welled in Kelly's eyes. She smiled tremulously.

Without a word, Chuck tugged at the hand he was clasping, pulling her closer. She fell against his broad chest, sucking in a shuddering breath as his powerful arms encircled her, holding her like he was never going to let her go. Surrounded by his familiar scent, secure in his embrace, Kelly clung to him.

"I love you, Chuck," she admitted in a shaky voice. "I've been wanting to tell you."

He eased away just far enough to see her face. "You love me," he said dubiously, "even knowing what I did?"

His vulnerability made her love him even more. "From the first night I laid eyes on you," she avowed.

He laughed at the irony. "That must have freaked you out."

"Totally."

"I couldn't keep my eyes off you that night," he admitted. "I kept thinking you were either an assassin or you worked for the FBI."

She smiled with irony. "They say your first guess is always the right one. Do you forgive me for lying to you?"

"Of course I do. A better question is do you forgive *me* for betraying my country?"

Compassion moistened her eyes. "You didn't really."

His brow furrowed, and he stared at her neck, fighting for composure. "Well, thank you for that."

She raised a hand to his cheek, bringing his gaze up. "I've missed you so much. And I've been *so* sad that you wouldn't talk to me"

He took her hand from his cheek and clasped it. "I'm sorry, Kelly. I've missed you, too."

The sound of her real name on his lips was a novelty. "It's my fault. I shouldn't have pushed you away with that lie about . . . I mean, I was kidnapped but, thank God, those boys never touched me."

He shook his head in disagreement. "I'm glad to hear they didn't touch you, but that didn't push me away, Munchkin. We could have worked through that. It was the embarrassment of being caught, then thinking everything we had shared was only in my head. You'd only gotten to know me so that you could corner me."

"No." She wiped a stray tear from her cheek. "Trust me, none of that was in my job description. Neither was falling in love with you."

He sent her one of his rare smiles. "Well, we can't turn back the hands of time."

"No, we can't," she agreed, smiling back.

"But we could take on the future together," he proposed.

She bit her bottom lip, eyes brimming with joyful tears at the images his words evoked. "Yes, we could."

A male voice floated across the parking lot. "For the love of God, just kiss her already." It was Austin, watching them from their balcony.

Kelly chuckled and rolled up onto her toes to throw her arms around Chuck. With the sky blushing a deep rosy hue, they kissed and kissed and kissed until Austin made a sound of mock disgust and went inside.

EPILOGUE

WARM WATER PELTED Austin's face as he stood in his shower, lathering his hair with shampoo. God, it felt good to be home in his own tub, scrubbing away the layers of dirt that had accumulated after days of travel. His last shower had been a mere wetting down under a trickle in a shower stall on a guided missile destroyer. By contrast, the spray coming out of his showerhead felt like an exotic massage. Dozens of individual jets caressed his lips, his neck, his groin, bringing back memories of Evelyn's kisses.

As he turned around to rinse the shampoo from his hair, a song sprang to mind that his parents used to play when he was a teenager: B.J. Thomas's *Rain Drops Keep Falling on my Head*. Austin started to sing it, belting out the line about the blues not defeating him. As he sang, his phone vibrated unheard on the sink. It buzzed until the caller was prompted to leave a message.

Toweling off two minutes later, Austin realized he had missed a call from Evelyn. His optimism soared. With droplets of water still sliding down his body, he accessed his voicemail, putting his phone on speaker so he didn't have to hold it against his wet ear.

"Hey, it's Evelyn, finally calling you back. I'm glad you're home safe . . . ." Her voice faded momentarily. "Sorry," she added, "there's an SUV parked in front of my house. My neighbors must be having guests over." He could tell she was in her car, probably just getting home from work.

"Anyway," He heard her motor shut off, heard her car door open as she presumably got out, "I just wanted to call and say hi." Her tone was friendly but not flirtatious. Call me when you—" She cut herself off abruptly, then said quickly, on a note of real concern. "There are some men coming at me. What do you want?" She was talking to them now, clearly fearful. Garbled noises followed. "Help!" Evelyn's scream seemed to come from a distance. Then fainter still, she cried, "Austin!"

Staring at his horrified expression, Austin heard the phone go dead, as if someone else had picked it up and ended the call.

"What the hell?" Austin breathed.

Sneak Peek of Book 2

LOST IN HER thoughts, Evelyn Haskins exited Little Creek Naval Amphibious Base, where she worked as a mental health counselor, and merged onto Shore drive, headed for home. It was Friday afternoon, yet the prospect of a relaxing weekend inspired little enthusiasm. A grim joylessness had taken up permanent residence in Evelyn's chest, so that she scarcely noticed the warmer weather or blossoming fruit trees. Local restaurants were beginning to gear up for a new tourist season, filling the ocean breeze with mouthwatering aromas. Evelyn saw and smelled nothing. She had been like this since banishing Austin Collins from her life.

The worry that she had made a mistake gnawed at her. How could her decision be wrong? Even Andrew, the last of her four stepfathers and her adoptive father, had told her not to get involved with a Navy SEAL. Not only was Austin a SEAL, but he was only twenty-five years old, compared to Evelyn's thirty. He'd been referred to her for counseling because he tended to get into bar fights. Okay, to be fair, he didn't fight just anybody. He punched out bullies in the belief that he was teaching them a lesson. His translucent eyes and his winning smile suggested his motives were pure, and Evelyn had reason to believe they were.

On the one hand, Austin was brilliant. He could speak half a dozen languages. On the other, he'd been diagnosed with ADHD, and he couldn't hold still longer than ten seconds, except when he *really* focused, which he seemed to do every time he looked into her eyes. He had an uncanny ability to read her mind and that disturbed her, as he'd quickly guessed her deepest insecurity.

You don't want to end up like your mother, he'd said one day.

Bingo. Yes, her mother was a hot mess. Susan had made a career of the military, not by serving her country, but by marrying a total of four Navy men, only to leave the last one for an Italian billionaire. Why would anyone want to be like Susan? But maybe Evelyn *was* already just like her and didn't realize it. After all, she was supposed to cure Austin of his issue with bullies; instead, she had used him to rid herself of an unstable boyfriend.

If she hadn't let Austin run Jeff out of her life, then Austin wouldn't have gotten the idea that *he* and Evelyn ought to go out. He wouldn't have kissed her and shown her exactly what she would be missing when she pushed him away.

But that was the right thing to do, she'd assured herself, over and over. She had sworn from a young age that she would never, *ever* date a military man, let alone marry one. That way she *couldn't* end up like her mother. Clinging to that logic, she had thrust Austin out of her life in the hope that she would soon forget about him.

But that was three weeks ago, and her resolve was crumbling. In all that time, Austin had been overseas on a super-secret assignment about which she was glad to know very little. In his absence, he had managed to leave several texts and two lengthy voicemails on her cellphone, all of which she'd forced herself to delete— after reading and listening to them several times. It had taken every ounce of her determination not to call him back.

And now he was back home. She knew that from his latest message. That knowledge had robbed her of her ability to focus, making her useless to her clients. Her entire being ached to see him, to return his call, but her conflicted brain told her she would eventually forget him. It hadn't even been a month!

Turning off of Shore drive onto the road that passed a marina and ended at her neighborhood of modern condominiums, Evelyn realized she couldn't recall even a portion of the four-minute commute. Driving this distracted was dangerous. Maybe she *should* return Austin's call if only to express her relief that he was back. She didn't have to date him. They could be friends. *Yes!* Relief crashed over her at the prospect of a compromise. She didn't have to cast him out of her life completely.

With a sob in her throat, she groped for her cell phone, while still several blocks from her condo.

Her heart threw itself against her breastbone as she accessed his number. She knew the sound of his voice would melt her and she steeled herself, only to have her expectations dim when his phone rang and rang, then bumped her over to voicemail.

"This is Austin," came the cheerful recording. "Say what you gotta say." *Beep.*

Evelyn focused on her message. "Hey, it's Evelyn, finally calling you back. I'm glad you're home safe . . . ." Her message faded off as she realized an unfamiliar black Suburban was parked in front of her home, along the curb. Its tinted windows made it impossible to see if anyone was in it. "Sorry," she added, "there's an SUV in front of my house. My neighbors must be having guests over."

She drove around it to park in the single-car driveway. "Anyway," she killed the engine of her old Volvo and pushed out of it with the phone still plastered to her ear, "I just wanted to call and say hi. Call me when you—"

Her voice died as three men stepped simultaneously out of the SUV and started across her tiny lawn headed straight toward her. The sky was still light enough that she could tell the men were strangers, short and barrel-chested with black hair and hostile expressions. Alarm licked up her spine. She backed away. "There are some men coming at me," she reported quickly. "What do you want?" she demanded as they surrounded her. One of them jerked her hand from her car, and her phone clattered onto the driveway.

As a cloth sack enveloped her head, Evelyn screamed, "Help!" But the cloth muffled her cry. Ruthless hands forced her arms behind her back A nylon zip-tie cinched her wrists together. She was shoved from behind and stumbled in her yard as they propelled her toward their vehicle.

"Austin!" Evelyn screamed, praying her voice could still be heard.

She felt herself hoisted and tossed before sprawling across a bench seat in a car that smelled of cigarettes. Her adrenaline spiked, and she kicked the man getting in behind her. In the next instant, her ears rang as he clocked her head in retaliation. Evelyn slumped against a second man getting in on the other side. Wedged between the two, she reeled, semi-concussed and helpless as a ragdoll.

The portion of her brain that was still alert registered three doors closing. The engine of the SUV roared to life and the vehicle pulled away from her curb, taking her with it.

Wake up! This can't be happening.

But it was. What on earth? She'd just been kid-napped! Stuff like this happened in places like Mexico, not here in Virginia Beach.

Please, she thought. Let Austin get her message and realize what had happened to her.

Other Books by
Marliss Melton

Echo Platoon series
LOOK AGAIN (novella #1, permanently free)
DANGER CLOSE
HARD LANDING
FRIENDLY FIRE
NEVER FORGET (short novel)
HOT TARGET
TAKE COVER (novella #2)

Taskforce series
THE PROTECTOR
THE GUARDIAN
THE ENFORCER

Navy SEAL Team 12 series
FORGET ME NOT
IN THE DARK
TIME TO RUN
NEXT TO DIE
CODE OF SILENCE, a novella
TOO FAR GONE
LONG GONE, a novella
SHOW NO FEAR

Warriors of York series (medieval romance)
THE SLAYER'S REDEMPTION
THE DARK KNIGHT'S REWARD

Made in the USA
Middletown, DE
02 January 2022

57444949R00235